A Foreboding of
PETRELS

PREVIOUS BIRDER MURDER MYSTERIES

ABOUT THE AUTHOR

Steve Burrows has pursued his birdwatching hobby on seven continents. He is a former editor of the *Hong Kong Bird Watching Society* magazine and a contributing field editor for *Asian Geographic*. Steve now lives with his wife, Resa, in Oshawa, Ontario.

A Foreboding of
PETRELS

STEVE BURROWS

POINT
BLANK

A Point Blank Book

First published by Point Blank,
an imprint of Oneworld Publications, 2022
Reprinted, 2022, 2023

ISBN 978-0-86154-175-1
ISBN 978-0-86154-176-8 (ebook)

Typeset by Geethik Technologies
Printed and bound in Great Britain by Clays Ltd, Elcograf S.p.A.

Visit our website for a reading guide
and exclusive content on THE BIRDER MURDER SERIES

Oneworld Publications
10 Bloomsbury Street
London WC1B 3SR
England

Stay up to date with the latest books,
special offers, and exclusive content from
Oneworld with our newsletter

Sign up on our website
oneworld-publications.com/point-blank

For Kelli and Jim:
Who have shared their story with us every step of the way

And for Marlene and the Harmer family:
Who now carry David's story into the future

1

The murdered man lifted his eyes and gazed upwards. Overhead, a white bird drifted on invisible air currents, heading for the thin crescent of light on the horizon. He watched it fading into the twilight until it disappeared from view, leaving behind only a pale, empty sky. The man knew the white bird would be the last living thing that he would ever see.

He lowered his eyes and looked around at the cold, inhospitable landscape that surrounded him. When the snow-mobile's engine had failed to start the first time, he had known he was in trouble. By the third turn of the key, he had known he was dead. But he hadn't known then that he had been murdered. It was only when he lifted the engine cowling that he saw the murder weapon: the severed fuel line. In the warm, well-equipped service bay back at the base, it would have been a quick fix. A cup of coffee, a shared joke with the others, and the new line would have been installed. Ten minutes? Fifteen at most? Out here, in the midst of this frozen wasteland five kilometres from base, the damaged line was a death sentence. And the clean, sharp edges of the cut meant it was murder.

He shivered and pulled his jacket closer around him. All that was left now was to wait for the approach of nightfall, when the plunging temperatures would rob his body of the last of its warmth, and death would gather him into its dark embrace. To wait; to hold on. But to do so without hope. That was the hardest part. Each moment seemed to stretch out, cruelly offering him a reprieve he knew would not be coming. And every second his fate was delayed, he remained in this strange state. Murdered. But not yet. Once more, he looked around. Nothing moved. Nothing existed. He was by himself out here, left to perform the loneliest vigil of all, the wait for one's own death.

The despondency had left him long ago, and even the last residues of anger that had replaced it had finally subsided. At first, his mind had refused to accept his fate. He continued frantically turning the key, even as the lifeless grinding of the engine told him his efforts were futile. If he only kept trying, kept hoping, the machine would miraculously spring to life. The fuel would vault the gap in the line, flood into the engine, and the snowmobile would speed him back to the warmth and safety of the base camp. But with the slow, building realisation that there would be no miracle, waves of despair had swept in, engulfing him. Hours had passed since then. Now with the milky twilight beginning to descend over the landscape, the last of his human emotions seemed to be ebbing away: his fear, his sorrow, even his desire to survive. There was nothing left inside him now but emptiness, a void as barren and featureless as the terrain that surrounded him.

He knew whoever had murdered him would return. There were many ways to kill a person out here, but only a few could be disguised. It would not be long before his absence was noted. Too long, yes, to save his life, but on the base, no one could remain missing for very long. And then? After a cursory check of the buildings, the search would begin. If his death was to appear accidental, his killer still had some steps to take. The cleanly sliced ends of the fuel line would need to be disguised in some way, to hide any evidence that the act had been deliberate. A radio, too, would need be placed in his survival kit bag, from which his own radio had been removed. Only after rearranging the scene to suit the narrative would the report be sent back. Subject found. No signs of life. Regrets.

And so his death would be attributed to a snowmobile that failed to start. Exhibit A: the key still in the ignition. The autopsy on the machine would reveal some previously undetectable flaw. In these temperatures, materials became brittle and unpredictable. Equipment could reasonably be expected to fail now and again, should be, in fact. Just bad luck, then. The autopsy on the human casualty would similarly reveal nothing beyond the expected: the impact of exposure to extreme cold over a prolonged period – hypothermia, frostbite, frozen flesh. The punishing conditions of this continent would have claimed another life. He would simply be one more victim, like so many others over the centuries, of the bitter temperatures, and the chilling, deadly winds.

He checked the sky again, but there was no sign of the bird against the gathering darkness. Had he really seen it? Perhaps it was a product of his imagination, a precursor of the hallucinations that he suspected would soon be coming, the delirium brought on by his body shutting down. The bird seemed to have appeared from out of nowhere, a white shape drifting across the featureless landscape, like an omen of his forthcoming death. His *death*. He understood how he had been killed, how a severed fuel line had left him stranded in the unsurvivable depths of an Antarctic winter night. And he knew why. So the only question left was *who?* Who among his colleagues had murdered him? Which one of the people he had spent the last six months living among had condemned him to death? Half a year they had spent together, clustered in the claustrophobic quarters of the base. Half a year without light, shut off from the outside world, with only each other for company, for contact, for companionship. He didn't know who had killed him, but he did know that they must have sacrificed something of their own soul to do it. That guilt would haunt them until the end of their days. Would it be enough? Would their demons bring the punishment they deserved? No. Their crime had to be revealed, so the world could deliver its own justice.

The man's shiver reflex had gone, and the cold was beginning to numb his thoughts. He could sense the decline of his responses, feel his vital signs slipping away. But a last spark of will still burned somewhere within him. Not for survival. Nor for vengeance. But for truth. He could still prevent his death from being a lie. He could still tell the world what had really happened.

Taking off his glove, he reached out and clasped the fuel line in his hand, laying the severed ends across his palm. His flesh, already on the point of freezing, showed white through the gap between them. He drew his fingers inwards, pressing them against the fuel line, making a fist that enclosed the two ends within it. The severed line would remain there now, sealing the truth indelibly into his palm, as the night temperatures froze it to his hand. He gathered the survival kit bag tightly under his arm, leaning down on the flap so nothing could be inserted. Then he hunched up closely against the snowmobile, nestling in so that the coming temperatures would fuse man and machine together into a single, frozen block.

The truth would be there, still, when his body was transported back to base, when, in the warmth of the camp's infirmary, his thawing fingers were unfurled and the sharp, clean-cut edges of the fuel line were exposed. It would be silent testimony to the deliberate act that had taken his life, but it would be enough. A message from beyond his frozen death, a clear and unequivocal statement to the world he had left behind. *I was murdered.*

2

The rhythmic clicking of the bicycle wheel was like the ticking of a distant clock, measuring the progress of the rider along the narrow path. It was overloud in the silence that hung over the marsh, seeming to emphasise the strangeness of someone cycling across this landscape in the dark. Even in daylight, this path was a challenging one. On a cloud-shrouded night like this, only the weak glimmer of the bike's lamp prevented the cyclist from drifting off into the standing water on either side.

A fugitive moon emerged momentarily, painting bars of grey light across the landscape, and the noise ceased as the cyclist paused to take in the surroundings. All around lay only a dark, sinister emptiness. But the rider was not concerned about the dangers this place might hold. Those who carry their own menace are not troubled by threats from elsewhere.

Ahead, the bulk of the wooden hide emerged from the surrounding night; a different darkness against the monochrome background. The rider headed for it now, passing veils of mist that hovered over the marsh like witnesses. At the clearing around the hut, the rider laid the bike down carefully on the grass, and began searching in a nearby thicket. The heavy can resisted the first pull, but emerged eventually, thudding to the ground and sinking into the mud. The rider lifted the can and opened it. The cloying scent of petrol escaped into the air.

The fuel was poured carefully, distributed around the base of the hide in a way that minimised the splashing, gulping noise coming from the neck of the can. When it ran dry, the rider drew a lighter from a jacket pocket and flicked it. The flame illuminated features taut with tension. Once again, the figure checked the surroundings, but this time with more purpose. Beyond the hut, away in the distance, a single white light burned bravely against the night. In the other direction, as far across the darkness as the light ahead, the faint yellow glimmer of a lamp was barely detectable. The rider had placed the lamp as a marker before setting out, insurance against becoming disorientated out here and heading off in the wrong direction once the night's work was finished. The lamp would show the way safely off the marsh, where the warmth of a nearby pub awaited. And an alibi.

Across the flat landscape, only two things stood between the light in the distance and the lamp behind. One was the cyclist and the other was the bird hide. The extinguished lighter was replaced in the figure's hand by a phone. Despite the surrounding silence, or perhaps because of it, the conversation was conducted in a hushed tone.

'It can't be this one.' The features tightened at the sharp retort on the other end of the line. 'Because it's on exactly the same bearing as the last one.' The intake of a sharp breath signalled the growing frustration. 'Of course it matters. The hides are all in a straight line. If this one is set alight, you may as well draw an arrow across the marsh pointing directly to the next target.'

Across the wetlands, a restless wind fidgeted, as if undecided whether it should linger. In the end it moved on, playing through the tops of the reeds as it passed. The voice on the other end of the phone was still querying the decision to abort the mission. The listener expelled another exasperated sigh. 'I realise the urgency, but we'll have to choose a different one, further afield, so they won't be able to detect a pattern.'

This time, the retort was instant. And so was the reply. 'Tomorrow night, or the night after, at the latest.' The rider shut the phone off abruptly and stuffed it back into the pocket of the dark jacket. The wind had returned now, picking up and riffling through the grasses. The yellow police tape beside the lamp would be flapping loudly. It would serve as another handy marker as the cyclist approached. Perhaps a visit to the pub was in order anyway, even if no alibi was going to be needed tonight.

As the figure bent to retrieve the can, a faint rustling came from inside the hide. It wouldn't be a person at this time of night, surely? It had to be an animal: a rat, most likely, or a fox. Some other creature for which a dark night on a marsh held no fear. Still, it was important to be sure. The rider edged towards the hide and lifted the door latch, pausing to listen for sounds. There were none. Extending an arm, the figure eased the door back with a flattened hand. It swung inward silently. A band of moonlight spilled into the space through a half-open viewing slat, but deep shadows still lurked in every corner. The rider listened again, not moving a muscle. It made no sense to call out. If no one had yet acknowledged the presence of this figure in the doorway, it was unlikely they would answer.

Once more, the wind moved through the tall grasses, whispering a warning. A flicker of movement shivered across the darkness of the hide's interior, before shrinking back into invisible stillness. The cyclist drew a steadying breath and took a step forward. A flash of whiteness exploded, sending the intruder recoiling through the doorway in shock. Rolling backwards, the rider flattened out against the boards of the hide's exterior, the petrol can slamming against the wall and falling to the ground with a metallic ring that echoed out into the darkness. From a half-crouch, the human watched as the white spectre disappeared across the marsh, the Barn Owl's steady wingbeats as silent as the landscape over which it now flew.

The cyclist bent and snatched up the petrol can, taking a gathering breath to flush away the embarrassment at being so badly startled. Concerned about guiding the bike with the petrol can now balanced precariously on the handlebars, the rider was too preoccupied to look back. The wide-open door to the hide went unnoticed.

But not from within. It was a few minutes before the sound of tentative stirring came from beneath the wooden bench. Unable to tell by sight, the raggedly dressed man had relied upon his ears to confirm that the intruder had left. Although he hadn't watched it happen, he knew it had been the Barn Owl that had come to his rescue. His friend had announced its presence in their shared space earlier in the evening; a chorus of soft clicks and purrs that had made the man smile to himself in the darkness. From beneath the bench, he had listened carefully as the owl stirred at the outsider's approach. He had heard it shuffling in readiness for flight as soon as the intruder tentatively pushed open the door, followed by the explosive flurry of the owl's escape, and the half-cry of alarm as the visitor ducked to avoid it. But before all that, the man had heard something else: one side of a telephone conversation that had revealed plans to commit a crime.

He considered for a moment the details he had overheard from beneath the bench. He knew the target. He knew

3

'Forty-five days.'

Detective Chief Superintendent Colleen Shepherd was aware she sounded like a doctor making a prognosis; one a patient might not be particularly happy to hear. Domenic Jejeune was standing in the doorway of his cottage, an outstretched arm on the open door still barring her entry. Shepherd peered around him into the hallway, and he took the hint, rolling back his arm to invite her inside.

The detective chief inspector led his boss through a warren of stacked boxes and half-packed cartons to the kitchen. 'Would you like a cup of tea?' he asked over his shoulder. He paused at a countertop piled high with the clutter and upheaval of a house move. 'The kettle's already gone, but I think there's still an old saucepan around somewhere. I could find it out if you'd like.'

Whether it was intentional or not, he made it sound altogether too much of an ordeal for a cup of indifferent tea. Shepherd passed. Outside the window, stars of light touched the tops of the riffling water in the wide, quiet sea. He loved the view from this kitchen window, she knew. It was one of the many things about this cottage he would miss when he moved out.

She nodded at the binoculars on the counter near the sink. 'Getting a bit of last-minute birding in? Anything interesting?'

'There were a couple of Eiders out on the water earlier, and a Little Stint went past just before you arrived.' He knew Shepherd would have no interest in the names of the species, but offering her the bare-bones response he usually reserved for non-birders would have been ungracious. Despite the news she had brought, her visit was an act of friendship, not one of duty, and he was aware he had not shown her how much he appreciated it.

Shepherd was silent for a moment before drawing a breath. 'Lindy?' she asked abruptly, as if perhaps she'd been looking for a way to approach the subject and come up empty-handed.

Jejeune nodded. 'Yeah. Doing well. She seems to be recovering nicely.'

'It wasn't a head cold, Domenic. She was in a hostage situation. She saw a man shot to death before her eyes. Nobody recovers nicely from that, certainly not this soon. She's going to need support as she tries to come to terms with everything.' She offered him a smile. 'Perhaps you could take a few long walks around the countryside up at this new place when you get there, let her know you're ready to listen whenever she feels like talking.'

'We take walks now,' protested Jejeune lightly. 'She comes birding with me.'

Shepherd looked doubtful. 'I'm not sure shushing her into silence every five minutes when a new bird pops into view is absolutely the best way of encouraging meaningful conversation.'

Disparaging references about his pastime were Shepherd's way of showing him their relationship was on an even keel. It hadn't always been the case. But it was clear, nevertheless, that she was genuinely concerned that his efforts to help in Lindy's ongoing recovery from her traumatic experience might be falling short of the mark.

She mistook his silence as a response to her news. 'I realise it's not quite the result we were hoping for,' she said.

He tilted his head. 'No.' Thirty days had been the consensus at the station. Even the notoriously cautious Danny Maik had suggested as much. *I can't see it being more than a month, sir. Not once they factor in the result.*

'Still,' continued Shepherd. 'It could have been worse. I've seen the removal of evidence from a crime scene end a career before now. Of course, there was never any intention to pervert the course of justice in this case. And that's why I made it perfectly clear to them that I believed they should base the penalty on the offence. Never mind about making an example of anybody, or sending messages to the rest of the service. Look at the offence, look at the intent, and rule accordingly.'

If Shepherd was waiting for a show of gratitude, or agreement, or any sort of a response at all, really, she was destined for disappointment. Domenic Jejeune was capable of some of the most disconcerting silences she had ever encountered. The way he was staring at her now, arms folded, leaning back against the kitchen countertop, seemed to echo with a dissatisfaction she knew he did not really intend. But Shepherd was never one to let an awkward pause to go unpunished. 'On the bright side, you'll have plenty of time to get the new place knocked into shape.'

'Plenty,' he agreed.

'There's that conservatory you were so keen on,' she said encouragingly. 'Didn't you say you were thinking of doing something with that?'

'I thought it might be a good spot to turn into an aviary. Get a few Strawberry Finches in, some Gouldian Finches, even. I'm not normally a fan of keeping birds in cages, but this would be different. They'd be free-flying, able to forage more naturally, perhaps even breed.'

'Sounds interesting,' said Shepherd dubiously.

'I'll let you know as soon as things are sorted. You can come over and have a look.'

'That would be nice,' she said cautiously. 'But perhaps it might be better to wait a while.'

'Forty-five days?' Jejeune's wan smile suggested he hadn't taken any offence.

'For appearances' sake. Not that there would be very much by way of shop talk to avoid, anyway.'

'Things are still quiet?'

Shepherd nodded. 'Mostly.' She gave him a look of concern. 'But you should keep your wits about you if you do go out birding. A hide went up in flames a couple of nights ago.'

'Really? Which one?'

'Abbot's Marsh. I'm surprised there's been nothing on your birding network about it. I understand it's normally very reliable.'

'I haven't checked the postings recently. I've been busy with the move. Was it deliberate?'

Shepherd nodded. 'A pretty thorough job, too. The outside was completely doused. All four walls. At least two cans of petrol used.'

'When was this, exactly?'

'The night before last. Leave it alone, Domenic.' The warning tone in Shepherd's voice was unmistakable. 'The terms of your suspension prohibit you from going anywhere near an active police investigation.'

'The suspension's not in effect yet,' Jejeune pointed out.

'No,' said Shepherd, drawing the word out. 'But the details of the fire are still under wraps for now. An astute observer, say one of your disciplinary panel members, for example, might wonder how you got hold of this information. They might further wonder whether someone from the department had been here to pay you a friendly visit, less than twenty-four hours before their confidential ruling was announced.' She fixed him with the kind of look that had ended a number of their discussions in the past. 'I know forty-five days sounds like an eternity at the moment, but the time will fly by, truly. Before you know it you'll be back at the station, setting the world to rights, as usual.'

On another day, he might have pointed out that she had just told him that the world, at least the criminal world in Saltmarsh, didn't need setting to rights at the moment. But she was doing everything she could to keep his spirits up, and he rewarded her efforts with a smile of gratitude.

'Well. I suppose I should leave you to your packing,' said Shepherd. 'Oh, one more thing. When you do finally hear the decision of the review board tomorrow, you might try to find a suitable expression from somewhere. Disappointment would be the preferred one, but I suppose even mild surprise would suffice. Only, to greet the news with your usual cold-fish look might give them the idea that perhaps you'd already been informed of their decision.'

'Mildly surprised disappointment it is, then,' said Jejeune with a smile. 'I'll start working on it.'

He walked her to her car, the burgundy paintwork of the Jaguar XF glistening in the sunlight as they approached. He looked around at the small front garden as if he hadn't seen it for a while. Or perhaps like someone preparing to say goodbye to it. Shepherd saw a shadow of sadness cross his face. And now, she thought, he wouldn't even have the distraction of work to take his mind off his move. 'Change can be a good thing, Domenic. It's a chance to put our past behind us.' She paused. 'It's what you need. Both of you.'

His expression suggested this wasn't the first time he'd heard this argument, but he managed another grateful smile. Shepherd was able to find a smile of her own in return as she said goodbye. But it was no more than a faint one, tinged with uncertainty. And perhaps something more.

As soon as the sound of the Jaguar's engine had faded away, Jejeune returned to the kitchen. He grabbed his binoculars and car keys, leaving through the back door and heading round to the side of the cottage, where his Range Rover sat. The vehicle he called The Beast was already filled almost to capacity with boxes and cartons and overstuffed bags. But he managed to find room to slide in behind the wheel and fire up the engine. There was no need to input his destination into the Range Rover's satnav. He had been there so many times, The Beast could probably have found its way to Abbot's Marsh all by itself.

4

Gayatri Monde settled into the plastic office chair and opened her laptop computer. The surface of her desk was bare apart from the device, the rest of her office equipment and documents stored away in the three small boxes stacked against the wall behind her. The laptop powered up and she spent a long moment looking at the screensaver image: a younger self staring back at her, an infant boy snuggled against her hip. There was a tap on the door frame and Gaya looked up to see a woman in a bright orange snowsuit standing in the open doorway.

'Scott said to tell you he'll be in for your boxes in a few minutes.'

'How's it going?'

Lexi Marshall shrugged. 'Like usual. Too much equipment, not enough room for the personal possessions.'

Gaya smiled. The move out was always the same. The woman saw the meeting reminder blinking on Gaya's laptop. 'Have you thought about what you're going to tell him?'

'I have to tell him everything, Lexi.'

'About the death, obviously.' The woman looked around and stepped into the room, easing the door shut behind her. 'But about the other stuff?'

'It will come out anyway. It's a small base. People see things.'

At the door knock, the two women fell silent. A man clad in a similar orange snowsuit to Lexi's opened the door. He pointed at the boxes. 'If those are going, Gaya, we'll need to get them into the Hagglund right now. Amy is almost ready to do the weight calculations.'

Gaya nodded. The reports out of McMurdo were suggesting the ice field was shifting, and cracks were beginning to appear. If they were going to be doing stress testing along their route, it would be important to have accurate weight readings for both the heavy-duty tracked vehicles and the equipment in them.

Lexi stood by in silence as Scott Della stacked the boxes on top of each other and edged past her to leave. She let her eyes trail after him. 'Yeah, well I'm sure people would be interested in what I've seen, too.'

'Concerning Scott?'

Lexi tilted her head. 'Like you said. It's a small base.'

The two women stared at each other. In the silence, Gaya could hear the sound of the wind outside. She had grown used to the creaks resonating from the walls, and the constant, eerie rattling of metal, but it had never seemed to carry such menace before. She checked her watch. 'It's time for my call,' she said.

Lexi turned to leave. Gaya didn't need to ask her to close the door. Privacy was a precious commodity in the close confines of an Antarctic base, and everyone understood that even the most innocent of personal communications might be guarded jealously. Not that the call Gaya Monde was about to make was personal. Or innocent. She stared at the screensaver image for another long moment and drew a deep breath. She clicked open her Zoom connection and waited. A grainy grey image appeared, glitching and time-lagging. But the features of Julien Bellaire were unmistakable nevertheless.

'Good morning, Gayatri.' Bellaire's voice carried the warped, robotic quality she had become accustomed to on these calls, but it was otherwise carefree and unguarded. She could see no evidence of anyone else in the room, but she needed to be sure.

'Are you alone, Mr Bellaire?'

There was a pulse of silence before he replied. 'I am.'

'And you are recording this meeting?'

Again, the question caused a moment's hesitation. 'As you know, Gaya, all communications to and from the base are recorded.'

This time, the silence came from the other end of the world.

'You may continue,' prompted Bellaire.

'There has been an incident.' She paused. 'Alex Kasabian is dead. The recording, Mr Bellaire... I wonder if—'

'Alex Kasabian? Dead? How? An accident?'

The pause from the base was so enduring, Bellaire checked to make sure the feed was still live. 'It does not appear to have been an accident, Mr Bellaire,' said Gaya finally. 'It seems Alex Kasabian's death was caused by a deliberate act.'

Bellaire's shock seemed to draw him towards his screen. 'What? No, this cannot be.'

For a fleeting moment, Gaya sensed the dislocation of a man confronted with a situation he could not control. Despite his immense wealth, circumstances had taken Julien Bellaire into a strange realm of uncertainty and insecurity.

'Alex had gone out to check his monitoring equipment. While he was out there, the fuel line on his snowmobile was severed. He froze to death.'

'Severed?'

'Cut through.'

'No,' said Bellaire again. 'I cannot accept this. There must be some mistake. It must have been an accident, surely? Perhaps if you were to examine the snowmobile again, more carefully... After all, a cursory check, in such challenging conditions...'

Who was he, thought Gaya, this man who had never visited the continent, to speak of the conditions out here? What did he know of the savage winds, of the cruel, flesh-numbing cold that buried itself into your core every time you ventured out? What did Julien Bellaire know of an Antarctic landscape that had claimed the life of Alex Kasabian with its stealthy, silent violence? 'Both the body and the snowmobile are still out at the site. But there is no mistake, Mr Bellaire. The line was cut in two.'

She waited, listening to the silence at the other end of the call. Thoughts now, then a response. It was Julien Bellaire's way of regaining control, of beginning to shape events again. Even through the snowy haze of the feed, Gaya could tell that he had looked away from the screen. She remembered the view beyond the large mullioned windows in his office; a gentle, rolling landscape of green fields dotted with oaks and beech trees. Whether Julien Bellaire would find anything out there to help him process the news, she didn't know.

'Could he have done this himself, perhaps? Accidently cut through the line while attempting a repair?'

'There was no tool lying anywhere near the body. His survival bag is tucked under his arm and cannot be accessed yet. It will be impossible to go through the contents until the body has been recovered and given time to thaw.'

'So it is possible there is a screwdriver in the bag, or some other tool capable of cutting through the fuel line?'

Gaya moved her head. 'It is possible.'

Through the pixilating reception, Bellaire may not have seen the gesture, but he could not have missed the tone in her voice that said otherwise. He chose to ignore it anyway.

'Then we shall leave the cause of his death undetermined for now,' he declared. 'But how can it be that no one noticed he was missing? Why was his disappearance not detected before everyone retired for the night?'

There was no window to draw Gaya's eyes from the screen, but even if there was, there would have been no rolling, sun-kissed fields to meet her gaze. All that existed beyond the corrugated shell of her dwellings was an unblemished expanse of whiteness, stretching as far as the eye could see in all directions. 'There was a 300-Club event that night,' she said quietly. 'Alex said he didn't want to be a part of it. Everyone assumed he'd returned to base after his monitoring trip and just gone straight to his quarters. He rarely took breakfast with us anyway, so it was not until mid-morning that his absence was noted. When we checked the shed and found that his snowmobile hadn't been logged back in, I went out to the station immediately. I found his body at the site.'

Bellaire began to speak, but the connection was interrupted momentarily. His twisted features were frozen on the screen until the connection was re-established and his tinny voice came through again. '...did not try to recover him? Or the machine?'

'Alex died with his hand clutching the fuel line. It is frozen to it now, impossible to detach. We're still in the middle of an extreme cold spell. I couldn't risk exposing a crew to those temperatures for the length of time it would take to dig out the body and the snowmobile together and load them onto a transport sled.'

'So the site has not been disturbed?' There was a guarded-ness about the man's inquiry. Even though the question had to be asked, perhaps the answer was something that held more uncertainty for Julien Bellaire.

Gaya understood. 'The team has been out to the site to pay their respects, but nothing was touched. I took photographs before the others arrived, to record everything just as it was when I found it. I am attaching the file now.'

She saw Bellaire lean forward to click the attachment. She waited as he examined the photographs and watched him turn his head away to look out of the window once more. What had he seen as he studied the image of Alex Kasabian's outstretched arm, of the blanched fingers clamping onto the fuel line? Was it the same things she had: the desperation, the suffering, the anguish of a man having the life slowly frozen out of him?

Bellaire's voice startled her back from her thoughts. 'I must report this, Gayatri. You realise that?'

'You understand we cannot stay on here,' she said.

Bellaire nodded. The cramped confines of the base would not be able to sustain the newly arriving crew and the one that had been scheduled to depart. To place so much strain on the meticulously calculated resources at the base risked the lives of everyone. 'With the colder temperatures, the window for the ship to depart will be narrow. You must proceed to your rendezvous with the *Oceanite* as planned. You will leave a liaison at the base?'

'Lexi Marshall has volunteered.'

'She and Alex were close, I believe?'

'Once. It ended. Not well.'

'And yet she now wishes to stay on?' Bellaire considered this for a moment. 'She understands that nothing at the site is to be disturbed. The weather conditions will improve soon. It will be easier for the new team to recover the body and bring it back to base.'

A violent bang against the outside wall of Gaya's office startled her. Something propped against the building ready to be loaded into the Hagglund had been caught by the wind and was being battered against the side of the structure. She heard Scott shouting urgent orders over the screeching sounds of metal on metal. The arrogance of wealth, thought Gaya, for Julien Bellaire to believe he could dictate from the comfort of his Elysian English countryside how matters would unfold in this untamable landscape.

'If you will forgive me,' she said, 'there is much to be done if we are to depart on schedule.'

Bellaire nodded. 'I will inform the police. Make your report to the authorities at Dumont d'Urville when you arrive, and brief the incoming base commander about the situation. Beyond that, discuss this with no one.'

The banging outside her office had ceased. Only the low moaning of the wind against the metal skin of the building could be heard now. She had heard that Antarctic research bases were the most remote human habitations that had ever existed on Earth. Never had it seemed more true to her than at this moment. Never had the distance between her steel hut and the soft green fields of England seemed so vast. 'I will do what needs to be done.' She looked back at her screen and saw that it had frozen again. This time the connection did not return; the link was abruptly terminated. Perhaps her final response had been delivered to dead air. But she knew Julien Bellaire had received the message anyway.

5

What this place needs, thought Colleen Shepherd, is a touch of freshening up. A splash of colour here, a lick of paint there. Perhaps even a plant or two. She gave a small sigh. When the decor of Saltmarsh station was foremost in her mind, it was a sign that the wait for a serious case had been going on too long. The day-to-day fare was being handled efficiently enough. With this group she'd expect no less. But unless something more worthy of their talents came in soon, getting the decorators in might at least provide a bit of a distraction.

Across the room, Detective Sergeant Danny Maik was tilting his imposing form towards a fresh-faced constable. Shepherd observed Maik carefully. He had suffered a serious injury in the incident involving Lindy, and if he showed no physical signs of it now, the DCS was still concerned about hidden wounds of another kind. But he seemed in good enough spirits today. Whatever wisdom Danny was imparting, it was bringing a smile to the constable's face. Maik liked to show his approachable side from time to time, she knew. It made it easier to get everybody's attention on those occasions it was necessary to trot out the other side of his personality.

Across from Danny, Lauren Salter was avoiding eye contact and sitting just far enough away to make sure everything stayed nice and discreet. From an admin point of view, having officers at the same station involved in a relationship wasn't something that could be allowed to go on indefinitely. But at the moment, there was no need for Shepherd to do any more than make sure the two sergeants were assigned to separate aspects of any investigation. For now, the relationship between Danny and Lauren Salter could remain that most unusual of situations in the workplace: open knowledge that everyone simply chose to treat as a secret.

Shepherd completed her survey of the room by settling her gaze on Tony Holland. He was seated on a desk near the window, his feet resting on the chair in front of him. If only the detective constable would unconsciously adopt some of Domenic Jejeune's more useful habits, she thought ruefully. Holland was engaged in the activity that seemed to occupy most of his time these days: regaling anyone who would listen with tales of his recent secondment. His constant references to his time at *The MET* had developed into something of a meme at the station, but Shepherd suspected Holland would happily accept that as the price for remaining the centre of attention.

The gentle indolence of the Incident Room suggested nothing major was waiting for Shepherd in the daily update, but there was only one way to find out. 'Right, let's get to it,' she said. The conversations died down and the small knot of officers turned to face their DCS. Maik handed her a wafer-thin docket and she disguised a look of frustration as she consulted it. 'This suspicious death out at Harland Corners?'

'Suicide, we believe, ma'am,' said Holland. 'We got the call because her lawyer said she'd made an appointment the day before to change her will. But the assistant who took the call confirms she only wanted to verify a couple of the terms. There was no mention of changing anything.'

'So nothing for us, then? Let's check it out to be sure. And nothing more on these vehicle break-ins.'

'Same M.O. at each. Quiet car parks, unlocked cars, valuables in sight. We've asked traffic to keep an eye out and step up runs past the more remote parking areas.' Maik inclined his head. 'Matter of time, unless they get bored and move on.'

Shepherd gave a short nod. 'Fair enough. This fire at the Abbot's Marsh hide.' She looked at them. 'Kids, we think?'

'I'm not so sure, ma'am,' said Lauren Salter dubiously. 'Tony arrives back from the Smoke and the next thing you know, there's an attack on the local birdwatching community.' She held up her hands. 'Just saying.'

'I've got nothing against birders. Listen, during my time at the Met...' Holland waited for the chorus of jeers to die down, '...I came to appreciate that there's room for us all to cohabit this planet in harmony.'

'No cause for alarm, ladies and gentlemen,' said Salter, holding up her hands again in mock appeasement. 'Tony's new girlfriend is into Taoism, apparently. He's just trying out some new material before he sees her tonight.'

'Kids?' Shepherd's tone suggested it might be time to get back to business.

Maik shrugged non-committally. 'If it was, they certainly came prepared,' he said. 'According to Bryan McVicar, there was enough petrol splashed about to have burned up three hides that size.'

Shepherd nodded. The local fire crew chief's word was not one to be doubted. 'But if not kids, then who...?'

Danny shrugged again. 'Hard to imagine who else would get any joy out of torching an empty hut. Or any motive other than vandalism.'

So possibly not kids, but no likelihood that it was anybody else, either. Shepherd sighed inwardly. If thinking like this was a by-product of Maik's newfound romance, it hardly boded well for the future. She was all for Danny finding some joy in his life, but if it was going to bring about this kind of non-committal drivel, this relationship was going to turn out to be a bloody nuisance.

'Okay. What else do we have?' Shepherd made a show of consulting the folder again before closing it and looking at Holland. 'Speaking of your new girlfriend, didn't she bring us something yesterday?'

'Oh, I don't think we need to give that too much credence, ma'am,' said the constable easily.

'What's this, then?' asked Maik. Even a lead so casually dismissed by Tony Holland had to be better than trying to turn a torched birding hide into a worthwhile investigation.

'A blog post,' said Shepherd. 'It showed up on a site run by North Norfolk University's Department of Global Climatology. Tony's girlfriend is a receptionist there.'

'Administrative assistant,' said Holland, 'at the Bellaire Institute, to be precise. It's affiliated with the uni because of its link to an Antarctic research station. It's Paige's job to monitor correspondence to and from the base. A couple of days ago, there was a blog post that seemed a bit dodgy. I told her it was probably nothing but she sent it over anyway.'

'Where it was duly logged into our system,' said Shepherd archly, 'which means we will now be taking a proper look into it. "*I will not live to see the storm petrels return.*" That was the message, wasn't it, Tony?'

'Yeah, but as I say, I'm sure there's nothing to it. I mean, it's a blog post. I don't think they're meant to be treated as gospel.'

'Storm petrels,' Maik said. 'They're birds, aren't they?'

'Pelagic seabirds,' said Salter, consulting her phone.

Holland pulled a face. 'Well, if it's about birds, we know who we should be asking. Where is he, by the way? Typical

– the one time some birding knowledge might be useful and he's nowhere to be found.'

'The inspector is not handling cases for the time being,' said Shepherd evenly.

'Oh, right. The suspension.' A look from Maik quelled the jauntiness in the constable's tone. 'Erm, so how long'd he get, then?'

'Still to be determined. The decision is being announced today.'

'He's lucky a suspension is all he's looking at,' said Holland earnestly. 'Removing evidence? They don't tolerate nonsense like that down at the Met, I can tell you. It's by the book all the way down there. He'd have been out on his ear.'

That, thought Shepherd, was highly unlikely. It seemed to her that any police department in the country would have done all they could to retain the services of an officer like Domenic Jejeune. But Holland's comment, she knew, was less about Jejeune and more about finding yet another opportunity to remind everyone about his recent sojourn down the Smoke. Perhaps it was time to remind him he was well and truly home.

'So we can leave you to follow that one up, then, can we, Constable? It's probably nothing, as you say. But just for the sake of appearances, let's be thorough. Dot all our i's and cross all our t's. Just as they would down at the Met.' The light glinted on the lenses of Shepherd's glasses as she fixed Holland with her patented over-the-rim stare.

'Right,' she announced brusquely, 'I'm sure the rest of you all have things to be getting on with. I'd remind you that paperwork is not an inconvenience, it's a vital part of our job.'

Shepherd crossed towards Danny, who was watching as the other officers departed. Like Shepherd, they had been hoping for something more substantial from the briefing. To say that they looked unenthused by the prospect of more paperwork would have been an understatement.

'I'm considering giving the place a facelift,' the DCS told Maik. 'Boost morale a bit until something major comes in. What do you think?'

Danny Maik had experienced more than his share of make-work projects during his army days, and he'd never known a new coat of paint to do much to lift anyone's spirits. 'I think a project like that might encourage a wide range of responses, ma'am.'

She gave a sigh. Not too long ago, she would have considered Danny Maik the last bastion of straight talk around here. Perhaps this was another sign that he was more at peace with the world these days. She hoped not. She would hate to see Maik's refreshing honesty become one more casualty of his romance. 'Everything okay with you these days?' she asked solicitously. 'I'm told you've completed your counselling programme. I trust it helped.'

Maik tilted his head non-committally. He wasn't sure that the mandated sessions had achieved any more than a couple of quiet nights down the pub would have, but he knew Shepherd was a strong advocate of such interventions. What *had* helped him was Lauren Salter's constant presence and companionship, but he saw no reason to share this with his DCS. He suspected she already knew anyway.

'Do you think Lindy will have benefitted from her own sessions?'

Maik gave the inquiry some thought before answering. 'She's been through a lot. The counselling will have laid some markers along the trail, but she'll have to find her own way back. She's got the mettle, I've no doubt about that. But it might take some time.'

Shepherd watched Maik carefully. He had locked eyes with death on more than one occasion. If there was anyone who would be an authority on what it took to come through something like this, it was him. 'And the support she's going to need, you're confident she'll have that?'

Danny Maik had been putting two and two together and reaching five for a long time now. 'It's a fine balance, giving her the time and space she needs and being ready to jump in when she wants help. I'm no expert on relationships, but I'd say she and the DCI have a strong enough foundation to weather this together.'

No expert, perhaps, but Danny had come a long way in a short time since he and Salter had started seeing each other. Not so long ago, it would probably have taken the sight of a man in a tuxedo and a woman in a long white dress standing at the front of a church before Danny cottoned on that there might be something going on between them. 'Right, well, I doubt things are quite desperate enough around here just yet for us to be classifying either this bird hide business or the blog post as a major crime, but that's not to say we avoid looking into them altogether. I just don't see the need to commit any unnecessary resources to them at this stage. Understood?'

Maik understood. Make a few lukewarm inquiries, but be prepared to drop them as soon as anything more worthwhile appeared on the horizon. He just hoped that day was coming sooner rather than later.

6

'Okay.'

Lindy Hey sighed. Domenic's response to her inquiry as to how he felt about the length of his suspension might have been expected, but it was no more helpful for all that. When the Choctaw people first introduced their subtly accented agreement to the rest of the world, it's unlikely they imagined anyone would be able to wring as many nuances from it as Domenic Jejeune. His version of *okeh* could mean anything from *spectacular* to *deeply disappointing*. Lindy had once told him he could get more mileage out of the word than most people managed in an entire speech. But even if she wasn't always able to pinpoint his exact meaning, she was fairly sure this response was a long way from the positive end of the spectrum.

'It will soon pass, Domenic. Six weeks sounds like a long time, but with all there is to do around here, it'll go really quickly. You'll see.'

'Six and a half weeks,' he said. He turned away from the window and looked around the room, awash with a sea of half-opened boxes and crates and laundry baskets pressed into service as makeshift moving cartons.

It will soon pass. Lindy realised DCS Shepherd had probably said much the same thing when she'd delivered the news.

'I'm sorry, Dom. I'm not making light of it. I know it's going to be difficult.'

'No, you're right. There's plenty to keep me busy.' As if to convince himself, Jejeune hefted a large box to waist height and began carrying it along the hallway. 'Bedroom One?'

'Two, I think. For now, anyway. Or better yet, the conservatory.'

She followed him and watched as he laid the box on the floor before pausing to take in the view through the large picture windows that ran the length of the room. They stood together for a moment, looking out at the mirror-calm waters of the inlet beside the house, faithfully reflecting the stand of leafy trees on the far bank. The moment was shattered by the doorbell chime, a sound so unfamiliar to both of them they looked at each other for a moment before recognising what it was. It was a small reminder of the newness of their surroundings. What other surprises would this house have in store for them?

Lindy's delight at seeing the figure at the door was genuine and fulsome. 'Danny! Come in. Dom's in the conservatory.'

Maik followed her in. He nodded approvingly as he looked around. 'Nice spot,' he said.

'We're thinking of turning this into my project room,' Lindy told him.

Though the topic of what Lindy darkly referred to as her *Projects* had come up from time to time, Jejeune hadn't been aware they'd agreed on any definite space for them. But it didn't really matter. The aviary idea was probably impractical, anyway.

'Fancy a cuppa?' Lindy asked Danny. 'I'll put some music on, too.'

She disappeared and, moments later, the tight up-beat of a Motown backing track came through the sound system.

Silky-smooth female vocals flowed in seamlessly. Lindy called from the kitchen, seeking Maik's approval. He'd have been happy enough with 'You Can't Hurry Love' at any time, but the fact that Lindy had clearly chosen the track to send her own cheeky message added an extra measure of delight.

Jejeune watched as his sergeant leaned back and settled into the music, the Supremes' subtle harmonies bringing a faint smile to his face. He gave himself a moment before turning to Jejeune and lowering his voice slightly. 'The DCS was wondering how Lindy's counselling went.'

'I would imagine between the two of them, they'd worked through the worst of the counsellor's problems by the end of the sessions,' said Jejeune.

Maik smiled. The comment had captured Lindy's persona to a tee, at least the Lindy the world had known before her ordeal. Jejeune craned towards the kitchen. He seemed faintly unnerved that she was out of his sight. Maik regarded his DCI carefully. In some ways, Lindy seemed to have handled the whole affair better than her partner, even though she had been at the centre of the terrifying events that had unfolded that day, and he had been only the latest of late arrivals.

Lindy returned with a tray of cups. She handed Jejeune his coffee. Colombian, Maik remembered, a favourite since the DCI's return from the country a couple of years before. The sergeant sat forward awkwardly in the chair and held his teacup and saucer on his lap. The delicate chinaware looked like a child's play set cradled in Danny's large, battle-scarred hands.

'So how's life?' asked Lindy brightly.

'Plenty to be thankful for.' Maik's faint smile said the rest. 'And you?'

Lindy nodded quietly. 'Yeah, you know, all good.'

Jejeune watched the interchange. There was a connection between them now that he knew he could never share. Together in that cottage they had stared into the face of death and survived. No one else could ever be a part of that. 'DCS Shepherd was telling me about the fire at the Abbot's Marsh hide,' he said conversationally, to remind them both he was still there.

Maik inclined his head apologetically. Both men knew she'd done so before Jejeune's suspension had been officially announced. Neither Shepherd nor anyone else in the department would be telling Jejeune about active cases for the next forty-five days. But Danny was keen to show he hadn't come empty-handed. He fished a piece of paper from his jacket pocket. 'Constable Holland offered to accompany me today. I suspect he may have wanted to run this by you, so I thought I'd save him the trouble.'

'Of seeing me?'

Maik smiled and handed Jejeune the paper. It was a transcript of the blog post from the Antarctic base. 'The constable's been tasked with getting to the bottom of it, but he's got other matters to attend to just now.'

'Anybody we know?' asked Lindy.

'I believe the young lady is new in town,' said Danny. Which, his look suggested, explained it all.

'*I will not live to see the storm petrels return.*' Jejeune looked up from the paper. 'This was everything? There's been nothing like it from this account, either before or after?'

'Not according to the person who sent it over, this same new acquaintance of the constable's, as it happens.'

'Is it okay for Dom to be having a look at this?' asked Lindy guardedly. If there was one person in the world she would want to protect from trouble besides Domenic, it was the man sitting beside him now.

'It's a preliminary inquiry. If it's determined there's cause to take it further, it'll become an active case. At that point…' Maik let his regretful expression make his point for him.

Jejeune nodded in understanding. 'Any idea how far Constable Holland's inquiries took him?'

'The account belongs to a man called Alex Kasabian, one of the researchers stationed at Camp Isolée in Antarctica. It's a climate research base affiliated with the university and an institute here. It has also been verified that the message was sent, or at least routed through, the ISP at the base.'

'I would have thought Wi-Fi time at those bases was precious,' said Lindy. 'I can't see anybody wasting it on a prank.'

'Nor can I,' said Jejeune. 'Has anybody attempted to contact the base?'

'Call's in, but the next satellite window is not until two a.m. our time. Even then, it's hit or miss, apparently. Depends on the atmospherics. So when would the storm petrels be likely to arrive in Antarctica?'

'Down there, he'd be talking about Wilson's Storm Petrels. Since the Antarctic summer is the opposite of ours, I'm assuming breeding migrants would begin to arrive around November. But if this person is there now, it means they've already been there all winter. An Antarctic winter is the lockdown of all lockdowns. I can't imagine anyone who had endured one wanting to stay on for a summer season that would take them into November. At least, not under normal circumstances.'

'From what I've heard, Antarctica doesn't involve normal circumstances very much,' said Maik. He reached for his tea again and finished it. 'Still, perhaps things will make more sense when we hear back from the base. So I can leave this with you then?'

'Of course you can,' said Lindy on Dom's behalf. 'I can even do a bit of background research at the mag on this facility.' She looked at Danny. 'That'd be okay, wouldn't it?'

'A private citizen can use any available legal resources for his research— Sorry, sir. I didn't mean to imply...'

Jejeune smiled. *A private citizen.* At least Danny hadn't told him it would soon pass. Maik eased himself to his feet and handed Lindy the cup and saucer. 'Thank you.' He took another look around the room. 'This is the right place, Lindy,' he said sincerely. 'This will get you there.'

Jejeune watched the exchange from the sidelines, content to be a bystander once more. In a strange way, Danny seemed to have gained something from his ordeal: a sense of purpose and direction in his life that caused him to seek out a new relationship. Would the prospect of transforming this new house into their home be enough to offer Lindy a similar road to recovery, he wondered.

He walked Maik to the door and lingered on the step as the sergeant went to his Mini. Before he got in, Maik looked back at his DCI. 'It occurs to me, sir, what with it being so quiet and all down at the station, if ever there was a time to be away from work, this would be it.'

Just right, thought Jejeune, and just enough. Typical Danny Maik. He nodded his thanks.

Lindy joined him on the step in time to watch the car drive away. As they turned to go back into the house, a Black-headed Gull drifted in over the inlet and executed a slow pinwheel turn on a downward-tipped wing. It was a manoeuvre of such breathtaking elegance, Domenic Jejeune stood in silent appreciation for a long moment. He could be happy here, Lindy knew. But he had to allow it, and she didn't know if he was ready to give himself permission while the spectre of a man called Ray Hayes hovered over them. 'No past, Dom,' she said. 'That's what we agreed. Remember? This is us, now: a new start, a new place.'

He did remember, sitting at the top of the drive in the Range Rover after completing their second walk-through. And afterwards, a silent drive to the estate agent's office to submit their offer. It was their pact, their agreement, codified in a legal document, signed before witnesses; this is us now, moving on, together.

The gull drifted back towards the mouth of the inlet. Lindy linked her arm with Domenic's, watching the bird's effortless glide as it headed out towards the open sea. 'New horizons, Dom,' she said. 'Let's see what they hold.'

7

The breeze was from the southwest. It was warm and carried the scent of white clover, still in bloom around the man's feet. There was not enough force in the wind to churn the nearby waters, though, so only the faintest sound of lapping against the shoreline reached his ears. He sensed the momentary shadow of a cloud passing overhead, in what must have been an otherwise clear sky, and listened to the bird calls that filled the air. When he stood still like this, it seemed to Arliss Dyer that he could draw the entire surrounding landscape into himself, filling his senses to capacity.

He was standing on a wide circular landmass at the foot of a sharp incline. Another slope, equally steep, rose up on the far side of the land. On either side of the flat expanse lay a different body of water, one fresh, one salt, separated by the land between them. He felt the footsteps approaching across the hard-packed ground. The voice, when it came, was the one he expected.

'Arliss, what a nice surprise. No doubt you've already heard those Redwings *sieep-sieeping* away overhead.'

'There a Meadow Pipit up there, too, I believe,' said Dyer.

Tori Boyd shielded her eyes from the sun with her hand as she turned her face skywards. Above the fast-flying Redwings she could see the pipit, singing sweetly as it spiralled downwards on half-closed wings. She shook her head, even though she knew the man could not see the gesture. 'Those ears of yours should be declared a national treasure. So to what do we owe the pleasure?' She looked at the man closely, taking in the stalks of straw clinging to the fabric of his jacket. 'You're not sleeping rough again, are you? I thought you had sorted a permanent place to stay these days.'

'Another refugee of the pandemic, I'm afraid. The lady I was lodging with passed, sadly, and her family decided to sell up. Means I'm footloose and fancy-free once again for the time being.'

'But that's terrible, turfing you out like that.'

'Can't blame 'em, I suppose, with the housing market the way it is. They did put me in touch with some organisation that might have a spot for me. It's just that...' Dyer turned his face into the gentle breeze.

'Those places tend to be in town,' said Boyd. 'And you'd miss your outdoors, wouldn't you, Arliss? But surely you don't intend on roaming the countryside indefinitely.'

Dyer smiled and shook his head. 'I've grown a bit too fond of my creature comforts, I'm afraid. No, I'll find somewhere soon enough when the weather turns. Have to say, though, there's still something wonderful about waking to the dawn chorus, hearing those Skylarks warbling their way up into the skies first thing in the morning. As a matter of fact, it's something I heard while sleeping rough that has me coming up here today, Ms Boyd. It concerns these hides: the Brackets.'

On either side of the flat land, a pair of wooden bird hides described long curves around the separate shorelines, each hugging the edge as it faced outwards. The man's gaze was locked unerringly on the site of the wooden structures. Mind maps, thought Boyd, memories of previous visits when he had gathered in the details with his other senses. But mind maps relied on accurate information.

'Things are quite a bit different from than the last time you were here, Arliss. We've removed the back walls of the hides and connected them into one large structure with a curved glass front and back wall, and a large frosted glass dome over everything. Most impressive it is, I assure you. It all houses a research facility now, the headquarters for a project we're involved in with the university.'

Dyer inclined his head to show he could picture the new layout. 'Sounds like there's no through passage between the hides any more, then.'

'The new facility stretches all the way from one side to the other now, but I can let you through the building and out the back if you wanted to go up the far side.'

Dyer didn't acknowledge the offer. 'Don't imagine the birders come down to the Brackets any more, then, either.'

Boyd allowed a note of sadness to creep into her voice. 'They haven't been bird hides for quite some time. We don't even call this place the Brackets any more. We're the Bellaire Institute now; officially the Julien Bellaire Institute for Climate Science.'

Dyer was silent for a moment, as if the information troubled him. 'I don't want to alarm you, Ms Boyd, but I believe some people are planning to set fire to one of those hides.'

'What?' She knew Dyer would have heard the panic rise in her voice. 'Where did you hear this?'

'Last night. I was up at Stirrat's Wood. Somebody was talking on a phone to another person, saying they were going to set fire to a hide here, after they'd done that one.'

'You were there? And you heard this person?' Could he hear the fear tightening in her chest? 'Are you sure they were talking about this facility?'

Dyer swayed his head. The gesture had a slightly mechanical quality to it. 'They didn't mention this place by name, but unless I'm mistaken, these are the only hides in a straight line with the ones at Abbot's Marsh and Stirrat's Wood. The idea was to make the fires look random. But they realised all the hides line up, dead straight across the landscape: Abbot's Marsh, Stirrat's Wood and here. Nothing random about that, is there?'

Tori Boyd stared out over the open lands. Across the expanse of fresh water, she could see the shallow depression of Stirrat's Wood. Beyond it, the distant waters of Abbot's Marsh glinted in the light. Although she couldn't see either hide, she knew he was right. Buildings, trails, topography: Arliss Dyer could probably navigate the countryside around here as well as anyone with full vision. It was one more reason he would want to stay local, she realised.

'Could it be that you mistook this person – I take it you would have said if you recognised the voice – this person's intentions? Perhaps it was someone's idea of a joke.'

Even to her, the casual dismissal didn't sound convincing. Dyer held his head to one side, as if listening to a recording in his head. 'They were serious. This person had come to Stirrat's Wood last night with the intention of setting fire to that hide. I could smell the petrol, hear them pouring it around the hide.'

'You were inside the hide?' Boyd slammed her hand to her mouth. 'Thank God they didn't go through with it.'

'Wasn't God that stopped them,' Dyer told her matter-of-factly. 'As I say, it was geometry. I was going to give Inspector Jejeune a call.' He fished a battered-looking cell phone from the inside pocket of his jacket. 'Got his number in here on speed dial. But I forgot to charge it at the pub last night. Dead as a doornail. So I thought I'd better get over here and tell you first.' He paused for a moment. 'You need to be careful, Ms Boyd. They said they were going to choose another hide, one in a more random spot. After that...' There was an awkwardness to the way he nodded as he concluded, but the point was made.

Perhaps the only thing Arliss Dyer was incapable of interpreting was silence. After a long pause, Boyd put a hand on his arm. She had found some calmness from somewhere and was closer to control now. 'I simply can't believe somebody is intending to attack this place, Arliss. I'm sure it must all be some kind of mistake. I mean, the Brackets aren't even hides any more. They're not even individual buildings. But this should be reported anyway. Let's go inside and we can call the inspector from there. You can use my phone. And we'll see if we can't find you a drop of something nice, too, by way of a reward.'

As they approached the large glass doors of the building, Dyer paused and gestured to a stand of trees at the top of the far rise. 'The starlings always did like those hornbeams,' he said. 'Be why that Sparrowhawk is hanging around, I suppose. He's just off to the west of them.'

Boyd looked up into the trees. It took her a moment to locate the dark shape. Had he really heard the hawk's low, repeated call all the way down here? The sightless inhabited a different world, she thought. Those who could see experienced life only as it happened, the immediacy of events as they unfurled before them. But Arliss Dyer's world was one of foreshadowing, of cues and hints and veiled suggestions. An approaching flock of Redwings, the impending strike of a Sparrowhawk, a forthcoming arson attack; it was almost as if Dyer's blindness had provided him with the gift of prophecy as compensation.

'Hello, Arliss.'

Paige Turner was surprised to see him enter the administration centre behind Tori Boyd. When it came to outsiders, the converted space was usually considered forbidden territory. And yet here he was, this shabbily dressed gent being guided in, hand on arm, as if he was a visiting dignitary.

The woman's voice seemed to startle Dyer. 'I didn't know you worked here,' he said.

'My day job,' she told him.

'You two know each other?' Boyd asked sharply.

'Arliss occasionally pops into the pub where I work at night,' Turner told her, in a tone that might allow the man to imagine an ironic smile.

'Can you get him a single malt? Make it a healthy one. Oh, and a nice glass, right, Arliss? Didn't you once tell me it makes the good stuff taste even better?'

Turner headed to Boyd's office at the far end of the glass-domed space. A *please* and *thank you* would have been too much to expect, but at least when she did this at her other job she got the occasional tip. By the time she returned, Boyd was just handing Dyer her phone. 'It's gone to voicemail,' she told him. 'Here, leave a message.'

'Hello, Inspector. It's Arliss... Arliss Dyer.'

The message was surprisingly lucid and concise, at least as far as Paige Turner was concerned. She'd encountered Arliss in the pub a number of times, and she'd never heard him speak with this kind of deliberate enunciation, either. To him, at least, the gravity of the report clearly warranted such eloquence. At the mention of a threat to their building, Turner flashed a look in Boyd's direction. But the other woman waved away her concerns. Dyer concluded his account with a heart-felt assurance: 'I may be a touch hazy on a couple of points, Inspector, but I can recall what I heard. Have no fear on that score. I can recall what I heard.'

He returned the phone to Boyd and finished off his whisky with a flourish. Perhaps there was something in the way he left his arm extended when he handed Boyd the empty glass that suggested he might not say no to a second one, but the offer wasn't forthcoming. The work of the Institute would always come first for Tori Boyd and, as important as Arliss's visit had clearly been, it was now time for him to be on his way. With one more round of effusive thanks, she ushered him from the building, and closed the door behind him. She turned and raised her eyebrows towards the other woman.

'These are not even bird hides any more,' protested Turner. 'You couldn't even get near the viewing slats if you wanted to, not with those banks of computers in front of them.'

'Exactly. Plus, with it being Arliss, and him likely having been sleeping one off at the time, I can't say I'm overly worried.' Boyd shrugged. 'I suppose we should keep an eye out for anything unusual, but now that it's in the hands of the authorities, I'm sure it'll all be properly looked into.'

Turner wasn't sure which of them Boyd was trying to reassure with this breezy dismissiveness, but neither of them was being taken in by it. She was well enough acquainted with Arliss Dyer to know he wouldn't have been here unless he was convinced about what he'd heard. And the way Tori Boyd was hurrying to her office now, jabbing at her phone even before she had closed the door, suggested she felt his warning was sufficiently concerning for her to loop at least one other person in. Which seemed fair enough. If there was a credible threat to the Julien Bellaire Institute for Climate Science, it was only fair to inform the man whose name it bore.

8

The dark line of the convoy trailed across the ice field like a black thread. The slow-moving fleet had been tracking across the vast, white expanse for hours, but it had now come to a halt. A pair of snowmobiles moved slowly across the ice in front of the idling vehicles, following a line of flags that stretched out into the distance. Periodically, a rider would lean over, cautiously assessing the ice thickness along the flagged route.

From the vantage point of the roof of the tracked Hagglund, the flags seemed to follow a safe path over the sea ice. A route like that, over frozen ocean several feet thick, would support equipment far heavier than the truck Gaya Monde was now standing on, even with its attached trailer. But she knew that new ice cracks could open spontaneously, so even a flagged route like this needed to be checked. The snowmobile team would find the narrowest of the cracks, and drill test holes beside them to see if the thinnest sections of the ice were still safe to traverse.

Scott Della climbed up the ladder and joined Gaya on the roof of the Hagglund. He lowered the scarf from his mouth and she could see his breath escaping in wisps of cold air. 'I don't like this, Gaya. The last McMurdo report was two weeks ago. You know how rapidly things can change at this time of year. The PGC maps aren't accurate any more.'

Gaya nodded. The Polar Geospatial Center's high-resolution satellite imagery would be more reliable, but it was not available to them before they left, and they had no way to access it out here. The same was true of the two other more reliable sources of information, drone flights over the area or word of mouth from a recent visit.

'The sheet is moving,' continued Scott. 'The thinning shelf ice is causing tidal cracks, and crevasses are opening up as interior ice drifts out into the new spaces. The team thinks we'll need to take the heavier vehicles further round.'

Gaya could envision the spiderweb of scars on the white canvas of the ice field out beyond their view. She understood the concern in his voice. Nobody liked having to abandon a flagged route across an ice field. But it was not just the safety aspect that concerned her. 'What will that do to our ETA at Dumont?'

Della shrugged. 'With luck, we can pick up the flagged route again further on, so a couple of hours?'

Monde sighed. And without luck? They would be many more than a couple of hours late arriving at Dumont d'Urville Station. The ship they were heading for would wait. There would be grumblings from the captain, perhaps even a formal complaint to Julien Bellaire, but even after a full day's delay, the extra pack ice that would have formed in the bay would still be comfortably within the *Oceanite's* icebreaking capabilities. But the incoming base crew would not wait. Gaya cast her eyes to the sky, where the clouds swirled like poured milk. Like everyone else on this continent, the team that had arrived on the supply ship would be acutely aware of the narrow windows of weather that permitted long-distance travel here. Whether Gaya was there to rendezvous with them or not, they would head out for the camp immediately upon arrival.

She raised a set of binoculars and watched as a member of the snowmobile team dismounted and planted a black flag. A dangerous spot, a new crack or seal hole; a place to avoid. Scott left the roof of the Hagglund to report the latest finding to the convoy's drivers. It crossed her mind that the role of field safety coordinator had recently belonged to someone else. In different circumstances, it would have been Alex Kasabian's job to oversee glacial travel. Though his death had been reported to the McMurdo Safety and Response Team before they had embarked on their journey, the US South Pole contingent couldn't get another expert to them at such short notice. Scott Della had reluctantly taken on the role of developing the field plan for the terrain. And the responsibility.

Gaya moved towards the vehicle's roof ladder, but before she descended she paused for one last look out over the ice field. Despite the overcast skies, the glare off the surface was intense. The crisp low wind had polished the plane to a sheer, gleaming shine. The whiteness altered one's perspective. There were no buildings or treelines to offer a sense of proportion, no backdrop to define one's field of vision, so that you looked out and could not tell if you were staring at an expanse one kilometre away, or five. But always on the horizon, even in the faded light of a day like today, was the faint shimmer of a mirage, floating like a promise. Of safety? Of comfort? She peered out over the featureless terrain. Without a visible sun, or anything to anchor a person to the landscape, it was easy to feel irredeemably, terrifyingly lost out here. How easy it would be to disappear into this inhospitable emptiness for ever, she thought. To be missed? Possibly. But never to be found.

Scott Della approached her again as she reached the base of the Hagglund's steps. 'They're not crazy about what they're seeing out there.' He paused for a moment. 'They're recommending we lighten the load by having some of the team members haul full sleds on foot. Maybe a hundred pounds each, plus our own weight.' He looked at her frankly. 'It could make a difference.'

The Hagglund fired up and began inching across the ice. Inside the trailer, Gaya had not been aware how loud the giant machine's engine was, but out here standing on the ice beside it, the throaty, guttural roar was almost deafening, like an alien presence that seemed to have no place in the pristine silence of this wilderness. Five team members were harnessed to small sleds carrying tightly packed loads. Each person was tethered to the sled in front, so the caravan made one long connected chain, with Scott in the lead and Gaya as last link.

They had been walking for an hour. The tracked vehicles had disappeared from view. But they were not far away. Before she had come here for the first time, Gaya had imagined the continent to be one vast, flat expanse of ice. But ridges and valleys stretched across the terrain, dips and depressions that would be capable of hiding a vehicle as large as a building a mere few hundred metres from where you stood. This was a landscape where you saw things that did not exist and missed those that did. How could anyone come to terms with a place like this?

Afterwards, the rest of them would agree that no one heard the crack. But Gaya did. The Antarctic's moving ice had a wide range of sounds: deep, sonorous rumblings that sounded like the stirrings of a sleeping giant, sharper reports that echoed across the landscape like a rifle shot, with a recoil that rolled across the frozen terrain. This one sounded like a sigh, a whisper of Antarctic breath that barely disturbed the air.

Perhaps Gaya's sled had already slipped into the crevasse by the time she heard it. The rope tightened so quickly she had no time to react, and in a second it had whiplashed her off her feet, so that she hit the ground with a jarring thud. It began dragging her backwards across the ice, and she waited for the jolt as the slack to Amy's sled was taken up. But it never came. The unsecured rope whipped out from around the metal runner of the sled in front and slithered along the ice behind Gaya. She could see Amy ahead of her, trudging across the ice, head bowed, concentrating on hauling the load attached to her own rope. She continued on without breaking stride, oblivious to the unfolding drama behind her.

Gaya's sled bounced off a ledge in the crevasse and began a freefall into open space, dragging her more rapidly across the ice. She scrabbled for purchase, grasping desperately at passing ridges, but the momentum was too strong for her, tearing her gloved fingers away, and twisting her over. She was pitching and half-rolling now, all the time being pulled relentlessly towards the gaping maw of the crevasse. She unhooked the ice-pick from her belt and frantically tried to jam it into the glassy surface flashing past her, repeatedly hacking away in her desperation to get purchase on the rock-like ice. It grabbed finally, halting her slide for a moment. But the respite was short. The relentless pull of the free-falling load stretched Gaya's arm out farther and farther until the axe was torn from her grasp and her slide towards the edge resumed at a faster pace than ever.

She had arched her neck, craning to see the approaching gap, when she felt the resistance. Not a stop yet, but slowing. She curled her neck forward and looked along the length of her body. At the far end of the rope, Scott lay full out on the ice, holding on desperately and calling over his shoulder for help. Gaya was still sliding towards the crevasse, now only metres away. If she went over the edge, she knew there would be no way to bring her back up. The combined weight of the load and her body was too heavy for a dead-lift, and the sled would be too far below her to be cut away. Even the entire team of four would never be able to hold the free-swinging weight until a pulley system could be set up over the mouth of the crevasse. At some point, the strain would become too great and, no matter how hard they fought it, they would have to let her go.

She slid again, and halted again. Scott was holding on for the moment, but he was losing the larger battle. The last slide had halved the distance to the edge of the crevasse and she was now so close she could feel the cold draught coming up through the opening, colder even than the surrounding air, as if a portal to a frozen netherworld had been opened. If she went through that opening, she knew, she would never return.

She felt the world juddering and heard a mighty roar. But it was not the beckoning call from any ice-clad Hades. The Hagglund was backing up. It did not attempt to approach the crevasse, where the additional weight could have been catastrophic, but instead angled towards Scott, so others could grab the rope as he held on to it and tie it to the back of the tracked monster.

With the rope secured, Scott slid towards Gaya on his belly to distribute his weight for fear of causing the crevasse to splinter into other cracks.

'Are you okay?'

Gaya couldn't nod. 'I think so. Yes,' she breathed.

'I'm going to come past your head and cut the rope. Get ready for a jolt as the sled lets free. Okay? On three.'

Scott made a cut with a single clean stroke and the liberated rope snaked down the crevasse in a blur. Released from the tension, the short remaining section whipped back across Scott's face, scoring his cheek. Gaya rolled over and spreadeagled her own weight out, inching back towards the Hagglund until it was safe for the others to help her to her feet. Her bulky arctic clothing had absorbed most of the shock of her drag and she was able to stand unaided, but her arm felt sore and weak.

Amy Della approached her. 'I'm so sorry, Gaya. The rope... It must have... I never felt a thing. Honestly.'

She helped Gaya to the Hagglund and hovered nearby as the base commander reached up to grasp the ladder to the cab. Gaya cried out sharply and recoiled in pain, drawing her arm in tightly. Amy reached out to her, but a hand roughly caught her sleeve. 'Leave her,' said Scott. 'Go back to the group. I'll help her.'

'I think I've hyperextended it,' Gaya told him. Her mind flashed back to the moment she felt her grip finally slipping away from the axe, her arm outstretched, desperately clinging on, straining every sinew, every muscle, until finally she could hold on no longer. It had felt like she was letting go of life. As she was being dragged towards the crevasse, with death closing in and the Antarctic winds tearing away her cries for help, she had lived Alex Kasabian's last moments. And just for a moment, she had known the terror he must have felt, the same despair as his life slipped away from him. She sank to the ice beside the Hagglund, the memory inside her, entwining itself around her heart. She clutched it to her, unwilling to let go. The tears were still frozen on her cheeks when Scott wrapped a blanket around her and helped her to mount the stairs to the waiting warmth of the cab.

9

Colleen Shepherd entered the Incident Room with a spring in her step that had been noticeably absent in her most recent visits. The lack of major cases might still be casting a pall over the station, but the onset of her new project seemed to have lifted her spirits considerably.

'The painters will be in tomorrow,' she announced by way of a morning greeting. 'I realise there might be some minor inconvenience, but they're going to try to keep disruptions to a minimum. They're starting with my office and the hallways, so we'll be okay in here for a couple of days. They'll be hanging plastic sheets up over the doorways to keep the fumes out.'

Maik's expression suggested he felt perhaps paint fumes weren't going to be his biggest concern with this project. He handed her the daily briefing docket and she extracted a sheet, waving it in their general direction. 'Another presumed suicide. We're convinced there's nothing more to this one?'

Salter nodded. 'There was a recent terminal diagnosis. She'd even discussed taking her own life with a neighbour.'

'Everything goes to a nephew in Vancouver,' said Holland. 'He wasn't even aware he had an aunt still alive over here.'

'And her prints were the only ones on the electric toaster found in the bathtub,' Maik added.

Three of them looking into the one case said a lot about the lack of serious crime coming into the station. But at least Shepherd was assured they had gone about the investigation with their usual thoroughness. 'We're sure, then?'

Maik had spent too long in the military to see any point in answering the same question twice, and he suspected under normal circumstances Shepherd would feel the same way about asking one. But these were far quieter times than normal, and Maik was in a generous mood. 'We are,' he said definitively.

'An actual toaster bath,' said Salter absently. 'Sorry. It's how the kids refer to suicides these days. Max told me. *Taking the toaster bath.*'

'Charming,' said Holland.

Salter shook her head sadly. 'Were we ever so cavalier about death, I wonder?'

'He's young,' said Maik. 'The further away it seems, the more liberties you feel you can take with it. Speaking of Max, he mentioned that he needs you to sign the permission form for his DNA test. For that ancestry project he's doing at school.'

'I'll get round to it,' said Salter offhandedly.

'I should get that done,' said Holland. 'Find out a bit more about my ancestors.'

'What, to see if any of them had opposable thumbs?'

'Right,' said Shepherd, her newfound indulgence in frivolity having reached its limit. 'Where are we on the hide fire? Kids still our best guess?' She eyed Holland. 'Now that we've eliminated the constable from our inquiries.'

'We can't hide from the fact we haven't made any progress,' said Holland. 'In fact, we haven't seen hide nor hair of any evidence. Once we have a suspect, though, there'll be nowhere left for him to hide.' He spread his hands and nodded his head to acknowledge applause that wasn't forthcoming. 'I should have known such sophisticated wit would be wasted on you lot. When I was at the Met, they thought I was hilarious.'

'I have no doubt you were a constant source of amusement down there,' said Shepherd drily. 'But back to matters at hand. Any new developments?'

'Erm…'

The others had spent enough time in the Incident Room with Lauren Salter to know that when she started a sentence tentatively like this, it was usually a sign that she knew the contents were not going to be particularly well received.

'Inspector Jejeune, ma'am… was he looking into the fire at Abbot's Marsh, at all? Only a patrol car reported seeing his Range Rover out there.' She flickered a glance towards Maik, and Holland realised she was wondering whether she should continue. 'We wondered if you'd sent him out there to look for something specific.'

'No, I did not,' Shepherd responded sharply. *In fact, I specifically told him to stay away*, she didn't add aloud. She sighed with exasperation. 'Honestly, that bloody man… When was this?'

'The day before yesterday. Around lunchtime.'

Maik eased forward as if to say something, and Holland saw Salter place a restraining hand gently on his arm. She would take the brunt of any frustration Shepherd might want to direct towards someone coming to the DCI's defence. The constable smiled to himself. *The course of true love*, and all that.

'I'm sure he just thought he might be able to help, ma'am,' said Salter, 'it being to do with bird hides and all.'

Shepherd paused and gathered herself. 'Let's be clear about this. As of zero nine hundred hours yesterday morning, Chief Inspector Jejeune began serving a forty-five-day suspension. He'll have our support during this time, and he will be welcomed back unconditionally once he has been reinstated to his duties. But in the meantime, he is to have no involvement whatsoever with any active cases. Understood?'

The silence suggested it was.

'So,' she said decisively, 'moving on. Anything more on that blog post from that base?'

The uneasy silence in the room continued and Shepherd sighed inwardly. Had even words like *yes* and *no* finally become unsafe in a workplace setting, she wondered.

'It's still being looked into,' Holland said guardedly.

Salter surmised that, in Shepherd's current mood, it might be in everyone's best interests to deflect her attention away from who, exactly, might be looking into it. 'I did find out that petrels get their name from St Peter, Tony, if that's any help,' she said. 'They can paddle across the surface of the sea as they take off. It looks like they're walking on the water. You know, like St Peter.'

Shepherd's expression suggested she wasn't entirely convinced this information was going to take them much further in their investigation. If this was an indication of their progress so far, she seemed to feel it might be wise to move on to other matters. Unfortunately, at this point, the only other matter of note was the arson at the hide.

'I'm wondering if there is another element to this fire,' she said cautiously. 'If perhaps somebody has something personal against bird hides.' She surveyed the room and clapped her hands together. 'Any takers? Come on, you lot, thinking caps on.'

'There was that old case from a long time back, remember?' Salter asked the room. 'That young girl. She was picked up by a squad car, naked except for a blanket wrapped around her, walking barefoot along the road. She said she'd been locked in a hide after a skinny-dip.'

'They took her to hospital, but she stole some clothes and ran off before she could be interviewed.' Maik nodded admiringly. 'Well worth a look, ma'am.'

Holland did his best to suppress the incredulity spreading across his face, even if he wasn't entirely successful. 'You've got to be joking,' he said. 'That case was donkey's ago. This is just kids, surely.' He turned to Maik. 'You said so yourself.'

Maik inclined his head. 'It was a lot of petrol to burn down one hide. And it's a good distance off the main road. There'd be closer targets if you just wanted to cause a bit of damage.'

Shepherd nodded. 'Danny's right. It's a long way to carry that much petrol. In my experience, vandals are not all that interested in activities that require too much hard work.' She lowered her head, silently acknowledging the fact that any option, regardless of its merit, becomes your chosen one by default when there are no alternatives. 'Fair enough, Sergeant Salter,' she said half-heartedly. 'Dig around. See if there's anything worth following up.' She drew a breath. 'Okay, let's stay on this Antarctic blog matter and see if we can't put it to bed quickly.'

As she moved towards the door, one further thought seemed to strike her. 'And let's make it easy for DCI Jejeune to observe the terms of his suspension, shall we? There is to be no discussion of active cases with him. In fact, it might be better if we were to give him a wide berth altogether for the next few days, until he's had time to come to terms with his situation.'

'I hope the DCI comes up with something on that blog post soon,' Salter murmured to Maik as they watched Shepherd leave. 'It's getting exhausting dodging and weaving every time she asks about it.'

'He's talking to somebody tomorrow,' said Holland. He gave a wry smile. 'Though I think he's going to have his hands full with this one. The call came in through the main switchboard, so it was put through to us. Julien Bellaire, no less, returning a call from the DCI.'

'The Billionaire Bicyclist?' Maik raised his eyebrows. He would have thought people as wealthy as Julien Bellaire might have other people who could return calls on his behalf.

'He said he had a window at eleven a.m. tomorrow, so I told him I'd email the DCI with the message.' Holland shook his head slowly. 'I still can't believe he actually said that. I mean, what kind of a prat tells a DCI that he has "a window"?'

'One that has enough personal wealth to retire the national debt,' said Salter. 'You don't think a bloke like Bellaire is going to be sitting around all day just waiting for somebody to drop in and ask him about seabirds, do you?'

'Seabirds that walk on water, let's remember,' said Holland. 'Here, perhaps we should call them a Jejeune of Petrels.'

'I think it's time you went to see your girlfriend,' Salter told him as she stood up. 'Your Taoism is starting to slip.'

10

A single pale sunbeam had escaped the cloud cover to play its light on the marram grass that grew tall along the cliff edge. The blades stood like the hairs of a paintbrush against the ethereal backdrop of the sea. Beside them, the hide loomed like something from a dream, the soft spangling of the water behind it dancing like a field of stars. Lindy would have readily admitted that Dom's birding occasionally provided scenes like this, that she would otherwise have missed. But that didn't necessarily mean the birding part was always worth it. Today, though, the visit to this clifftop hide at least had another worthwhile purpose.

Perhaps Lindy saw it first, but by the time she spoke Domenic had already stopped and placed a protective arm across her chest.

'Dom, there's somebody sneaking around the hide.'

He nodded. A figure was creeping along the side of the hide, keeping low where it would be out of sight of the viewing slats. They squatted near a fringe of shrubs and tall grasses. At this distance, there was a good chance the figure would not see them unless they drew attention to themselves by moving. But Jejeune had been around these parts long enough to know that sound carried on still morning air like this. He leaned in closely.

'There's an arsonist who's been targeting bird hides lately,' he said in a low voice. 'I think this could be him.'

The figure appeared again, flickering in and out of view through the tall grass like a pale shadow. 'There are vehicles in the car park, Dom,' whispered Lindy. 'There must be people in that hide. We have to warn them.'

She moved to stand up, but Jejeune laid a hand gently on her arm. 'We're too far away. If he is intending to set fire to the hide and we alarm him, he may panic and do it anyway.' He studied the figure closely. It was a man, he was sure of that now. 'We need to get closer. If I can get between him and the hide somehow, I might be able to ward him off.'

'You can't go after him yourself, Dom. He could be armed.'

Jejeune shook his head. 'Arsonists don't usually carry weapons. It's not normally a crime that needs them.' He watched as the crouching figure moved around towards the far side of the hide. In a moment, Domenic would lose sight of him. 'We need to move now. As soon as you see I've got between him and the hide, you go in and get those people to safety.'

'Dom. You need to call this in.'

'We can't wait, Lindy. Once he sets it alight, it may be too late to get everyone out. We have to go now.'

Jejeune was already up, moving towards the hide as fast as his low crouch would allow, using the fringe of vegetation as cover. Lindy stood to follow, but her movement alerted the figure, and he began to sprint away from the building towards the path leading from the hide. From here, they couldn't tell if he had already set a fire or not. As Domenic peeled off to give chase, Lindy headed for the hide.

'Everybody out,' she shouted as she crashed through the door.

The small knot of startled birders stared at her.

'Now. The hide is about to go up in flames.'

There was a chaotic scramble as the small group thrashed around the cramped interior, grabbing equipment and belongings and hurrying from the hide. Lindy heard Dom call out, and through an open slat she saw him flash past in pursuit of the fleeing figure.

Lindy was the last to leave the hide. She emerged to face a sea of hostile faces.

'What's the meaning of this?' asked a woman, shouldering a heavy 'scope.

'I thought you said there was a fire?' said a small man, his arms filled with binoculars, bird guides and a Thermos. He laid them on the ground carefully and looked around. 'I don't even smell smoke.'

'We saw someone skulking around the hide. We thought he was planning to set fire to it.'

'It's probably just another one of those idiots after the cars,' said the woman tersely. 'Somebody should go and check on them.' She marched around to the far side of the hide as a taller, bearded man with a shock of white hair joined the group.

'No sign of fire anywhere around the hide, thankfully,' said Quentin Senior.

'So it was a false alarm?' said the man. He turned to Lindy. 'What do you think you're playing at, scaring us like that for no reason?'

'I can assure you, David,' said Quentin Senior, 'if Ms Hey sounded the alarm, it was because she genuinely believed we were we were in danger.' He looked to Lindy.

'There was a man. He took off when we arrived. Dom's gone after him.' She gestured weakly in the direction the two figures had disappeared.

They heard the woman call from the car park. A car door was open but nothing had been taken. It looked like the thief had been disturbed, but the incident, combined with Lindy's startling warning, seemed to have shaken the other birders enough to convince them it was time to leave. They silently dispersed to their cars and drove away.

'I'm so sorry,' Lindy told Senior. 'Dom thought…we were convinced…'

'You weren't to know.' The man reached to take Lindy's hands in his own large paws, his blue eyes shining with delight. 'It really is so very good to see you, Lindy. Truly.'

The simple sincerity of Senior's words touched Lindy deeply. Since her ordeal, she'd had plenty of practice at accepting people's expressions of concern and comfort. But Senior's unaffected joy at seeing her left her struggling to produce any response at all.

'I take it your young man didn't bring you up here purely for the birding,' said Senior with a kindly smile. His teasing about her aversion to the pastime had been a feature of their conversation in the past. He was keen to show that, despite her long absence, nothing had changed.

'I think he wants to ask you about petrels.'

'Petrels.' Senior turned his eyes to the sea. They both knew that whenever Lindy mentioned a bird, Senior saw it as an opportunity to show off his knowledge. Though she had no real interest, she would never deny herself a few minutes of the man's infectious enthusiasm. 'Ah, well, there's a few out there, no doubt, but sadly, they rarely drift close enough to afford us more than a quick glimpse. Consummate fliers, you see, beautifully proportioned to ride the winds of the world's oceans. No need to come to land at all, except to breed. That said, we do have something called the European Storm Petrel that shows up on a fairly regular basis.' Senior stroked his luxuriant white beard, searching his memory. 'There was a presumed White-chinned, too, a couple of years ago, that stirred quite a bit of interest. Don't think the inspector was about that day, though.'

Lindy was quiet. Not all of Jejeune's absences from the Norfolk birding scene were for reasons she wanted to dwell upon. She was trying hard to look engaged but, in truth, the colour of a petrel's chin was not uppermost in her mind. 'There's no reason you can think of that anybody would need to be concerned about petrels showing up, is there?'

'Oh, most certainly.'

Lindy looked surprised.

'Storm petrels are held to be portents of bad luck,' said Senior flatly. 'Devil birds, the sailors call them. It's felt that the birds can predict disasters, you see. They foreshadow the coming of high seas, shipwrecks, any number of maritime catastrophes. At sea, the appearance of storm petrels off a ship's bow has all sorts of sinister connotations.'

Before Lindy could reply, Jejeune arrived to join them. He was breathing heavily and his hair was matted with sweat. He shook his head. 'Too many places to hide.' He indicated the stands of tall grass that surrounded the hide. 'All you have to do is lay low in this stuff and you're pretty much impossible to find.'

'Did you get a good look at him?'

He nodded. 'Good enough. But he wasn't carrying anything.' He turned to Senior. 'Did you find any petrol cans lying around?'

'It seems he was just after valuables from the cars,' said Senior. 'Undoubtedly another in that recent spate of break-ins at car parks.'

Jejeune nodded. 'Yes, probably that,' he said. 'Of course.'

Even to Lindy it didn't sound convincing. 'You should have been here five minutes ago,' she told him to deflect the older man's quizzical gaze. 'There were petrels everywhere, right, Mr Senior? Big groups of them, or gangs or whatever the collective noun is?'

'D'you know, I don't believe I've ever heard one for petrels. I did once hear someone suggest a gallon.' Senior barked a laugh and slapped his thigh with a meaty hand. 'A gallon of petrels. And they say birders have no sense of humour.'

Lindy's expression suggested she might still be looking for evidence to the contrary. She turned to Domenic. 'Wouldn't work for your lot back home, though, would it? They'd need to be gasoline birds, and I suppose it'd have to be a *litre* of them.'

'There is such a family as oilbirds,' pointed out Senior. 'A litre would work perfectly well for them. A Litre of Oilbirds,' he pronounced, nodding with satisfaction. 'Yes, I'd be all right with that one. But as for petrels,' he tilted his head slightly, 'I am happy to leave our charming wordsmith here with the task of coming up with one.' He turned to Jejeune. 'Seems a bit of an odd time of year to be looking for petrels, Inspector, if you don't mind me saying so. You'd be better off up at Mousa during the breeding season. Ever seen that spectacle?'

Jejeune hadn't.

'The birds nest in an Iron Age tower. The calls from their nesting chambers seem to be coming from everywhere, bouncing off the walls in an eerie cacophony the like of which you've never heard. And against this soundtrack, you've a twilight sky filled with birds swooping in and out in a never-ending stream.' Senior pointed a gnarled finger at Jejeune. 'As soon as you can, Inspector, promise me. It's a show not to be missed.'

Jejeune nodded. 'At the moment, though, I'm actually more interested in the breeding behaviour of Antarctic petrels.'

'Antarctica, eh?' Senior nodded. 'Ah yes, well, you've got a plethora of them down there, all right. Some beauties, too. Black-bellied, Soft-plumaged. Further out you'd have your Mottled, and your White-chinned, of course.'

'Wait,' said Lindy, 'isn't that the one you said had been seen here? A bird all the way from the Antarctic?'

Senior nodded, delighted that his point had been made. 'The world's great wanderers, the petrels. There's probably no ocean in the world where you're not likely to encounter one.'

'I was wondering if you knew of anything unusual about the breeding season of Antarctic storm petrels,' said Jejeune.

Senior stroked his prolific beard again and stared at the ground thoughtfully. 'There'd certainly be enough Wilson's Storm Petrels down there. Millions, in fact. One of the great wildlife spectacles, the Antarctic's Wilson's.'

'But as far as you're aware, there's nothing notable about the timing of their return.'

'I can't imagine they'd dither about, either arriving or leaving. The window for successful breeding is short enough as it is in that part of the world.' Senior smiled. 'You know, they say creatures need a certain kind of mettle to survive in the extreme climates. Beyond the physical attributes. There has to be a determination about them, a certain obduracy. Two of the three species of birds ever seen at the South Pole are petrels: the Antarctic and the Snow. That should tell you something about them.' He peered out over the sea. 'Looks like the haze is lifting a bit,' he announced. 'Fancy an hour in the hide at East Point?'

Jejeune declined with a regretful shake of his head.

'Just be careful,' said Lindy. She turned to Domenic.

'She means this hide fire at Abbot's Marsh,' he told Senior. 'I don't suppose you've heard anything from the birding community?'

Senior looked at him for a long moment. As with the vehicle break-ins, the police had already questioned the local birders on this point. The detective's inquiry seemed to suggest any answers had not been shared with him. Senior had no idea why this might be. He just knew there was a lot about today's proceedings that was not adding up. Something of his wariness came through in his guarded response.

'No, but I'm sure it won't deter them. Especially the older ones. Time is a relentless foe for a poor old birder, Ms Hey,' he said, turning to her. 'We can improve our knowledge and experience as we get older, but each season our old friends seem to slip ever so slightly further from our grasp. A field mark fades, a flash of colour dims, a call grows fainter. At this time of year, every birdable moment is a gift to be cherished.' He looked back to Jejeune. 'They'll not likely fritter them away worrying about some half-baked threat to their hides.'

No, thought Jejeune, *and neither will you. But you should.* 'Could we meet later, to go over the list of hides in the area?' he asked. 'I'm pretty sure I have most of them, but there may be one or two I'm overlooking.'

'Indeed,' agreed Senior magnanimously. 'How about here, tomorrow evening? Get a few twilight pelagics in with our chatter?'

Lindy wasn't sure what a twilight pelagic might be, but Domenic looked happier than at any time since he'd returned from his fruitless chase. He may not have caught the fleeing suspect, or received the information he came here for, but an opportunity to spend time birding with Quentin Senior was obviously no bad substitute.

11

'I still can't see what this has to do with combatting climate change.' Paige Turner straightened from her kneeling position beside the wharf and wiped her brow with the back of a gloved hand. In front of her, the waters of the bay riffled like a skein of dark-blue silk.

'We're just covering all our bases,' Tori Boyd told her. She gave a mirthless laugh. 'Which is a nice way of saying we're proactively defending the Institute against criticism. Descaling the buoys vastly reduces the amount of rust being released into the oceans.'

Just below the surface of the water, a large metal cradle filled with sea buoys lay submerged, like a sleeping sea monster. Leaning forward, Turner grabbed a chain affixed to one of the corners of the cradle. From her position beside her, Boyd reached out to a control panel mounted on a post and flipped a switch, causing the heavy-duty motor of an overhead crane to spring into life. She lowered it to a point where Turner could attach the chain to the large hook dangling from it.

The manoeuvre completed, Turner looked out over the bay. Mottled bands of grey cloud were beginning to gather, stealing the colour from the water. Closer to the shore, a field of other buoys bobbed gently, waiting to be corralled for their own descaling. 'I realise it would be a significant amount of rust we're talking about,' she said, 'given the size of the Institute's operations, but it must be massively expensive to bring in all these buoys and then redeploy them again afterwards.'

'When you've been around Julien long enough, you realise it's not about money.' Boyd indicated the grid and the large collection of buoys. 'If it takes all this to avoid the charge that he is polluting the oceans at the very same time he is striving to give the planet cleaner air, he'll happily pay it.' She looked at the other woman significantly. 'He really is genuinely committed to the cause, you know. This Billionaire Bicyclist thing isn't just for publicity. He truly does feel by cycling to the various sites on the estate he's practising what he preaches by lowering his carbon footprint.'

Turner reached out to grab the last of the corner chains on the cradle and slipped it onto the hook. With all chains attached, Boyd grasped a lever and began manoeuvring the crane's arm upwards until the hook took up the slack. As it continued its slow rise, Turner watched the giant cradle emerge from the dark waters, dripping an unbroken stream of silvery run-off into the bay. Inside the cradle, the sea buoys bobbled and leaned uncertainly. Boyd expertly set the payload on the ground beside them. 'We need to get that grid on,' she declared. 'We have to make sure the buoys don't bang together during the electrolysis process.'

'Surely they're pretty robust,' said Turner dubiously. 'I mean, the battering they must take at sea.'

Boyd nodded. 'But with them all bumping together like this, it would be easy for some of the monitoring hardware to become dislodged. Watch out while I lift the grid.'

The mechanical noise kicked in again as Boyd manoeuvred the crane to hoist a metal grid and swing it over the cradle, juggling the motor in short spurts until a grid square was positioned neatly over the neck of each buoy like a rectangular collar. She lowered the grid gently until each square securely cinched over an individual buoy, effectively separating it off from its neighbours. Turner moved in and fastened the edges of the grid to the cradle and Boyd then swung the entire cargo out over the bay again, resubmerging it until only the lip of the grid was visible. The newly secured buoys rocked slightly, but remained stable and upright.

'Would people really criticise him for that?' Turner asked. 'The rust being released by the buoys' harnesses?'

'When you're trying to establish a reputation as the leading environmental defender of your generation, there will always be people out there looking to denounce you,' Boyd told her. She lifted two large electrical connectors attached to the ends of heavy-duty cables coiled on the wharf. 'The sceptics will seize on anything to undermine this project. The scope of the work the Bellaire Institute is doing is a clear threat to their efforts to derail progress on climate change. I'd say the Institute, and Julien personally, are just about their number one targets.' She laid the connectors beside the grid and turned towards the admin offices. 'Coming?'

She headed off, following the course of the electrical cables that were snaking their way across the ground back towards the building. Turner fell into step beside her. 'You don't think they could have had anything to do with what Arliss heard?'

Boyd gave a cold laugh. 'Arliss is hardly the most reliable of sources. It was probably all in his imagination.'

'I'm not sure it was,' said Turner uncertainly. 'I spoke to him in the pub last night.'

'You did? Was he coherent?'

'Enough. He seemed pretty consistent on the details. Particularly this idea that the hides were all in a line.' She shrugged. 'If he's right, it does sound like one of the hides here is being targeted.'

'If he's right,' emphasised Boyd dismissively.

The cables led back to an electric panel attached to the outside wall of the admin building. Boyd fished a key on a chain from round her neck and opened the box to flip a switch inside. A faint electrostatic hum filled the air. She began walking back towards the far end of the bay and Turner joined her again.

'So you don't think anybody would be targeting the facility, particularly.' She smiled. 'Or even you personally. No deep, dark secrets in your past?'

'Oh, I'm sure we all have those, don't we?' said Boyd, not returning the other woman's smile. 'Take you, for example, popping up here out of nowhere on your bike. Just you and your Taoism.'

Turner nodded to acknowledge the point. 'It helped me through a difficult time.'

'An unhappy relationship?'

'Yeah,' Turner said, nodding again. 'With my childhood.' She seemed reluctant to provide any further details. It was Boyd's cue to continue with her work. Having reached the wharf again, she picked up a connector from each cable in a gloved hand and held them apart. Spreading the jaws open, she snapped them onto the grid.

'Okay, done,' she announced. 'Now it's back to the data.'

But Turner stayed for a moment, taking in the surroundings as if assessing where a threat might come from. On either side of them, the land rose steeply to higher ground. Down here, the wide flat expanse of land flanked by its different bodies of water seemed suddenly exposed and vulnerable. She looked around. Not for the first time, she was struck by the evenness of the circular landmass they were on. To her, it resembled perhaps nothing more than a giant helicopter pad. 'Do you think this is a natural feature?' she asked. 'It just has a slightly man-made feel to it, don't you think?'

Boyd shrugged. 'If it was, it was constructed a long time before any of us appeared in this landscape.' She looked at Turner significantly. 'By people who treated the planet a good deal better than we are.' She shook her head. 'We've made such a mess of things. That's why the work of the Institute is so important.' She cast a long glance out over the bay, where the current was stealthily doing its work on the submerged cradle of sea buoys. 'And why we really can't afford to let anyone stop us getting it right this time.'

'This Inspector Jejeune,' said Turner, as the two women set off back to the office building, 'is he a friend of Arliss's, or something?'

'A birding acquaintance, I suppose you might call him. Arliss really does have the most fantastic hearing. He detects birds we'd have no chance of seeing otherwise. Why do you ask?'

'Arliss says he's going to speak to him.'

'What on earth for?' The news seemed to agitate Boyd. 'He's already told him everything he knows.'

Turner shook her head. 'He seems concerned that the DCI won't believe him. *I can recall what I heard.* Remember yesterday, he said it a couple of times?'

'I'm afraid I wasn't exactly hanging on every word. Did he say where he planned to meet the inspector? Or when?'

Turner shrugged. 'As soon as he can, presumably. Does it matter?'

'The last thing we need is a police inspector getting in the way of things down here while he determines the whole thing was down to Arliss's Scotch intake.'

'So you're convinced there's nothing to it, then?'

'You really have nothing to worry about, Paige,' said Boyd firmly. 'The only person I know who has anything against this project is my ex. And he's hardly what you'd call a threat. To anybody.' She paused, but Turner's questioning glance encouraged her to continue. 'The truth is, Glover may have resented the fact that I'd rather spend my time on the project than with him, but he lacks anything like the backbone to do something about it. Besides I have my own little guardian angel to protect me when it comes to Glover.'

'Julien Bellaire.'

Boyd smiled enigmatically. 'A story for another day, I think. We need to get back inside. The data from the latest set of readings will be coming in shortly. I want to be on hand to process them right away.'

12

Julien Bellaire owned things. It was there in the way he entered a room. His eyes moved from item to item, assessing its worth. The fact that he did so even with the items in his own house told you possessing them mattered little to him. It was the knowledge that he was in control of these things that was important. He had the final say on their fate; this room, this house, this world in which he moved.

'Inspector, thank you for coming. Please sit.' He indicated an armchair beside the fireplace. 'You'll take coffee with me. I understand you are something of an aficionado.'

If the comment was meant to impress, it served its purpose. Less than forty-eight hours had passed since Jejeune had called to request the appointment. Prior to that, as far as he was aware, neither he nor his interest in coffee had ever come to Julien Bellaire's attention.

Bellaire returned to the door to speak to an assistant and Jejeune took the opportunity to study the man. Were it not for his assured demeanour, there would have been little about Julien Bellaire to distinguish him. He was of a height and build a few inches shorter and a few pounds heavier than Jejeune. He was also, as Lindy might have said, a study in beige. His mousey-brown hair was the exact colour of his eyes, giving him a curiously coordinated appearance. The fawn silk shirt and pale mushroom trousers that complemented it were equally well matched. He wore no socks but the exquisite leather latticework of the tan shoes looked more than soft enough to compensate. The only note of incongruity was the heavy silver Richard Mille watch on the man's left wrist. It was such a flamboyant accessory, to Jejeune it had the feeling of something Bellaire might have felt compelled to wear: a gift from somebody important, a wife, perhaps. *Perhaps?* It was a sign Jejeune had received no prior official briefing on Bellaire, a whispered reminder that, regardless of the courtesy with which he had been received, he was not here on police business.

Bellaire had barely crossed to the other armchair when there was a discreet knock on the door. The assistant held the door for a maid who entered bearing a tray. 'Ah, the coffee. We will take it here.'

Jejeune watched the maid carefully. She possessed a quiet confidence that suggested she was not nervous in Bellaire's presence. Both unobtrusiveness and competence would be prerequisites for employment here. Bellaire did not need to instruct the maid to close the door on her way out. He took a cup from the tray and offered it to Jejeune courteously. 'Not Colombian, but bird-friendly nonetheless. It's from a plantation in Costa Rica, shade grown.'

Whether it was a specific reference to Jejeune's interests, or merely the statement of someone wishing to display his own green credentials, it was one more sign that Bellaire's preparation for this meeting had been a good deal more thorough than his own, thought the detective. He took a sip of the coffee before setting the cup down on the tray.

Bellaire left his own cup untouched and strolled towards the fireplace. Despite his stature, the mantel was at a perfect height for him to rest his elbow. Jejeune suspected the fireplace would have been custom built to allow Bellaire to strike just such a pose as this when the mood struck him. The man leaned forward and touched the edge of the mantel with his fingertips.

'It is my sad duty to inform you that Alex Kasabian is dead,' he announced simply. 'He had gone off-site to check on some monitoring equipment. Travelling unaccompanied is a breach of our operating protocols, but he insisted on going alone. While he was at the monitoring station, it appears he inadvertently cut the fuel line to his snowmobile. Unable to return to the base, he froze to death. His body was discovered the next morning.'

Jejeune was silent. It was a concise account, delivered in the emotionless tone of a man who felt no personal connection with the victim. If and when a more sympathetic rendition was required, for team members or colleagues, for example, Jejeune had no doubt Bellaire would be capable of producing one. But for this visiting detective, he had reduced his report to the pertinent facts.

'May I ask which day Mr Kasabian's body was discovered?' The inquiry sounded a touch formal, but Jejeune sensed that a man of Bellaire's affectations would welcome such a level of decorum.

'The day before yesterday.'

'And when did you become aware of it?'

'You're wondering why I waited until now to report it?' Bellaire's eyes met Jejeune's. 'I tried to reach you yesterday. I did not consider this news to be left in a voicemail message.'

Jejeune nodded, accepting the man's point.

'I received a video call from the base commander.' Bellaire reached for his phone and tapped a couple of keys. 'I have just sent a copy of the recording over to you. It is unedited. Our policy at the Bellaire Institute is to ensure open access to all our records.'

Jejeune checked his phone but did not open the file. Through the large mullioned window behind Bellaire's desk, the late-morning sunlight lay easily upon countryside. Long shadows of stately beech trees dappled the meadows. Such gentle beauty seemed a long way from an Antarctic landscape where a man had frozen to death.

Jejeune turned to Bellaire. 'Were you aware Mr Kasabian had posted a blog predicting that he was going to die?'

'We will all die, Inspector. Since Alex did not stipulate how or where, I am not sure his blog post constitutes a prediction. Extended periods of isolation and confinement can cause severe psychological problems. This has been studied in astronauts. Perhaps Alex's post was the product only of the endless months of an Antarctic winter.'

'I couldn't find any evidence that he had posted anything like this before. Did he speak to anyone at the base about mental health issues? Did he inform his family?'

'Alex had no family. He was an orphan, a refugee. It seems he rarely spoke to the others at the base about personal matters. He was very much a person who kept to himself.' Bellaire turned to stare out of the window. The view seemed to hold his attention for a long time, but Jejeune could see nothing out there besides the soft, bucolic countryside stretching away from the house.

'Who discovered the body?' Jejeune asked the man's back.

Bellaire turned to face him. 'The base commander, Gayatri Monde. When Alex was discovered missing, Gaya went directly to the monitoring station, where she found the body. It was not possible to recover it. Alex Kasabian's hand is frozen to the snowmobile's fuel line. But she did take photographs. They are appended to the file I sent you.'

Jejeune bought himself a moment to consider the information he'd just learned by taking a slow survey of the room. From every corner, exquisitely appointed items caught his eyes: an onyx coffee table, a Parnian Hollywood desk, a Tiffany lamp. For all its lavish furnishings, though, the room had a feeling of being incomplete in a way he couldn't quite put his finger on. 'Is there a large cohort of researchers at the base?' he asked. 'Only I would have thought someone's absence might have been noted before nightfall.'

'It is a small group. Some have worked for me before: Gaya, Alex, a Canadian couple, Scott Della and his wife, Amy, an Australian, Lexi Marshall. The others are new. They were hired by Gaya, each as a specialist in his or her own field. Alex's failure to return was overlooked, Inspector, because it was assumed that he had returned from his inspection and gone to bed.'

'Assumed?'

'The others were all involved in something called a 300-Club event.'

'Isn't it almost spring down there?'

Bellaire looked surprised. 'You know of this practice? Perhaps they have it in Canada, also?'

'Not as far as I'm aware. Was there a particular reason for organising one that night?'

Bellaire shrugged. 'Perhaps they felt it would be good for morale. There had been some unpleasantness, romantic entanglements, jealousies…' He gave a wave of his hand, as if to imply such trivialities were beneath his interest. 'We strongly encourage team members not to become involved during their stay at the base. But humans are humans; the days of isolation are long and dark. If they are discreet, then perhaps there is no harm done.'

'But that wasn't the case here?'

'I have no further information on this. If you feel this line of inquiry is important, I will instruct Gaya to provide you with whatever insights she may have.'

Jejeune said nothing but his expression suggested that in the unexplained death of a man on an Antarctic ice shelf ten thousand miles away, every line of inquiry was important. 'Although it's affiliated with the University's Department of Global Climatology, I understand Camp Isolée is an independently run operation,' he said. 'I imagine maintaining and operating a research facility in Antarctica must present a lot of logistical challenges.'

Bellaire had not moved from the window. He stood as if framed on a stage, with the vast expanse of the English countryside rolling away behind him. 'In the days of our forefathers, it took a lifetime to accumulate a fortune. Now dotcom startups and other online enterprises mean you can do it in your twenties. But having everything you could possibly want at such a young age is less satisfying than one might imagine. Indeed, it can be dangerous. Boredom is a hazardous thing for those with the resources to indulge any whim they choose. Much better to find a cause and focus on it, use the skills that made you successful in one field to yield benefits in another. For a number of years now, climate change has been that cause for me.'

Jejeune nodded thoughtfully. He had the impression it was a speech Bellaire had delivered before. 'Will you be able to continue your work at the base without Mr Kasabian?'

The man took a step towards Jejeune and looked at him frankly. In other circumstances, the gesture might have been intimidating, but it seemed he only wished to emphasise his point. 'Those who know me understand two things about me, Inspector. First, my commitment to affecting the course of climate change is real, and, secondly, I have the resources to see my goal through. The immense scope of our data-gathering will be at the forefront of climate science for decades to come. We will be able to inform decisions and influence global policymaking in a way never before possible. The important work at Camp Isolée will continue, regardless of the tragic circumstances.'

Jejeune looked around the room again from his seat. As before, he had the impression that this was a man who indulged his vast wealth, yet did not celebrate it. But once again, he could not escape the feeling that there was something missing. 'Would it be possible for me to talk to this base commander?'

Bellaire thought for a moment and gave a short nod. 'This may be arranged. The crew is in transit to Dumont d'Urville Station, to rendezvous with a supply ship. It is a long and difficult trek from the base, even if the weather holds, and there are no channels for external communication. I will pass on your request to the authorities in Dumont. Gaya will contact you when it becomes possible. If you have specific questions for her, I can pass those on, too.'

Jejeune declined the invitation with a smile.

'It is my organisation's intention to provide you with all the facts, Inspector,' said Bellaire frankly. 'We can do no more. If, in the end, the gaps that remain are too great for you to put together a picture of what happened to Alex Kasabian, the fault will not lie with us.' He reached for Jejeune's coffee cup. In another man, the gesture may have seemed brusque, but he managed the moment in a way that seemed to imply it was Jejeune who must have other pressing business, and Bellaire was simply accommodating him.

After the large oak doors closed behind him, Jejeune stood for a moment on the portico of the Bellaire mansion and reflected on the meeting. There had been a faintly adversarial tone to their exchanges. Jejeune looked at the rack of bicycles beside him: practical road bikes, mountain bikes, and one or two that looked like they would be capable of winning races. Perhaps all Julien Bellaire's interactions were contests to be won. But at times it had seemed almost as if the man was defending himself against charges Jejeune had not levelled. In a meeting that had already set a couple of warning bells ringing for Domenic Jejeune, that was perhaps the loudest siren of all.

13

It should have been dark. A bank of low clouds closeted the moon, robbing the night of its light and leaving an inky void that arced across the sky. Not even the normal field of glittering stars was in view tonight. The surrounding landscape should have mirrored this sky, cloaking the marsh in the sullen depths of its darkness. But instead, the night was lit from below with a red glow. Flares of orange and sulphur-yellow burst upwards into the sky. And arc-lighting flooded the scene with the intense, penetrating whiteness of artificial daylight.

There was noise, too, to accompany the light: machinery and shouting voices. Danny Maik stood a short way off from the scene, watching the movement of the men between the patchy shadows. He saw someone walking his way, the silhouette of the bulkily equipped figure temporarily blocking out most of the glow behind him. Maik shielded his eyes as the person approached, but he was still unable to identify the figure until he spoke.

'It's a hot one, Danny,' said Bryan McVicar.

'Arson again?

Danny saw the man's helmet tilt forward slightly in a nod. 'We're having trouble getting close enough for a proper look, but one of the lads thinks he's caught sight of a couple of petrol cans.' The crew chief turned and surveyed the ferocious blaze behind him. 'A couple of gallons would be enough.'

'Similarities?'

'No differences, as far as I can tell. We'll have a better idea when we can see things in the daylight, but for now, I'd say if this person didn't set the one at Abbot's Marsh, then they were likely there, watching how it was done.'

Maik looked at the three fire engines. 'Big response. Were you expecting more than this when you got the call?'

McVicar shook his head. 'With the weather we've been having recently, the vegetation round here is like tinder. It doesn't need much encouragement to go up. And if this fire starts to run, it'll be a bugger to bring under control. We've got one unit on the hide and the others wetting down the grass around it to make sure it doesn't get away from us if it does jump.'

Maik nodded. Having only one unit on the fire itself explained why the hide was still burning with such intensity. It showed little signs of being brought under control yet. Both men took a step backwards as the blaze sucked in an updraught of air and flared outwards, making the hide glow red against the night. In a way that Maik couldn't have explained, the surrounding darkness seemed to intensify the heat coming from the burning structure.

'Any idea how long it's been going?'

McVicar shrugged. 'Hard to say. They all have different personalities, fires. Some are at it right from the off, some hesitate first. I've even seen some that looked like they were going to pack it in altogether, and then come roaring back the next minute. Best guess? A good twenty minutes by the time we turned up. Who called it in, by the way?'

'Passing motorist,' said Maik simply. 'Anonymous.'

In the distance, he could see the faint reflection of shimmering red tinting the pools of water that the hide used to overlook. His eyes flickered towards a crew playing their hoses over the surrounding vegetation. 'If your people could do what they can to preserve what's left of those cans when they're done...'

McVicar nodded again. 'Though if they left the cans here in the first place, it probably suggests there's no prints on them.'

Everybody's a detective, thought Maik ruefully. He was thankful, though, that this man was prepared to concentrate on his own area of expertise just at the moment. He had turned to stand shoulder to shoulder with Danny now, staring at the blaze. In the glow of the flames, McVicar's skin took on a reddish hue, but Maik could still see grey smudges of smoke on his cheeks and forehead. He wondered if these thrill-seeking kids would be as keen to set a fire if they could see the price it exacted on men like Bryan McVicar. But then, when were kids like that ever interested in the human costs of their actions? If this was kids, that is. 'Did those tracks on the path look like bike tyres to you?' he asked.

'If they were, it wasn't us. We came by fire engine.'

Maik rewarded the comment with a smile. A firefighter came over and handed McVicar a scrap of charred paper and an open combination lock. Maik couldn't hear the conversation, but it was short, and the man was heading back to resume his duties in less than a minute, pulling on his protective gloves once again as he went. McVicar set the items into Maik's open palm. 'It's hard to tell for sure, but we think they came off the door.'

Maik took out his phone and studied the singed paper carefully by its light. Perhaps he could make out a couple of letters? Handwritten? It was too difficult to tell in these conditions. He'd have another look later. The lock itself was scorched and blackened, but it still showed small patches of silvery newness in places. He examined it for a moment, then slipped it into his pocket. Seeing as it had been through at least three sets of hands by now, an evidence bag seemed pointless. 'Since the lock isn't fastened, I'm assuming the hide was unlocked when it was set on fire.'

McVicar shrugged. 'All we can say is, by the look of it, the door was definitely closed. There are scorch marks on the outside. I'd go so far as to say that was likely the point of origin, though I'll be happier once the fire investigations crew has taken a look in daylight.'

The ringtone on McVicar's phone was startlingly loud, piercing the darkness even over the roar of the fire. The crew chief listened intently, then shut off his phone without comment. He called over the crew sub-officer and leaned in, speaking loudly, to overcome the man's ear-protection equipment. Only when the man had moved off did McVicar turn to address Maik.

'We've got a five-alarm down in Sheringham, all crews requested immediately.' He paused. 'I'll leave Crew Three here until the hide is out, but they'll need to wrap things up and get over there as soon as possible.' He shook his head. 'There's less threat of this one spreading now, and there's rain on the way, by the look of it, but it still wouldn't hurt if somebody stayed around to keep an eye on things for an hour or so after the crew has gone, just in case.'

Somebody, thought Maik wearily. That is to say, the only person who would be left once the firefighters had departed. McVicar looked at him and even in this light, Maik could see the white streak of a grin through the grime on his face. 'Sorry to have to ask, you being a family man now and all. But I'm sure Lauren Salter will understand.'

In front of Maik, the last of the fire was smouldering to its death. A few silvery wraiths of steam rose from the wet, blackened wood, but there was no sign of glowing embers, nothing that looked likely to burst into life again should a sudden gust of wind sweep in from the coast. The site was safe now, but Danny would watch for a while longer anyway.

In the quiet darkness following the departure of Crew Three, he'd let his mind wander over the possibilities of why someone would want to set fire to a couple of hides, of use only to a disparate group of birdwatchers. He kept coming back to the same question. Was it mischief, or something more? The multiple cans of petrol, the thoroughness of the job; they didn't feel right for kids. And all the way out here? He knew this area well. There wasn't a dwelling for a couple of miles in any direction. It was a long, inconvenient distance from anywhere after a drunken night in the pub. The call had come in from an anonymous source, but that could mean anything, or nothing. A passing motorist on his way home from the club, with the evidence of one too many on his breath, a cheating spouse slinking home from the wrong direction in the early hours. There were any number of reasons someone might want to report a roaring fire in the middle of a field but not want to hang around to offer their personal details. But nevertheless, the anonymity added one more layer of uncertainty to all this.

He went back to his car and flicked on the headlights, trapping the glistening pile of blackened timber in their beams. It would be cool enough by morning for the jackdaws and the crows to come, searching through the rubble for anything worthwhile. And then, when it was cooler still, it would be the turn of a police team to do the same thing. At first light, he'd call in some uniforms to secure the site, tape it off until the fire investigations officer could get in for a better look, too. But there was no point in troubling anybody else now. It was enough that one poor sod had to be out here. *A family man.* Was that what he was now? He thought about texting Lauren, but it was late. Better she got a good night's sleep and woke refreshed and ready to face the chaos of getting Max off to school in the morning. Besides, if she had learned about a fire at Canon's Cross from the duty officer, she would have guessed he was out here. The fact that she hadn't called him suggested she was safely settled in for the night.

He stared again at the ruins in the headlight beams. The site seemed to simmer with menace. What was it, this message it held for him, this warning? Danny had attended dozens of fires in his time. Some had been set in anger, others in revenge, some had just been a bit of nonsense that got out of hand. But this one didn't feel like any of those. There was a point to it, a purpose. Perhaps it was the sense of deliberate planning that had gone into it, but something about this fire was making him edgy.

He flipped off the headlights and got in the car, letting the darkness settle over the scene once again. Now that the fire was out, the night air had turned cooler, though not enough for him to roll up the windows. He sat quietly, listening. And in the silence it came to him, the reason for his uneasiness. He wasn't alone. He could sense the presence of somebody else out there, as surely as if he could see them. The arsonist, perhaps? Sometimes they liked to stick around, watch the results of their handiwork. But there was nothing to see here. A single wooden hut, barely a building at all, had gone up in flames. No dramatic rescues, no fleeing survivors running screaming from the building. No media, no cameras. Not even a fire brigade any more. And the hide itself was now nothing more than a sodden pile of charred timbers. He looked around the dark countryside. If it was the arsonist, he must be disappointed. If it wasn't, Maik had no idea who it could be. But someone, or something, was out there.

He got out of his Mini and took a flashlight from the boot, playing it around the area carefully, in front of him, around him, behind. Everything within the beam was still; everything beyond, darkness. He flipped off the light and stood, motionless. The silence was heavy with danger. No wind. No birds. No night calls. Yet still, this feeling that he was not alone here.

He was about to return the flashlight to the boot when he remembered the items in his pocket. Using a handkerchief, he took out the combination lock and inspected it carefully. Despite the scorch marks, it was clear to him that it was brand new. He returned it to his pocket and withdrew the singed note, carefully laying it across his palm and securing it with his thumb. With the other hand, he played the flashlight beam over it. It was not possible to make out any words, but he recognised one or two of the letter shapes. He should do. He had seen them often enough.

14

The cloudless sky stretched over them like an awakening. After the months of winter night, the impossible endlessness of the blue expanse seemed to overpower the senses of the group gathered beside the quay at Dumont d'Urville Station. They stared up in silent awe at the dome of daylight above them, each with thoughts they chose not to share.

On the hillsides around them, outcrops of bare rock pushed through the snow cover, like patterns on the unrelieved whiteness that had been their domain for the last few months. The strange topography was one more thing to become accustomed to now that they had left their base camp on the far side of the ice sheet. But the disorientations of the natural world paled in comparison to those brought on by the human activities. The busyness in the port area was overwhelming. Everywhere they looked, groups of people hurried from one place to another, into and out of the red-roofed Nissen huts, between the stacked-up containers. And the noise; the whirring of machinery, the clanking of the ship's loading gear, shouts, roaring engines, confusion. The sensory overload of their reintroduction to the outside world had them all longing, momentarily at least, for the solitude and silence of the base that had been their home until so recently.

Beside them at the quay towered the formidable, scarred metal sides of a 200-foot-long icebreaker that was to be their new home, temporarily at least. The *Oceanite* sat low in the water. It would sit lower still once it bore the passengers, crew, and the equipment now being loaded onto it. Around the ship, drawn by the promise of food that accompanied human activity, South Polar Skuas swooped in, their pealing cries carrying far on the cold, still air.

A man approached the group along the quayside, bare-headed despite the cold. Gaya recognised him as the head of station here, a hard, uncompromising man, shaped by the unrelenting harshness of this remote place, and seemingly suited to it. Perhaps it was a sign of the strangeness of this outpost in the Antarctic wilderness that, despite having seen him on three or four previous visits, she didn't know his name. She left the group and walked over to meet him.

'You talk to a Jejeune?'

Gaya shook her head.

'UK cop. Wants you to contact him. Left a number.'

Gaya shrugged evasively. 'Perhaps later, when I'm on board.'

'Up to you.' He scratched an unshaven cheek. Somehow, the gesture managed to imply the matter was urgent.

'I want to ensure my team and equipment are all on board safely first,' Gaya told him.

'We do that.' The man looked out over the water. Deep lines creased his weather-beaten face. His eyes showed a lifetime of squinting in the glare from the land, or perhaps looking out at sea, waiting for the next set of problems that might be arriving.

Gaya was silent for a moment. 'We left him,' she said eventually. 'Just left him.'

'You couldn't have brought him here,' said the man, still looking out at the water. 'The fuel cost to tow that extra load all the way here would have put you all at risk.' He clenched his jaw. 'Alters your perspective, this place.'

He was right. It was hard to believe now, watching them fill the immense bladders to be towed to McMurdo and beyond, that the special Antarctic mix of fuel was such a precious commodity. But it was prized over just about all else at base camps. From the furnaces to the generators, everything ran on it. Over the nine-month winter when it was too cold for any kind of resupply mission, fuel meant life, and the lack of it meant death. *Altered perspectives*, she thought. The perspective that said it was okay to abandon a man's body to the elements and leave it for the new occupants of a camp to retrieve. A perspective that allowed you to dispassionately report via a video chat that a colleague with whom you had worked and lived for the last six months had frozen to death. Could the all-pervading coldness of this place really seep so deep inside a human soul? Alex Kasabian's death told her it could.

The man's radio crackled and he took the call. He listened for a moment, then turned to Gaya. 'Be a delay getting you out. A man's been hit by a Pisten Bully. Backed up over him.' His report was as dispassionate as the rest of his conversation.

'Will he be okay?'

He shrugged. 'We save the ones we can.'

Gaya watched him leave, his pace measured and purposeful but not hurried. She looked around at the port, the activity temporarily suspended as the workers migrated to the site of the accident. Danger was a way of life out here, and there were many ways to die. Her eyes fell on a stone cairn holding a brass plaque, erected two years before to a man who perished after falling in the water. It had taken him only about ten seconds to die. If he had climbed out of the water, the icy winds would have chilled his body instantly, killing him in half the time. And yet he had still struggled until his dying breath to scramble back on to the shore. Survival is the most basic of human instincts. How long had Alex Kasabian fought his approaching death before the coldness had numbed his senses, and shut his brain down to save him from the torture? She would never know. The answer, like all of Alex Kasabian's other secrets, had died with him.

She returned to the present in time to see Amy Della approaching along the quayside.

'I just wanted to tell you again how sorry I was about what happened out there.' She reached out and touched Gaya's sleeve. 'We could have lost you. I don't know if I could bear that, so soon after Alex.' She paused for a moment. 'They are saying he cut the fuel line himself. Accidentally. Do you think that's what happened?'

Gaya said nothing.

'After what went on between Alex and me,' said Amy. 'The argument. I said some things… I just wanted to say, if you heard raised voices, that's all it was. A disagreement. We're all aware of the stress of living in those conditions. People blow up at each other over the smallest things.'

The two women shared a look. Amy was correct that it was not unusual to have disagreements in winter at an Antarctic base. The close confines, the boredom, the sheer absence of normalcy could lead to bitter, sometimes vitriolic arguments. But whatever had happened between Alex Kasabian and Amy Della was more than just a disagreement. And both women knew it.

'Julien Bellaire is requesting any information about personnel be reported to this detective, Inspector Jejeune.'

'Report what you like,' shouted Amy, angry now. Her eyes filled with tears. 'I have to live with the knowledge that those hateful words were the last thing I ever said to him.'

She saw Scott approaching and turned her head away. He made no attempt to hide the fact that he had noticed his wife's anguish, but he made no inquiry about it. In fact, Scott Della paid her no attention at all. When he spoke, he looked only at Gaya.

'Delay's over. We're ready to board.'

'Were they able to save that man?'

Scott nodded. 'He was one of the lucky ones.' He turned away abruptly and walked towards the gangway.

Gaya smiled her sympathies to Amy for the way her husband had treated her in her moment of distress.

'Yes, go on,' said Amy bitterly. 'Do that. Report everything.' Her tear-filled eyes bore hard into her husband's departing back. 'And while you're at it, ask Lexi about what she saw. Include that in your report, too.'

She moved off in the direction of the gangway before Gaya had a chance to respond. But it was clear from Amy's dagger stare at her husband that whatever Lexi Marshall had to report, it was going to involve Scott Della. And it was going to bring trouble.

Gaya stood at the stern of the boat and watched as it eased away from shore. Somewhere out there, the new team was already traversing the ice field on their way to the base camp. Did she envy them? Did she wish she was going back again, accompanying them across that unbroken sheet of whiteness that would be the only colour they saw until the steel-grey sides of the camp buildings rose in the distance? It didn't matter. Gaya Monde had a different destination now. One she could not change.

The ship made its gradual curl around the headland and headed out to open water. The wind out here was stronger, bringing bitingly cold air that numbed her skin. But still she stood there, watching the port of Dumont d'Urville recede into the distance. Under the clear blue sky, a mist of sorrow descended over her. She did not share the others' excitement, their sense of joy and anticipation at seeing loved ones again. Nor their sense of liberation from their confinement. They spoke of doing their time at the base as if it was a prison sentence. How could they feel that way? Even as you loathed the isolation and stultifying boredom of an Antarctic winter, it was almost inevitable that you would grow to love this continent. There could be few places on Earth where it was possible to form such a bond with the land itself, with the sheer beauty, the peacefulness, the undisturbed constancy that put you in touch with the aeons of ice accumulation on which you were standing.

The churning wake that trailed the boat had already stretched away from the shore. They were heading for the Île des Pétrels archipelago. The Island of Petrels would be her last sight of the continent. After that it would be open ocean, the empty seas ever increasing the distance between Gaya and the body of Alex Kasabian. She gently rubbed her injured shoulder and drank in one final sight of the fading landmass. Like a departing emigrant, her eyes dimmed with sadness for what she was leaving behind. Because she knew she would never see it again.

15

There were many kinds of silence, thought Domenic Jejeune as he sipped his coffee: the sinister, uneasy quiet of the marshes at night, the preternatural stillness of a cathedral-like stand of white pines back in Canada. But this silence was something different. There was soul-settling calmness about the cove on a morning like this. The waters were as still as smoked glass. As Jejeune watched, the dark shape of a single Velvet Scoter appeared, trailing a white wake behind it. But the bird's presence did not disturb the tranquillity of the scene. In a way he couldn't have explained, its seemingly effortless glide across the water only added to it. He watched the scoter for a moment longer until it disappeared from view, and then returned to his work.

Jejeune hunched forward with a magnifying glass, studying an image on his computer. Against the dazzling whiteness, Alex Kasabian's contorted body melded to the snowmobile like a bizarre, abstract sculpture. He had gripped the fuel line in that manner to tell them something, thought Jejeune. And perhaps he had managed to do so, even if it was not in the way he had intended.

Lindy entered the room. 'I've been thinking,' she said, leaning over to ease the lens out of Domenic's hand, to ensure she had his full attention. When he was engrossed in his work like this, it was by no means guaranteed. 'It might be better if everything in Bedroom One was in Bedroom Two, and then everything in Bedroom Two could go into Bedroom One.'

Jejeune leaned back in his chair and looked at her. 'Couldn't we just renumber the bedrooms? Then everything would already be in the right place.'

Lindy put her hands on her hips and fixed him with a stare. 'It won't take long. Unless, of course, you think this recent lack of activity has left you too weak and flabby for physical labour.'

He smiled at the faintly exasperated expression. She was coming back to him. Perhaps the stained grey T-shirt and untidy red bandanna weren't part of her normal appearance, but the attitude, the confidence, this look that he had missed so much, they were all the Lindy he had known before. He knew there was still some way to go, but the falterings, the fierce overcompensation, the sheer, careering inconsistency of those early days after the incident; Lindy had clearly decided she wasn't having any more of that.

She shuffled away a stack of documents to make room for herself to perch on the corner of the desk. 'I meant to ask, how did your meeting with Quentin Senior go?'

'He didn't show.' Jejeune tilted his head slightly. 'Nobody seems to know where he is. He's not been seen in any of his usual haunts for a couple of days. Not the trails, not the hides. Nowhere.'

'So he's like super-missing, then,' she said with a mischievous smile. He'd suspected this fad of super-imposing, as she called it, would eventually attract Lindy's scorn. On a hike a few days earlier, they'd come across the desiccated corpse of a long-deceased squirrel. After prodding it with her toe, Lindy had shaken her head sadly and pronounced it to be *like super-dead*.

She looked at him through the magnifying glass. 'Maybe when you've sorted this case, you should turn your sleuthing skills to finding him.' She lifted one of the papers she had displaced. 'Wow, printouts. You really have gone old-school on this one. What are these, meteorological reports?'

Jejeune nodded. 'For Antarctica.'

'I'm not sure you need a printout for that. I'm going to go with *Cold*.'

'I've been looking at the weather for the days around the time the base decided to hold their 300-Club event. I'm wondering why they settled on that particular day.'

'Can't help you, I'm afraid. Not least because I haven't got the foggiest idea what a 300-Club event is.'

'It's a tradition among those stationed at the South Pole. They wait until the outside temperature reaches minus 100 degrees Farenheit. Then they heat a sauna to 200 degrees Farenheit and after spending a few minutes in there, they go straight outside for a walk, thus joining a small group of people who have experienced an immediate three-hundred-degree swing in temperatures.'

'They go outside naked?'

'Except for boots. Though I think you're allowed to put your hands over any parts you don't want frostbitten.'

'I don't think I'd have enough hands. And they do this just so they can be part of some club?'

'I think it's generally seen as some sort of bonding activity. Which is why it might be significant that Alex Kasabian wasn't part of it.'

'Perhaps he's the only one that had any sense. Apart from anything else, it must be incredibly dangerous to subject your body to extremes like that.'

Jejeune nodded. 'You risk hypoxia and frostbite if you're out more than five minutes. And breathing in air that cold can cause severe damage to your lungs, especially if you exert yourself.' He peered at the photo of Alex Kasabian thoughtfully. 'The thing is,' he said, 'I think in this case, the whole event may have been set up as a distraction.'

'Really?' asked Lindy in mock surprise. 'And just what could anybody possibly find distracting about a line of naked people parading across the ice in minus 100 degree temperatures?'

'But that's the point. It wasn't minus 100 degrees, it was minus 96. Which meant the sauna had to be 204 degrees. The whole purpose of the event, I would suggest, is to say you have experienced those two exact extremes: 200 degrees above and 100 degrees below. Humans like rounded numbers. Nobody celebrates adding the two hundred and fourth bird sighting to their list, or sprints ninety-six metres. All I know is this event has the feeling of being cobbled together just to get everyone at the base to participate. Everyone except Alex Kasabian.'

'But if everyone else took part, it's hard to see how any of them could have killed Kasabian. And I have to say, exposing your naked skin to a three-hundred-degree temperature swing in the presence of a bunch of other people is what I'd call establishing an alibi the hard way.'

Jejeune nodded thoughtfully. 'Possibly. But I think somebody did use this event, somehow. Did you have any luck looking into Julien Bellaire, by the way?' he asked.

'We had a file on him at the mag, as a matter of fact.' Lindy drew a breath and exhaled. 'Bottom line: Julien Bellaire is one seriously wealthy man. A billionaire many times over. I mean, this bloke makes more money per year than our landscapers.'

Jejeune smiled. They were in the process of getting estimates for minor work to the garden at the new place, and Lindy's outraged disbelief at the quotes had become an ongoing theme, so much so that the crew had taken to delivering their appraisals directly to Jejeune. Via email.

'French national?' asked Jejeune.

'Born there. French is still his first language. He uses it for important stuff like naming his playthings, you know, a pair of supply ships, Antarctic research bases, mansions, stuff like that. He's been here a while now. Not sure if he's a dual citizen, though.'

'Anything about how his climate research operations are run?'

Lindy shook her head. 'Not much, but he seems to go out of his way to show he's not one of those come-and-go philanthropists. His grandiose pronouncements might sound a bit OTT, but then I suppose you need that sort of self-importance if you're going to take on the job of becoming the planet's self-appointed saviour. I have to say, though, his commitment to environmental causes does seem genuine. That Costa Rican coffee he served you, for example, comes from his own plantation, run to the highest imaginable ethical and ecological standards. It's probably fair to say you'll never drink a cup of more environmentally friendly coffee in your life. And of course, he does have that whole Billionaire Bicyclist thing going. He even goes to local meetings in town by bike if the weather is nice enough. Granted, he's probably followed by a security detail in an armour-plated Mercedes that gets about four miles to the gallon. But it's the thought that counts.' She became serious. 'Do you really think he's involved?'

Outside the window, the inlet was still and silent. The scoter had gone and apart from the flickering movement of the leaves on the far bank, there was nothing to distinguish the scene from one captured in a painting. Jejeune looked back at the image on his computer screen. There was a grotesque elegance in the way Kasabian's arm arced across the space from his body to the snowmobile's fuel line, literally frozen in the air between them. It was as if he were imploring someone to come to his aid. Perhaps now, too late, someone was.

'Yes,' he said, 'I do.'

'But somebody else must have killed him, obviously,' said Lindy thoughtfully. 'The problem is, at those temperatures, nobody could possibly have cut that pipe without wearing gloves, could they?'

Jejeune shook his head. 'They would have risked freezing their skin to any of the metal parts if they removed their gloves, even for a few seconds.'

'So no fingerprints,' said Lindy. 'And no tracks because of new snowfall. And due to the insulated clothing, no hope of any DNA at the scene either, I'm assuming. I hate to say it, Dom, but if someone down there did commit this crime, it might just be the perfect one.'

But Jejeune knew better. The perfect crime was not one somebody got away with. It was the one no one even knew had been committed. In this case, the body had been found, and photographed. And Alex Kasabian had told him what had happened. It meant Jejeune had all the information he needed to know he was now investigating a murder.

16

The Brackets. In truth, Danny Maik had never really warmed to the locals' name for the two hides at the bottom of the incline below him. For one thing, brackets were supposed to enclose something. All that had ever been between these two hides was a wide space that you could traverse to begin climbing up the slope on the far side, if that kind of rigorous exercise was something that interested you. More often, though, he'd seen people sprinting downhill; birders clattering along with their bins and 'scopes and tripods in tow, alerted to a rare sighting from one hide or the other.

The Julien Bellaire Institute for Climate Science. He wasn't in love with the current name of the site. Any time people started building structures and naming them after themselves, it sent the kind of message that didn't really sit well with Danny. Of course, whatever people chose to call this place these days, there was now one name that was more fitting than any other: *Crime Scene.* What had once been the hide that overlooked the sea was a blackened tangle of timber and plastic and glass. From the top of the rise, Maik couldn't see the extent of the damage to the new central section of the facility, but the hide on the far side that overlooked the marsh appeared to be intact.

He left his car in the circular driveway of the house at the top of the incline and began the steep descent down. It crossed his mind how difficult it would have been for the firefighters to get equipment down this slope. It was little wonder the fire had done so much damage before it was put out. Although the slope had continued to narrow on both sides as it descended, the land fanned out considerably once it flattened out. He'd forgotten how much room there was down here. He regarded the new structure carefully. In the greyscale palette of the overcast skies, the contrast between the weathered planking of the remaining hide and the glass of the new adjoining structure was jarring. To spend millions retrofitting the hides and leave the outside appearance untouched like this didn't make much sense to Danny. But then, he was no expert in architectural design. Since the renovations had all been funded by Julien Bellaire, Danny supposed how the finished project looked was really no one's concern but his.

In the bay on the seaward side of the property, the large metal cradle containing the buoys rose and fell with the gentle tide. As he approached for a closer look, the bitter tang of smoke rose towards him, as if the water somehow still held the odour of the fire.

'In for maintenance,' said a voice behind him. A woman stepped out of the charred debris of the burned-out hide, slapping the dirt from her gloved hands against her left thigh. 'The buoys. We pass an electric current through them to descale the rust.'

'Must cost a fortune in soda crystals. For the electrolyte,' added Maik, at the woman's puzzled glance.

'We manage to scrape by.' She removed her glove and offered her name along with her hand. Tori Boyd was probably in her early forties, but had the kind of beauty that had deepened with time. She had a presence about her that suggested she was at ease dealing with men's interest, as if it was to be expected. She saw Maik glance at her heavily bandaged right leg, the dressing showing dark smudge marks from the smoke residue. She smiled and nodded. 'Yes, I know. My doctor is not going to be very happy with me, is he? I just wanted to see what was salvageable.' The smile faded. 'Not very much, I'm afraid.'

Maik could just make out the remains of electronic equipment among the ruins.

'Computers?'

Boyd smiled sadly. 'Plus a couple of stand-alone servers and some fairly sophisticated monitoring hardware. The Bellaire project has deployed a vast network of sea buoys in oceans around the world, all fitted with ultra-sensitive temperature detection hardware. The coverage is exponentially greater than any other project of its type and as a result, the data we collect is more comprehensive and more accurate. Its value to the world's climate monitoring efforts is incalculable. All of that data is collected here.'

It sounded almost as if she was reciting the information from a brochure, but Maik had already realised she was a person for whom crisp efficiency would be important. He looked at the central block and the hide on the far side. 'Was there much damage to the rest of the facility?'

She shook her head. 'Thankfully, no. As a recent build, the central block had cutting-edge fire-retardant materials, all well above code, as you would expect if you knew the owner. Luckily, that prevented the fire from spreading any further.'

Lucky escapes always made Maik suspicious, especially when it seemed to him that there would have been room in the burned-out hide to comfortably house a lot more equipment than he could see. It was a question worth asking, at the very least.

'Air-gapping, Sergeant. It's a process that ensures no one can access one network through another. When we started out, the data was collected by satellite-based passive microwave sensors, like the ones used to detect sea ice concentrations. Those readings were transmitted directly to the Department of Global Climatology at the uni. But with the recent trend of high-tech hacking, Julien, the owner, felt the risk to the university's databases was just too great. So now, once the sea temperature data is received from the buoys, I have to download it onto a hard drive and carry it all the way over to another bank of computers housed in the hide on the far side of the building, and manually upload it from there.' She laughed at his expression. 'I know what you're thinking. It's all a bit Neanderthal for a state-of-the art operation like this. But it really is the best way to keep the university's databases secure.'

Maik had been accused of a Neanderthal approach himself, at times. The difference was, his efforts usually had the desired effect. He surveyed the scorched timbers of the hide. 'Unfortunately, this air-gapping was no defence against a low-tech attack, was it? I imagine this has set your research back quite a bit.'

Boyd brightened. 'That's about the only positive in this whole situation. The data is cloud-saved once it's been transmitted. None of the information has been lost, only this hardware. That can always be replaced.' She looked back at the hide. 'It's the data that holds the true importance in what we do. And that, at least, is safe. I suppose that's the main thing.'

'Plus, no one was hurt.'

'Yes, of course,' she said thoughtfully. 'That too.'

'Were you working here when the fire started?'

She shook her head. 'No, I was at home.' She indicated the house at the top of the incline behind Maik. 'I saw an orange glow down here and I knew immediately what it was. I came to see if I could put it out myself. Though I fear now that I might have wasted valuable time trying to get down here with this damned thing slowing me down.' She pulled a face and tapped the heavy bandaging around her knee. 'More nuisance than pain. Can't do anything, though, certainly not in a hurry. As soon as I got down here and realised the size of the blaze, I called the fire brigade, but it had completely taken hold by the time they arrived.'

Without the DCI's steel-trap mind to capture the details of the operations here, it occurred to Danny he might be well advised to write a few things down. He took out a notepad and pen. 'Is this air-gapping system common knowledge?' he asked.

'We make no secret of it. Julien feels that if people know the system can't be compromised, it might prevent them from trying.'

Maik jotted down a few lines. 'Any candidates for somebody who might have tried anyway?' he asked eventually. 'Any recent threats made against the facility, either directly or online?'

'Online? The product of a brief fling between an opinion and a keyboard is hardly going to keep me awake at nights. But yes, as a matter of fact, I did receive one indication that the facility might be in danger. A man named Arliss Dyer came to see me. He'd heard someone discussing the possibility of setting fire to a hide that might have been one of these. It all sounded a bit vague and improbable at the time.' She paused and set her hands on her hips, surveying the charred ruins in front of her. 'Of course, I'm beginning to wish I'd taken his warning more seriously now.'

Maik nodded slowly and made another entry on his notepad. 'It's a pity no one thought to pass this information on to the police.'

'Oh, but he did, Sergeant. He called DCI Jejeune. Did the inspector not mention it?'

There were times when Maik was grateful he'd never traded in his notepad and pen for a digital recorder. Without his head bowed like this, even Danny's normally stoic features might have revealed a touch of surprise. His measured response, though, when it came, betrayed none. 'I've not spoken to the inspector recently. Are you sure this Arliss Dyer reported it?'

'I was with him. In fact, he used my phone to leave his message for the DCI.'

'Why would Mr Dyer call the inspector, instead of the station?'

'He knows DCI Jejeune personally. We both do. Arliss is something of a local celebrity among birders.' She looked at Maik carefully. 'Are you quite sure the inspector didn't report the call? It was light on details, admittedly, and Arliss did mention he'd been drinking earlier in the evening. I suppose it's possible he didn't think the information was credible.'

'I'm sure the DCI would have given it due consideration,' said Maik non-committally. 'Do you happen to know where I might find this Mr Dyer?'

'He could be anywhere. He's currently wandering about the countryside, sleeping rough, apparently. Arliss is blind, Sergeant, I may not have mentioned that. But he knows this landscape as intimately as anyone I've ever met. As I say, Inspector Jejeune is acquainted with him. Perhaps you can ask him if he knows where Arliss is.'

Maik's smile thanked her for the advice. He looked out at the bay again and nodded towards the buoys. 'Don't they usually use chains to secure sea buoys to anchors?'

Boyd nodded. 'We use Dor-Mor weights, and a Halas embedment system simply because there's nothing better, but by using polypropylene ropes instead of chains we can significantly limit the abrasion to the seabed. Unfortunately, we have to fasten the ropes to the buoys using a metal harness, which means we have to retrieve them periodically and bring them back here for descaling.' Boyd seemed to hesitate for a moment. 'You know, Sergeant, if you are looking for suspects for this fire, you could do worse than consider my ex-husband. I wouldn't have thought of him normally, but his name did come up in a recent conversation. Glover believes my dedication to the project is what broke up our marriage. He's wrong, of course, but I know he has always resented me working at this facility.'

Danny took in the smoke-blackened remains of the hide. A lead was a lead, but they rarely just fell out of the sky like this. 'Has he been around lately?'

'He gave me a lift home from the hospital on Tuesday night.' She looked at him frankly. 'You can imagine how thrilled I was about having to ask him, but I couldn't drive myself. As a rule, though, he'd rather stay away from here.'

'He opposes the kind of work you do?'

She shook her head. 'Oppose is a bit strong. It's all just a bit beyond him. Glover spent his whole life among academics, trying to disguise the fact that he was an imposter. The one time he did try furthering his education, a paramedic course, he found it all too overwhelming and packed it in after the first year. The truth is, my ex-husband has always operated on a more visceral level. If he can't buy it dinner and bed it, it's not likely to hold his attention for very long.'

It was not what Maik would call the most disinterested assessment of a suspect, but it was worth following up. At this point in the investigation, anything was. He thanked Boyd and closed his notepad. As he was turning to leave, he took a look out over the marsh. A string of ducks sped inland on

17

Danny Maik was aware as he stood at the threshold of the Board Room that he was about to bid goodbye to an important touchstone of his past. Having weathered countless storms that had battered the north Norfolk coast over the decades, the Boatman's Arms had been overcome, finally, by the economic tempest brought by the pandemic. The pub had stood at the centre of Saltmarsh social life for so long the local community felt its loss keenly. At first, there had been rumours that the property had been purchased, and that its new owners had plans to restore it to its former glory. But there were no signs of life any time Maik passed by, merely shuttered windows and boarded-up doors that seemed intent on permanently closing one more chapter of his life. And so, it was on to the Board Room; a new venue for the off-duty officers to meet and mingle and solve the world's problems. With a sigh he would never have acknowledged, even to himself, Danny reached for the handle and opened the door.

He saw Tony Holland at a table in the far corner of the room as he entered, and, drawing nearer, he noticed Lauren Salter seated behind him. She was wiping tears from her eyes. Danny's expression made his inquiry for him.

'Tony's just been trying his hand at Taoism.' Salter exploded into laughter again and he waited patiently until she dabbed her eyes and took a deep steadying breath. 'He said we shouldn't judge any man until we've spent some time living in his shoes.'

'As the sole tenant, presumably,' said Maik.

'She knows what I meant,' said Holland irritably. 'I'll get them in. They've got their own craft beer on. See what you think.'

Maik sat beside Salter and she dissolved into one more giggling fit before finally bringing it under control. 'God help me, I did miss him,' she said. 'Whatever you do, though, don't tell him. Anyway,' she swept an arm around to indicate the space, 'what do you think?'

The room was a good deal brighter than many pub interiors Maik had been in. The walls were lined with aged oak shelving neatly stacked with books and board games. From large stone fireplaces in opposite corners, healthy fires were suffusing the room in a pleasant amber glow. Maik would have said the place was pitched to a much younger crowd than himself, but the clientele argued against it. Many of them were hunched over board games, staring intently at game pieces or cards. The absorbed study of the players made for a much quieter pub than he was used to, but that was all right with him, too. The ambient hum of conversation was low enough to speak to the person across the table from you without having to strain forward over the din. On the whole, Maik decided he could be happy enough here. All that remained was to see whether the beer was up to scratch.

Holland returned from the bar cradling three glasses in his hands. He set them down on the table and whipped his leg over the seat of the chair to sit saddle-style, with the back against his chest. As he distributed the drinks, Maik raised a finger to indicate the song coming over the system. If the

Board Room was intent on winning him over, playing 'How Sweet It Is' by Marvin Gaye was certainly going about it the right way.

It was the same tune Holland had heard Maik whistling when he came into the office the other day. Even if it wasn't exactly his cup of tea, it was at least an indication of where Danny's heart was these days. After the dreary regimen of losses and loneliness Maik had subjected Holland to before he left for London, the upbeat side of Motown was a welcome change.

Salter checked a text on her phone. 'Have either of you heard anything about Quentin Senior?' she asked. 'That's the second person today I've had asking whether there's been any news on him. Nobody knows where to find him.'

Holland pulled a face. 'He's probably off chasing some lesser-spotted something or other. You know what these birders are like when there's a rarity about.'

Maik took a sip of his cloudy beer and set it down on the table again, wincing. 'If it is a rare bird he's after, I daresay he'd have let the DCI in on it.' He turned to Salter. 'Why don't you check with him? While you're at it you can find out how his meeting with Julien Bellaire went.'

Holland sipped his own beer, continuing on long past the point Maik had reached his limit. 'He undoubtedly told him that there was nothing to it. Pound to a penny, it was just somebody's idea of a joke.'

Undoubtedly. It was not a word you heard very often when Domenic Jejeune was investigating something, thought Maik ruefully. *Possibly, probably*, the DCI would have been able to live with those. But a word that suggested doubts were out of the question? The DCI would most certainly have had doubts about a message from anybody predicting their own death. Even one from Antarctica.

Holland nodded towards Maik's beer. 'You haven't got very far with that one,' he said. 'Did you want to try something else?'

In place of a reply, Danny gave a slight cough.

'You all right, Sarge? You look a bit pale.'

'Fine. Just those paint fumes on my chest.'

Salter nodded. 'I know what you mean. I've had a headache all day myself. I suppose it's too much to hope that Shepherd is going to lose interest in all this redecorating nonsense.'

Maik inclined his head. 'You know the DCS. Once she starts something, she likes to see it through. My guess is that we're in for a good couple of weeks of this, unless we can catch a decent case.'

Salter pulled a face. 'Then all I can say is thank God for plastic sheeting.' She held up her glass. 'I'll have another, Tony, if you're going.'

She watched Holland make his way to the bar. One upside to having his new girlfriend working behind the bar was that he didn't need much encouragement to get the drinks in, even when it wasn't his round. As her eyes flickered towards the door, Salter fixed on a smile and spoke through clenched teeth. 'Hey up, look like we've been discussing colour schemes.'

Maik spun in his seat to see DCS Shepherd standing in the doorway surveying the room. She saw them and began heading over, noticing Tony Holland deep in conversation with the barmaid as she passed. 'I thought I might find you in here,' she said as she arrived. She looked over her shoulder. 'I see his flirtation with Taoism didn't last long.'

'No that's her, ma'am,' said Salter. 'She works at the Institute during the day and then does part-time evenings here.'

'Pity she can't tell us anything about the fire up there,' said the DCS sourly. 'An attack on a climate change facility.' She shook her head slowly. 'I imagine this has set their research back years.'

'As a matter of fact, they didn't lose any data,' said Maik. 'It was all hardware, damaging enough, but replaceable.'

Holland joined them, setting a large glass of white wine in front of Shepherd and another near Salter.

'All in all,' continued Maik, 'the fire might not have too much long-term effect on their operations. In fact, I'd say with this Dr Boyd in charge, they'll be up and running again in no time.'

Shepherd's eyebrows climbed in surprise. 'Tori Boyd?'

Holland gave his DCS a puzzled glance. 'Tory, like the party?'

'Tori. Like Victoria with an attitude,' said Shepherd tersely. 'She runs the Bellaire Institute?'

Maik nodded. 'It's privately funded, but she's the director. Do you know her, ma'am?'

'By reputation. She was one half of a glamour couple on the local scene, back in the day. There'd be a picture of them in the paper every once a while: Tori and Glover Boyd, dressed to the nines, toting a glass of champagne at some university function or another. I believe she was considered the genu-ine article, a high-flier in the academic world. The husband was always regarded as a bit of a hanger-on, all style and no substance. Fancied himself as something of a ladies' man.' She paused. 'It all ended in a vitriolic divorce, I seem to remember.'

'She did put her ex-husband forward as a possible suspect,' said Maik. 'There didn't seem to be much love lost between them.'

'Disgruntled ex, out to destroy the wife's work?' said Holland. 'Wouldn't be the first time, would it? Any previous between them, I wonder?'

He looked expectantly at Salter, who was staring at her phone. It was not like her to miss an opportunity to contrib-ute to local folklore, so he could only conclude she had never heard of the Boyds. It was certainly possible. He had lived around here as long as anyone, and he couldn't recall any previous mention of them.

'Sergeant,' prompted Shepherd. 'The Boyds. History?'

'Oh, er. One verbal confrontation at the university,' she said consulting her phone. 'Formal caution for the husband. Nothing else. I did run a background check on that girl, by the way. The one in the hide.'

Judging by Shepherd's reaction, as changes of topic went, this one certainly had something to recommend it.

'Nothing on her identity,' said Salter, 'but when she ran away from the hospital, she left the blanket. It was filed as possible evidence in a crime, but it wasn't tested for DNA because there was never any case brought. Surely there would be some on there, though. We could send it off to find out.'

Holland shook his head dubiously. 'I don't know, ma'am. I'm wondering if this isn't a straightforward case of sabotage.' He looked at Maik, but the sergeant seemed to be finding something about the tabletop fascinating.

'And what makes you say that, Constable?' Shepherd could sense the awkward dynamic between the two men, but she couldn't quite put her finger on what was going on.

Holland left a long stare on Danny, but when the sergeant raised his eyes to meet it, Holland apparently didn't see what he was waiting for. He shrugged. 'Just intuition,' he said lamely.

Shepherd cast her own look Danny's way, but he met it full on, leaving her with nowhere to go. 'Yes, well, I'm not quite sure that'll get us over the line on this one, Constable,' she said stiffly. 'Still, at least we've got a couple of things to look at tomorrow; the blanket... And the husband.'

But not the sabotage, thought the watching Salter. Though judging by the way Tony Holland was looking at Danny, that topic too seemed like it might be rearing its head again before too long.

18

The choreography had not varied, but the dynamics had. Domenic Jejeune now had a crime to pursue, and that would colour everything he asked, everything he heard, everything he thought. He wasn't sure whether Bellaire was aware yet of the shift; he suspected not. But as he was led along the hallway into the room, Jejeune felt a new electricity coursing through him, sharpening his alertness.

The two men had waited in silence as the uber-efficient maid once again served their coffees to Bellaire's exacting standards without the slightest mishap. There was no reference to the coffee's origins this time. It was no longer necessary to establish Bellaire's green credentials. He knew Jejeune would have conducted a thorough background check on him by now. Small talk was not necessary either. Both men knew the detective's visit was not a social call.

'You have made progress in your investigations.'

It was difficult to tell whether Bellaire's words were a statement or a question. 'Some. I left a message at Dumont d'Urville, but the base commander didn't contact me.'

Bellaire nodded at the news. 'It was a question of opportunity, not evasion, I assure you. Communications are not always easy around Île des Pétrels. Connections are at the whim of the weather and atmospheric conditions. Now they are on board the *Oceanite*, you will hear from Gaya at the first opportunity. We are, as I said, anxious to make sure our operations have been as open as possible.'

Indeed Bellaire had said, thought Jejeune, a couple of times now. It would be interesting to see if this openness was officially declared among the goals for the project. Or even the vision. Outside the window, a Nightingale was working its way along a split-rail fence. Jejeune wondered what was causing this normally shy, secretive bird to venture out in the open like this. He hoped it wasn't ill or injured. In birds, as in people, an unusual pattern of behaviour was often a signal that something was not right. 'I couldn't find any reference to an interest in Antarctica prior to your involvement with this base,' he said. 'It seems like a considerable investment in an area that is new to you.'

'The continent, yes. But my association with climate research is long-standing.' Bellaire took a sip from his coffee cup and set it down on the table between them, leaning forward slightly as a prelude to an elaboration. 'Temperatures in the Antarctic are generally less susceptible to short-term impacts brought about by individual events. Given their relative stability, they provide a reliable baseline against which changes in other parts of the world may be measured.'

'Even so, I can't imagine the idea of establishing a privately funded research facility down there would be well received by the international scientific community.'

Bellaire tilted his head. 'Perhaps, but there is no official body to oppose it. Some countries have claimed areas of Antarctica, but those are just territorial conventions. They are not recognised as legal jurisdiction. Over eighty percent of the continent is not claimed at all. The land on which we established our facility belongs to no country, and therefore none has any authority to prevent it.'

Bellaire rose and strolled across the room. Jejeune was struck again by his nondescript appearance. Perhaps it was Bellaire's unremarkable physicality that had provided the drive to stand out in other areas. 'They could still have made it difficult for you logistically,' said the detective. 'If they had blocked access to Dumont d'Urville, for example, it would have been impossible to supply your base with the resources it needs to operate.'

Bellaire shrugged easily. 'Since I do not have the scientific background to be able to justify my presence on the continent, my contribution has been more… practical.'

Jejeune nodded slowly as the understanding came. 'The two supply vessels.'

Bellaire smiled. 'The *Oceanite* and the *Mouette*. They are placed at the disposal of all the research teams down there. Each ship has a research lab and heliport on board. Neither is fast, but they have the heavy-duty motors needed for those conditions. Most importantly, they are double-hulled and ice-strengthened. They both hold the highest possible ice-breaking designation.'

The motors were 2,500 kilowatts each, on two shafts, and the icebreaking classification was +1A1. In Jejeune's experience, pride of ownership was often manifested by an indulgence in the details. Bellaire's casual account of the ships' specifications showed that he was aware of their capabilities only to the extent to which they were of use to him. Despite his satisfaction with the ships' fitness for purpose, they were possessions, not passions, chosen for their ability to meet the needs of their owner, in this case, as a quid pro quo for establishing a research camp on the world's most remote landmass.

Jejeune looked out of the window again. The Nightingale had gone. The split-rail fence looked different now, as if the gnarled wood was more of a structural feature and less a part of something natural. He looked back at Bellaire, who was standing behind his desk, studying something of interest in a document. 'Would Mr Kasabian's research at the base have involved proprietary information?'

Bellaire looked up at him and tapped his lips with his forefinger. 'You don't believe Alex was responsible for his own death.'

'There was no sign of any tools that could have cut through a pipe in the photographs I saw.'

'Until the body is recovered, his survival bag cannot be checked. Until then, such a premise cannot be ruled out. Once the body has been allowed to thaw, a thorough search of Alex Kasabian's clothing and survival bag will be conducted. You will be provided with a complete inventory of the contents.' He smiled tightly and set the document down on the desk. 'If your question is related to a possible motive for someone else to kill him, though, I fear I must disappoint you on two counts. Alex dealt with no proprietary information. Indeed we have none.'

He paused and stepped towards Jejeune, as he had done previously. There was no more menace in the gesture than last time, but it was a curious way of emphasising your point. 'It is our responsibility as human beings to effect positive change, is it not? Our duty? The Bellaire Institute can effect that change, *will* effect that change. The repercussions of our work will be felt for generations. But we live in a world where reliable information is becoming harder to identify. Findings are selectively mined for helpful phrases, contradictory ones are ignored. Opinions are presented as facts, facts as opinions. It is important to reassure people that there aren't contradictory realities, only one. But the only way people can accept this is if they are able to see things for themselves: information, complete and unfiltered. Therefore we feel it is our duty to make the data we gather available to everyone. After all, our work belongs to the world. Are we not all shareholders in this planet?'

With the Nightingale gone, Jejeune looked around the room for a new point of focus while he marshalled his thoughts. There was a jarring incongruity to the collection of objects, he now realised. It was as if people had been dispatched with instructions to purchase the best of everything, with the definition of the word left up to them to decide. It had resulted in pairings like an antique jade desk set with a Montblanc Meisterstück pen in the holder, and a Penn executive leather chair behind the Hollywood desk. The only unifying theme in this room was a price tag.

Bellaire noticed Jejeune's interest in the furnishings. 'Our generation won't be revered for the possessions we accumulate, Inspector. That way of keeping score belongs to the past. We will be judged on how we have changed the world, what impact we made on humankind, on history.' He closed the distance between them still further and leaned forward again. 'Not schools, not libraries.' He brushed the suggestions away with his hands. 'I mean vast, ambitious projects, undertaken by individuals with the resources and the skill and the vision to realise them. We cannot change our past, but the future, that vast great commons of humanity,' he nodded, 'it is on this that we must inscribe our legacy. And we will.'

His sincerity radiated from him like an energy, lighting his eyes with such overwhelming conviction that the subject no longer mattered. The sheer potency of his belief obliterated any doubts you had. This was his closing pitch, Jejeune realised, how Bellaire concluded his business deals, clinched his agreements, with the dynamism and power of a personality that were compelling and irresistible.

'You said two counts,' Jejeune reminded him.

Bellaire gave a tight smile. 'I have had it confirmed that everyone else at the base was involved in the 300-Club event at the time.' He spread his hands. 'So you see, it cannot be that anyone else was involved in Alex Kasabian's death.'

'As base commander, would it have been Gaya who arranged the event?'

'She would have signed off on it, but I know the Canadian, Scott, was the driving force behind it. He had participated in one before.'

'You know, I spoke to someone who had participated in a 300-Club event at the South Pole,' said Jejeune. 'He said he was surprised they went ahead with one so late in the year.'

Bellaire shrugged. 'They were in a spell of extreme cold, and with the departure deadline looming, perhaps they saw this as their last chance. The external temperature would have been quite cold enough to make the experience memorable, I would have thought.'

Jejeune nodded. Quite cold enough to kill a man in an insulated snowsuit, five kilometres from the base. Bellaire's personal assistant appeared silently in the doorway, summoned, Jejeune suspected, by some device he had not detected. What else about Julien Bellaire's world had he failed to pick up on during his visits, he wondered.

'Just one more thing, Mr Bellaire. When would you expect the results of the inventory to be available?'

'The new team will have warmer temperatures and more daylight to work by. They will recover the body as soon as it is safe to do so. A few days at most.'

'I would like to request that the entire process is also videotaped. Both at the site and back at the base.'

Bellaire spread his hands. 'As you wish. The recording will be supplied to you with the inventory.'

Jejeune stood up to take his leave, looking in the assistant's direction. 'At some point, it may be necessary for us to speak again.'

Bellaire bowed his head slightly in understanding. 'An appointment will not be necessary, Mr Jejeune. You are most welcome any time. I close my doors only upon my enemies. Why should they ever be closed to you?'

19

Outside the windows of the Incident Room, the sunlight flooded across the landscape like honey. Deep shadows lay beneath the line of Corsican pines that marked the far boundary of the fields, and pockmarked the ditches and furrows in the fields. It was a scene of peace and tranquillity that was not mirrored by DCS Colleen Shepherd's features. 'I've just got off the phone with the press liaison office,' she said curtly. 'Apparently somebody has been putting locks on the local bird hides, along with a note that gives the combination and asks users to make sure the hides are re-locked after use.'

'What sense does that make?' asked Holland. 'Why bother locking them, if you're going to give the combination?'

'Those hides were set ablaze from the outside, anyway,' said Salter. 'If it's to protect them from attacks, what's the use in locking them in the first place?'

'Exactly the questions the press are asking,' said Shepherd irritably, 'with some justification, it seems to me. They wanted to know if we were aware of this latest development.' She looked at them. 'We weren't. And so, in the absence of anything resembling actual progress in the case, I wonder if we could at least find out who's behind this nonsense.'

Maik fished a piece of paper out of his pocket. It was a copy of a receipt from a local hardware store for locks and other hardware. The equipment had been sold to one Domenic Jejeune. Shepherd's already unhappy expression seemed to take a turn for the worse. 'I can just imagine what the Community Liaison Office will have to say if it comes out that it's one of our own involved in this idiocy.'

'A suspended one at that,' added Holland, whose newfound interest in Taoism apparently didn't preclude him piling on.

'I doubt it's likely to have much effect on the public's opinion of us,' said Maik. 'What with them already holding us in such universally high esteem and all.' He had already booked the fragment of the charred note and the singed lock into evidence, pending the formal examination of the site at Canon's Cross, but he saw no pressing need to inform the DCS of this just now. Colleen Shepherd looked vexed enough as it was.

'He is supposed to remain away from all police-related activities,' she said, her voice rising with frustration. 'Not meddling in ongoing investigations. Clearly somebody needs to remind him that he's still under suspension.'

In Maik's experience, when a superior officer decided that somebody needed to do something, he was usually the some-body they had in mind. But in this case, he'd be happy to take on the responsibility. It would be preferable to having the DCS deliver the message herself, especially in her current frame of mind.

'Right,' she said, consigning the matter to the *Completed* folder, 'moving on. We now have a couple more leads on the fire at the Bellaire Institute. The ex-husband's name has come up.'

'Whoever set that fire probably knew the lie of the land,' said Holland. 'It would be no small job to come down past the house at the top of the hill, carting a couple of full cans of petrol, without being detected. Even at night.'

'Glover Boyd would know the layout,' said Shepherd, nodding. 'He does seem to be our most promising lead at the moment.'

'I'm not sure about that, ma'am,' said Salter dubiously. 'Based on the point that girl was picked up by the squad car, the Brackets would have been the closest hides.'

'To be fair,' said Maik, 'if we're going that way, they do still look like hides. The outsides were left untouched during the retrofit.'

Holland's stare had already been on the way to disbelief. Danny Maik's support for the idea ratcheted it up to a new level. 'This again?' he said. 'I told you, it's ancient history.'

'Your intuition still telling you it was sabotage, Constable?' asked Shepherd.

'No ma'am. It's more than that.' He stared at Danny in the same way he had at the pub. And as before, Maik met his gaze evenly.

Shepherd sighed impatiently. Enough of this. If they had something, she needed to hear it. 'Yes,'

'There was a phone call, wasn't there, Sarge?' asked Holland. 'From the Institute?'

Maik hadn't distributed his own notes of his meeting with Tori Boyd, so Holland could only have received this information from Paige Turner. But compromised into it or not, he recognised that the time had come to share the information.

'A couple of days before the fire, ma'am,' he said evenly. 'A man named Arliss Dyer reported overhearing a plan that seemed to imply that one of the hides up there was being targeted, and the previous hide fires were being set to disguise it.'

Holland drew his eyes away from Maik and fastened them on Shepherd. *Sabotage*, his look said. Shepherd fixed her own wide-eyed stare on Danny. 'This was reported? To us?'

'To Inspector Jejeune, ma'am. He and Dyer are acquaintances, apparently.'

Sometimes, Shepherd's volcanic reactions were preferable to when the ice formed over her like this. A muscle worked in her cheek as she fought to control her emotions. 'DCI Jejeune was warned of a potential threat to a climate research facility, and he did not pass on that message? Has this been verified?'

'Tori Boyd's phone records show a call to the inspector's number at the correct time and date. Be about the right length for the message they reported hearing Dyer leave, too.'

'Perhaps he just assumed Dyer would report it to us as well,' said Salter. Sometimes it was hard not to admire her loyalty, thought Holland, though he recognised her efforts were as much to excuse Danny's own failings as Jejeune's.

'No, Sergeant,' said Shepherd, 'what the DCI assumed is that we would continue to stumble around on this thing until he came to lead us all out of the darkness.'

A quest for personal glory didn't sound much like the Domenic Jejeune they knew. Catching someone who was threatening the local birding community, on the other hand – they could all see how he might not want to leave that to anyone else, especially given their lamentable progress in the case so far.

'I want him questioned,' said Shepherd. 'And I want a record of his answers on file.'

'Perhaps if I just gave him a quick call, ma'am,' said Salter. 'I mean a formal interview... while he's on suspension. The way it might look—'

'How it might look is irrelevant,' said Shepherd exasperatedly. 'If Chief Inspector Jejeune has decided to put himself squarely in the middle of our inquiries, then he can bloody well live with the consequences.'

'Still, though...'

'All right,' said Shepherd with dangerously caged patience, 'I'll run through this one more time and you can stop me at the part you think sounds like a suggestion. You will ask him what the hell he thinks he is playing at visiting a crime scene when I explicitly gave him orders not to. You will further ask him what in God's name he's doing interfering in an ongoing investigation by posting notes and putting locks on hides. And finally, you will ask him to explain why he chose to withhold information about a potential crime. Clear enough now?'

She had almost reached the plastic sheeting across the doorway when she turned for a final comment. 'And just because we're supposed to be pursuing some actual police work here as well, let's see if Glover Boyd has an alibi for the night of the fire at the Institute.'

The sheeting had not even settled back into place before Holland was out of his chair and following her into the corridor.

Colleen Shepherd looked up as Tony Holland knocked on her open office door. Her anger had been quelled somewhat by a text she had just received. 'A friend is asking me if I can find a home for this,' she said, turning the phone to him. 'I was thinking it might go next to that droopy fig thing near Danny's desk.'

Holland studied the image carefully. 'A castor oil plant?' He gave a short laugh. 'Be right up Danny's street, that one. Remind him of his youth; a dose now and then to keep him regular.'

Shepherd shut off the phone and turned her attention to him. 'So what is it, Constable? More tales of how things are done down at the Met? Let me guess, when they need a sketch artist, they give Banksy a call. I suppose it's too much to hope that you've come to tell me there's some news on that Antarctic blog.'

Holland's earlier buoyancy seemed to leave him like a punctured balloon. 'Yeah, about that.' He scratched the side of his head tentatively with his fingers. 'The thing is, I'm not quite sure where it stands, to tell you the truth. I believe Sergeant Maik asked the DCI to look into it.'

In Holland's experience, Shepherd was not given to theatrics, so he could only assume that putting her head in her hands like this was a genuine gesture of despair. 'For God's sake, what is wrong with you people? Are you all really so utterly convinced that we can't get by without him for a few weeks?'

'Well, what with it being birds and all,' said Holland reasonably.

'And with you being too busy romancing the Tao out of your new girlfriend to find the time.' Shepherd left her steely gaze on him for a long moment. 'At least tell me he's getting somewhere with it.'

Holland shrugged. 'Last I heard he was due to speak to Julien Bellaire.'

Shepherd shot him a glance.

'He owns the base.'

'As well as the institute that has just been set ablaze.' She nodded thoughtfully. 'Well I suppose if he'd found out anything we'd have heard about it by now. Tell Danny when he goes to see the DCI, he can thank him for his contributions and inform him that his services are no longer required. We'll get it back here and we, as in you, can take up the inquiry again.'

She gave him a tight smile, in lieu of a formal dismissal, but Holland made no move to leave. 'Erm, there is one other thing, ma'am. It's about Danny. And Sergeant Salter.'

The DCS's look asked him to consider if she really, really wanted to hear this. She offered him an open palm to indicate he should sit across from her. As he did so, he let his eyes stray around the room for a moment, as if it might be easier than meeting his DCS's gaze.

'This is not me having a pop at anybody, ma'am. You know I think the world of them both, but this business of having Danny and Lauren seeing each other and working together…' He shook his head.

Usually when Holland said it was not about him being in here to criticise someone, it was safe to assume the opposite. But the troubled expression the young constable now wore suggested that, just this once, she might be able take his comment at face value.

'This theory that Lauren is floating,' he said tentatively, 'about the girl in that hide. If I'd have come up with an idea like that, Danny would have kicked my arse from here to Cromer, and rightly so. But instead, he's carrying on as if he believes there might actually be some merit to it.'

'The fact that we now know the previous hide fires may have been set to disguise this one at the Institute doesn't necessarily mean it couldn't have been this girl who set them,' Shepherd pointed out. 'The scene of a crime can be very evocative for a victim. It wouldn't be the first time someone wanted to destroy a place where something traumatic had happened to them.'

'Yeah, but not somewhere that has been so completely repurposed that it no longer bears even a passing resemblance to the scene of the crime. I'm no Sigbert Freud, but even I know that much. Danny's only indulging Lauren in this business because he doesn't want to tell her she's wrong.'

'Yes, thank you Sigbert, I had got that far. But if it was sabotage, they weren't very good at it, were they? They didn't even get all of the computers, let alone the data. Besides, where's the fanfare? As we know, people who target facilities like this usually like to make a song and dance about it afterwards, but as far as I'm aware no one has claimed credit for an attack.' Shepherd drew in a breath. 'By all means look into it, but until we've definitely ruled this girl out, I'm ruling her in. If there's nothing to it, Lauren should be able to eliminate it as a viable line of inquiry within a day or two.'

She stood up with a decisiveness that suggested that this time, the meeting was indeed at an end. Holland took the hint and stood as well. As he reached the doorway, Shepherd called out to him. 'Oh, one more thing, Constable. This business about the phone call. There's usually a method to Danny Maik's madness. In future, if you want to know why he's choosing not to let everybody in on something, maybe a quiet word first?' She gave him a tight smile. 'I'm not sure how they feel about teamwork down the Met, but we're quite big on it up here at Saltmarsh.'

Holland nodded sheepishly.

'Right,' she said briskly, as he turned to go, 'I'll tell my friend we can take her *Ricinus communis* plant off her hands. And if Danny doesn't like it, I'll be sure to tell him who recommended it.'

20

The sun shone on a cobalt sea, the nearest clouds a grey mass banked on the horizon like a distant mountain range. The ship was heading in their direction, but the clouds seemed to be showing no inclination to close the gap, so it would be some hours yet before the *Oceanite* sailed into them. Gaya was leaning on the railing of the ship, an iPad tucked tightly against her side. The freshening wind had lost some of its Antarctic bite, but there was still enough chill to redden her cheeks and set her skin tingling.

The iPad bleeped and she tugged off a mitten with her teeth to answer the video call.

'Inspector Jejeune. I am Gaya Monde.'

Jejeune might have expected a more guarded greeting than the welcoming smile the woman offered. He returned it and added a question. 'Just as a point of clarification. I take it our discussion will be recorded?'

Gaya offered a pained smile. 'Our organisation's commitment to openness means no secrets. But sadly, no privacy, either.' She brightened. 'There are many birds out on the sea just now.' She turned the iPad towards the bow and Jejeune could see the small black and white birds dancing like butterflies over the foam-flecked wave tops. 'They are Wilson's Storm

Petrels. I took the trouble of finding out. I am told you have an interest.'

Bellaire, thought Jejeune. What else had he told Gaya about him? For the billionaire to offer unconditional access to his Antarctic base commander suggested he was not worried about the information she would provide. But as always, it was the information that this woman chose not to provide that would interest Jejeune most. 'I imagine you must all be anxious to get home after so long away,' he said. 'I was surprised to learn the team will be taking the ship all the way. I had thought you'd be sailing only as far as Ushuaia or Cape Town and then flying back to the UK.'

'Seeing the world without people in it changes your sense of who you are. In the busyness of the modern world, it is easy for a person to lose sight of this. But in the solitude of Antarctica, you can discover yourself once again. Perhaps some are not comfortable with what they find. They prefer to hurry home to the fictitious selves they become there. I choose to remain who I truly am. This will not change regardless of my final destination.'

Perhaps her ambivalence was simply a response to the disquieting process of relocation she was anticipating. Jejeune had heard stories of soldiers returning from service in remote areas finding great difficulty in adjusting to the urban surroundings they'd known all their lives. 'I was hoping you could tell me more about this 300-Club meeting that was held the night Alex Kasabian died.'

She nodded. 'There is a different rationality down there, Inspector. Many of the things that anchor one to reality in the rest of the world do not exist. Behaviour and actions that would be considered illogical or foolish find acceptance in such a place. But it was harmless. Scott had taken part in one before. I was happy to green-light it.'

'So no one else was involved in the planning or preparation?'

She shook her head. 'No one. Scott took care of all the logistics. Participation was completely voluntary, of course, but everyone took part.'

'Except Alex Kasabian.'

She was silent for a moment. 'Yes. Except Alex.'

'How was it organised?'

'Three groups of three at ten-minute intervals. Women first, then men, then a mixed group, two women, one man. I was the beacon. We were at a period called nautical twilight. Artificial light was needed to make sure no one lost their way.'

'And you were there the entire time?'

'The beacon is the most crucial role in this event. The five minutes of the walk takes a human body to its limit. If anyone wandered off course, it would almost certainly result in their death. I sat astride a snowmobile with its headlight on one hundred metres out. As soon as they came out of the hut, they headed directly for the headlight beam. Once they reached it, they circled me and returned towards the base.'

Jejeune nodded thoughtfully. It was the kind of report a man like Bellaire would appreciate: concise, detailed and, as far as he could tell, complete. The problems it raised for him were not of the woman's making.

The dark blade of a whale's fin broke the surface of the water and Gaya stared at it intently. In the nutrient-rich waters of the bay at Dumont d'Urville such sightings were common, but out here on the open seas, they were less frequent and she had learned to value them. She sensed that the information she had given Jejeune had caused him some difficulties. And she believed she knew why. He already suspected Alex Kasabian was not responsible for his own death.

'It ended,' said Jejeune. 'You said in the video that Alex Kasabian and Lexi Marshall were together once, but it ended. Did it end on the base?'

Gaya nodded. 'Alex began a relationship with Amy.'

'Scott Della's wife? Did he know?'

'In such close confines, it is impossible to keep a secret like that for very long. In the end, they stopped trying.'

'Were Kasabian and Mrs Della still together when he died?'

'Amy tried to pretend so. But everyone could sense the tension between them. When we got home, they would have gone their separate ways, I am sure of it.'

'And the relationship between Scott Della and his wife?'

'Over. Scott is not a man to forgive such a betrayal.'

So Kasabian had ended a relationship with one woman and begun another with the wife of a fellow researcher. And for her part, Amy Della had sacrificed her marriage for a man who had become intent on ending their relationship. Jejeune was silent. In the incestuous, isolated world of the station, this could have given any one of three people a motive to want Alex Kasabian dead. However, while at the moment he was no closer to uncovering the ultimate reason for the man's death, he suspected it ran much deeper than fractured relationships. If Kasabian's behaviour was part of a pattern, that might lead somewhere, but it would not be the final answer. His death wasn't the result of the spontaneous anger of passion. It was planned carefully, with preparations set up well in advance.

The boat pitched sideways and Gaya rocked, reaching out to the handrail to steady herself. 'The seas are building,' she said, 'but still those little birds play as if they had not a care in the world.' She spun the iPad again and Jejeune saw that more birds had joined the storm petrels around the ship's bow. Were they omens of further misfortune, he wondered. Or had this woman and her team already endured enough tragedy?

'Mr Bellaire tells me you have asked for a list of Alex's possessions, when his body is recovered,' she said suddenly. She looked out to sea for a moment before returning her eyes to the camera. 'But I think you do not believe you will find anything among them that Alex could have used to cut the line.'

Jejeune made no comment, but the look in the woman's eyes told him that she agreed. 'Did you ever hear about points of inaccessibility, Inspector?' she asked. 'They are places on the globe, on land or in oceans, which are the most distant from human civilisation. When Camp Isolée was established, the point of inaccessibility for the continent of Antarctica changed. What a powerful thing it is that by merely existing, humans can change the dynamics of isolation, don't you think? It can only be measured in terms of other life elsewhere, you see.' She paused for a moment as a wave of sadness seemed to pass over her. 'Antarctica is a harsh place. And unforgiving. But there is such beauty there, too. A death like Alex's should have no place there.'

Jejeune nodded solemnly. 'Would the rest of the team be willing to share their written recollections of events shortly before and after the body was discovered?' he asked.

'Julien Bellaire insists that we all cooperate fully with you in your investigation. They will send you their accounts, and they will leave nothing out. You have my word.'

She stared into the camera once more. 'You must discover who did this, Inspector. Alex deserves justice, even in death.'

The weather had begun to turn by the time Amy Della emerged on deck. The wind had become stronger and more erratic, showering the deck with an occasional burst of sea spray. The air had turned colder too, and she tugged the fur-lined hood of her jacket around her face tightly as she approached Gaya. She joined her in watching the storm petrels flitting around the bow. 'Those poor little birds,' she said. 'How are they going to survive out there?'

Gaya looked at them for a long time as they darted in and out of the surf, dancing on the wave tops as they took off. 'This is their home. They belong here.'

Amy held her phone out in front of Gaya. 'Have you seen this?'

'The incoming crew's inventory?' Gaya nodded.

'When I did my check the day after Alex went missing, one of the radios was not there. I had assumed Alex had it with him in his bag.'

'And yet the new base commander reports all radios are accounted for. How do you explain this?'

'I don't have to explain it,' said Amy Della testily. 'The radio was missing. If it's there now, it's not on me. Maybe Lexi returned one to inventory and forgot to sign it in. I don't know. But you need to ask her. I don't want this coming back on me. I did my job properly.'

'I haven't been able to establish a link with Lexi yet. I will have to ask Julien Bellaire to contact her from the Institute.'

Amy was quiet for a moment. 'So she hasn't told you about Scott?'

Gaya looked at her. Amy lowered her eyes to the deck, as if she found the intensity of the base commander's stare too much to withstand. 'Lexi saw him returning a snowsuit to the store room the morning after Alex's death. But he had been working inside all day, preparing for the move.' She looked up into the other woman's eyes. 'So why would he have needed one?'

Gaya met the woman's questioning stare. The gusting winds whipped her hair about her face, but she did nothing to prevent it. 'The inspector wants all personnel at the base to send him a report. You must include in it everything you know, Amy. Everything. Do you understand? Julien will instruct Lexi to do the same.'

'This detective,' said Amy. 'Do you think he will find out what happened to Alex?'

Gaya paused for a long time before answering. Out at sea, the little birds were still flitting around, untroubled by the uneasy rise and fall of the waters. 'Yes,' said Gaya finally. 'I suspect he will.'

21

'I see the nineties have finally caught up with Norfolk, then,' said Tony Holland. 'They don't dress soft-tissue injuries that way any more down the Smoke.'

The officers in the Incident Room turned their attention away from the computer screen to look at Holland, who was standing behind them. They had been watching footage of Glover and Tori Boyd returning to her home from the hospital, but the private CCTV cameras had struggled with the darkness, and the footage that had been sent over was grainy and low-quality. Holland's comment had provided a welcome distraction.

'Medical expert as well now, are you?' asked Salter.

'I took a first aid course when I was down at the Met. Learned all about the newest techniques. They like to make sure their officers all have an up-to-date first aid certificate, so they sent me on the course as soon as I got there.' He offered Salter a lavish wink. 'Graduated with honours from the kiss of life section, of course.'

'I can't imagine there's much satisfaction in kissing a rubber-lipped dummy,' she said.

'To be fair,' said Maik, 'I don't suppose those dolls had a choice.'

Holland nodded indulgently. 'You know, they say timing is everything in comedy. Unfortunately you two are about a hundred years too late to join the Marx Brothers.'

Shepherd entered the room, the overpowering smell of fresh paint that drifted in after her causing Danny to give a slight cough. He couldn't remember ever being so badly affected by paint fumes. Things had got so bad recently, he'd even considered pulling out the mask he kept in his desk drawer, a reminder of those strange times when those who wore them were considered the good guys.

At the front of the room, Shepherd waited for quiet. Her expression ensured it wasn't long coming. She turned to Maik. 'First order of business. Have you spoken to Inspector Jejeune yet?'

'Today, ma'am.'

'Well while you're at it, ask him if he's heard anything from Quentin Senior recently. We've had yet another call from a concerned neighbour. Apparently, it's not like him to just take off without letting anybody know. Besides, Eric assures me that there is nothing around at the moment that an experienced birder like Senior is likely to be off chasing.'

'If he hasn't shown up by now, I suppose we should consider opening a missing persons file,' said Salter.

Shepherd thought for a moment. 'Give it another twenty-four hours. If there's still no sign of him, start one then.' She turned her attention to the image frozen on the screen behind her. 'What's this?'

'We're looking at Glover Boyd, ma'am,' said Holland cautiously. 'We thought if the Bellaire fire was set by the same person as the other two, it wouldn't hurt to check whether Boyd had an alibi for either of them.'

It wasn't an accident that he had gone for the team approach. He couldn't see any objections to this line of inquiry himself, but it hadn't slipped his notice that the DCS had consulted her partner about rarities Senior might be chasing, rather than the other resident birding expert around here. He knew from personal experience that once you were in Shepherd's bad books, it could be a long stay.

'And?'

'This footage the hospital sent over is time-stamped the twenty-first,' said Salter. 'That's Wednesday, the night of the Canon's Cross fire. If that date is right, it gives him an alibi for the second hide fire at least.'

'Tori Boyd told me they were at the hospital on the Tuesday,' said Maik.

Shepherd shook her head uncertainly. 'I don't want to eliminate him until we're sure. Let's get over there and have a chat with him. See what he has to say for himself.' She looked at Salter. 'You and the constable.'

'A bit heavy-handed, isn't it, just for a quick chat with an ex?' said Salter edgily. 'I imagine Tony could handle that by himself. My time might be better spent looking into this Bellaire Institute. See what I can turn up there.'

Holland looked at her quizzically, but he wasn't the only one. It wasn't like Salter to try to reassign the duty roster like this. Still, at least she hadn't offered to stay around to work on the girl-in-the-hide angle. Perhaps even she could see that was a dead end by now.

'If you are going to be staying close, perhaps you can get that DNA permission form for Max over to the school,' said Maik easily. 'He mentioned it again last night.'

'I'll get to it, Danny,' said Salter testily. 'I've already said I would. I am actually capable of taking care of my own son, you know.'

'Nobody's saying you aren't, Lauren.'

Maik's use of her name resonated around the room like the concussion from a bomb blast. A look of regret flickered across Salter's features. 'Sorry, I've just got a lot going on at the moment.' The smile she offered wasn't one of her best, but Maik accepted it anyway.

The entry of the desk sergeant into the Incident Room during a briefing session was a notable enough event to draw any lingering attention away from Salter's outburst. The gravity of his expression told them what was coming. 'A body, ma'am. Just been discovered in the ruins of the hide fire. Uniforms have secured the scene, awaiting further instructions.'

'I don't understand,' said Shepherd, looking at the team. 'SOCO have been over that Bellaire site with a fine-tooth comb. Danny, you were there, too. How on earth could anybody have missed it?'

'Not the Bellaire site, ma'am,' said the desk sergeant. 'The one at Canon's Cross.'

Danny had been at that one too. But as far as he was aware, no one else from here had been anywhere near it since the fire department was called away and he was left alone to watch over it.

'Okay, all hands out there until we see what we're dealing with,' said Shepherd urgently. 'Fast as you like, people. We've lost enough time on this one already.'

No one needed to be asked twice. The scraping of chairs as officers stood and grabbed their jackets threatened to drown out Shepherd even before she had finished speaking. After days of sitting around waiting for it, they finally had their proper crime. The suppressed energy of the orderly rush to get out of the Incident Room exploded into a sprint along the corridor to the car park. At last. Action.

In the daylight, it looked like a scene from a different planet, thought Maik. The darkness the last time he was here had hidden most of the destruction. What he'd been able to see through the red glow when he'd stood on this spot talking to Bryan McVicar had told him the arsonist had done a thorough enough job, but the beams of his headlights later gave him no indication of the scope of the destruction. The sides of the hide had collapsed inwards, bringing the roof down on top of them. The pile of scorched timbers now resembled a demolition site more than a building. There didn't seem to be a single piece of wood that had escaped incineration. He thought back to Bryan McVicar's comment about fires having personalities. There was an anger about the one at the Bellaire Institute. The fuel had been splashed high up the walls to make sure the fire burned fiercely, a scorching rage that would consume everything in its path. This one felt more sinister. The burn pattern suggested it had approached the hide from a distance, skulking along the ground like a predator before springing in for the kill. Literally.

He heard the heavy slamming of a car door and saw Colleen Shepherd approaching, carefully picking her way over the muddy terrain. She joined him, taking in the mounds of damp grey ash that surrounded the central pile of scorched timbers like devotional offerings. Somewhere in the centre of all this devastation lay the remains of a human being. 'Found by a couple of birders, they tell me,' said Shepherd.

'They'd come out to take a look at the damage, apparently. One of them noticed there was a lot of activity from some crows in the back corner, so they decided to investigate.'

'The police tape around the site too subtle a hint for them, then?' She sighed. 'Still, I suppose it's a good thing somebody was doing our job for us. Do we know who our victim is?'

Maik indicated the medical examiner, down on his haunches on the top of the pile of burned wood. 'Not a lot to go on, apparently. But he's just about done. He'll give us pre-liminaries before he leaves, if there are any.'

'Well, let's get the body moved as soon as possible once he's finished here. We don't want any accusations of insensitivity as well as incompetence.'

Maik understood her ire. She knew she was facing a torrid press briefing as soon as she got back to the station. The palpable lack of progress in the arson at the Bellaire Institute was bad enough. The discovery of a body at a site the police had already attended would have things quickly sliding towards accusations of ineptitude. Now she had to go out in front of the press and assure them she would soon be able to reveal answers she didn't have, claim progress they weren't making, and promise a result that had never seemed further away. So, yes, Maik could understand the DCS's testiness. He was beginning to feel a bit that way himself. He knew, too, that Shepherd wouldn't tolerate any more blows to the reputation of the department. And that meant, among other things, she would be looking to put a stop to the meddling of one under-suspension DCI with immediate effect.

Shepherd surveyed the charred ruins again and shook her head slowly. 'Well, we knew it would come to this sooner or later if things continued.' She was still looking towards the burned-out hide, a black scar against the surrounding greenery, but she seemed to be focusing on something beyond. 'Everything we've got, Sergeant. I want these hide fires sorted before there's any more loss of life.'

'Yes ma'am.'

'Now, if you'll excuse me, I have to go and explain to the ACC how it was that a body lay here undetected all this time at a site we knew to be a crime scene.'

Maik watched her make her way back towards her car. Holland approached from the other direction. It could have been Maik's imagination, but the constable seemed to have hesitated until the DCS had departed.

'Tallish. Older. Male. That's about the best the ME can say for now,' said Holland. But his expression suggested he suspected a lot more. Maik did too, now.

'There's enough tissue to get plenty of DNA, so if he's on file we should know who he is soon enough. Though...' Holland pulled a face.

Maik nodded and lowered his head slightly. 'Let's not get too far ahead of ourselves, Constable. There's a few people on that missing persons list who would match that criteria.' *Before we start considering anybody who was about to be added to it*, his eyes said. 'Let's keep the description to ourselves for the time being.'

Holland nodded. Anybody who heard it would undoubtedly come to the same conclusion he had. But only one person might be tempted to take it upon themselves to do something about it. For now, Danny Maik was obviously trying to make sure Domenic Jejeune didn't get the chance.

22

Jejeune was scrutinising the photo on his computer screen with his magnifying glass again when Lindy entered, barefooted and brushing pastry flakes from her skirt. 'Croissants,' she said, 'the glitter of the pastry world. They were good, though, if I say so myself. Especially given the state of that kitchen. The under-floor heating hardly compensates for the fact that the place is a deathtrap. There's wires and extension cords everywhere, Dom.'

'It's only temporary. The wiring seems to be out on the one wall. I've called an electrician. He'll be here tomorrow.' He smiled. 'Until then, I doubt it'll hamper your culinary genius.'

She returned his smile. She was enjoying baking again. After her ordeal, she had abandoned all her hobbies. Somehow, they had all seemed such a pointless waste of the precious time she'd won back with her reprieve from death. But gradually, she'd given herself permission to enjoy them again, and pottering about in the kitchen was one of her favourites. As long as the kitchen didn't look like an electrician's workshop.

She leaned in to look at the image Dom had been studying. It was the same one as before, Alex Kasabian, arm outstretched, clutching the fuel line. 'Looking for clues,' she asked, 'or are you just checking to see if there are any birds in the background?'

Jejeune grinned. 'There rarely would be, down there. It's a point Kasabian makes in a blog entry – see.' He pointed to a printout on his desk and Lindy picked it up to read it. He had circled one of the entries.

> *I havent been posting anything lately because theres nothing to report. Nothing out of the ordinary has happened except that a white bird flew over the base today, which some people found interesting.*

'What do you notice?' asked Jejeune, still scrutinising the photograph through the magnifying glass. 'Other than the missing apostrophes, of course.'

'It's a blog, Dom. I think grammar is what they call an optional extra. Like spelling. But it's clear this man doesn't understand what a blog is. A weblog is supposed to recount what is happening on an ongoing basis. You don't just wait for exciting events before you post. That would be like… it'd be like letting the tale wag the blog.'

She punched him hard in the shoulder, looking so pleased with herself he could do nothing but let her enjoy her moment of glory before replying. 'Kasabian said some people found the bird interesting. He doesn't say he did. And he calls it a white bird.'

Lindy looked puzzled.

'It would have been a Snow Petrel,' said Jejeune. 'An early summer flyover.'

'Not everyone is an expert, Dom. This might come as a surprise to you, but I daresay researchers at an Antarctic base have better things to do than memorise the names of all the different species down there.'

'There aren't that many,' said Jejeune. 'And "Snow Petrel" is hardly "Southern Beardless Tyrannulet", is it? I think most people could manage to remember it, even…'

Lindy eyed him narrowly.

'…someone uninterested in birds,' he continued benignly. 'The point is, I don't think Alex Kasabian cared about birds at all, and I'm betting he wouldn't know a storm petrel if one landed on his shoulder. It seems unlikely he'd tie a threat to his life to their return.'

'He said storm petrels, didn't he?' asked Lindy. 'Not just petrels. Or is a storm petrel and a petrel the same thing?'

Jejeune shrugged. 'Petrels are all part of the same order of Procellariiformes, but the fulmarine petrels and the gadfly petrels are a different family to the diving petrels, while the storm petrels belong to another family altogether. I suppose you'd say all storm petrels are petrels but not all petrels are storm petrels.'

'Well there's a couple of minutes of my life I'll never get back,' said Lindy, shaking her head. 'Honestly, you lot really need to find somebody who's better at classifying these birds. From an outsider's perspective, whoever's on the job now is hardly covering themselves with glory. Speaking of which, is there any further news on Quentin Senior?'

'There's been no sign of him anywhere on the local birding circuit, and nobody's heard from him. He just seems to have vanished.'

'Not much cop at this detective business, are you?' She nodded at the screen. 'Let's hope you have more luck down there. Are you any closer to discovering what happened?'

'Perhaps.'

It was a typical Domenic Jejeune response, less helpful than silence. Lindy let it go. She looked at the image again. 'That poor man,' she said. 'To die like that. And how terrible for his family, knowing he was so far away. They don't even have a body to bury yet.'

'He had no family,' said Jejeune. 'He was orphaned during the Armenian conflict. He left as a refugee and although he was resident here in the UK, he retained that status.'

'How awful. I can't imagine what it would feel like to be stateless like that, how disorientating it must be.'

Jejeune nodded his agreement. 'Though it's not as unusual as you might think. According to the UN, there are currently around twelve million stateless people in the world. Many of them orphaned children, as Kasabian was.'

'And yet from that sort of start in life, he ended up at an Antarctic research base.' Lindy shook her head sadly. 'To have overcome such odds, he must have been brilliant.' She looked at Kasabian's photo again, but saw something else there now, a vast, milling crowd of dislocated people with nowhere to call home. 'There must be so much genius penned up in those refugee camps,' she said quietly. She sighed and eased herself back from the screen. 'But, that's a sadness for another day. I'll go and get dinner started.'

Jejeune watched her disappear into the kitchen, her bare feet slapping on the tiles. Could she really compartmentalise her sorrow like that? The way she had consigned her recent trauma to her past suggested she could. He envied Lindy her gift. Separating out strands of this idea or that inquiry to the exclusion of everything else was incomprehensible to him. For him, everything was interconnected. And those connections were soon going to cost him his investigation. The recent fire at the Bellaire Institute meant he would be forced to hand over this case to the active investigations unit. No one could plausibly argue any longer that there was no connection between the two matters. Julien Bellaire was the connection. He owned both facilities. Even though there were no grounds to take this inquiry from him, Colleen Shepherd wouldn't see it that way. He was sure he was only days, perhaps hours, from having to turn everything over to a team he now knew beyond a shadow of a doubt would be unable to bring the case to a successful prosecution.

Lindy returned to find him deep in thought, his expression troubled as he gazed unseeingly out of the window. It didn't matter that she misinterpreted the cause; she would have handled it the same way anyway. It simply wasn't Lindy's style to tiptoe around the edges of an issue. If there were elephants in the room, her approach was to grab a broom and try to usher them outside as quickly as possible. 'You know, it'd be okay for you to show a little more anger, if you felt like it,' she said. 'Or resentment, or frustration.' She flapped a hand. 'Whatever you wanted, really. Nobody expects you to be happy about your suspension.'

Jejeune looked up at her and flashed a short smile. 'I'm fine.'

It was the reflexive response of someone who normally chose his words with great care. Lindy wasn't sure what it signalled, but if brooms didn't work, perhaps elephants sometimes responded to the lighter touch. 'A certain Mr Shakespeare had some advice about being in disgrace with fortune and men's eyes,' she told him. 'You've probably never heard of him out in the colonies, but he was very popular over here at one time. He seemed to have an astonishing insight into the human condition, almost as if he had a window into the soul.'

'Sort of like an English Leonard Cohen, then.'

Lindy gave him a stony stare. 'Anyway, instead of sitting around beweeping your outcast state, Shakespeare's solution was to think about the one you love. And that, such wealth brings, that then you'd scorn to change your state with kings.'

'I'm sure I would,' he said. 'Especially if she had any more background information on Julien Bellaire. I meant to ask, why does the magazine have a file on him in the first place?'

Lindy inhaled deeply and exhaled. 'Well, for a start, there are not too many billionaires with connections to this area. Other than landscapers, of course.' She gave him an impish grin. 'And then there's the whole Billionaire Bicyclist thing. But the main reason was that there was a rumour about the Institute's equipment. It was supposed to be breaking down at an unusually high rate. A lot of local businesses supply infrastructure to the project and we wondered if it might suggest that the organisation had been cutting corners. Or worse, using bogus repair and supply contracts as a way of distributing a few backhanders to people. The magazine assigned one of their top investigative journalists to look into it. Actually their top one.'

'And what did you discover?'

Lindy took a small bow. 'Nothing. The organisation offered me complete access to all requisition and maintenance records, pointed out that all their procurement processes followed the required protocols and generally exceeded expectations across the board. They even invited me up to the facility to see for myself.'

'So you've been there?'

She shook her head. 'No need. Once I'd been through the receipts and invoices they sent over, and made calls to suppliers and repair shops, it was clear there was simply no evidence whatsoever that their equipment was malfunctioning any more often than normal.'

'So where did the rumours come from, then?'

Lindy shrugged. 'Probably just malicious gossip. When you set yourself up as a bastion of environmental integrity like Bellaire has, there's always going to be somebody wanting to take you down a peg or two.'

The stove dinged and she padded into the kitchen, still barefoot. He heard the crash of a pan and Lindy's startled cry. When a second call came, more panicked, he was already halfway to the kitchen.

Lindy was standing on a small island of dry tiles, surrounded on all sides by a pool of water. The lead from the electric kettle draped like a black snake from an extension cord onto the floor. The end was resting in the water, still and deadly.

'Dom' said Lindy, fighting for calm, 'the water, it's coming closer.'

The edges of the spilled fluid were creeping inexorably inward, merging with more still draining slowly from a large pan lying on its side. In moments, the water's edges would flow together to engulf the tiny patch of dry flooring Lindy was standing on. Jejeune looked around, but there was no way to reach across to unplug the lead without stepping in water.

'The electricity, Dom. You have to shut off the power. Hurry. The water's still coming.'

But hurrying wouldn't do it. There wasn't time to reach the fuse box before the water reached Lindy's bare feet. He looked around for something to lay down across the pooling water, but there was nothing to hand. The fluid continued to ebb closer, seeping inwards, encroaching inexorably on the dry tiles.

'You have to jump, Lindy,' he called urgently. 'To me. I'll catch you.'

Lindy looked at her feet. Her voice rose in panic. 'I can't, Dom. It's too far.'

'No, I'll grab you. Come on, now. It's almost there. Jump.'

She lifted off from one foot, flailing so far forward she almost dragged her toes in the water. Jejeune grabbed her outstretched arm and yanked her viciously behind him, sending her skidding into the kitchen wall. She scrambled to her feet and ran from the room.

With the power off, cleaning up the kitchen and restoring things to normal didn't take long. But by the time he returned from switching the power back on, Lindy was huddled on the living room sofa with her feet tucked beneath her and a blanket draped over her knees. She was cradling a large glass of wine, but Domenic could see that she hadn't drunk any of it.

'Well, that was interesting,' she said. The brave smile couldn't disguise its fragility, but there was no lingering fear behind it. Her brush with danger had shaken them both, but it had not taken them back to where they once were. Lindy's alarm had been real enough, but she had been in control of her fate this time, able to make her own decisions. And if seeing Lindy in danger had still jolted Domenic's heart almost out of his chest, this time he had been there, ready to help, instead of arriving only in time to pick up the pieces. The incident had reminded them that life was uncertain and they would face other dangers, other threats. But it told them, too, that these did not have to define them, to control the way they went about their daily lives. As unlikely as it was, it seemed to have driven away some of the residue of Lindy's earlier trauma and given them a brittle new confidence that they could one day put it behind them.

23

Lauren Salter stood at the base of the incline, taking in the office block and the glass dome that connected an intact hide and the burned-out shell of another one. She'd brought Max down here a few times when public access was granted to the Brackets. He would run down the hill between the hides, shouting and waving his arms, sometimes to the chagrin of the birders if there was something rare in residence. Neither she nor her son had been here since the climate facility had been established and the connecting building constructed, though.

Tori Boyd limped towards her as she entered through the door of the glass-domed admin block. 'Sergeant, how can I help you? More questions? Your colleague came the day after the fire.'

'Just a few points to clear up,' said Salter pleasantly.

To her left, she could see a wall of hastily erected perspex screens running floor to ceiling, the full width of the room. On the far side of them lay a sodden, charred tangle of blackened timbers, the aftermath of the recent blaze. 'The temporary arrangements are all up to code, I can assure you,' said Boyd. 'Fully compliant with all workplace regulations as well.'

It struck Salter that Boyd's inordinate concern with showing how law-abiding the operations were here was the sort of thing you might expect from someone who'd faced accusations in the past that this wasn't always the case. It was something to look into when she got back to the station.

The way Boyd was standing expectantly before her now told Salter she was keen to get on with things. The sergeant was happy to accommodate her. 'You told my colleague your ex-husband drove you home from hospital last Tuesday,' she said.

Boyd nodded. 'That's correct.'

'The hospital records show your visit was on Wednesday.'

'It was Tuesday, surely.'

'No ma'am. It was Wednesday, the night of the hide fire at Canon's Cross. If he was with you that night, it would mean he couldn't have been involved in it.'

'Then yes, Sergeant, as much as I would like to deny Glover an alibi, I can confirm he was with me at the hospital on the Wednesday. He never once left my sight. He even conducted his flirting with the nurse fully in my line of vision.'

'The CCTV footage from the house shows him leaving a full hour after he dropped you back there. Can I ask why he stayed so long?'

Boyd sighed theatrically. 'My ex-husband may have been unable to complete his paramedic course, but he had the annoying, fussing side of things down pat: a blanket this, a hot drink that. Eventually I had to send him on his way, he was driving me mad.'

Salter nodded. But even if that gave her ex-husband an alibi for the other fire, it didn't necessarily clear him for this one at the Institute. 'Your separation. It was not on good terms, I understand.'

'Nor was the marriage, frankly. Glover was entertaining enough at first, but his appeal tarnished over time. In the end, his charm simply wasn't enough to compensate for all the affairs.' She looked at Salter candidly. 'I am not one of those women who believes the failure of a marriage is a failure on both parts, Sergeant. Not that I hold the other women responsible, either. They were of no consequence to Glover, frankly, discarded as soon as they were conquered in favour of the next one.' She paused for a moment. 'Perhaps it would have been better if there had been one person. There may have been less emptiness at the thought of the relationship ending if there was at least an identifiable reason behind it, one particular individual to point to. But there really wasn't. Just an endless stream of petty betrayals and deceit. In the end, they just eroded away any love I may ever have had for him.'

Salter's uncomfortable expression suggested she was not too interested in hearing any more about the failure of the woman's marriage. She indicated the charred wood visible through the perspex panels. 'Do you really feel your ex-husband's resentment of your work could cause him to want to do this to the facility?'

Boyd sighed. 'At the Uni, I'd stay late because it annoyed him. It was my weapon against him. All this scholarly study, it made him feel inferior, you see.' She gave a cold smile. 'I'd usually try to make sure one or two younger male colleagues stayed on as well, treat them to lavish, wildly expensive meals on his credit card. That's the problem with being unfaithful, of course: it leaves you unable to trust any one else. And a weakness like that is easy to manipulate.' She sighed. 'Small victories become important when a relationship is falling apart, but such pettiness diminishes us, doesn't it, in the end? Sometimes I think that's where you can really tell the true extent of a relationship's breakdown, in the meanness, the malice, the small things we do that cost us so much of ourselves. Afterwards, one wonders why we do it.'

Because revenge rarely stops by the logic counter for advice, thought Salter sadly. But again, she gave Boyd no outward sign that she wanted to pursue the line of inquiry any further. 'The man who made the call from here, Arliss Dyer. You know him, I understand?'

'He comes here every now and again. Or at least he used to, when they were hides. He enjoys finding us birds that, quite frankly, we wouldn't get to see on our own, Inspector Jejeune included.' She looked momentarily puzzled. 'You know, given the inspector's connection with Arliss, I have to say I'm surprised it isn't him up here, following up for himself. No offence, of course.'

Salter's short smile showed there was none taken. 'The inspector isn't available just at the moment.'

'He isn't?' The news seemed to disconcert the woman in a way that Salter couldn't quite identify. 'Of course,' she said. 'He's just bought that new place, hasn't he? I suppose he's taken some time off to fix it up.'

Salter smiled again. If you were patient enough, people often came up with their own explanations. Whether they were accurate or not was another matter entirely. 'Just to be clear, Ms Boyd, these birds Arliss Dyer identifies by sound, you do see them for yourselves?'

'Most of the time.'

'But not always?'

'Just because we can't find one doesn't mean he was wrong. If you're looking for someone who would question Arliss's hearing abilities, Sergeant, I would suggest it's going to be a long, fruitless search.'

'And there's nothing else about the message he left that comes to mind. Nothing you didn't already mention to my colleague?'

Boyd shook her head. 'No. It's all exactly as I reported it. Light on details, sketchy on connections, something about the alignment of the hides across the marsh.' She let her eyes fall on the perspex sheeting, and the tangled mass of blackened timbers on the far side. 'And all, we see now, completely accurate.'

She gave a short, sad laugh. 'Dear Arliss. It's funny. You could hardly find a greater contrast between my ex-husband and a man like him. In fact, he's the kind of person Glover utterly despises. Someone with enough resolve to not allow his blindness to define him, enough courage to make his way independently in the world and, perhaps most importantly, enough nous not to be taken in by Glover's shallow charm. I suppose my obvious affection for him is not something Glover has ever found particularly pleasing either.'

Salter nodded as if to suggest she'd heard more than enough about the failings of Tori Boyd's ex-husband for one day. 'Well, I'm sure you have plenty to be getting on with,' she said, standing up. 'Thank you for your time. I'll see myself out.'

Salter had almost reached the base of the incline when she noticed the woman cycling down the hill towards her. 'Hi. Paige, isn't it?' said Salter, as the woman dismounted. 'I'm Sergeant Salter, Lauren. A friend of Tony's.' She looked around the yard as if to remind them both they were alone. 'I'm wondering if you might have a few minutes for a chat.'

'Sure,' said Turner guardedly. She indicated a low stone wall along the wharf and wheeled her bike over to it. Salter followed her. They sat side by side, facing the water.

'Tony tells me you're new in town.'

'Not long, yeah.' Turner's husky voice had an almost masculine quality to it, but Salter imagined Tony Holland found plenty to like in it all the same. Besides, it was what a voice said that mattered. The woman turned to indicate the building. 'The Institute doesn't pay much, so I'm bartending as well until I can get on my feet. Plus, it's close to home. I've got a place up by where the old library used to be.'

Salter nodded. 'I know it. Near the marsh. It's nice up there. Lots of trails.'

'Yeah, I'm not really what you would call the outdoorsy type, but I do take my bike up there every now and again. I suppose it's just nice to know that it's there. I can't get over how easy it is to find some green space out here that doesn't feel like it's going to have disappeared by the next time you visit.'

Salter nodded. 'That's the way we like it. You must have met Tony just after you got here.'

Turner smiled at the memory. 'One of the punters was giving me some grief and things got a bit heated. Tony was having a drink at the bar and he stepped in to calm things down. He told him gently that his behaviour was borderline harassment, and having that on his record was something that would follow him around from then on. He said besides, he could tell him from experience that when a woman said no the way I was saying no, there was no chance I would be changing my mind.' She smiled again. 'He was so good; authoritative and yet compassionate at the same time.'

'Tony? Constable Holland?' Salter's surprise was genuine. 'Blimey, that spell down the Smoke really did change him.'

'What, you mean, "*His time at The MET*"?' quoted Turner. She laughed and shook her head. 'I've told him he's got to stop saying that. People will start thinking he's an opera singer.' She became serious for a moment. 'I think talking about himself so much is just him overcompensating for all that praise he missed not having a dad around.'

'He told you about that?' asked Salter.

'You didn't know?'

Salter nodded. 'But I'm surprised he confided that to you. I mean, you know, so early.'

'What can I say, I'm a good listener. Still, I imagine not having a father around can be really hard on a young boy, so I suppose we shouldn't judge him too harshly.'

The air turned cooler for a moment as a shadow passed over the bay. Salter looked up. There weren't many clouds in the sky, but one had managed to trace a path across the sun anyway. Life in a nutshell, she thought. 'I was wondering if you could tell me anything more about a telephone call you overheard. One made by a Mr Dyer.'

Turner's eyes flickered towards the building. 'Arliss?'

'You know him?'

Turner nodded. 'He's a regular at the Board Room. You're talking about that message he left when he called the inspector?'

'That'd be the one.'

Turner gave a small shrug. 'Not much to tell. He said he had overheard somebody discussing setting fire to a hide, and he thought they might have been talking about one of these here. That was about it, really.'

'And you're sure it was DCI Jejeune he was calling?'

'I distinctly remember Tori telling him it had gone to the inspector's voicemail when she handed over her phone.' She looked at Salter. 'She had to dial for him, you see. Arliss is blind. She was surprisingly nice to him, as a matter of fact. I hadn't seen that side of her before. It was a bit out of character.'

Salter's expression showed interest. Turner looked out over the water for a moment. 'Don't get me wrong. She's extremely good at her job. As a private facility, the Bellaire Institute is not subject to the same oversight procedures as most scientific operations, but she makes sure everything complies with all the standards anyway. If anything, she overcompensates, probably to put the scientific community's mind at ease about the legitimacy of the work we're doing here. But sometimes, she seems to think showing a concern for the health of the planet means she doesn't need to show much for the other human beings on it. Tori Boyd is the kind of crusader who checks her humanity at the door when she clocks on.'

Salter searched the woman's face for signs of some deeper-seated malevolence but found none. People and their bosses, she thought. 'Getting back to the call, did you get the sense that Mr Dyer was telling the truth?'

'Was he lying?' Turner shook her head. 'No. But one hundred percent convinced about what he'd heard? Let's just say I'd imagine it's been a long time since Arliss Dyer fell asleep sober. If the voice woke him out of a drunken sleep, you know, all fuzzy and groggy, it might be hard to be sure what he'd heard. I have to say, he did seem to be going out of his way to convince the inspector he wasn't mistaken. To me, it sounded like he was afraid he might just dismiss his message out of hand.'

And consequently, not pass it on, thought Salter. She looked around as if getting her bearings. 'You know, there was an arson attack on another hide recently, not too far from the Board Room. It would probably be the closest place for somebody to pop in for a settler before heading out for their night of crime. Last Wednesday, it would be. You were on duty that night, I believe. I don't suppose you noticed anything unusual?'

'Like somebody acting nervous, or smelling like they'd recently filled a can with petrol?' Turner pursed her lips and shook her head. 'Just a normal night, as far as I can remember. Other than Arliss leaving early. That was a bit odd. He went just after I came on shift. I wasn't there long myself, though. It was a slow night and the gaffer let me go early. I didn't mind. I had some laundry to catch up on.'

Salter sighed inwardly. She done all she could. She supposed she had been hoping that either of the women, or both, would want to change their original account, or at least be more equivocal, not quite remembering a detail, or being unsure about something. But both witnesses were quite sure about all aspects of the message, and their accounts matched. Sitting here in the bright Norfolk sunshine looking over a glittering body of water, Salter could find no reason to doubt the word of either one. The call had happened. And that meant it was time to hand over her information to Danny and leave him to do what had to be done. Namely visit DCI Jejeune, on the record.

24

Not so long ago, thought Tony Holland, Glover Boyd would have been something to see. The man staring at him now from the doorway of his modest house was still in the kind of shape many men half his age would have been content with. He was tall and slim, his frame accentuated by the elegant striped shirt and expensive tailored trousers. He wore his wavy, grey-flecked hair longer than a man of his age should have been able to get away with. But on him, it looked right, complementing the high cheekbones and deep-set brown eyes with their faint character wrinkles at the corners. There was a hint of powder on the collar of his shirt, but if he used it on his skin it was well disguised. Glover Boyd's casual, slouching pose against the door frame added the perfect touch of raffishness to what was clearly a carefully cultivated image.

He led the way along a short corridor into a living room decorated in a style Holland might have called casual neglect, a movement that seemed to him to be exclusive to men like this. Nothing was actually dirty; it was more a case of shambolic disarray, with various items of clothing left over the backs of chairs, and dishevelled piles of papers strewn over table surfaces, as if to suggest the occupant had no time for such frivolities as hanging up sweaters and storing documents neatly. In the corner of the room was a loosely arranged stack of indifferent watercolours. Boyd saw the constable look at them as he took his seat.

'Thought I'd try to indulge my artistic side, discover whether I had one, more like.' He gave a dry smile. 'The answer is clearly not.' He pointed to a shelf piled with photography equipment. 'Paintbrushes have gone the way of that lot now. Never quite had the patience to wait for that perfect shot, or, let's be honest, the talent to capture it.'

Boyd's apologies didn't extend to the state of the room, and he similarly made no gesture of hospitality. No offer of a cup of tea, or something stronger. 'Out of Saltmarsh station, you say?' His voice had a rich, textural quality that infused even mundane inquiries such as this with impressive gravitas. 'Knew a young constable there once. Lauren. Salter, I think. Many moons ago now, though. Probably long since moved on.'

'She's still there,' said Holland. 'She's a sergeant now.'

'Is she, indeed? Well done her. No surprise though, really. She was a bright young thing, as I recall.'

The direction of the conversation was threatening to become uncomfortable and, having already abandoned any hope of even so much as a digestive biscuit, Holland was keen to get down to business. He set his recorder down on the coffee table between them.

'As I say, sir, your name came up in connection with a series of hide fires. I just have a couple of dates to run by you. If you could provide us with your whereabouts, we can eliminate you from our inquiries. How about the eighteenth?'

'Last Sunday, that'd be? Home. Alone. The dull life of a single man, eh, Constable? If I'm not mistaken, you're cut from the same cloth. Love the ladies, but not so much the commitment?'

It disturbed Holland that Boyd could identify this in him. Even without the background of the man's reputation, he would have recognised the traits in Boyd immediately. But it had never occurred to him that it would be just as easy for the other man to spot someone of a similar disposition. 'If we could just get back to the questioning. How about the nineteenth?'

Boyd gave a wan grin. 'Same, I'm afraid. Not doing very well, am I? There are a lot of empty spaces in a life like ours, Constable, and I should tell you, the older you get, the more that emptiness does tend to echo. Still, at least you've got your career. Closest I ever got was studying to be a paramedic.' He shook his head with what might have been genuine regret. 'Wasn't for me, unfortunately. Turns out I'm not very good with the sight of blood. Or even seeing someone in pain, come to that. Still, the greatest ambitions are usually the first to die, eh, Constable.'

Holland didn't return the man's smile. It was a signal that they could dispense with the editorials from now on. 'So that's no alibi for the eighteenth or nineteenth. How about the twenty-first?'

'Wednesday? Depends when. I was alone earlier in the evening, but I did go out for a couple of hours later on. I had to pick up my ex-wife at the hospital. Knee ligaments or something. She had no way to get home, so she gave me a call. I was happy to help. Always am. We didn't part on the best of terms, you see. I wandered,' he said simply.

'A bit of a surprise that you'd be her first call, then. There was nobody else she could ask?'

Boyd shrugged. 'My ex-wife is a formidable intellect,' he said, with something approaching admiration, 'but like many of her ilk, it can leave her a touch intolerant towards us lesser mortals. You'd think by the time a woman had reached Tori's age she might be able to understand that there are nuances, that things aren't quite as cut and dried as they seem. But she won't have any of that. Either you're as wholeheartedly committed to the cause as she is, or you're on the dark side. The cause in this case being climate change, of course.' He pulled a face. 'I'm afraid it's an approach that does rather mean she doesn't have many friends she can call on in a crisis.' He paused and looked away for a moment. 'There was never really anything in it, by the way, between Constable Salter and myself. A couple of dinners, consenting adults…'

'Your ex-wife must have been grateful, I take it. For the lift. Especially at such short notice?'

'Didn't say. She was on the phone the whole time to that man she works for.'

'Julien Bellaire?'

'Spent the entire trip sitting in the back of the van discussing the extent to which her injury would incapacitate her.' He gave another of his mirthless smiles. 'A hint, Constable, not at all.'

'According to my colleague, she can hardly even weight-bear on that leg. Are you saying she thought she wouldn't need any time off at all?'

'You've not met Tori, I presume, or you would not be surprised that she felt a trifling thing like damaged knee ligaments wouldn't derail her efforts at combatting climate change. It was that sort of all-consuming commitment that put paid to our marriage.'

'Not the wandering, then?'

'Well, that didn't help, obviously, but I would have stopped it in a minute. Those other women never meant anything to me. They were a way to relieve the boredom, that's all, something to do to keep at bay the unremitting loneliness of being stuck at home while Tori was out saving the world.'

Holland noticed a business card under the glass of the coffee table in front of him. It was perforated vertically, just beyond the G and D of the man's name. Boyd noticed his look and withdrew the card, tearing it along the perforations. He handed it to Holland. With the G and the D removed, it read LOVER BOY.

'A bit of fun,' said Boyd matter-of-factly, 'delivered with a wink and a smile to show it was all in good part. But I can state categorically that I never promised to leave my wife for a single one of them.' He looked at the constable frankly. 'It was something of a point of pride with me.'

Holland's blank expression suggested that if Boyd was looking for some sort of approval for his noble conduct, it might be a long wait. 'There's a report that you confronted your wife at her workplace at the university once, sir. Was that to do with the amount of time she was spending there?'

'Ah yes, the Great Debate. Possibly the only time in my life I ever showed anything approaching a bit of mettle. My credit card bill had just come in and the red mist descended. I was spoiling for a fight and I went there to have it out with her. And where did it get me? A caution and, I now see, a go-to point any time my name comes up in connection with a police inquiry.'

'Just to be clear, that's the only reason you went to her place of work. It wasn't because you had a problem with the nature of the work itself, for example.'

'Ah, I see. No, Constable, nothing like that. It happened at her place of work because I knew if I waited until she came home, I'd never have had the resolve to see it through.' He gave a wan smile. 'I may lack a university education, but I'm not completely oblivious to the fact that Tori's work is hugely important for the future of our planet. For one thing, my mother is continually at great pains to point it out.'

'Your mother?'

'Gayatri Monde, the base commander at Camp Isolée, Julien Bellaire's Antarctic research station. That's how I met

Tori. She was a graduate student of Mother's; one of the best she'd ever seen, possibly *the* best. *You need to grab this one, Glover,*' he quoted, *'and hold on tight. She's destined for great things. Only don't damage her. The world would never forgive you if she failed to live up to her potential because of your nonsense.* But of course, I didn't hold on to her. Not in my DNA. If there's any saving grace at all, it's that Tori went on to achieve everything she'd promised the world anyway, in spite of me and my wandering ways.'

'Not so good with dates, though, is she? Originally she claimed she was at the hospital on the Tuesday.'

'It was Wednesday, Constable. I'm sure it was a genuine mistake.' He gave one of his stock laconic grins. *Or perhaps not*, it said.

Holland looked around the room, taking in the sad, shambolic desolation of the man's life. He couldn't remember ever being in a cluttered space that seemed so empty. The need to get out of there rose in him like nausea. 'Just one last question, sir,' he said. 'Can you account for your movements on the night of the twenty-second?'

'That would be the night of the fire at the Institute? Ah, now, for that one I did have some company. We had dinner in a restaurant.'

'Local?'

'The woman, yes, the restaurant, no. A discreet little place in Happisburgh.' He gave another of his patented sad smiles. 'Wouldn't care to provide any further details, though, if it's all the same to you. She's married, you see. Part of the attraction for us, isn't it, the idea that they're already attached? Means we see a way out, an escape route for when the time comes. I suppose she's settled down now, Sergeant Salter. Husband, kids.'

He waited, but it was clear Holland had no intention of revealing details about the personal life of a fellow officer. 'I hope so, anyway,' continued Boyd. 'It's how I'd like to think of her ending up. Happy. Not alone. I was going to ask you to pass on my regards, but I think perhaps it would be rather better if you didn't.'

Holland tucked away his recorder and stood up to leave. There hadn't been much about this interview where he had felt he was on the same page as Boyd, but, on this point at least, they were entirely in agreement.

25

The bird swept past them quickly, flying close to the shore. Lindy shielded her eyes with a hand to follow it. Domenic kept his bins on the shape until it had disappeared from view.

'Petrel?' she asked,

Jejeune lowered his bins, looking surprised. 'No, but close. It was a Fulmar. They're from the same family: the tubenoses. They're quite closely connected to the petrels, as a matter of fact.'

He seemed so delighted with the apparent progress in her birdwatching skills, she hadn't the heart to tell him she was being flippant. She was always happy enough to join Domenic out here on this wild stretch of coastline. For her, the sheer magnificence of the crumbling clifftops and the seascape made the trip worthwhile. But she knew, too, how important his birding had been to him during those times when, as with other people, most pastimes were denied him.

Far out to sea, a patchwork of marbled clouds drifted almost imperceptibly landward. A cloud of Knots crossed the sky, the tight formation wheeling and swirling in a dazzling display of aerial agility. They landed on the rocky beach at the base of the cliffs and Lindy inched forward to risk a peek over the edge. Foaming waves pounded the rocks, crashing themselves into oblivion in explosions of white spray. Above them, the cliffs showed the scars of recent collapses: deep grooves in the crumbling red clay, as if the sea had tried to claw them back into her clutches.

'It would be easy to blame it all on the rising sea levels, wouldn't it? Okay, the melting ice caps aren't helping any, but the erosion of these cliffs has been going on for a lot longer than humans have been warming the planet. You want better evidence of our impact on this world, you don't have to look much further than that.'

She pointed to the beach, where the Knots were picking through a trail of debris deposited by the incoming tide: pieces of styrofoam, a skein of green string, and piles of empty plastic bottles.

Lindy's eyes dimmed for a moment at the sight, but her spirits were raised again immediately as a man began approaching them from the car park near the abandoned priory. It wasn't a long walk, but even this journey over the flat, tussock-strewn field seemed to have winded Danny Maik. 'You all right, Danny?' asked Lindy with concern as he arrived. 'You look a bit out of puff.'

'Paint fumes,' he said. He turned to Jejeune. 'The DCS is having the station redecorated.'

Jejeune smiled his sympathies. 'Still waiting for a major case, then.'

Danny said nothing, and an uncomfortable silence fell between the two men. Normally quietness rested easily between them, but something was different this time. There was a hesitancy about Maik, something that went beyond the awkwardness of Domenic's inquiry. Lindy didn't know what it was, but when a battle-hardened warrior like Danny Maik started looking like he would rather be somewhere else, it was time to take notice.

'A body has been found. In the remains of the fire at Canon's Cross.' Danny wasn't a person who averted his eyes to avoid embarrassment, but Lindy was aware of how long it had been since the fire, and she could see the sergeant's discomfort that the discovery had taken this long.

'We don't have an ID, yet,' Maik continued. 'The remains are too badly burnt.' He lowered his head slightly to deliver the rest of the news. 'Only… we have had recent reports of a missing person.'

Lindy's eyes widened in horror and she let out a small sob. 'Oh, Danny. No, please…' Tears welled up as she stood beside Jejeune, one hand on his shoulder and the other pressed to her chest. Jejeune's stare found the ground, but he remained silent.

'The individual appears to have been in the hide when it was set alight. All we can say so far is that the victim is male, substantial build, older, probably.'

Lindy pressed her hand to her mouth and curled forward, while Danny carried on along his excruciating path, as only he could; methodical, professional, sorrowful. 'That misper, sir, it's for…'

'Quentin Senior?'

Lindy was weeping openly now, tears streaming down her cheeks unchecked. She seemed not to know what to do with her grief, turning away from them, putting her head in her hands, turning again, sinking against Dom's shoulder. He gathered her into him, stroking her hair softly.

'The ME was able to get DNA samples from the victim's remains,' said Maik. 'We're still waiting on the results. I just wanted you to know. In case…'

Jejeune was silent for a moment. He lowered his head. 'I can't think of any reason Quentin Senior would be in that hide, Sergeant,' he told Maik. 'There'd be no bird activity out that way from dusk onwards: no Nightjars, no owls. And nothing currently in the area that might require an early morning sighting, the kind that might necessitate an overnight stay in the hide.'

Maik nodded solemnly.

Jejeune drew a breath. 'I don't think the body in that hide is Quentin Senior. I believe your victim is a man named Arliss Dyer.'

Lindy lifted her head to stare at Dom. She smudged away the tear tracks from her cheeks with the heel of her hand. But her voice was still fluttery and uncertain, as if she didn't trust herself to believe yet. 'Dom, are you sure?'

'He'd match the description, sir, Dyer?' asked Maik.

Jejeune nodded. 'The last time I spoke to him, he told me he was sleeping rough, in hides in this area.'

Lindy turned to Maik. 'How soon until we can know, Danny?' she asked impatiently, 'For sure?'

'We should have the results back later today. I don't suppose you'd have anything with Arliss Dyer's DNA on it would you, sir? It would help speed up the ID process.'

Jejeune managed to find a small smile from somewhere. 'If you're asking whether I knew him, Sergeant, I did. He was a friend, of sorts, a birding acquaintance. He had the best birdcall ID skills I have ever known. But I didn't know him well enough to have any of his personal possessions.'

Maik's expression acknowledged the clumsiness of his manoeuvre. It wasn't the first time he had failed to slide one past his DCI, nor likely to be the last.

'Can you let us know, Danny? Please? As soon as you hear?' Lindy had recovered herself slightly now, but had done nothing further to remove the tear streaks. They remained, dried by the wind out here on this open clifftop, a testament to her affection for a friend she thought she had lost.

Maik nodded. He fell silent but made no move to leave. He stood on the windswept edge, stoically looking out over the sea. 'You need to be careful up here. I played on these clifftops as a boy, but a good deal of them have disappeared since then. Most people's childhood memories recede into the past. Mine are crumbling into the sea before my very eyes.' He paused again.

'Another question, Sergeant?'

'A couple, sir, yes. Particularly since you believe the victim to be Arliss Dyer.' His look suggested regret that he couldn't give Jejeune time to process his grief at the loss of his birding acquaintance. 'You said the last time you spoke to him, he indicated he was sleeping rough.'

Jejeune nodded. 'He called me to say he had heard a Curlew Sandpiper up at Morston, so I went up to meet him. He mentioned it then.'

'And when was this, sir?'

'About ten days ago.'

'And you've had no contact with him since?'

'No.'

'Of any kind.'

'Aren't I entitled to a phone call, at some point?' Jejeune knew better than to expect a smile from anybody. No one was really in the mood for jokes. The three of them stood in silence for a long time, listening to the rush of the wind in their ears.

'Danny wouldn't ask if he didn't have to, Dom,' said Lindy, finally caving in to the pressure of the emptiness between them.

'A lock, sir, with the combination written nearby. Strikes me, the only person that would work to keep out of a hide was someone who couldn't read the note. Or see it.'

A shadow passed over Jejeune's features. Of regret. Of failure.

Maik couldn't tell his DCI about the open lock that had been recovered at the Canon's Cross hide, along with a fragment of the note. He couldn't tell him, either, that it suggested he was now dealing with murder in the case of the man in the hide; the man they knew, even without confirmation, to be Arliss Dyer. But he saw in Jejeune's eyes that he didn't have to. His DCI was already there.

'There's a report, sir, that Arliss Dyer called your number and left a message. Three days ago.'

Jejeune shook his head. 'He didn't.'

'We have two independent witnesses who can verify that they heard, and saw, him do so.'

'I didn't receive any message from Arliss Dyer, Sergeant.'

Lindy looked on as if hypnotised. She knew the two contradictory statements could not both be true. And yet she knew they were.

'He gave you a warning that someone might be planning to set fire to a hide, possibly one of those up at the Bellaire Institute; the Brackets, as was.'

Jejeune offered no response. He had denied receiving the message twice. He wouldn't do it a third time. They both knew there was only place left to go: Domenic's phone. Danny Maik could request to see it. Or Domenic could offer it to him. She could see in the eyes of the men what it was costing each of them to wait for the other to act. But she knew that neither would. And she knew, too, what *that* would cost them.

Maik looked at the clifftops, letting his eyes rest on the ragged tufts of windblown grass for a moment. 'Sir,' he said finally, 'can you think of any reason why two people would want to fabricate evidence about Mr Dyer calling you?'

Jejeune looked directly at Maik and the two men stood for a moment, staring at each other, unblinking, while the clifftop winds played about them. 'No, Sergeant. I can't.'

Maik flipped his notebook shut and said goodbye, with another forced smile. Jejeune turned and raised his bins once more to scan the sea for birds, but Lindy kept her eyes on the departing figure for a long time. As the sergeant trudged his way back to his car, she couldn't ever recall seeing him looking so sad; a bowed, solitary figure crossing a tawny landscape as empty as a lonely heart.

26

The seas heaved upwards in vast oily swells, the waves rolling towards the ship like an advancing army. A blast of icy air shredded the tops of the nearest waves, sending foam flecking across the steely water.

'Those little birds have gone,' Gaya Monde told Jejeune through the iPad camera. The connection was grainier than before, with thin white interference lines threading through the image. 'Perhaps they sensed the coming of the storm.'

More likely, the *Oceanite* had moved beyond the range of the Wilson's Storm Petrels, thought Jejeune. Behind Gaya, the sky was an unbroken expanse of grey, leaden clouds hovering menacingly over the sea. Gaya was bundled against the weather, but her head was uncovered. 'I am told my son has been questioned about the murder of a man in Saltmarsh,' she said dispassionately.

'Your son?'

'I am Glover Boyd's mother. You didn't know.'

Even in his exiled condition, Jejeune was aware that the only current murder inquiry in Saltmarsh was that of the man now confirmed as Arliss Dyer. There was no reason he should have been informed who the detectives were looking at, but he was surprised no one had mentioned to him that their suspect was related to Gaya Monde.

'I've always believed it would require a certain strength of character to kill another human being,' she said pensively. 'You must be aware of this, Inspector.'

Jejeune didn't say.

'You should know that Glover does not possess, and never has, the steadfastness it would take to murder someone, especially in such a terrible way.'

'If he had no involvement, I am sure that will be established during the course of the investigation,' said Jejeune. He was unsure why he hadn't told her it was not his case. Was it because he was afraid of losing this one? It bothered him that he did not really know.

She shook her head regretfully. 'It is strange though, is it not, that a man who cannot bear to see the pain of others brings so much of it through his actions.'

The swirling winds buffeted the microphone of Gaya's iPad in a never-ending stream, fluttering the sound in and out and making it hard for Jejeune to hear her. 'It sounds like the wind is picking up, Ms Monde,' he said. 'Perhaps it would be better if you went inside.'

'The reception is unreliable inside.'

Jejeune suspected the privacy she found out on deck, the cherished isolation that she had been forced to sacrifice when she reached Dumont d'Urville, was of as much importance to Gaya Monde as the signal strength. A bird drifted past in the background of the camera view, no more than a mottled cross against the deepening grey canvas of the cloud cover. A Cape Petrel? Jejeune was unable to tell for sure, but their position suggested it was possible. The location the satellite tracking was giving him put them somewhere off the western coast of South Africa. He was struck once again by the course they were plotting for home, swinging so far out into the open seas.

'Have you received the reports you requested?'

Jejeune confirmed that he had.

Gaya nodded, as if to herself. 'This is good. You must know everything if you are to understand what happened, Inspector.'

'This business of the radio in the inventory,' said Jejeune. 'Who would have had access to the store room?'

'Besides Amy, only I have a key. But the door is left unlocked at times, and others occasionally come and go. Theft is not an issue in such a small community. There is nowhere to hide things and nowhere to run.' She looked out at the sky, dark and overcast. 'We leave one winter only to head into another,' she said. 'I read a poem about winter by William Carlos Williams. "These". Do you know it?'

Jejeune shook his head.

'He speaks of dark, desolate weeks in "*an empty, wind-swept place without sun, stars or moon*".'

For a long time, neither of them spoke. 'Am I right in assuming a team member would be required to come to you if they had any concerns?' asked Jejeune finally.

'As base commander, I should have been the first to be informed. But it has been known for people to ignore the chain of command.'

A sudden gust of wind rocked the boat sideways and a burst of icy spray exploded over the deck. Gaya stutter-stepped on the slippery surface as the boat fought to right itself. The iPad swirled to show Jejeune the caged anger of the darkening sky before Gaya regained her balance.

'You should go in, Ms Monde. It's getting dark out there.'

She smiled at his advice. 'In populated places, we find darkness so disconcerting,' she said. 'Driving around the empty streets of a town at night, the unlit buildings look like something dead, something from which the soul has departed. They make us uneasy. But in Antarctica, one learns to embrace the darkness. You realise it holds no terrors. It cannot harm us. Only the darkness inside humans can do that.' She paused for a moment. 'Mr Bellaire tells me you have requested a record of the analytics of Alex's blog postings. Perhaps you will find what you are looking for in there.'

Jejeune nodded. 'Perhaps.'

'You must discover what happened, Inspector Jejeune. You must bring some closure. For Alex. For all of us.'

Gaya Monde's last, long imploring look into camera suggested that she felt perhaps, finally, the time was approaching when he would.

She turned from the dead screen of the iPad to find Scott standing on deck beside her. His heavy woollen hat was already sodden by the spray, and he had his collar turned up against the icy blasts of wind gusting across the deck. The air hung heavy now under the brooding, uneasy skies, and the atmosphere stirred as if an electric current was thrumming through it. When the storm came, it would unleash all its pent-up energy with devastating force. On the vast stage of the ocean, even a Category +A1A-rated icebreaker would be meagre shelter against an onslaught of such raw power.

'You should come in, Gaya,' he said. 'It's getting cold out here, and those clouds are getting ready to let loose.'

Gaya turned to him. 'Amy says you were seen returning a snowsuit to the store room. The morning after Alex was killed.'

He shook his head and turned his face into the wind. 'You shouldn't believe everything Amy says about me, Gaya. You know that.'

'It was not her who saw you.'

Scott looked over the churning waters. He nodded. 'Okay, yeah. I found it on the floor of the sauna changing room the morning after the event.' He shrugged. 'Maybe someone wore it in there as a joke? There was a lot of vodka going around the night before, as I recall.' He paused and turned to look at her, grabbing on to a handrail to steady himself as the ship rolled. Beneath his feet, the deck was slick with seawater.

'Kasabian was always an odd guy, wasn't he? He was never really part of the group. Not like the rest of us. You know, together.'

Was he saying it was all somehow Alex Kasabian's fault for not fitting in, not being a part of their stupid, frivolous activities? His fault that he froze to death, with winds biting into his flesh until his blood could not flow any more? Was this Scott asking for absolution, wondered Gaya, for himself, for her, for the rest of the group? Absolution for them, sitting in a sauna less than five kilometres away, drinking vodka from the bottle to toast themselves for their courage in going out into those conditions? And their success in returning safely from them? She shook her head. No, there was no absolution. There was only guilt, as dark and encompassing as an Antarctic winter. Guilt for the death of a poor terrified man who had met his end in the cold, silent darkness. Alone.

'The inspector has requested a report on the analytics of Alex's blog postings,' she told Scott.

He shrugged. 'I'm pretty sure it didn't have a very wide following. Probably only the staff of the university department, the people at the Institute, a couple of other climate monitoring organisations. Perhaps he's just looking for a new angle to try to find out what happened to Alex.'

'Perhaps.'

27

The onshore breeze swirled Lindy's long blonde hair around her head as she straightened up from the 'scope, and she corralled the wayward strands with a hand. 'Okay, I must admit, Mr Senior, over the years you have shown me some absolute belters. That bird is not one of them.'

'Yes, I'm afraid the female Rose-coloured Starling is a bit drab compared to the male. He is truly spectacular. In the world of birds, as you have probably realised, the males are generally brighter.'

'Those wacky birds, huh,' said Lindy drily. 'Talk about an evolutionary disadvantage.'

Both smiled to acknowledge the delight they shared when Senior served up such fare as this for Lindy to volley back over the net. This time, though, Jejeune suspected the man had been as keen to show Lindy the bird as much as a way to free himself from her embrace as anything else. As they had approached the shambling figure on the headland, Lindy had raced ahead and given him a tight, enduring hug. If he remained unaware why she was so relieved to see him, he accepted her affection with his usual equanimity.

He turned to Jejeune now. 'D'you know, Inspector, I can't apologise enough for not making sure you got my message.

The bird was on private property in the Scilly Isles, but the owner had said he'd accept a maximum of four birders to look at it. We had one spot left on the plane, so after I didn't hear anything from you, I left a message on the rare bird line to say first one to meet us at the airport snagged the spot. I thought it was a touch strange when I got to the airstrip and no one was there. I was airborne before I realised I'd had the damned phone on mute. By then, of course, it was too late to do anything about it.'

'So was it worth the trip?' asked Lindy.

'Indeed it was. Eastern Orphean Warbler. A rare prize indeed.' He paused, looking guilty at his momentary indulgence. 'Don't worry, Inspector. I can't imagine it'll be the last that shows up. Possibly even be one in these parts one of these days. So, nothing further on that terrible business of Arliss's death, I take it?'

If Senior's abrupt change of subject to escape the awkwardness of the moment was transparent, his interest in the new topic was genuine enough. As was his sadness. 'I shall miss old Arliss,' he said. 'He once told me he had learned to recognise not the birds' calls, but their voices. That way, even a sound from the bird, a broken-off part of a repertoire, would be enough for him, the same way you might recognise the cough of a person in another room, even without a word being spoken.' He turned to Lindy. 'Never met anyone more adept at call ID. Birding by ear is no easy task,' he assured her earnestly.

'You're telling me,' said Lindy emphatically. 'I've never even seen a bird's ears. I don't know how you'd go about using them to identify one.'

Senior barked a laugh. 'There is something about the soaring flight of a bird that can lift the sadness from your soul,' he told her, shaking his head slightly. 'A conversation with you,

Ms Hey, has much the same effect.' He smiled at her gratefully. 'Given any more thought to the collective term for petrels?'

'You know, you're not wrong about their reputation. They must be one of the few bird species that doesn't even have a pub named after them, which in this country must say something about their unpopularity. Given their penchant for foreshadowing trouble, I'm thinking perhaps a foreboding might work.'

'A Foreboding of Petrels,' said Senior, trying it out. He nodded his head slowly. 'Now, that's something I could get behind. Well done, Lindy. Well done.'

'I suppose you heard about the fire up at the Bellaire Institute while you were away,' said Lindy, following her normal practice of deflecting any praise. 'Another bird hide,' she said significantly.

'I did,' he said. 'Though sadly, they are no longer active hides. Haven't been for a while now.' He turned to Jejeune. 'Did you ever take Lindy up there during the glory days?'

Jejeune shook his head.

'Shame.' He turned to Lindy. 'It was a beautiful spot, the way the buildings on either side curved around the water's edge. George Melchiot had them built. One of us, you see, a birder. Had the means to go along with the interest. Constructed two long hides, one facing the sea, the other facing the marsh. We used to whip across from one to t'other based on a shout. Always something interesting tootling past on the saltwater side, and the freshwater marsh was productive, too. One of the best locations in the area to see Water Rail. Get an eyeful of Black-tailed Godwit close up, too, that you'd rarely be treated to unless you went down to somewhere like Cley.' He shook his head sadly. 'Great loss to the birding community, I have to say.'

'Do you know much about how things operate up there now?' Lindy asked with a wide-eyed innocence Domenic had long since learned to be wary of. She didn't even bother with a glance in his direction. He needed to know these things but he was being prevented from asking them. If he was fortunate enough to overhear a conversation between two private citizens, however, there wasn't a thing Colleen bloody Shepherd or any police disciplinary board could do about it.

Senior shook his head. 'Not much, I'm afraid. We were hoping we would still be granted access after that rich fellow took it over, but alas, no. Wanted it all for himself, it seems.' He brightened. 'Still, hard to argue with being booted off a patch for such a worthy cause, isn't it? Climate change is the one fight we have the same vested interest in. Lose that, and it'll be hard for any of us to find a decent place to live. I have to say things certainly seem to be in the right hands, though.'

'You mean Tori Boyd?' asked Jejeune.

'Remarkable woman,' said Senior with evident admiration. 'I never could settle to the husband, frankly, but no such reservations about her. The whole package, that one. Brilliant to the nth degree, well connected, engaging personality. Fine-looking woman too, as you well know, Inspector. You've spent enough time birding with her.'

Lindy cocked her head on one side to fix Jejeune with a momentary stare.

'On the whole,' continued Senior, 'I'd say the climate science field is damned lucky to have her. One gets the impression a woman like that would have succeeded no matter which field she chose, be it politics, industry, whatever. Puts me in mind of another formidable female not a million miles away from here.' He looked at Lindy and offered a wry smile. 'Though the Boyd woman's a good deal older, of course.'

'I think Tori Boyd is only about forty-two,' said Jejeune.

'As he said, darling,' said Lindy, patting his arm gently.

Below them, a boat with a brightly painted hull drew up on shore, sending a small fling of Dunlin skittering. A group of young adults clambered out carrying large blue rubbish bags. 'Clean-up crew,' announced Senior. 'I called 'em yesterday. I couldn't believe how much plastic had accumulated in the few days I was gone. Unfortunately, they couldn't make it until today and last night's tides have taken a lot of it back out to sea.' He sighed. 'Still, it will all show up again soon enough.'

'And if it doesn't, there'll be plenty more plastic to replace it,' said Lindy. 'There's an island of the stuff three times the size of France out there somewhere.'

Senior nodded sadly. 'It's the seabirds I worry about most.' He looked at Jejeune for confirmation.

'Study after study is finding plastic in the digestive systems of dead birds all around the world,' Jejeune told Lindy. 'It's discovered in huge numbers of birds every year. Even those that survive develop catastrophic health problems.'

'Ever hear of Point Nemo, Ms Hey?' asked Senior. 'It's a spot in the South Pacific considered to be the most remote place on the planet. When the space station orbits, the astronauts are closer to that point than any humans on Earth.'

The ultimate point of inaccessibility, thought Jejeune. He suspected he knew where Senior's aside was leading, and he already felt sadness for Lindy's coming distress.

'Do you know what they found at Point Nemo during a scientific survey? Microplastics. Seventeen parts per million. More than two thousand kilometres from the nearest occupied land. Is it any wonder so many of our seabirds die from ingesting the stuff? There appears to be quite literally no place on Earth that is free from it.'

Lindy cupped her hand again to rein in her wind-blown hair, but it could just as easily have been a gesture of despair. 'Will our planet ever forgive us?' she asked, shaking her head.

It wasn't a question to which she had expected an answer, but when she looked across at Jejeune, it seemed that he might be considering it. And then she recognised it, the look that told her that Domenic was closing in on something. The synapses were firing, making connections that hadn't existed before, lighting up pathways, to new questions, perhaps to answers. But whatever maze of ideas Domenic currently found himself in, he wasn't ready to share them. Yet.

Senior moved off for a brief chat with the clean-up crew and they watched him go, negotiating the steep bank with difficulty. His right hip had given him trouble for as long as they had known him, but it was undeniable that age was taking its toll on the great old body, too. Jejeune could see again in Lindy's expression the relief that they hadn't lost him to the hide fire at Canon's Cross. He had rarely seen her so upset as the day she thought Danny had brought them the devastating news. But she was back now, as resilient as always. And as soon as Senior was gone from their sight, she turned to Jejeune.

'I wonder if you'll still think I'm beautiful when I reach forty-two.'

'I'll think you're beautiful no matter what your IQ is.'

Jejeune took a step to the side, just in case, but Lindy had another agenda to pursue. 'I was thinking, when the case is wrapped up perhaps we could go away for a while, somewhere warm, maybe to just relax and take our minds off things. I mean, you have the time off. We may as well use it.'

'Perhaps we could go to see some petrels,' said Domenic.

'Where? Mousa?' Lindy's eyes widened as she noted his grin. 'Antarctica?' She seemed unable to move, or even take her eyes off him. 'Really, Dom? Ant-bloody-artica?'

'It would be a wonderful experience,' he said. 'It's so remote.'

'So is Felixstowe. The closest motorway is in the Netherlands. That doesn't necessarily mean I'd like to spend my holidays there.'

'It would be the trip of a lifetime.'

'It would be sodding cold, is what it would be. I said somewhere warm, Domenic. Antarctica is manifestly, demonstrably not warm.'

'It's not as cold as it used to be. In fact it's predicted that climate change will raise the average temperature in Antarctica by three degrees by the end of this century.'

Lindy's look told Jejeune what she thought of his information. It was not a good look. She shook her head anyway, just in case he'd missed it. 'Sorry, darling. Stomping around in the frigid wastes of Antarctica is not on my bucket list. Not even close.'

Jejeune nodded. 'Got it. Lindy: not frigid. Message received.'

She stuck her tongue out at him. 'Perhaps the deliciously attractive Tori Boyd would like to go to Antarctica with you instead.'

But his smile now told her he wasn't serious. 'As much as I'd love to go to Antarctica, I wouldn't be able to get anywhere near that base. It would require special permission. And I think it's fair to say that Colleen Shepherd is not going to sanction a trip like that for a suspended detective.' He shook his head. 'No. Any answers I'm going to get will have to come from much closer to home.' He slipped into a thoughtful silence for a moment. 'Alex Kasabian was monitoring climate data. You'd have to assume everyone else at the station is equally committed to climate science. It's hard to believe one of them would want to suppress his findings. But it wouldn't hurt to be sure.'

Lindy thought about the trail of plastic on the beach, in the shadow of a cliff face showing millennia of history that did not reveal a single trace of human-made waste. For her, that the victim in this case was somebody who cared so much about what humans were doing to the planet only seemed to make Kasabian's death more tragic. If Domenic needed somebody to have a look around to see if there was something going on with the data at the Bellaire Institute, it seemed like the least she could do.

28

'Constable Holland.' Glover Boyd peered through the chain-wide gap at the person standing beside Holland. 'And?' He raised his eyebrows.

Such frippery was not likely to find favour with Maik in his present mood. He had been coughing quietly for most of the journey up here and his breathing was still a touch laboured.

'Sergeant Maik,' supplied Holland.

Glover Boyd closed the front door in order to disengage the chain. This moment had always held a frisson of uncertainty for both police officers. Would the door reopen, or would they hear the click of a lock being fastened against them as the person tried to escape out the back? It had gone both ways over the years. Constable Holland would undoubtedly end up handling the athletic side of things if Boyd did decide to do a runner today, but the fatigue that seemed to be ever-present these days made even the prospect of writing up a flight-and-pursuit report more than Danny really wanted to be bothered with. In the end, there was the satisfying rattle of the chain being released, and Glover Boyd swung the door inwards to allow the two men to enter.

The living room was a good deal tidier than on Holland's last visit. It was amazing what a call ahead from the police could do, he thought wryly. But the hosting showed no improvement. As before, Glover Boyd settled into his leather armchair without any mention of even a cup of tea. He seemed utterly at ease with the officers' visit. 'Another quiet evening alone, as you see, Sergeant,' he said. 'Rather glad of the company, truth be told.'

Maik didn't respond. His practice of never taking an instant dislike to anyone was being severely tested by Mr Glover Boyd. 'We're wondering if you've ever heard of a man named Arliss Dyer,' he said without preamble.

Boyd thought for what seemed be about the right amount of time before shaking his head slowly. 'Can't say I have. Who is he? Please don't tell me he's an irate husband.'

'Your ex-wife seemed to believe you'd know him,' said Maik testily.

'My ex-wife's wounds run deep, Sergeant. I try to be understanding. As the person who inflicted them, I suppose I'm at least partly deserving of her efforts to cause me problems. To my knowledge I've never laid eyes on this man Dyer, nor even heard of him.'

There was a carelessness about the response that was difficult to ignore. Boyd wasn't trying to convince anybody of anything. It simply didn't seem to matter to him one way or the other whether he was believed or not.

'The fact that your ex feels the way she does about you, though, that must make things a bit awkward for your mother, working in the same field and all,' said Holland. 'I imagine it's difficult for them to avoid coming into contact.'

'On the contrary, they remain close. It's me my mother doesn't like. I suppose we are what you would consider the classic dysfunctional family.'

Holland didn't know why people didn't just say *family*. He couldn't ever remember coming across what you would call a functional one.

'My mother feels responsible for the way I treated Tori, you see. A mother always feels she should have been able to correct the behaviour of her children, don't you find? Fathers seem so much more willing to accept that their children are flawed.'

It was Holland's turn to fall silent, so Maik stepped in. He leaned forward in his chair, the effort making him wheeze slightly. 'The constable mentioned you're claiming you have an alibi for the night the hide at the Bellaire Institute was torched, but you'd rather not give up the name.' He made little effort to hide his disbelief.

Boyd shifted uneasily. 'As I explained to the constable, the lady in question is not... unattached. I have no doubt she'll try to save her marriage at some point. The knowledge that she was with me wouldn't help her cause.'

On the side table beside Maik's chair lay an untidy pile of books. There were titles on winemaking and gardening, and on the top, a book on birdwatching. It crossed the sergeant's mind that you might be able to tell which hobby Boyd had pursued most recently based on its position in the pile. The same was probably true of the other equipment stashed in the corner: a discarded fishing rod, a set of golf clubs, a bicycle.

Boyd followed his gaze. 'Story of my life really, Sergeant,' he said, 'flitting from one thing to the next. In truth, I've always admired the discipline it must take to apply yourself to one vocation, as my mother and my ex-wife have done. Sadly, I never had that kind of dedication to anything. Turns out I'm pretty useless overall.'

'Like flirting with a hospital nurse while your ex-wife is lying there in pain? That kind of useless, you mean?'

Glover looked at Maik without anger. 'You've known it, haven't you? Not yourself, but someone close to you. Injured by someone like me. Whoever it was, don't judge them too harshly. Perhaps they were driven to it, as I was. Infidelity always has a backstory, Sergeant.'

Maik leaned further forward. Even from where he was sitting, Holland could hear the tightness in the sergeant's chest brought on by the effort. If Danny felt as bad as he sounded, it was no wonder he was miserable. Having to work so hard to breathe wouldn't do much for Holland's disposition either.

'At the moment, sir, you're in what I like to think of as a neutral state,' said Danny. His voice dropped into a range even someone who had never met him, like Boyd, might recognise as hazardous. 'From here, things generally go one of two ways. You can either talk yourself out of suspicion by telling us what we want to know, or stay quiet and move yourself deeper into it. I can appreciate you'd prefer your indiscretions remain discreet, but you might want to consider the alternatives at this point.'

Boyd's normal insouciance seemed to leave him for a moment. 'I can give you the restaurant's number. I'm sure the staff can confirm I was there from about eight until well gone eleven. I wonder if perhaps their testimony might be enough, without having to drag anyone else into this. It's not for myself, you understand, I fear I am long past the redemptive power of shame. But one lapse in judgement shouldn't destroy this woman's marriage. I really am not worth that. I'll get you the number.'

Maik was on his feet by the time Boyd returned. He looked at the paper briefly and seemed to find a sliver of his normal courtesy from somewhere to thank the man. But he clearly wasn't keen on spending any longer in Glover Boyd's company than he needed to, and his goodbye was crisp enough to border on being curt. Holland hurried along the hallway after him. Given Boyd's performance as a host so far, he wasn't expecting him to walk them to the door.

As they climbed into the car, Maik shook his head slowly. 'He's in it,' he said, 'right up to his powdered neck. He's at the centre of all this.'

'It's hard to see how, Sarge. If this alibi for the Bellaire fire checks out, that's two of the three he's off the hook for. I mean, the CCTV footage we have makes it pretty clear he couldn't have had anything to do with the Canon's Cross fire.'

'Private CCTV footage can be manipulated easily enough,' said Maik tersely.

Holland said nothing further until he had eased the Audi TT away from the kerb. It was hard to see where Maik's conviction was coming from unless he had something else, something he was keeping to himself for now. There was a lot of that going on in this case. Maik's phone rang with a tone Holland recognised. That song again, the one from the pub: 'How Sweet It Is'. He didn't need any secondment at the Met to deduce who was calling; he'd heard the same tone on Lauren Salter's own phone yesterday. Maik confirmed to her that the interview was over and he was heading home. And yes, he would stop in to see her on the way.

Holland nodded to accept the new destination and settled in for the ride. The Audi's suspension would ensure it was smooth. He wasn't sure the conversation would be.

'So if you like Boyd for this, presumably that means the girl in the hide is off the table now,' he said, trying for as much nonchalance as he could manage. Maik was silent, but a place on Danny Maik's team was not for the fainthearted, and Holland pressed on. 'I never saw that one as having any legs, to be honest. Not unless I'm missing something.' But his delivery suggested that Tony Holland was quietly confident that he hadn't missed anything at all.

'We pursue all avenues, Constable,' said Maik shortly. 'You know that.'

'It's probably none of my business,' began Holland tentatively. His progress was stalled for a moment by Maik's look, which suggested that people who began a sentence that way were usually right. 'But you're not doing Sergeant Salter any favours by pretending this is a viable line of inquiry. She's not made of glass, sir, as the metaphor goes. She's not going to shatter if you challenge her on this.'

'Metaphors, Constable? Take a language course as well, did you, during your time at the Met? Or more likely, date some young lady who did?'

When Danny Maik started dodging the substance of a conversation, it was time to put the subject to bed. Holland knew he could take things no further now, and both men settled into silence. He asked his phone for some Motown to see if that might brighten his sergeant's spirits. Something called 'Love Child' swelled into the Audi through the car's speakers.

'Not this one, if you don't mind, Constable,' said Maik gently. 'I never did care for it. Besides, they weren't just the Supremes by then. They'd become Diana Ross and the Supremes. Somehow that just never sat right with me.'

If there was a message there for Holland, something to do with teamwork perhaps, or knowing your place, he didn't feel like decoding it. He asked his phone for another selection and it offered up one called 'It Takes Two'. Holland had never heard of this one either, but it seemed to find favour with Danny, providing a lively background to whatever he was mulling over as he stared through the window.

It left Holland alone with his own thoughts. Boyd had not mentioned that his mother was in charge of Julien Bellaire's Antarctic base, meaning that, as far as Holland knew, he was the only officer working the case who was aware of the connection. He wasn't sure why he hadn't shared the information yet, but he knew it wasn't an accidental oversight. In his quietest moments, Tony would have admitted he was no Domenic Jejeune, but even he could see the two investigations were heading to a crossing point. Somewhere in the not-too-distant future, Tony Holland was going to face a decision. The time hadn't arrived yet, but it said a lot about the complexity of the situation that he wasn't sure yet what he would reveal, or when. Or even to whom.

By the time he pulled up outside Lauren Salter's house a remarkable transformation had taken place in the man sitting in the passenger seat. Danny had climbed into the car as a man wearied by the world and his own years. He had looked ill, dispirited, old. But the sight of the woman who shared his ringtone waiting on her doorstep seemed to rejuvenate him. It was a more sprightly Danny Maik who now eased himself out of the car, one with energy and vigour. He drew himself upright and found a spring in his step as he approached the house, returning Salter's smile with one of his own.

Holland drove off, contemplating the restorative power of love. Whether the transformation was real, or just a show Maik had somehow found the strength to put on for Salter, it didn't really matter. What would it be like, he wondered, to glow inside at the prospect of seeing somebody like that, to be so filled up, so completed by them, that being with them could turn you into someone else? Or at least make you want to be. The trouble with that kind of love, though, was it had the power to transform other things, too. Like your judgement.

29

No matter how many times you stood up here on this cliff edge, thought Lindy, the light would find another way to show the view to you. It had rained earlier that morning, a fine mist so gentle it had settled on the stalks of the grasses without bowing them. Now, pale clouds lay across the sun, diffusing its light into a soft pink haze. She wasn't sure what it was that kept drawing Domenic back to this same spot, when there were so many other places he could be birding. All she knew was that it had some connection with the case. Domenic would surely have conceded that much, though she doubted he even knew himself what it was.

Jejeune watched a bird flying near the cliff edge. In Canada, it was a Black-legged Kittiwake; here it was known only by the latter part of that name. He followed it with his bins as it rode the updraughts from the cliff face, tipping a wing or tilting its tail, or simply catching the right current and gliding effortlessly on the air. Such mastery of its aerial domain meant the Kittiwake was able to nest on the sheerest of cliffs, where footholds for birds were mere millimetres wide and, for predators, non-existent.

Lindy waited a little way off, on a patch of dry ground that posed no threat to her dress shoes. She checked her phone for the time. 'So if you're okay walking home from here, I'd better be off. We don't want Joe and Carla making the announcement about the baby without me, do we? Wish me luck.'

'Luck?'

'Statistically speaking, I'm more likely to die from a gender reveal party than I am from a shark attack. Bye.'

He watched her pick her way gingerly along the gravel path to the car park. Part of him still worried about her going out alone, where he wouldn't be able to protect her from the world. But she had been so obviously happy at the prospect of seeing her friends, her enthusiasm for her afternoon out laid his fears to rest. At least for now.

He watched until her car had disappeared from sight and then turned his attention back to the shoreline. The Kittiwake had returned, tracking along the cliff edge once more. He recalled the excitement when one of these birds occasionally showed up along the Lake Ontario shoreline, far from the sea, and possibly as far inland as any of its species in the world. For these were true sea gulls. He'd often told Lindy that there was no such bird as a seagull; they were gulls, and they were coastal. But the Kittiwake, spending the most time out on the open seas, was probably more entitled to the term than any other bird. He lowered his bins. A sea gull. A seagull. He shook his head slowly and smiled to himself. Seagull. No more accurate in any other language, but the key he had been looking for. Or one of them, at least. He took out his phone and turned it on, hoping he would find one of the area's fugitive mast signals. He googled his query as soon as the page loaded. And in the time it took the search engine to summon up its response, he had his answer.

Lindy came in to find Domenic sitting at the dining table. He looked up as she fumbled through the doorway and set her bag down. Like so much else about the new place, the shelf by the door had insinuated itself into their routines almost without their awareness. It was conveniently located for depositing whatever was in your hands as you came through the front door, and had already become the go-to repository of post, car keys and the occasional heavy bag.

'Good time?' he asked.

She teetered a little as she paused in the hallway to remove her high heels, supporting herself against the wall. 'Good enough that you'll need to give me a lift over there to pick up my car tomorrow.' She gave him a tipsy smile. 'It's going to be blue.'

'What will a baby have to be sad about?' Jejeune gave her a grin, and Lindy could see there was more to it than simple good humour.

'You're looking pleased with yourself. Did a bird of paradise fly by after I left?'

'No, but a Kittiwake did.'

Lindy padded over to the couch and curled her legs up beneath her. Her eyes shone with the wine, and with the pleasure of an evening out among friends. She was in the perfect mood to listen to Dom tell her how clever he was.

'The names of those two ships of Bellaire's,' he said. 'The supply ships that go to Antarctica.'

Lindy nodded. 'The *Oceanite* and the… other one. The *Mouette*. What about them?'

'Do you know what "mouette" translates as?' Jejeune didn't wait for a guess. '"Seagull".' He held up a hand to still Lindy's protest. 'I know. Trust me, there are no more seagulls in France than anywhere else. But it's the other name that matters, the *Oceanite*.'

Lindy looked blank.

'Storm petrel. Alex Kasabian's blog wasn't talking about the return of the birds. It was the ship, already en route, and no more than four days out when that post was made. The entry that predicted he would be dead before it arrived to take him home.' The entry, Jejeune's look said, that was spot on.

'Well done, you,' said Lindy, genuinely enthused. She rose and approached the dining table. He could smell the sweetness of wine as she draped her arms around his neck and leaned in to kiss his cheek. 'And did this clever Kittiwake tell you what all this means for your case?'

'Something important, I think.' Domenic touched his fingers to a cutlery setting lined up in a row on the table in front of him. 'Let me show you.'

Lindy took a seat beside him and he picked up the fork.

'Starting with the premise that Kasabian knew he would die before that ship arrived, and it was only a couple of days out, it's only natural he would be wary.'

'Of course it is. Super-natural, even.' She smiled at him and put her finger to her lips. 'Sorry, I'll be super-silent from now on. Carry on.'

'But if so, there's a logic triangle that doesn't hold up.' Jejeune set the fork down carefully. 'Firstly, he sends a message saying he's going to die before the ship arrives. Secondly, he learns the exact arrival date of the ship. Gaya's notes confirm that every member on base was informed so they could prepare for their departure.'

Jejeune lifted the spoon and set it down to represent an adjoining side of a triangle. Lindy noticed that the white plate she had left out earlier had been pushed aside, unused. When Domenic's mind entered the labyrinth of a crime, food was often an afterthought.

He picked up the knife. 'And then, two days before the ship is due to arrive, he goes out alone, in dangerously cold conditions.' Jejeune set the knife down so it completed the triangle.

Lindy stared hard at it. 'He couldn't have made things any easier for a potential killer if he'd tried,' she said. 'Why would he have done that?'

'Exactly. So if the logic of the triangle doesn't hold, we need to find out which piece is flawed. Let's go backwards. Did he go out that night?' Jejeune touched the knife. 'Yes, he did. Next, did he know when the ship was due to arrive?' He tapped the spoon authoritatively. 'Again, we can answer with certainty that he did. So the only question left is...'

'Did he know he was in danger?' Lindy put her hand to her mouth. 'Oh God, Dom. You don't think he did. You don't think he sent that message. But if not him, then who?'

'Someone who knew Alex Kasabian was going to be killed before the *Oceanite* arrived. And since no one issued any warning, we can only assume that was the killer.'

'But why announce it? What if Kasabian had somehow become aware of the blog? As soon as he found out about the plan to kill him, he would do everything he could to try and stay safe.'

'Agreed, it makes no sense to run the risk of alerting him. But the English version of the ship's name might have been used so he wouldn't understand the message even if he did come across it. One thing is clear, though: whoever posted that blog must have had access to Kasabian's personal account to do it.'

Lindy sat upright. 'If this was about his work with climate data, anything private he'd recorded, any notes, any suspicions, this person would be able to read it all.'

'Exactly. And the timing of his murder suggests he needed to die he before he returned to the UK, or even before he boarded the *Oceanite*. Somebody didn't want him to have the chance to contact the outside world about whatever he'd discovered.'

Lindy put a hand to her forehead, as if trying to disperse the fog of the alcohol for a moment. 'But surely he could have already done that, couldn't he? All he had to do was send a message on social media.'

Jejeune nodded. 'Except all communications from the base go via the Institute. If no messages from Kasabian were ever posted, either he didn't send one, which means he didn't want somebody at the Institute to see it, or he did send it, and somebody there intercepted it. Either way, it's going to be worth taking a look at what goes on up there.'

'But you can't do that, Dom. It has to go to Shepherd now. You know that. It's become an active case and you have to hand it off.'

He shook his head. 'At the moment, this is all just theory. Technically, I don't have to hand it over until I have evidence that there is a prosecutable case.'

'Oh, well, that's okay, then,' said Lindy sarcastically. 'We all know what a fan Colleen Shepherd is of technicalities. I'm sure she'll be all over an explanation like that.'

Lindy would be the first to admit she was a couple of glasses of wine away from a clear head, but even so, one thing was perfectly clear. From the way he was staring at his cutlery triangle now, Domenic was long past the theory stage. Evidence or not, there was no doubt at all that he was closing in on Alex Kasabian's murderer.

30

Tony Holland normally enjoyed the peace and quiet when everybody else was off pursuing inquiries, but today he wished there was somebody else in the office. The way Colleen Shepherd entered a room told you a lot about her mood, and today's forceful arrival suggested she wasn't here for a casual catch-up. She barely paused to sweep away the plastic sheeting across the doorway and Holland got the impression that if it hadn't moved aside, she would have been just as happy to barrel right through it. 'Nobody else around?' she said, scanning the room. 'Don't tell me they're all off doing their jobs. Frankly, I'd have trouble believing that today.'

Holland looked around the room himself, but the abject potted plants lining the unpainted walls behind Danny's desk seemed unlikely candidates to help deflect her ire. 'Anything I can help you with, ma'am?' he asked benignly. In the past, even his genuine contributions had occasionally been mistaken for sarcasm, so he gave the concerned tone a little bit extra, just in case.

'I've just had a phone call from the manager of the Board Room. Me, Constable, the detective chief bloody superintendent, receiving information on a case directly from a concerned member of the public. He said he had something he thought he should mention about Arliss Dyer, and he's been waiting for somebody from here, I'd hesitate to call them a detective, to show up so he could tell them.'

'I believe it was on our list to pay him a visit, ma'am,' said Holland, instinctively reaching for the safest unarguable response.

Shepherd fixed him with a look that suggested he might have tiptoed dangerously close to the sarcasm he'd been trying so hard to avoid. 'What are you doing here, anyway? No leads to pursue?'

It didn't seem the time to say he was in the middle of setting up an elaborate joke for Danny, so Holland picked up a couple of papers from his desk and waved them vaguely in the hope that she might interpret it as evidence of productive employment. 'May I ask what the information was?'

'Yes, Constable, you may. On the night Arliss Dyer died, an envelope was delivered to the Board Room. It contained enough cash for a bottle of top-quality single malt and a generous tip, and a note to say the bottle should be given to Arliss Dyer when he came in. Shortly after he arrived, Dyer received a call on the pub phone, after which he took his bottle and left the pub.'

'I don't suppose the manager saved the note.'

Shepherd gave him a look to ask whether they normally received that kind of luck. Holland was quiet. They both knew what this meant. If Dyer had stumbled into the unlocked hide in a drunken stupor and died in an arson blaze, he was the unfortunate victim of an unrelated crime. But if somebody had deliberately provided him with enough alcohol to render him unconscious, and then contacted him to make sure he went to the unlocked hide, it was a premeditated act of murder.

'It's interesting, don't you think, that Paige Turner has thus far failed to mention any of this to us?'

She was no longer his lady-friend, he noted, or even Ms Tao. He didn't need Shepherd's tone to remind him that you graduated to formal first-and-last-name status when you moved up the scale from witness to suspect.

'I'm sure she would have, if she knew about it,' said Holland reasonably. He shook his head. 'There's no way she has anything do with this.'

Shepherd's silence provided the counter-argument. The next step was clearly to establish who was correct. He was in no doubt that this was now a task that would not be entrusted to him. 'If she's anywhere near this, Tony, if Paige Turner's acquaintance with Arliss Dyer has gone even a baby-step further than serving him drinks when he came into the Board Room, you understand you can no longer be part of this investigation.'

'I swear, ma'am, she has never mentioned anything to me.'

Shepherd weighed the constable's words carefully and decided, as always, that trusting a member of her team was a risk worth taking. 'I'll get someone out there to have a word with her. I suppose it'll have to be Lauren. Danny Maik seems to think he's on to something with the Glover Boyd lead. Though, frankly, I'm not sure what that could be. Doesn't Boyd have an alibi for the night in question?'

Holland nodded. 'We've just received the CCTV back from the lab. Verified genuine. Which means we have time-stamped video at either end of the trip from the hospital, showing him picking up his ex and dropping her off. We also have two separate accounts from people who received calls from Tori Boyd while he was driving her home. She was on the phone for virtually the entire trip, which is backed up by pings from phone masts along the route. CCTV has the two of them arriving at her house at 9:47; exactly the right time for the journey from the hospital. If there's a tighter alibi than

Glover Boyd's, I haven't seen it.' He looked at her directly. 'He isn't our killer, ma'am.'

She nodded thoughtfully. 'But still Danny doesn't seem to want to let him go?' She nodded to herself. 'Okay, get over there and talk to the manager of the Board Room. And do not, under any circumstances, speak to Paige Turner about any of this until we've been able to confirm that she is in the clear. You do understand what it would mean if you failed to follow this order, Constable, even by accident?'

Holland nodded solemnly.

Shepherd had already begun to leave when Holland's call came. She turned back to look at him. 'What is it, Constable? More wisdom from Sigbert?'

Holland regarded her cautiously. He had dodged the bullet of her formidable temper, but now a different kind of uneasiness seemed to steal upon him. 'Erm, ma'am, this bloke Glover Boyd,' he began slowly, 'he told me he knew Sergeant Salter, Lauren, when she was a new constable.' He tugged at his ear hesitantly. 'The thing is, ma'am, I'm just about certain he plated her.'

Shepherd pulled a face. 'Is there perhaps not a better way we could put that, Constable?'

'Probably there is, but that's the point. This would have been no starry-eyed love affair between two innocent waifs, ma'am.' It was there in Holland's eyes when he looked at Shepherd, but he felt the need to say it anyway. 'I know how it works. With a bloke like Boyd, once you have them, it's not about the one you're with any more, it's about the next one. He would have seen her, pulled her and moved on. I'm not saying she would have been looking for any happily-ever-after herself, necessarily, only...' An itchy eyebrow became the focus for his hesitation this time. 'I'm pretty sure Danny knows about it.'

Shepherd looked at him frankly. It wouldn't have been unreasonable to judge his motives based on some of his past visits to her office, but in his 'previous', in the terms of the trade, those motives had always been fairly easy to spot. This time, as in his chat earlier about Salter, there was a pained awkwardness about his delivery that suggested a sincere reluctance to bring these ideas forward.

'Danny can hardly be surprised that Lauren Salter has a past, Constable,' said Shepherd reasonably. 'She has a child, which is a bit of a giveaway.'

Holland shifted his weight slightly. 'Yeah, but we all know his views on that type of behaviour, don't we?'

On Holland's type of behaviour, he meant. Despite their close working relationship, Maik had never made any secret of his disapproval of Holland's lifestyle. We are all hostages to our childhood and Danny had been raised in a household where his father's infidelity had exacted a high price on his mother. Shepherd gave the idea some thought. His intolerance of the kind of behaviour Boyd indulged in would certainly colour his view of the man. But it was unlikely a seasoned professional like Danny would allow it to fester to the extent that it produced a murder suspect where there was evidence to the contrary.

'You know I would never normally question the sarge's judgement,' said Holland into the silence. 'I mean I think he's a great copper, brilliant. It's just in this case, he might not have the distance he needs. Boyd spotted it right away, the effect Danny's old man had on his perspective. Interesting bloke, that Boyd. I tell you what, he may have been crap as a paramedic, but he could have made a living for himself as a psychologist, being able to read people like that.'

Shepherd's thoughts seemed to drift elsewhere and it was a long moment before she returned. 'Point taken, Constable,' she said. 'Leave it with me.' She looked at him. 'All?'

All. Holland nodded an awkward goodbye, and grabbed his jacket to head out to the Board Room.

Shepherd looked around the empty room. But the dissatisfaction on her face wasn't a result of the half-finished decoration. It shouldn't be necessary for her to have a word with Danny. If he was intent on pursuing inquiries against a man for whom they had established a cast-iron alibi, there would need to be more to it than just his disapproval about Boyd's lifestyle choices. Surely Danny's fixation on him couldn't just stem from the man's earlier relationship with Lauren Salter. But whatever was going on, it was compromising the investigation, and she couldn't allow that. She realised she couldn't put things off any longer. It was time to red-ring a date on her calendar for the departure of one of her detective sergeants.

31

Salter's first reaction was that it was a bomb. But there was a different kind of tension in the air as she pulled up. The concern on the faces of the people milling around in the car park revealed less wariness, but more fear. It was the kind of reaction that came with the presence of a hazmat team. And an armed guard at the door of the police station.

She skewed her car to a halt in a half-hearted attempt at parking, and sprinted towards a gaggle of officers gathered in the far corner of the car park. 'What's going on?' she asked.

They turned their eyes towards their DCS, standing in their midst, but Salter noted that Shepherd didn't bring her own eyes up to meet Salter's inquiry. 'What? What is it?'

'Possible hazardous material has been detected in the station,' Shepherd said finally. 'The team are checking it out now.'

'Hazardous material? What, sent in the post, you mean?'

'Left,' said Shepherd flatly. 'Danny found something on his desk when he came in this morning. A small bowl with crushed seeds in it from the castor oil plant. He thought it might be a symbol of something, so he googled it.' She finally met Salter's eyes. 'As soon as he found out what it was, he evacuated the building and called in hazmat. Lauren, it's…'

'It was a bit of a lark, that's all,' said Holland. He looked devastated and she could see tears welling up in his eyes. 'DIY castor oil, that's all it was meant to be.'

Salter looked puzzled.

'Castor oil plants, Lauren,' Shepherd told her, 'the seeds. They release ricin.'

She rounded on Holland. 'Ricin? You put ricin on Danny's desk? And Danny's been exposed. You bloody idiot, what have you done?'

'I didn't know. It was all in fun...'

'Oh God. How is he?' She fumbled for her car keys. 'Which hospital have they taken him to?' And it was then that she realised what all the lowered heads meant, all the downturned glances. 'Where is he?' she asked, although she already knew the answer. A pit of fear gaped open in her stomach. 'Tony. Where's Danny?'

Holland seemed incapable of finding words. Shepherd stepped in. 'He insisted on staying,' she said. 'He's hoping the plastic sheeting the painters hung up will have contained it in the office area. He wouldn't let anyone else enter.' She tried a small smile. 'You know Danny. When he insists on something...' The smile never had much chance of succeeding, and it faded away without a trace.

Salter was struggling to come to terms with the news. 'He's still inside? I've got to see him.'

She turned towards the building but Shepherd grabbed her arm. 'He's showing symptoms of exposure, Lauren. Ricin constitutes a grade one hazmat threat. No one can go near him for now.'

Salter struggled to free herself. 'I have to. I can't let him be alone.' She broke away from Shepherd's hold and ran to the building, taking the steps two at a time and bursting past the guard at the door before he realised what was happening. The others sprinted after her, led by Shepherd. As they reached the top of the steps, they heard the uproar coming from inside: shouts of alarm and angry, barked orders. 'The containment zone's been breached. Somebody get some screens up, for God sake.'

The guard had recovered enough to bar entry to the rest of the group and they were still standing on the top step, pressing back against the firearm across his chest when the white-suited hazmat commander emerged in the doorway of the building. The fury in his eyes was apparent even through the face shield. He flung a finger in the direction of Shepherd and the others. 'Sergeant, get these people back now. I want a ten-metre exclusion perimeter established. Nobody in or out until I say so.' He eyed the crowd gathered below him. 'You understand? Nobody.'

'I'm DCS Shepherd. This is my station.'

'Then you and I are going to have words, Superintendent. Just as soon as I've sorted out this bloody mess your officer has created. For now, I want you back.'

Over the man's shoulder, Shepherd could see the commotion in the building as some of the hazmat team tried desperately to reattach the plastic sheeting over the frame of the doorway while others raced in various directions, shouting unheeded orders at each other.

'You heard him,' said the guard. 'Fall back.' He gestured a gentle shove towards them, with his weapon at arms.

Shepherd ushered the rest to the base of the steps, but stood her own ground. 'That's my officer in there,' she said, her voice straining for control. 'I need to get her to safety.'

'It's too late for that,' the commander told her. 'Now that the containment barrier has been breached, both your officers have been exposed. Neither you nor anyone else will be allowed into this building until further notice. For now, you are under orders to clear this area. You need to step back with the others.'

With a last look at the frantic containment efforts going on inside the station, Shepherd retreated to the foot of the stairway. She drifted slowly backwards until she rejoined the group huddled on the far side of the car park. Not once did she take her eyes off the building where her two officers were facing possibly the gravest threat of their lives.

Tony Holland was pacing around the outside of the small knot of officers in a daze. 'I didn't know. I didn't know,' he repeated. He was holding his head in his hands, his fingers dragging through his loose blond curls as he wandered around, repeating the mantra. He stopped suddenly and clutched the sides of his head more tightly. 'Christ, what have I done?'

He was falling apart, thought Shepherd. She needed somebody to fetch his girlfriend, someone who could talk to him, calm him down. She looked around the car park. Who would she normally send? Danny? Salter? Jejeune? What had happened to her team? Her world was imploding and here she was standing alone at the centre of it, her unit vapourised into nothingness. She suddenly felt so isolated, so exposed.

Time seemed to take on an elasticity. Minutes stretched out agonisingly. Conversation among the waiting group had ceased completely, each of them now wandering around aimlessly or staring off into space, nursing their own thoughts. Holland sat on a low wall in silence, head bowed, his eyes locked on the ground. An ambulance made a slow, ponderous turn into the car park, lights flashing but no siren. A good omen? A bad one? Two medical crews in full masks and protective gear approached the building and were waved forward by the guard to duck under the yellow tape and climb the steps. They disappeared inside, watched by all sets of eyes.

More elastic time passed before the first white-suited medical team reappeared at the top of the stairs. One or two of the group approached the makeshift tape barrier as they descended. Two medics carefully carried a stretcher between them. 'Danny,' said someone quietly, though the features of the figure on the stretcher were hidden so completely behind an oxygen mask it was impossible to tell. The second stretcher team emerged, and descended the steps with their burden as cautiously as the first. When both were in the ambulance, the doors closed with an overloud metallic clang. The gathered group watched as the vehicle slowly pulled away, lights flashing as before, still no sirens. Nobody was in the mood to speculate on omens any more.

By the time Shepherd had turned from watching the departure of the ambulance, the hazmat commander was walking towards the group. He halted as he reached her. 'Before I submit my report, I'm going to need a full account from you, Superintendent, with particular emphasis as to how and why a hazmat-secured zone was breached by one of your officers.' He paused. 'The review committee are going to need to be able to understand how the situation got so badly out of hand when we'd given explicit instructions that the site was to be sealed, secured and evacuated.'

Shepherd said nothing. She didn't care for his tone, or the fact that this conversation was being held in front of junior officers, but she understood. Lauren Salter had not only risked her own life by rushing in and breaching the containment zone. She had also endangered this officer's team. Shepherd would have felt the same way if somebody had put her own people at risk like that. And she would probably have reacted the same way, too.

The commander continued. 'We're taking air samples now. Nobody will be going in or out until the readings come back at safe levels. The dish has been sent off for analysis. The plant has been removed as a precaution, obviously.'

'Those bloody plants go tomorrow, all of them,' said Shepherd firmly.

The commander saw Holland sitting on the wall, head still bowed, staring at the ground. 'You need to hang your head, Constable. You're the one responsible for this mess, I understand. You could be looking at a professional misconduct hearing here. Negligent handling of hazardous materials. They'll be particularly interested to know if you have any knowledge of chemistry, I should imagine.'

Holland looked up at him. 'New line for you is it,' he asked bitterly, 'predicting the future?'

'I can predict yours, son, if you don't change your tone.'

Shepherd approached and stood between the two men. She hadn't been able to protect many of her people today. She wasn't going to miss the opportunity when it came up.

'Perhaps it's better if you and I discuss this later,' she said.

'Just telling you how I see it.' The man shrugged and looked back at the building. 'Things will be far worse for the sergeant, though, if any of my people come down with anything. She'll be looking at charges.' His expression softened a touch. 'Still, I suppose that's the least of her worries at the moment. I hope your people both make a full recovery, DCS. Wish them that much for me, would you, at least.'

The commander moved away to oversee the packing up of the operation. Holland watched him for a moment and then turned to look at his DCS. 'A hearing, ma'am? What am I going to say?'

'Nothing today, Constable. I think that's best. Don't you? If it needs to go further, you can have your union rep with you.'

She walked off to attend to arranging some transport to the hospital. Holland stared for a long moment at the façade of the police station. Behind the yellow tape barrier, strangers moved around, entering and exiting the station from which its officers were banished. That was his doing. With all that had happened today, his senses weren't at their best, but he was sure the DCS had used the word *if*. He felt so hollow inside, he didn't really care whether a hearing went ahead or not. What he wanted to do now was to get to the hospital, to face the real consequences of his actions.

32

Shepherd hurried along the hospital corridor to meet Jejeune and Lindy, speaking in the hushed tones that the setting encouraged. 'Lauren is showing no symptoms of exposure, and her tox screening confirms there is no ricin in her system. We'll be allowed in to see her in a few minutes.' But there was a shadow behind her relief. They waited. 'Danny is still in isolation for now. He is symptomatic, but they think there might be something else going on with him, too. They're waiting for some lab reports. No visitors at this time,' she pronounced solemnly.

The three made their way back towards Salter's room. Tony Holland and Paige Turner were leaning against the wall outside, arms linked as she gently stroked his shoulder. He introduced Jejeune and Lindy before drawing the two senior detectives to one side.

'I never meant for this to happen. I swear I had no idea about ricin and castor oil.'

He looked at his superiors, but both remained silent. 'The hazmat commander said there'll be an inquiry. Possibly a disciplinary hearing.' Holland's face clouded with confusion. 'He said they'll want to know if I have any background in chemistry.'

Shepherd looked to Jejeune. 'Higher-level ricin produc-
tion requires more than just crushing seeds,' he said. 'The
intent to cause harm would be easier to prove if you had some
basic knowledge of chemistry. They'll also want to know about
your working relationship with the sergeant; whether there
was any bad blood between you, other incidents in the past.'

'What? No, I think the world of him, you know that, sir.
He's the best man I've ever known.'

Jejeune's expression suggested these weren't necessarily
questions to which he'd need answers himself.

'And that's what will come out in the hearing, Tony,'
Shepherd told him. 'I don't see this going any further than preliminary inquiries. It was a mistake, yes, stupid, possibly, but
the harm was unintentional. People can forgive that, as long as
everyone comes out unscathed.'

Only Jejeune had noticed her inadvertent glance at Salter's
room, a place where forgiveness might not be so easy to come by.
Shepherd had called the consequences of Holland's misjudged
act unintentional. But Lauren Salter's actions had been anything
but. She had recklessly ignored established safety protocols and
compromised the ongoing containment operation. Perhaps her
desire to see Maik, to be with him, was understandable. But a
police officer was required to stay in control at all times, and that
included control of your emotions. Salter had selfishly indulged
her own feelings, and put other people's lives at risk as a result. It
was not something Shepherd would forget. Today was for gratitude that the worst seemed to have passed, and tonight would
be for healing; wounds, and illnesses and troubled spirits. But
the time would come to cast a cold, dispassionate eye on what
had transpired today. And once that had happened, Colleen
Shepherd would take the action she needed to.

A nurse emerged from Salter's room. Her look took them
all in, but rested longer on Paige Turner. 'You can all go in now,

but just for a few minutes. And stay behind the screens at all times.'

The group shuffled in and pressed back against the walls of the confined space. A perspex screen surrounded the bed. Salter was sitting up. Her complexion was flushed, and her cheeks bore the marks of the oxygen mask she'd recently had removed. There was a tap on the door and a doctor entered. He was clearly surprised by the crowd in the room, but his questioning glance to the nurse was met by a frank stare. There were times when visitor quotas could be waived, at least for a few minutes. The nurse made room for the doctor, squeezing in next to Paige Turner.

'Don't I know you?' she asked.

'I don't think so,' said Turner. 'I work at the Board Room. Perhaps you've been in there?'

The nurse shook her head. 'A couple of shifts in here on a Saturday night is enough to put anyone off alcohol for life. No, you just remind me of someone I went to school with, that's all. Sorry, my mistake.'

The doctor came round to the side of the bed and addressed Salter directly as if the others weren't present. 'Well, the good news is you look to have escaped any exposure at all. We want to check your vitals a couple more times, but if everything remains stable we can probably give you the all-clear to go home later today.'

'And Danny?' she asked.

His tone changed. 'We're not sure what's going on, so we're keeping him overnight for some tests.' He tilted his head slightly. 'He's not showing the signs we'd expect, but something's put him here in intensive care. We'll know more when the results are back this evening.' He straightened. 'Right, well, I'll let you get on with your visit.' He turned to the nurse. 'Not too long, though.'

Shepherd's phone gave a shrill ring and she answered it before it got to a second one. The doctor made to leave but she held up a finger for him to remain. She listened for a moment in silence, nodding once and thanking the caller before shutting off the phone and turning to them all. 'Preliminary indications are that ricin-binding antibodies were absent from the air samples taken.'

Holland looked at her. 'Absent?'

'As in not present,' she said drily. 'We've been cleared to re-enter the building.'

The doctor nodded. 'This is good news. It means at most Danny's exposure can only have been residual or low-level.' He looked at Salter. 'That's not to say you don't need to take things easy for a while.'

'Domenic,' said Shepherd. 'A word? Outside?'

'I should go, too,' Turner told Salter. 'Let you have some quality time with Tony.'

Paige Turner held the door open for the doctor and followed him out. Lauren Salter didn't take her eyes off her until she'd gone.

Shepherd and Jejeune retreated to the far end of the corridor, where they stood beneath the bright glare of a fluorescent bulb. 'Have you spoken to Danny recently?' asked the DCS.

'He came to see me a couple of days ago.'

She nodded. 'To ask you about a phone call, I take it, from Arliss Dyer?'

Jejeune returned her even stare. 'I told him I hadn't received one.'

Shepherd kept her eyes on him. He must know, surely, that they had already verified the call from Boyd's phone with the service provider. Why would he persist in this denial? Was there something about his relationship with the man that he felt he needed to conceal? 'You knew him, I understand, Arliss Dyer. My condolences.' Shepherd pursed her lips. 'I'm told he enjoyed a drink. Or two.'

'I believe he did.' Jejeune's flat tone invited Shepherd to get to the point.

'And presumably your birder friends would know what his favourite tipple was.'

'Arliss Dyer knew a lot of people besides birders.' If this was going to be an interrogation, Jejeune would treat it like one. Shepherd would need to ask specific questions if she wanted specific answers.

She looked around but there was no activity in the corridor, only the ambient noise of hospital business humming in the background: doors swishing, carts clattering, the occasional tinny announcement over the paging system. 'I'm told that you were asked to look into that blog post from the Antarctic base,' she said finally. 'Anything to report?'

'I am convinced that Alex Kasabian didn't send that post,' he said.

'Do you know who did?'

'Someone else who had access to his account.'

Sometimes it was hard to tell whether Jejeune was being deliberately obtuse. Especially when he had his back up, as he appeared to now. If he did realise Shepherd was asking for a more specific identity, his impassive features gave no sign.

'And is this just your theory, Domenic, or do you have proof? Because I would remind you, they are not one and the same thing.' Except, when he looked at her with this frank stare of his, she knew they were.

'Alex Kasabian is dead,' he said. 'He went out to check some readings and he froze to death when his snowmobile failed to

225

start. The fuel line had been cut. It can't be proven yet whether he had the tools in his possession to do it accidentally.'

Procedurally, there was no reason for Shepherd to have been informed of this before now, but it was clear from her expression that she was in no mood to entertain an argument like that. Her complexion darkened as she seemed to be considering how much she wanted to reveal to him. 'We're working on the theory that Arliss Dyer's death might be connected to the fire at the Bellaire Institute. And that, as you will know, connects to this Antarctic death through Julien Bellaire. It's time for you to step aside, Domenic. We need to begin an active investigation into Alex Kasabian's death.'

Jejeune shook his head. 'You can't do that,' he said, using the reasonable tone that she found so maddening at times.

She eyed him critically. Her DCI might not have ever been too open about his thought processes, but he'd always had a healthy respect for the team's abilities. Did he truly believe they weren't up to the task, all of a sudden? 'I'd urge you to consider the bigger picture here, Domenic. Continuing to investigate what is now an active case is a breach of the terms of your suspension. If you'll remember, I asked them not to make an example of you when they passed down their judgment. They'll be keen to ensure you don't receive any leeway, either. And they will even more keen to be able to show it. The rest of the team are perfectly capable of taking this through to a prosecution.'

'It won't be prosecuted.'

'What are you talking about?' Shepherd checked over her shoulder, but whether it was because she thought her voice had already been a touch too loud, or might be about to become so, wasn't clear. She felt her temper starting to rise. It wasn't enough that Jejeune didn't trust anyone else at Saltmarsh to see the investigation through. Now, he wanted to do the

Crown Prosecution Service's job for them as well. She lowered her voice, straining for patience. 'It will be up to the CPS to decide whether a prosecution can be brought, Domenic, not you. The role of the police service here, again, not yours, is merely to submit a viable case.' She paused and looked at him. 'I will expect your notes and any supporting information on my desk tomorrow morning. Shall we say nine?'

'Alex Kasabian was a refugee,' said Jejeune evenly. 'He was killed in a location where no country has any legal jurisdiction. Without a claim through the citizenship of the victim or sovereignty over the crime scene, I don't believe any judicial system in the world has the authority to prosecute this case.'

Shepherd fell silent. Holland and Lindy emerged from Lauren Salter's room. The constable left to catch up with Turner, but Lindy stood outside the door, at the far end of the corridor, watching Domenic and his DCS intently.

'I need to get a legal opinion on this,' said Shepherd finally. 'In the meantime, I would strongly suggest you don't pursue this any further. Are we clear? No inquiries of any kind.'

Jejeune greeted the directive with his customary silence.

Lindy approached as soon as she saw a break in the conversation. 'So, Lauren was saying some DNA had been identified off an old blanket. It belonged to Arliss Dyer.' She seemed to realise the implication and held up a hand. 'Oh, she wasn't talking to me. She told Tony Holland. I was just there. I couldn't help overhearing. Sorry,' she said without a hint of remorse.

If Jejeune had any reaction to the news about the blanket, he was keeping it to himself. Lindy shifted her look between the two officers, but if she had intended it as an opening for the DCS to invite Dom into the case, it didn't go the way she had planned. Whatever had gone on before she arrived, the distance between them seemed greater now than ever.

'We should go,' Jejeune said. 'If you are allowed to see Danny, please tell him I'll come to see him as soon as I can,' he told Shepherd as they left.

She watched the brightly lit tunnel swallow up the diminishing figures, but she left her gaze on the empty corridor long after Domenic and Lindy had disappeared from view. Even if she wasn't best pleased about Lindy's ham-fisted efforts to keep Domenic in the loop, she had more important matters to contend with just now. Not least, whether the only person she knew who was capable of solving a crime committed ten thousand miles away could be allowed to continue his investigations.

33

It was no surprise that the plants were gone. Maik had made a point of checking the bins behind the station before he came in, but Shepherd wasn't petty. She wouldn't have taken out her anger and frustration on a few potted plants. They would be stashed in a spare room somewhere, probably the warehouse down the street they used for evidence that exceeded the space of the small lockup downstairs. Wherever they were, Danny Maik knew they would be off-site, nowhere near him. Even if his deductive reasoning hadn't been able to tell him this, his new, unlaboured breathing would. Laid low not by ricin, then, merely a weeping fig. One more threat Danny would need to be alert to for the rest of his life. The list was piling up.

The painting in the Incident Room had been completed, and done well. With so much having spiralled out of her control recently, Shepherd had been keen to exert her influence in any area where she still had some, and the results showed it.

But for all the page-turning potential the newly decorated room offered, it could do nothing about the palpable tension that hung in the air. No one could forget the events of the last time they were in this building together, and even if Danny, the principal actor in the drama, had assured them that he was fine and everything was back to normal, no one was buying that line today.

Shepherd would expect them to go about their duties as if they were, though. Whatever lingering uncertainties hung in the atmosphere today, there were still crimes to solve. 'Right, let's get down to it, shall we?' she said. 'We now have a statement from the manager at the Board Room telling us that Arliss Dyer received a bottle of whisky and a phone call shortly before he left the pub on the night of his death. He also confirms he let Paige Turner leave early that night, as it was slow.'

'She had no reason to harm him,' said Holland quickly. 'It's pretty clear she really liked the bloke.'

'Or so she claims. We have no independent witnesses to testify about the nature of their relationship.'

On another day, Holland might have risked telling the DCS her line of inquiry was ridiculous. Not the DCS personally, never that, but she would allow her ideas to be challenged once in a while. But it was not another day. It was the day when Lauren Salter was sitting meekly in a corner, avoiding eye contact from Shepherd that was unlikely to have been forthcoming anyway. It was the day when Danny Maik seemed content to benignly watch proceedings from the sidelines, instead of getting involved. So if anybody was going to come to Paige Turner's defence, it would have to be Tony Holland. Only Shepherd's expression suggested he had better go about it carefully.

'With respect, ma'am. Why would she want to kill Arliss Dyer? She's only just shown up here.'

Shepherd regarded him coldly. 'The organisation she's working for suffers an arson attack, and she has a self-confessed connection to a murder victim. If she wasn't going out with somebody in the department, do you think this is a person we might be looking at anyway?'

Holland went quiet. Shepherd looked down at the folders on the desk beside her. She was silent for a long time. 'The thing I'm struggling with here is motive. Dyer specifically told DCI Jejeune in his voicemail message, in front of two independent witnesses, that he did not recognise the voice at the hide. So if he is telling this to anyone who'll listen, what threat did he pose? He's already told people everything he did hear. What possible benefit could there be to killing him after the fact?'

'Unless, of course, he did recognise it.'

Everyone turned to Holland again. 'I mean, we've all been taking Dyer at his word, but really he was just some dodgy drunk who was down on his luck. You know what they're like, people who have nothing. They come across a bit of information, they're going to try and milk it for all it's worth. Say he did recognise the voice that night. Is he really going to ignore a nice little earner like that?'

Maik inclined his head. Though he was only floating this as a way to deflect suspicion from his girlfriend, Holland had raised a valid point. Shepherd, though, seemed less convinced. 'Then why report it at all, if he planned to blackmail the person?'

'Maybe the call to the DCI was just to raise the odds, apply a bit of pressure.'

Shepherd shook her head. 'I'm sorry. It's all a bit thin.'

Maik could understand her reluctance. While she'd be willing to concede that it was an idea that needed looking into, Holland's proposal not only expanded the suspect list to now include people Dyer may have known after all, it also gave each of them an equally plausible motive to want him dead. But Danny suspected Holland wasn't quite finished yet. When you were trying to shift suspicion from one individual, it helped if you had a specific target in mind to move it to.

'Julien Bellaire, ma'am—'

Wherever Holland was intending to go with his comment. Shepherd was keen to ensure he never reached his destination. 'Can you really see a person with his resources getting involved in something like this? You'll have a reason, presumably, as to why the Billionaire Bicyclist would want to murder a homeless man in a hide?'

Holland spread his hands. 'All I know is, he's all over this. He owns the facility that Dyer heard being threatened. He owns the base in Antarctica where the other murder occurred.'

'The other death.'

'With respect, ma'am, we can't ignore the fact that two bodies have shown up at facilities owned by him. All I'm saying is it might be worth checking into the activities of that institute a bit more closely.'

'I already did,' said Salter, finally breaking her silence. All eyes turned to her. 'It seems to me every time anybody talks about this project all you hear is compliance this, openness that. Almost as if somebody was going out of their way to emphasise how above-board the operation is. We all got the same impression.' She looked at Danny and Holland, who were both willing to support her on this with a nod. 'The thing is, with these global temperature measurements, we're dealing with razor-thin margins. A quarter of a degree one way or another is incredibly significant. Given the scale of the Bellaire operation, it wouldn't take much to shift the dial by altering some results.'

Shepherd's look encouraged her to continue.

'I mean, part of me wants to say so what if they are fudging the numbers a bit. You need to get people to see the truth one way or another. Even if the temperature readings were inflated a touch, it can't be wrong to make sure people are being alerted to the realities of climate change.'

Shepherd wasn't in the mood to discuss the ethics of lying for a good cause, but she did seem to be warming to the idea that they might actually be getting somewhere. 'Your findings, Sergeant.'

'The Bellaire Institute's policy of transparency means their data is some of the most accessible in the world. I spoke to a local investigative journalist who's just finished an in-depth review of their records.' She paused and took in the room with her look. 'Nothing. If there was a pattern of inconsistency with other readings around the world, it would have been flagged. The Bellaire data are entirely in line with every set of readings from other global monitoring programmes.'

Shepherd made no attempt to hide her disappointment. It would have been something, finally; but like everything else in this case, it just vanished into thin air as soon as you took the time to look into it closely enough. Elsewhere in the room, there were plenty of expressions giving Salter credit for trying, but Shepherd simply looked down at her folders again. This far into the investigation, a briefing that increased the number of suspects and eliminated promising leads was hardly going to find favour with her. 'Right, well, if there's nothing else.'

Salter's voice came just as she turned to leave. 'Ma'am, can I say something?'

Shepherd half-turned and made a show of looking at her watch. She gave a curt nod. 'My office.'

'No ma'am, here. Now. To everyone.' Salter stood up and the group settled to silence, all eyes turned once again in her direction. But she didn't speak. She simply looked back at them, at the group, at individuals. The silence built, through their indulgence, through their discomfort, to an unbearable, unrelieved pressure. But still Lauren Salter stood there, upright, jaw firmly set, unspeaking.

'I made a mistake.' The words were slow when they came, but the voice was steady and firm. She shook her head slightly, and perhaps allowed herself the smallest of ironic smiles. 'It's such a small word for what I did. I could have put the lives of everyone here at risk. And I regret doing that, as much as I can ever remember regretting anything.'

She looked around the room, seeking eye contact, holding it wherever she found it. This was not, she was telling them, one of those mealy-mouthed apologies that put the onus on other people's sensibilities: *if* she had offended anyone, *if* anyone was upset or put out. This apology didn't imply that it was their standards that were at issue. Only her conduct. This was Lauren Salter telling them she was wrong.

Maik's heart was breaking for her. She looked so vulnerable as she stood up there, all alone. But he knew that she didn't want his support at this moment. This wasn't his time. It was hers. She didn't want him to rise from his seat and walk up to stand beside her, to put a comforting arm around her and tell her that it was all right, that everyone understood. It wasn't all right. She wasn't asking for their understanding. Perhaps she wasn't even asking for their forgiveness. She was here to give them something, not take anything from them. And in their attentive silence, their willingness to meet her eyes when her gaze sought them out, the group were telling her that they recognised this, too.

'I have thought about what I did every day since it happened. I'll probably think about it every day from now on. But it will be a small price to pay if it reminds me that I can never again take actions that potentially put the lives of my colleagues, people I care about, at risk.' She looked around the room, locking eyes with each individual in turn. There would be no attempt to defend her actions, they realised, no attempt to justify them, or even explain. That was not why she was standing here. Only to say this. 'I'm sorry. And I always will be.'

There had been some dumbfounding moments in this room before. Domenic Jejeune's astonishing revelations had been responsible for more than a few of them. But Maik could never remember a silence so profound. It reverberated round the newly painted walls, an empty, echoing hiss that threatened to suck them all into its void. It wasn't simply the heartfelt sincerity of the apology, the genuine remorse in every drawn-out word. It was an acknowledgement that what had been broken that day could never be repaired. It was a realisation that change was coming.

34

A sunny, crystal-bright day greeted Lindy when she went outside to meet it. She sat down on a rock beside the cove, steaming mug of tea in hand, and slowly took everything in. The air was so clear she could see the silhouettes of droplets on the dew-glazed leaves. The briny damp-moss scent of seaweed drifted towards her on a breeze so gentle the grasses barely bowed their stems to acknowledge its passing. In front of her, the water was as calm and untroubled as a sleeping child.

It still surprised her that this could be the same body of water as the roiling white-caps that raced past just the other side of the point. It was as if the sea, its energies spent in other battles, now sought refuge in this placid cove. Perhaps this was what Lindy wanted now too, she thought, a place to shelter from the world's turmoil, somewhere to instead let life slowly drift in towards her, where she would meet it on her own terms.

She was still enjoying the quietude when she heard the crunch of tyres on gravel, and she turned to see Colleen Shepherd's Jaguar draw up. The DCS saw Lindy and came over to her, looking over her shoulder at the car as she approached. 'I know, but it's my last fling with fossil fuels. I'll be going electric with my next car. I might as well treat myself to this one a bit longer.'

Lindy smiled. 'He's up.'

Shepherd knew they were both early risers, and such early morning drop-ins were not unknown when they lived at the cottage. As they moved towards the door, Shepherd paused to look at the cove. 'It's a lovely spot, Lindy.' She looked at her. 'It was the right move, you know. However difficult it might have been. You needed to put the past behind you.'

Lindy nodded but said nothing. For all the eye-rolling at Shepherd's recommendation for counselling sessions, she knew the DCS truly did have her best interests at heart. The same was true for Domenic, though there were times when it was harder for him to see it.

'I bring you greetings from the ACC,' said Shepherd brightly as they entered Jejeune's temporary office set-up in the conservatory.

'I can only imagine the form those greetings would take.' Jejeune smiled as he said it, but Lindy could see that this business of having people visit him here as if he was some housebound invalid was starting to wear thin.

'I should leave you to it,' she said tactfully. 'I'll go and put the kettle on.'

Shepherd looked around and nodded approvingly. 'Nice space. So this is where you're planning to have your aviary, is it?'

'We've had a rethink about that,' he told her. 'Apparently.'

Shepherd smiled at his thwarted plans. She suspected the conservatory would gradually morph into some undefined space for both of them to use. The evolution would be imperceptible. They would simply find themselves one day in a place that they had not realised was forming around them. It was the way houses became homes.

'I just came by to tell you I ran this Antarctic business by the ACC,' she told Jejeune. She cast a sour look. 'I'm not sure international geopolitics are his forte. He once told me he'd always wanted to see the Great Pyramids of Gaza. However, he did get legal to weigh in and between them, they've come up with this.'

She produced a piece of paper from her briefcase and handed it to him, waiting in silence while he perused it. He seemed to be spending an inordinate amount of time going over what was a single-page document, and Shepherd knew he was weighing what it did not contain as much as what it did.

'It's not an eye test, Domenic,' she said finally. 'As you'll see, the legal opinion is that, given the location and victim's statelessness, this is a crime scene without any jurisdiction. As such, you're free to pursue your inquiries, as long as they don't cross paths with any open investigations.'

Lindy returned and busied herself setting out the tea things. But it didn't stop her casting a side glance at Domenic. She suspected his investigations had already taken him well beyond the parameters of this agreement. His delayed response to it would be because he could see no way to pursue them any further without agreeing to the terms.

'That's *any*, Domenic,' emphasised Shepherd. 'The moment it touches anything the North Norfolk Constabulary are involved with, or any other police department for that matter, you are to immediately cease all further inquiries and hand everything over to Saltmarsh station.' She waited expectantly. 'I can assure you this is not negotiable.'

'Okay,' he said finally. He handed the paper back to Shepherd, nodding as he did so.

'I'm afraid it will need something more formal than that.' She pushed the paper back in his direction. 'They want a signature.'

She waited while he found a pen and scrawled his signature at the bottom of the page and handed the paper back to her.

'I thought the country of an accused killer could make a claim for jurisdiction,' said Lindy as she handed Shepherd her tea. 'You know one of the people at the base camp did this. They must have. Couldn't their home country claim jurisdiction and prosecute the case?'

'There were eight different nationalities at Camp Isolée,' said Shepherd. 'The likelihood of those countries launching a cooperative investigation when there is a one-in-eight chance their own citizen was involved are about as remote as that base itself.' She looked at Jejeune. 'Unless you have any proof as to which one of them is guilty.'

Jejeune shook his head. But even if Shepherd didn't see that faint shimmer behind his eyes, Lindy did. And she knew what it meant. Sometimes, one little word made all the difference. Even a big little word like *proof*. In the absence of evidence, it meant a confession. Domenic didn't have that. But he did know what had happened out there. And how. Lindy was sure of that now. So no, not proof, perhaps. Just answers.

Shepherd sipped her tea and looked at him. 'Just one more thing, Domenic. Should your inquiries in this matter take you anywhere near Julien Bellaire you are to back away immediately. It's hard to overstate the influence a man like Bellaire has with the upper reaches of the North Norfolk Constabulary, and since there is no possibility of a conviction anyway, you risk making yourself, and us, a dangerous enemy unnecessarily. So wherever you go with this case, it will not be there. Do I make myself clear?' She stood up. 'Right, well, I should be going, let you get on with your day.'

'I'll walk you out,' said Lindy. 'You can stay here and get on with some work,' she told Domenic, 'now that you've been given the all-clear.'

Shepherd had been doing the job too long to suspect that Lindy's unexpected offer was simple courtesy, but her escort didn't say anything until they reached the DCS's car. 'That business at the hospital the other day... about the blanket... I wanted to apologise. I was just...'

'...trying to provide Domenic with information he wasn't entitled to.' Shepherd gave her a wry smile. 'We will get there, Lindy, without him. I can appreciate that Arliss Dyer was a friend of his, but it really is best for everyone that he stays clear of our investigations.'

'I just thought he might be able to help. I mean, the killer who left Arliss that whisky obviously knew him well. I thought if Dom knew anything about this old case with the blanket, he might be able to make the connection between Arliss and this person.'

Shepherd inclined her head slightly. 'I saw a show on TV recently where they'd discovered a document that they were convinced was some sort of medieval treasure map,' she said, reaching into her bag for her car key fob. 'They had the paper and the ink tested and both came back as authentic, so they were celebrating the fact that the document was genuine...'

'...when really all they had was a document written on paper from that period using ink made with techniques from that period. It could have been written the day before.' Lindy nodded in understanding. She frequently told friends there were a lot of similarities between investigative journalism and detective work, but she was beginning to appreciate that there were a few differences, too.

'It's not as easy as it looks,' said Shepherd. 'At the moment, there's no way we can even prove that the person who left the bottle is the killer. Perhaps it was just an act of kindness. It could be that somebody else who wanted Dyer dead saw it and exploited what they saw as a perfect opportunity.' She gave Lindy a kindly smile. 'That's the problem with evidence. If you're not careful, it simply leads you where your heart wants to go.'

'Like love, then,' said Lindy, with an ironic grin.

Shepherd made a face. 'About as reliable, too.'

But Lindy knew better. Your heart would never let you down. You just had to learn how to listen to it. And hers now was telling her that Domenic was heading for trouble. Shepherd wasn't going to be happy when she realised he had withheld what he knew. She would rescind his permission to continue the investigation. And when he continued anyway, as Lindy knew he would, any protection he might get from her would be lost.

When Lindy returned to the conservatory, Domenic was looking at the trees on the far side of the cove. But he wasn't seeing them. His focus was on something not in view; an internal mirror that he was now holding up to himself.

'You failed to mention, under questioning, something which you may later come to rely on,' she intoned gravely. 'I can't help feeling this may harm your defence. When Shepherd finds out, I mean.'

'What I have wouldn't be enough for anybody else,' said Jejeune. 'No country would consider opening a case against its own citizen based on a few random thoughts of a suspended police officer.'

But this was no longer about bringing the case to a successful prosecution anyway, she knew. Domenic would still pursue this case after the last hope of that had long vanished. A man had been murdered. He had died stranded and alone, thousands of miles from home, without even a country to claim his body. In life, no one had been there to protect Alex Kasabian. Now all anybody could do for him was to discover the truth about what had happened. And Domenic Jejeune would do that. Because to get the answers, to solve the case, to finally understand what had gone on out there in that Antarctic wilderness, would be to offer some meaning to the man's death. It would show the world that Alex Kasabian had mattered enough that someone cared sufficiently to find out why he had died.

35

Tori Boyd was limping around the fringes of the rubble, sweeping away debris with a wide garden broom, as Lauren Salter made her way down the incline. The sergeant could see a bright white dressing on her leg. 'I see you got rid of that old one, then?'

Tori Boyd looked down at her leg. 'Oh, yes. I had a friend of mine who's a nurse come over and do it. I didn't dare go back to the doctor with the filthy state the other one was in. He's not the most sanguine of men at the best of times.'

The doctor must be one of the few men around here Tori Boyd wouldn't have been able to get to come around to her point of view, thought Salter, especially if she put her mind to it.

'Still no Inspector Jejeune?'

'He won't be here any time soon,' said Salter.

The other woman's wide-eyed look seemed to invite further disclosure. Salter imagined it would have worked wonders on Tony Holland, but she had no difficulty staying silent on the matter.

'Well, I don't know what else I can add about the fire,' said Boyd airily. 'Do you have any new leads?'

'We're looking into the possibility that it was a targeted attack.'

'Sabotage, you mean?'

Salter nodded. 'Only, seeing it now, it is surprising they didn't go for higher-value targets. I mean, if they knew anything about the air-gapping and the online data storage, they're going to know taking out a few computers isn't going to put you out of business for very long.' She nodded in the direction of the bay. 'Those buoys, though, with all that sensitive monitoring equipment on board. If they'd got in among that lot things could have been far worse for you, couldn't they?'

Even the thought seemed to make Boyd uneasy. She shifted around, finding a more comfortable position for her bandaged leg. 'They could still be replaced,' she said, trying for a carefree tone that didn't quite come off. 'It's the data that is the crucial component to our work, not the hardware.'

'Still, that is a very large number of buoys you've got out there.'

'They were all deployed as a single batch. It makes sense they'd all need descaling at the same time.'

There was more defensiveness in Boyd's response than the observation should have generated. 'Just seems strange that there's so many, that's all,' said Salter.

Boyd spun on her. 'Instead of looking for faults with our procedures, you might try showing a bit more gratitude that someone like Julien Bellaire actually cares enough about the planet to do something about saving it. Government after government has failed to deliver on their promises. But fortunately for all of us, one individual with the resources and power to make a difference has decided to take on the responsibility.'

'Nobody is questioning Mr Bellaire's commitment here,' said Salter reasonably. 'I have a ten-year-old son at home. I'm as grateful as anybody that Julien Bellaire is interested in putting the good of the planet above profit.'

Boyd nodded a faint apology, even if she couldn't bring herself to utter one. 'I just get a bit tired of it, frankly, having our operations questioned, undercutting the valuable work we're doing. There's the potential to achieve great things here, and it's all down to the vision of one man. He deserves better than the constant sniping and cynicism he receives.'

It was clear Tori Boyd's devotion to the project was absolute. If she felt anyone was threatening it in some way, Salter could see her having it in her to do something about it. But that wasn't the case, was it? Not only did Arliss Dyer pose no threat, all the data was still intact on the cloud. She'd lost physical equipment but no research. 'When I was here last, you said your ex-husband knew Arliss Dyer. But he told my colleague he's never met him.'

'I regret to say it is entirely possible he wouldn't recognise him by name. Humans simply don't register with him unless he has a use for them. That said, even for Glover, missing a man of Arliss's uniqueness is a bit of a new standard.'

'But you implied that he strongly resented Dyer. It would have obviously put him in the frame as a potential suspect in his death.'

'Really? That's not the way I remember it. I merely said Arliss was the kind of honest, straightforward person Glover would have trouble with.'

In the video interviews Salter had been forced to pursue during the pandemic, it was always as if there was a faint veil of separation between her and the other person. In the case of this woman, Salter couldn't help the feeling it was still there, despite the fact that she was standing directly in front of her. Tori Boyd may not have been guilty of anything, but she was a long way from being innocent.

She smiled at Salter disdainfully. 'Look, if Glover says he never met Arliss, then I'm sure he didn't. I certainly have no recollection of seeing the two of them together. Besides, I thought we had already established he was with me at the time, giving me a lift home from the hospital.'

'Eventually, yes, but not at the first time of asking.' Salter looked at her squarely. 'Deliberately trying to incriminate someone in a crime is a criminal offence itself, Ms Boyd.' She didn't need to point out this was the second time the woman had tried to direct suspicion onto her ex-husband. Her expression told Boyd that the Saltmarsh police department wouldn't tolerate a third.

Boyd surveyed the ruins of the hide again and shook her head slowly. 'It's such a cowardly act, arson, isn't it? Non-confrontational. Unwilling to look your victim in the eye. The act of someone exactly like my ex-husband. I suppose that's why I thought of him. But the fact remains that somebody destroyed all this. If the police are convinced Glover was not involved, I suppose they need to start looking elsewhere.' She looked back towards the office building. Through the glass, they could see Paige Turner working away diligently at her desk. 'You're from around these parts, Sergeant. It's always amused me how outsiders pronounce the name of those cliffs down the coast.'

'You mean Happy's Burg, instead of Hayes-boro?' Salter remembered the suppressed grins at the station the first time Domenic Jejeune had said it.

'Unusual, don't you think, that somebody who's only just arrived here should be able to get it right first time? And have such a good knowledge of so many other aspects of local history.'

Like where the old library used to be, thought Salter. And just like that, as quickly as her ex-husband had been eliminated as a suspect in Arliss Dyer's death, the woman had managed to conjure up another one. Boyd stared at the blackened ruins of the hide again. 'Of course, on reflection, I see now that it's unlikely to have been Glover who did this. He simply lacks the sort of commitment you'd need to act on anything, destructively or otherwise. Even when he speaks, it's all *quite* this, *rather* that. He's unwilling to take a stand one way or the other even in language. It's no wonder he's such an utter bloody disaster at relationships.'

Salter gave no sign that she wanted to discuss Glover Boyd any further. Or at least that was what she had intended. But Boyd had seen something, a flicker in her eyes, perhaps, a faint turning of the head. And she knew.

'Oh my God, you were one of them, weren't you?' She looked at Salter, who remained silent, trying to look the woman in the eye. 'Not recent, though was it? You're far too clever now to fall for his nonsense. No, he would have harvested you when you were young, when you still believed in things like true love and fairy-tale princes in striped shirts with jokey calling cards. Relationship on the rocks, was it? Just feeling a bit lonely and left out? Vulnerability, you see, Glover always knew how to spot that.' She looked at Salter coldly. 'I suppose I should feel something for you, pity, perhaps. After all, you were as much a victim of Glover as I was. You all were, his other women. But I have no sympathy for you. Glover was married and you all knew it. He never tried to hide that fact, ever. And you went along with it anyway. You all did.' She shook her head. 'So no, I don't feel sorry for any of you.' She turned her back on Salter and spoke over her shoulder as she limped away. 'If Inspector Jejeune has any more questions, I suggest he sends somebody else.'

As she made her way back up the incline, Salter reflected that she was not as stung by Boyd's remarks as she might have been. She understood the woman's anger towards her, and that helped. She had made a mistake, but she had known what she was doing. If she had regrets now, it was too late to do anything but learn from them. As a police officer, you saw a lot of people who had made bad choices. It was the way they conducted themselves afterwards that really mattered. What troubled her more was the way that Tori Boyd had been able to exorcise her relationship with her ex-husband so completely. Salter had seen the photographs: the galas, the parties, the gatherings. They had looked happy, genuinely pleased to be in each other's company. The coldness in Tori's voice now made it hard to believe she could ever have had any feelings for her ex-husband at all.

Could love be so utterly erased, she wondered? Wasn't there always some residue of the feelings a couple had once shared, as there was between Salter and her own ex? Wasn't that what added to the pain, the idea that there had once been something?

But if Tori Boyd's feelings for her ex-husband had disappeared completely, was the same true for him? Closure does not necessarily come from a signature on a form. If he truly believed the work here had caused the breakup of his marriage, perhaps he *was* capable of trying to destroy the place, despite what his ex-wife believed. He couldn't have done it on his own, though, not with the alibi he had. He would have needed an accomplice. But then, thought Salter bitterly, Glover Boyd had always had accomplices, hadn't he? Once upon a time, she had been one of them.

36

If the rising waves and gusting winds of Jejeune's last video call had been the storm's overture, the conditions now suggested it had raised the curtain on its performance. Billowing sheets of spray swept in and cascaded onto the ship's deck. The fierce winds whipped and tore at the tarpaulins covering the mechanical equipment, the manic, frantic flapping adding its own noise to the din. Behind Gaya, an unbroken blanket of malevolent grey cloud cover pressed down, trapping the ship between the low sky and the dark, seething water.

'I don't think it's safe for you to be out there in those conditions,' called Jejeune over the noise of the storm. 'You should go back inside. We can do this later, when the worst has passed.'

'You are a kind man, Inspector, but there is no need to be concerned.' Gaya smiled. 'I am told my son is not a suspect in the death of that man any more. He has an alibi.' She nodded slowly. 'Glover always has an alibi. This man who died, he was your friend, I understand.'

'Yes, he was.'

'Then I am sorry for your loss.'

Jejeune acknowledged the comment with a tilt of his head. 'I have a question about the access to the communications systems, Ms Monde.'

But she didn't seem to hear him over the roaring of the wind. 'Yesterday a bird tracked us for a long time. I didn't see it flap its wings once. It was remarkable, the way it floated across the surface of the ocean, suspended between the two worlds of the sea and the sky. The captain said based on our position, it was likely an Atlantic Petrel.'

Jejeune nodded. Near Tristan da Cunha, it was possible. But there would be no birds following the ship in these conditions. The Wilson's Storm Petrels that had flittered around the bows in the Antarctic waters, the Cape Petrel that had painted its silhouette against the greying storm clouds, the Atlantic Petrel that had delivered it final portents yesterday; they had all abandoned the *Oceanite* now and left it to its fate.

'The personal communications from the base, Ms Monde, I'm assuming there were set times, when other traffic was unlikely to place a demand on the system.' He saw Gaya lean forward to hear him and raised his voice over the noise of the winds on deck. 'Who would have been in charge of monitoring access to the network?'

Gaya nodded and smiled to herself, as if Jejeune's inquiry brought her some kind of satisfaction. 'Lexi Marshall. Battery power is vital down there. It may be needed for an emergency message or a signal beacon, so she was under my strict orders to observe time limits on personal usage.'

The ship lurched under the force of a great heaving swell and Gaya staggered backwards, grabbing at the ship's rail with her free hand as she fought for her balance. It was a moment before she righted herself and drew the iPad up to her face again.

'*I will not live to see the storm petrels return,*' said Jejeune. 'I don't believe Alex Kasabian was responsible for that blog posting, Ms Monde. I think someone else posted it from his account. A personal account must be one of the few places at the base a person can enjoy some privacy. It is hard to believe Alex Kasabian would have shared his password with anyone.'

Gaya nodded her head. 'I agree.'

'But it would still have been accessible to certain people. Someone who set up the log-in protocols, or with administrator privileges. Who would that be, Ms Monde?'

A giant slab of grey water pounded against the sides of the ship with juddering force. Behind Gaya the rigging ropes thrummed in the constant winds and, somewhere offscreen, the manic flapping of material kept up its incessant rattle. 'Anyone in senior administration at the Institute would have access to retrieve this data,' said Gaya, raising her voice over the noise.

'And at the base?'

'Only Lexi Marshall. And myself.'

The conservatory seemed unnaturally quiet amidst all the turmoil onscreen. Towering waves were crashing down upon the churning seas like collapsing mountains. The ship was climbing great walls of glassy green water before cresting through the white foam and cascading down the far side. 'I wonder if you should go inside, Ms Monde. The conditions are not safe out there.'

The ship seemed to twist as the torsion of a wave caught it and the vessel's metal sides groaned in protest. Jejeune heard a tortured screech somewhere in the background and Gaya turned her head sharply at the sound. Urgent shouts filled the air and there was the heavy pounding of running feet on the deck.

'Some cargo has broken loose,' said Gaya evenly. 'A skid loaded with machinery is sliding around the deck. The crew is trying to secure it.' She turned away from the screen to watch the operation. There was another ear-piercing shriek and

Jejeune heard more agitated calls. He could understand the crew's concern. The ship with its rotund icebreaker hull was no sleek frigate capable of slicing through these walls of water. It would roll and lurch even in moderate seas. If the load wasn't secured, all that heavy equipment sliding around could cause the ship to pitch violently. Or worse.

Gaya took her gaze out over the roiling seas and then into the camera once again. 'I am told the recovery team has managed to bring Alex's body back to base,' she said. 'You will receive the video and the inventory of Alex's possessions within twenty-four hours.'

Jejeune nodded. If it crossed his mind to wonder why Bellaire had not informed him directly, he didn't let it show. The shouting behind Gaya had stopped now. It meant the cargo had been secured once more. Despite the conditions, the lashing spray, the fierce winds, the crew had done what they had to do. They'd had no choice. 'The reports from the other team members,' said Jejeune, 'they confirm your own accounts. About everything: the missing radio, the snow-mobile suit carried by Scott Della, the arrangements for the 300-Club event.'

'These things are all true,' she said. 'Tell me, Inspector, once you have received the video and the inventory, do you think you will have your answers?'

'Yes, I believe I will.'

She nodded her head thoughtfully. 'Good,' she said slowly. 'Then there will be no more empty places for you, no more darkness.' She gave a strange smile, as if some kind of safe harbour had been reached, a sanctuary against some inner storm. 'This has been my hope from the beginning. That someone would understand what happened out there.'

A wave crested the side of the boat intact and slammed onto the deck, as if it had been poured from a bucket. Gaya rocked on her feet and a panoramic view of the deck swirled into view as she spiralled backwards. Jejeune saw streams of free-running water cascading over the grey material of the deck.

'You cannot stay out there any longer, Gaya. The conditions are becoming too dangerous.'

'The storms now seem so much more severe than they used to be.' She offered a wan smile. 'Perhaps these, too, will be mitigated by climate control measures.' She looked out at the heaving, foam-flecked seas. 'I miss Antarctica. It held a peace for me that I have not known since we left. We spoke of a poem, Inspector, before. "These". You must take the time to read it. It explains so many of the mysteries of Antarctica: *"an empty, windswept place/ without sun, stars or moon".'*

There were tears on her cheeks when she turned back to the camera, but they weren't for the poetry, Jejeune knew. 'I cannot stop thinking about the final moments of Alex's life, *the* final moment, when the heart inside him stopped beating for the last time. One last heartbeat and then... no more. There are such small margins between life and death, aren't there, Inspector? It is true of our planet, too. Entire island populations could lose their existence to a quarter-of-a-degree increase in global temperatures. How awful to have to exist on such a razor's edge, and to know your continued existence relies on the wisdom and benevolence of a stranger like Julien Bellaire in some far distant land.'

The noise of crashing waves swirled into the wind in a roar that threatened to drown out the audio. A fresh assault of wind-driven spray splattered all around Gaya, matting her hair to her scalp and leaving dark tails of hair snaking over her forehead.

'You need to go back inside, Gaya. It's no longer safe for you to be out there. We can pick this up again once the ship is on the other side of the storm.'

'Is there such a place, Inspector? I wonder. It seems to me on the far side of a storm there is always another one waiting. Do not worry about me. You will have your answers. And then, everything will be fine.'

The explosion of another huge wave against the ship's side sent a white mist of spray over the deck. Whether it was this that severed the connection so abruptly, or simply Gaya's own actions, the feed went dead before Jejeune was able to say goodbye.

37

Paige Turner unquestionably looked at home behind the bar of the Board Room. She had an easy assurance about her that translated into an unflappable affability. She would handle expressions of undying love from affection- ate drunks and the brusque impatience of business lunch A-types with the same indulgent courtesy that the best bar- tenders brought to the role. So quite why the appearance of Danny Maik should bring such a flicker of concern to her face was unclear. 'Sergeant, hey, great. I mean, nice to see you. All better now?'

Maik confirmed that he was. He declined Turner's offer of a drink. 'I wouldn't mind a chat, though. Outside?'

Turner looked around for her manager, but he was nowhere in sight. 'My break's not for a while yet. I've only just come on. Can we talk here?'

'Paula,' said Danny. 'That was the girl the nurse was thinking of. You remember? At the hospital, the one who thought she recognised you? Sergeant Salter mentioned it. Paula was the name of the girl you reminded the nurse of. Paula Turner.'

Paige Turner surveyed the room of empty tables. 'Five minutes,' she said.

They sat at a small table in the corner of the beer garden, under an evening sky fading to lilac. In the distance, Danny could see the low, open spread of the marsh at Canon's Cross, glinting faintly as the dying light caught its pools of surface water. It was no great distance for someone accustomed to walking these fields. Even someone without the gift of sight. But it was an even shorter trip by bike.

Paige Turner sat opposite him, slowly rotating the base of her wine glass with her fingertips. At least a couple of the five minutes had already passed, but neither of them had spoken. Danny had the impression that once she started, though, the time limit might prove flexible.

'I thought it was clever, you know, the name,' said Turner finally. 'All symbolic and whatnot. Part of the makeover. Leave here at fifteen as Paula Turner: one more runaway from a group home, unmissed, unloved. Come back as a happy, confident woman with no baggage: Paige Turner. Page Turned.'

A lot of Paige Turner's earlier assurance had disappeared. In its place was hesitancy, reluctance. But at the same time, Maik sensed in her a need to explain things. He would wait. He had learned a lot over his time as a police officer. Lesson one was if somebody wanted to talk, you gave them as long as they needed.

'It wasn't malicious. At least, not at first. Me and a couple of other girls, townies, a bit older than me. We left our clothes in the hide and went skinny-dipping. When we got out, they grabbed my clothes, shoved me in the hide and locked it. I'm sure they didn't mean for me to be in there all night. Perhaps something prevented them from coming back.' She shrugged. 'I never found out,' she said simply.

The memories had taken her back there now, to the time, to the place. She stared at the tabletop with unseeing eyes. 'It was cold, I remember that. There were lots of spiders, and creepy-crawlies, and then, when it got dark, the rats came out.' Her resolve seemed on the edge of deserting her. She reached out and touched the edge of the table with her fingertips. 'Still to this day have a bit of a problem with dark, confined spaces. The Taoism helped with the other stuff, though.'

Maik's silence offered her a safe place for her feelings, a sanctuary where she could unburden herself. She accepted it, moving towards his calmness tentatively. 'It was already light when Arliss lifted the latch on the hide. I hadn't slept a wink. I just sat there huddled in the corner, looking at him, this shabby old bloke, standing in the doorway with a blanket wrapped round his waist. He didn't come in at first. He just stood there asking who was inside. *I do know somebody's in here*, he said. And I could tell that he did.'

'Did you answer him?'

Turner shook her head. 'Not for a long time. He told me to please myself and just came in. He stood between me and the door and rolled himself a loose-leaf. I just sat there, all hunched up, terrified. And then, without turning his head or even looking up, he tells me matter-of-factly that he knows I'm naked. He says he can smell my skin.' She forced a brave smile that didn't really come off. 'As you can imagine, it wasn't the most reassuring comment I could have heard just then.'

For the second time, her composure seemed to desert her. She drew a feathery breath that left her unable to say anything for a few moments. Maik said nothing. If Turner failed to answer any of the questions he had, there would be time enough to ask them afterwards.

'I asked him not to hurt me. I pleaded with him. He just laughed. And that's when I lost it. I started crying. A really good one, five minutes at least. And all the time he just stood there, not speaking, not moving, not even turning his head in my direction.'

When Turner raised her head again, Maik noticed her eyes were glistening. But she wasn't going to let tears close the distance she'd managed to put between herself and that hide on that morning. If the sergeant could judge anything about this woman in the short time they had been together, it was that she would determine who, or what, controlled her now.

'When I was done with all my sobbing and pleading, I just sat there as quietly as I could. And that's when he came towards me. He started unwrapping the blanket from around his waist and held it out in front of him. "I believe you're going to need this," he said. And then he was gone.'

'He didn't hurt you?'

'He didn't even touch me. I was terrified to go outside in case he was waiting for me, but eventually I summoned up the courage and stepped out of the hide. He was nowhere to be seen. I made it as far as the road, barefoot with the blanket around me, before a squad car picked me up and took me to the hospital.'

Maik had been prepared to offer a wide range of responses once Turner had finished her account. Absent from them was relief that she'd received only kindness from Arliss Dyer. 'So you had no reason to want to harm him?'

'Harm him? God no. When I think about what could have happened in that hide, and all he did was give me just about the only possession he had. He was just a nice man with fantastic hearing who liked a drink.'

She had been trying for a flat, dispassionate delivery, but her voice caught as she spoke about him in the past tense. Maik watched carefully as she fought to recover her composure. Done properly, affection for a murder victim was an excellent way of suggesting your innocence. The trouble was, it wasn't always easy to distinguish between genuine emotion and a very good copy. The best deceivers were those who told their lies sincerely.

Danny didn't know this woman well, and he would have to spend a lot more time with her to be sure, but as far as he was concerned, the odds were favouring her at the moment. Just.

'You must have been surprised when he came in here,' he said. 'Did you tell him who you were?'

'I didn't need to. He recognised my voice as soon as I spoke.' She shook her head. 'I probably only said fifty words to him in that hide, and yet, out of all the voices he must have heard in the intervening time, his could still pick out mine. No wonder the birders were always banging on about what incredible hearing he had. We chatted now and then afterwards, but we rarely mentioned the hide after that first time. He said he was happy I had managed to get over it, I thanked him for his blanket, and we left it at that.'

'I take it you haven't told Tony, Constable Holland, about any of this, about Paula Turner, or how you knew Arliss Dyer?'

She gave her head a small shake. 'At the moment he thinks my only connection with Arliss is shoving drinks in front of him. When the time is right, though. I'll tell him. All of it.'

Maik had been around a few people who were facing a point where they would have to confess a secret to somebody they cared about. Few had conveyed this kind of faith that all would be well afterwards. But perhaps Tony Holland would forgive her for keeping her past from him. Perhaps now he had returned from the Met, all wise and mature, he too would understand that we all have secrets that we need to keep from the ones we love.

'Did Arliss Dyer ever tell you he felt somebody might want to harm him?' Maik asked. 'Or that he'd received a threat from anybody?'

Turner shook her head. 'He never mentioned anything, and he didn't act like it either. If I had to testify, I'd have to say he didn't seem to be aware that he was in any danger at all.'

Maik gave a slight smile at the mention of testimony. Paige Turner was bright enough to realise that he hadn't come all the way down here just for some background information. The problem was, when a witness realised they were giving evidence that might end up being used in a case, they sometimes became selective about what they were prepared to offer.

'I'm just wondering,' he said casually, 'you know, the way these things turn out sometimes, coincidences, small world and all that. Would Tori Boyd be one of the girls who locked you in the hide that night?'

'Tori?' Paige gave a delighted laugh. 'Those girls were only a couple of years older than me. They'd be about twenty-five now, twenty-six tops. Tori Boyd couldn't pass for twenty-six in a dark room wearing a mask.'

Another lead cauterised, he thought ruefully. Revenge against a person who had caused so much grief in the past was a motive Danny could have lived with for the fire at the Institute. But, once again, his inquiry had led to nothing. So many avenues, so many dead ends. This case was nothing but.

'I saw one of those girls in here recently,' said Paige, looking over her shoulder towards the pub. 'She was with her husband and another couple, laughing and joking, without a care in the world. She didn't recognise me, of course. I've changed quite a bit since then, but I don't think it would have mattered even if I'd introduced myself by name. I'm sure she has completely forgotten about the incident. That's the thing about cruelty, isn't it?' she said sadly. 'It only ever seems to leave a mark on the victims.' She took a deep shuddering breath and pulled herself together. 'Well, I suppose I should get back to my shift. I hope I've been of some help, Sergeant. There's really not anything else I can tell you.'

Maik stood up as she left, a frisson of old-fashioned courtesy from days gone by. But he didn't leave right away himself.

He stayed in the beer garden, watching the slow, inexorable approach of a soft late-summer evening. And thinking. There weren't that many motives to begin with in this case, and every time he asked a question, it seemed to eliminate one more. For all Shepherd's histrionics, they were undeniably missing DCI Jejeune's input on this case, but even he couldn't produce motives out of thin air. And that left Danny with only one option now. According to Sherlock Holmes, once you eliminate the impossible, whatever remains, no matter how improbable, must be the truth. In this case, it would have to be one of the most improbable things he had ever known. But in the absence of DCI Domenic Jejeune, thought Danny, who was he to argue with such an authority on matters?

38

Lindy had spent a long time in the bedroom, not because what she wore mattered particularly, but because she found she was enjoying the process of preparing for an evening out. It had been a while since she'd riffled through her wardrobe like this, dangled jewellery against her outfit, blown a lipstick kiss to herself in the mirror. She emerged looking stunning, and headed for the front door, reaching for a jacket from the coat rack.

Jejeune hung up his phone to speak to her before she left. 'Danny's home. It was an allergy to ficus plants.'

'Those weeping fig things you see in offices all the time?' said Lindy. 'They're all over the place. How could he be allergic to them and not know it?'

'Apparently it's quite a rare condition, but the reaction to prolonged exposure can be very severe. Just to be on the safe side, they're getting rid of all the plants at the station permanently.' He smiled. 'Danny says he doubts Colleen Shepherd will even allow green tea in there any more. They're looking for someone to take them off their hands.' He paused. 'They were wondering about the conservatory.'

'It's my project room, Dom,' protested Lindy.

'You don't have any projects.'

'I'm getting some.' She shrugged on her jacket. 'Anyway, we can talk about it later. I'm off for drinks with a couple of the girls from the mag. A bit of a catch-up. We haven't seen each other in person for ages. You can order in, if you like, and I'll nuke it when I get home.'

'Okay.'

He tried a smile to tell her that he was no longer worried about her going out alone, but it didn't really come off. She stopped in the doorway and came back into the room. 'I still think about it too, Dom,' she said, approaching him and taking his hands in hers. 'Of course, I do.' She paused and took a small breath. 'A man died and I was there. I saw it happen. There was other bad stuff, too. Plenty of it. But Ray Hayes can't control my life because of what happened in that house. I won't allow that. I own my life, not anybody else. Me. And I have chosen to be.'

'To be?'

'As opposed to "not to be".' She let go of his hands and smiled. 'It's from Shakespeare. You remember, we talked about him? Popular English writer from a while back? "To be, or not to be, that is the question." Hamlet is talking about topping himself, but there are many ways not to be. You just let your fears control you, take over your life. You stop going out, stop interacting with people.' She paused. 'You just stop *being*.' She shook her head firmly. 'Not me.'

'"To be or not to be",' quoted Jejeune. 'Sounds like two questions to me. And you're saying this guy made a living as a writer?'

Everything was fine, he was telling her with his weak joke. He was settled now, reassured. And she should go out and have a good time with her friends, and leave her unworried boyfriend at home. Lindy was right. Though he remained convinced Ray Hayes would eventually resurface in their lives at some point, every day between now and then that he spent fearing it was a day with this vibrant, beautiful woman that he would lose to Hayes. That couldn't be allowed to happen. Besides, he had troubles much closer to hand to deal with just at the moment. And now he had the silence of the empty house to use as a sounding board for them. He cued the recently arrived video on his computer screen and settled in to watch it one more time.

Jejeune was outside when Lindy returned home, staring at the thunderclouds rolling in from the sea. Great billowing masses of bruised cotton were stacking up over the inlet; a prelude to the rainstorm they were about to unleash.

'Looks like I got back just in time,' said Lindy, coming to stand at his shoulder. 'This is going to be a good one.' As if in answer, a sudden gust of wind tore at the treetops on the far bank, setting them shivering. 'I had fun, by the way, in case you were wondering. I still can't get over how good it feels to be able to go out again, to talk to people. I really did miss it.'

Jejeune smiled, but his mind was elsewhere. Lindy recognised the quiet intensity in him. He was searching for something that was hovering just out of reach, waiting until it finally drifted close enough for him to grasp it. Except perhaps this time, this elusive piece, whatever it was, might not be coming. She raised herself onto her toes and kissed him on the cheek. 'Don't be too hard on yourself, Dom. No evidence, no witnesses, no access to the crime scene, even. You've done brilliantly to even get this far.'

'Yes, I have, haven't I?' said Jejeune thoughtfully. He turned towards her and shook his head slowly, the dark clouds like a purple halo behind him. 'Nobody should be able to do this well with a crime scene ten thousand miles away. As you point out, there's been no forensics, no access to any evidence, no witnesses. And yet here I am, coming up with answers, uncovering secrets, barely even missing a beat. Let's face it,' he said, 'I've made progress any other detective on a case like this could only dream of.'

Lindy looked at him. 'Steady on, Dom. It is my job to keep you humble, remember? Let's just say you've been less rubbish on this one than you usually are.' She stared out over the inlet and the answer rose to her from the depths of the dark waters. 'Oh my God, you think somebody's deliberately been leading you along?'

He nodded. 'From the very beginning. I've been given answers to questions I didn't ask, access to private worlds I would have never known about. The directive to the team from the start was to give me complete accounts of their rec-ollections. They were to leave nothing out, change nothing, protect no one. It was the perfect way to make sure I got any information they needed to give me.'

'In order to lead you exactly where they wanted you to go?'

Jejeune nodded again. The winds came up, riffling the sur-face of the water in the cove, driving the first black waves up against the rocks along the shoreline. The sky had darkened unnaturally as the cloud cover gathered and the temperature seemed to have dropped a degree or two. Lindy tugged her jacket more closely around her. 'We should go in.'

But Jejeune made no move. He continued to stare out at the building storm, as if somewhere in the midst of the tur-bulent, menacing air masses might lie the answer to the final question. *Why?* He had it all now; the radio, the snowsuit, the blog account, even the 300-Club event. But he did not know why. He did not know the reason Alex Kasabian had died. All he knew was, it was the key to everything.

'It seems a strange way to go about setting somebody up,' said Lindy, 'feeding you clues, letting you arrive at your own conclusions. If you ask me, it's a bit of a clumsy way to frame an innocent person.'

A distant growl of thunder rolled to them from out on the sea. Jejeune looked out towards it for a moment. He shook his head. 'Not innocent.'

'What? You mean you think this person is pointing you in the right direction?'

'I know they are.'

Lindy had a stare like a javelin when she chose to use it. She turned it on Domenic now. 'That video, it's the proof you needed, isn't it?'

He looked out over the water.

'Dom, you have to turn this over,' said Lindy. 'You know you do. You have to tell Shepherd right away. This person can make a statement. It would be the evidence they need. This person can actually identify the killer.'

'It is the killer.'

Lindy stared at him incredulously, unable to speak. Almost robotically, she held out a hand as Jejeune handed her his phone. The light from the screen lit her features with a pale glow as she raised it:

> *an empty, windswept place*
> *without sun, stars or moon.*

'It's from "These" by William Carlos Williams,' said Jejeune. 'Gaya Monde told me I should read it, that it would give me the answers I needed. On top of all the information she's given me, the poem is virtually a confession.'

Lindy stopped reading and looked up. 'You think Gaya Monde killed Alex Kasabian? And then led you to herself? Out of, what, guilt?'

Jejeune nodded. 'I think so, yes.'

Lindy regarded the swollen clouds. A sinister stillness hung in the air. She read the poem again, holding the phone in her hand for a moment afterwards, staring silently at the screen. She shook her head. 'I think it's more than a confession, Dom,' she said quietly, handing the phone back to him. 'If this woman's heart has plunged to a place without sun, stars or moon, the bleakness must be unbearable. I think this is Gaya Monde's suicide note.'

Domenic was silent for a long moment. A flash of lightning split the darkness and the crack of thunder echoed round the cove.

'We need to get inside, Dom,' said Lindy. But he remained, staring at the poem on his phone. 'I need a map,' he said. 'Let's go.'

The first tentative raindrops began splattering heavily onto the ground around them as they reached the door of the conservatory. By the time they made it inside, the clouds had opened up and torrential rain was pounding down violently over the inlet.

Jejeune moved over to his makeshift desk and flipped on a lamp against the unnatural darkness that had descended outside. From a drawer he unfurled a large shipping chart. On it, the route of the *Oceanite* was mapped by a jagged red line. He checked his watch and traced the route with his finger. Hastily drawing out his phone again, he googled an inquiry. Returning to the map, he stabbed at a point on it and dragged his finger back towards the red line. He looked up at Lindy.

'Come on. We have to get over to Julien Bellaire's house.'

Lindy looked outside, where sheets of rainwater were streaming down the conservatory window. Beyond them, the surface of the cove danced like a boiling cauldron under the relentless tattooing of the raindrops. 'Now?'

'He needs to get the captain to confine Gaya Monde to her quarters,' said Jejeune, grabbing the keys to the Beast from his desk. 'If you're right, and this is a suicide note, she's going to do it tonight.'

39

The road wound its way along the coastline, exposing the Beast to the worst of the storm's savage power. Swirling sheets of wind-driven rain swept in from the sea, machine-gunning against the coachwork of the Range Rover. Violent winds rocked the vehicle on its frame. But the Beast pushed on relentlessly, its wiper blades hurling heavy swatches of rainwater from the screen with every pass. Through the watery curtain, Jejeune caught sight of a light on the top of a hill, and he turned the Range Rover sharply onto a side track, gunning the motor to urge it to begin the steep climb towards Julien Bellaire's estate.

The bulk of the granite mansion shielded the forecourt from the worst of the storm-driven winds, but the relentless rain still hammered down with enough force to drench Lindy and Jejeune to the skin by the time they had reached the shelter of the portico. They squeezed in beside the rack of Bellaire's shiny bicycles, as pristine and dry as when Jejeune had last been here, and he rang the doorbell.

If Bellaire's unobtrusive personal assistant ever took time off from her duties, it wasn't during evening hours. She greeted them at the door and listened to Jejeune's breathless request as their clothing dripped onto the age-worn bricks.

The woman's eyes repeatedly flickered to Lindy, whose intense silence seemed only to reinforce the urgency of Domenic's request. They were left standing outside as she went to consult the master of the house, but it was not, as Lindy surmised, because the woman was trying to avoid pools of rainwater in the tiled lobby. The assistant had already realised the quickest way to deal with the situation was to have Bellaire come to them, rather than the reverse.

He emerged from the house moments later, dressed in a heavy yellow oilskin cape and carrying two more. He handed one each to Jejeune and Lindy as he spoke. 'The communications equipment is all located in the admin building at the Institute,' he shouted over the noise of the rain. 'Tori Boyd is the only one with access. She will meet us there.'

Jejeune held out his rain gear in a question. 'It will be faster on foot,' Bellaire told him. 'There is no road access to the facility from this side, only a bicycle track. Even if you drive around to the far side, the incline down from Tori's house will be impassable for a vehicle in these conditions.

He set out almost before Lindy and Jejeune had pulled on their rain gear. They caught him up, heads bowed, hoods grasped tightly around their faces, and the three of them trudged on into the onslaught of the storm. The drumming of the rain against their oilskins made conversation impossible, so they fell into single file, Lindy behind Bellaire and Jejeune bringing up the rear. Every time she turned to check on him, he saw the rain streaming down her face, plastering strands of hair to her forehead. Even above the noise of the storm, he could hear the savage flapping of the heavy oilskins as the winds snatched at them.

As they approached the incline, the last of the covering vegetation disappeared, exposing them to the full force of the storm sweeping in off the sea. Fierce winds buffeted them as they began to descend the narrow ridge, their footing made treacherous by channels of running water and slick, heavy mud. Jejeune saw Bellaire stumble and begin to slide dangerously towards the edge of the path. Lindy reached out a supporting arm, but he managed to right himself unaided, and resumed his ponderous descent, choosing a route further towards the centre of the slope.

As the incline widened out at the base, they were able to pick up their pace until they reached the burned-out hide. The slippery, rain-slickened rubble required care to navigate around, and the rain seemed to pummel them with even greater intensity during their slow progress. It kept up its relentless assault until they reached the front of the building, where they huddled together under the meagre shelter of the narrow glass awning.

The roar of the swirling winds was still loud enough to drown out a human voice, so Bellaire grabbed Jejeune's wet sleeve and pointed. A watery beam of light was descending towards them down the far incline: Tori Boyd. She fumbled in her pocket as she arrived and had keys at the ready as soon as she reached the front door. She held it open, fighting the wind gusts that would have torn it from her grasp, and dragged it shut behind her, flipping on the lights as she sealed them indoors.

In the narrow lobby, they all shrugged off their sodden rain gear and shook off the worst of the excess water. Boyd pointed to a suite of offices towards the back of the open-plan space. 'Through there. I'll get some paper towels.'

Bellaire led the way silently through the maze of desks and tables to an area with a long rosewood bench. A bank of three monitors sat side by side, with a computer tower for each on the floor below. Nearby, a server housed in a wire cage blinked its metronomic light at them. Through the rain-streaked rear windows of the offices, the darkness was complete, save for a single tiny beacon of light up at the top of the rise: Bellaire's estate. Though it had seemed almost an eternity in the conditions, it had probably taken them less than ten minutes to get here on foot. Jejeune had not been aware the man lived so close to the facilities.

Tori Boyd limped towards them and distributed a roll of paper towels to each. She set about establishing a link to the ship while the others dabbed the moisture from their faces and hair. One of the monitors burst into life with a snowy grey image and a hissing sound. A disjointed series of morphing soundbites gradually resolved into an audible track.

'...tain Jerrold. Is ...Institute?'

'It's Tori, Captain. Tori Boyd,' the woman told the image ghosting in and out of the scatter-grey background. 'Julien Bellaire is with me.'

Bellaire stepped into the line of the video camera. The image of the captain was resolving now, and they could see the stark, brightly lit background of the ship's bridge behind him.

'Captain, are Gaya Monde's whereabouts known at this time?'

'Everyone has been advised to remain in their quarters. We are riding out a strong storm. Force-ten winds, twelve-metre seas. It would be the safest place for her to be.'

'Can you have someone check and confirm immediately? If she is there, please make sure she is placed under guard. We have reason to believe she may be in danger. We will stay online while we await your report.'

The captain was a man of the seas. Navigating his ship through the height of a mid-Atlantic storm, the course of action was to obey orders, not question them. The explanations could come later. 'As you wish.' He moved from the video's line of sight and they heard him issue a crisp order to dispatch a junior officer to Gaya's quarters. He did not return into view and the four people in the Institute's headquarters stared at an image of an empty bridge, listening as the captain and his crew redoubled their efforts to combat the storm they were sailing through.

Lindy took advantage of the silence in the room to introduce herself, offering a newly dried hand to Bellaire and Boyd in turn.

'You're that journalist, aren't you?' asked Boyd. 'The one who won the award.'

'I'm *a* journalist.' Lindy was used to dealing with Domenic's public recognition by now, but had never quite come to terms with her own. But whether her name resonated with Boyd simply because of the award, or because of her earlier interest in the operations here at the Institute, was left unresolved as the captain appeared on camera again.

'No sign of her in her cabin or anywhere below decks,' he said, staring intently at the camera. 'My officers are making inquiries among the passengers and crew to find out when she was last seen, but I can't risk my men above decks until we're through the storm.'

Jejeune, whose own stare had remained locked on the screen throughout the captain's absence, leaned in to speak. But Bellaire was already there. 'Understood, Captain. We will wait here for news of your inquiries.'

There was a palpable air of tension to the waiting now. All joined Jejeune in staring at the unmoving view of the bridge on the screen, each locked in their own silence. Outside, the worst of the storm had rolled inland, leaving behind only a veil of light rain. Distant flickers of lightning still lit up the countryside, but the space between them and the rolling sounds of thunder that followed increased with every flash.

The silence in the room endured. The faint hiss of fluorescent lights overhead and the hum of the computer's fan filled the air, the only other sound coming from the light pattering of the rain on the glass dome above. No one moved. No one spoke. It was as if they were frozen in place, awaiting the appearance of a human onscreen again to free them. But when Captain Jerrold did appear, neither his expression nor his demeanour provided any kind of release.

'The last report of a sighting was at 21:15. Gaya was seen heading up on deck, towards the bow. A crew member advised her all passengers were confined below decks, but he says she just smiled at him – oddly, as he describes it now. She was still standing at the foot of the stairs when he left her.' He paused. 'A roped-off section to the bow appears to have been untied. It was secure when it was last checked at 21:10. It appears to have been undone deliberately.'

Tori Boyd seemed unable to take the news in. She reached a hand and placed it gently on the top of the monitor as if, without even this feeble support, she might not be able to stand.

'The timing, Mr Bellaire…' said the captain, fighting for an impassive delivery and not quite finding it. 'It would have been at the height of the storm, and we were heading directly into the teeth of it. Ten-metre waves were breaking over the bow at that time. Anyone who was out there unsecured…' He took a deep breath to compose himself. 'I'll institute a full search as soon as it's safe, but anyone who was above decks during that time would have been in extreme danger, especially at the bow.' He paused one last time and, perhaps in deference to the crystallising feed of the connection, perhaps in an effort to avoid any misunderstanding, or perhaps because he simply needed to say it, the captain added, 'I would not be hopeful of their chances.'

Silent tears escaped Boyd's welling eyes and trickled down her cheeks. 'Oh, Gaya! No. Please tell me you didn't. No.'

Lindy gathered an arm around her shoulder. Bellaire thanked the captain for his information, and leaned forward to terminate the connection. But just before he did so, Jejeune intervened. 'The location of your ship, the coordinates at which you believe Gaya Monde disappeared, it would be around latitude 24.18 and longitude −43.37?'

The captain's voice crackled a solemn confirmation through the rapidly fading connection and the call ended. The sudden disconnection and the sight of the blank screen seemed to sever the final strands of hope Tori Boyd had been holding on to, and she collapsed forward, supporting herself on the desk as her body heaved with her deep, shuddering cries. 'Poor Gaya,' she sobbed. 'Oh, my poor Gaya. What did you do?'

Lindy guided her gently to a seat and hunched down before her to whisper consolation.

'You knew the location?' Bellaire made no attempt to conceal his surprise. 'I think perhaps you have more to tell me, Inspector.' He looked at Tori Boyd, still bent forward, holding on to Lindy's arm, as if it might stop her from slipping away into her sorrow. 'But here is not the place.'

Bellaire led the way to the front door and stepped outside. Jejeune followed and the two men stood beneath the building's awning, watching the fine veil of rain falling over the compound. The passing storm had left a landscape glistening with wetness. A half-moon poked out shyly from behind a bank of trailing clouds, lighting the shining skins of the buoys in the bay.

Julien Bellaire took in the scene silently, deep in his own thoughts. Had he been expecting this, wondered Jejeune, or did he greet all human tragedy with this same sanguine response? Perhaps he was a man whose passions were reserved only for great schemes and visions.

'The location...' he said finally.

'Latitude 24.18, longitude −43.37,' recited Jejeune. 'It is at the North Atlantic's point of inaccessibility.'

'And this was a significant place for Gaya, you believe?'

'I think she wanted to experience what Alex Kasabian must have felt. To die alone and isolated, in a place as remote from the rest of humanity as possible.'

'As what? Penance? You believe she was responsible for Alex Kasabian's death?'

'She told me she was.'

'She confessed?'

'She told me she was the person who approved the 300-Club event. She also confirmed she had access to the supply room, where she could have replaced a radio after Amy Della had completed an inventory the morning after Kasabian died. And she controlled the server information required to retrieve passwords. Whoever killed Alex Kasabian relied on each of these elements. Only Gaya Monde had access to them all.'

Bellaire nodded slowly. 'For someone of Gaya's moral code, there could be only one way to properly atone for taking the life of another human being. She would not have wanted to spend her life in prison. This would not have been punishment enough.' He looked out over the bay. The buoys were rolling gently on the calmer waters. From moored boats that were not visible to him, Jejeune heard the clanking of the lanyards over the quiet winds. 'But she did not tell you why she killed him, did she, Inspector? This secret, I think she has taken with her.'

Jejeune followed Bellaire's look out towards the buoys. 'I'm told the preferred route for ships returning from Antarctica to the Atlantic is to go up the west side of South America and through the Panama Canal. Even if you choose to come back through the South Atlantic, hugging the western coast of Africa for as long as possible would protect a ship from the worst of the storms. Your ship, though, the *Oceanite*, the *Storm Petrel*,' emphasised Jejeune, 'is following a route right through the middle of those rough Atlantic waters.'

Bellaire turned sharply to look at Jejeune. There was a momentary anger in his eyes. He spoke slowly and without emotion. Perhaps he was trying for the same tone that he had used in their previous meetings, but there was a cold detachment to his words that prevented anything else from coming through. 'You know, it has been said that it is easier to dethrone a king than to bring down a billionaire. I told you before I didn't consider you an enemy, Inspector Jejeune. That still holds true. But perhaps we are to become adversaries.' He tilted his head slightly. 'I very much hope we do not. I can assure you, it is not a contest I would lose.' He looked back at the building. 'We should go inside. I believe Tori will be in need of my support now.'

40

Outside the window behind Colleen Shepherd's desk, the high, blue Norfolk sky bore only the faintest paintbrush strokes of white cloud. It was not a sky that promised thunderclouds. Those came from DCS Shepherd's expression, as she glowered at the man standing on the other side of her desk.

'What in God's name did you think you were playing at? You went to the offices of the Institute? Where you met Julien Bellaire? And we now we find out that, all this time, the woman you've been talking to is the mother of someone we've actively considered in this investigation? She threw her hands up in exasperation. 'How could you not see a connection?'

'I was never formally advised that Glover Boyd was a person of interest in the Arliss Dyer case,' said Jejeune reasonably.

'Nor should you have been. Open cases are supposed to be none of your bloody business.'

It didn't help Shepherd's mood to realise that somehow, Jejeune might have a point. Like most administrators, she preferred it when a subordinate's transgressions were black and white. With Domenic Jejeune, everything always seemed to stray into the grey areas. That the uncertainty usually seemed to play out in the man's favour rarely did anything to improve her disposition, either. But she was on firmer footing with Jejeune's errant conduct than with his justifiable ignorance.

'Then let's talk about this business of having Lindy go around and look into the data filed by the Bellaire Institute. *A local investigative journalist,* I believe was Sergeant Salter's phrase. Good God, Domenic, do you think we're really all that stupid? Do you realise what you've done here? You may very well have compromised an active murder investigation. For someone as bright as you, there is the occasional lapse, isn't there? I mean, am I the only one here who is concerned about your career?'

Her ire spent, Shepherd began shuffling through her papers with exaggerated care. Jejeune was put in mind of the scene when a bomb tech examined the site of an explosion. It was an exchange they'd had a thousand times and it always ended up the same way, Jejeune silent and Shepherd frustrated. But this time, he knew he had to give her more, something he wasn't really ready to part with just yet.

'I believe Arliss Dyer's death is somehow connected to me.'

She looked at him over the top of her steel-rimmed glasses. 'Is this you wanting a connection? Or is it based on sound reasoning?'

Was it? Enough to bring everyone along to the point where they would accept his deductions? No, he was still just too far away. But he had to offer something, because if he exasperated his DCS to the point where she decided protecting his career was no longer worth the effort, he would lose any chance he had of finally getting the answers he needed.

'I told Sergeant Maik I hadn't received a call from Arliss Dyer. I would have recognised the number. I gave Arliss that phone. But just to be sure, I contacted my provider and requested a list of the calls to my phone that day. There were none from Arliss, but there was one on there from a number I didn't recognise. Tori Boyd's.'

Shepherd stared at him incredulously. 'Well, of course the call came from Boyd's phone. Did no one mention that to you?' She threw up her hands in despair. 'God Almighty, who's running things out there, the Muppets? So you're now telling me you did receive a voicemail message from Dyer that day, after all?'

Jejeune shook his head. 'There was no message. Only dead air. Unfamiliar number, no sound.' He shrugged. 'I deleted it as soon I checked it.' He looked at her. 'I think now that Tori Boyd dialled my number, and then muted the phone before she handed it over to Arliss. She got lucky with it going to voicemail. I'm convinced if I'd have answered, she would have found some other way to abort the call.'

'Why on earth would she want to do that?'

'She suspected Arliss was going to tell me something she didn't want me to hear.'

'There was nothing in that message, Domenic. I can't show you a transcript of the witness interviews, for obvious reasons, but I can assure you the message contained nothing you might have considered actionable information, nothing at all. Arliss Dyer only seemed concerned you would think he was mistaken about what he'd heard.'

'Mistaken? Why would he think that?' Jejeune's mind took him back to the last time he had seen Dyer, in a sunlit meadow with the long, slanting shadows of afternoon laying deep pockets of cover. The other man had turned his head slightly at the inspector's approach.

'No sign of that Curlew Sandpiper, Inspector?' he asked.

Jejeune remembered making an effort to keep the disappointment from his voice. 'No. As far as I'm aware, nobody has found it yet. Few people doubt you were correct, though.'

Arliss had shrugged. 'In flight. A long way up,' he had said simply. 'But I can recall what I heard.'

Shepherd's voice brought him back to the present. 'No more, Domenic. You're off this as of now. Do you understand? No more Alex Kasabian, no more Arliss Dyer, no more Julien Bellaire. Stop by and give everything you have to the team on your way out. Then go home, see out the rest of your suspension, and pray this doesn't go any higher.'

She looked out through her window to the offices beyond before turning to him again. As was often the case, Shepherd's look carried more kindness than her voice had done. 'I understand he was your friend, Domenic. And I can't stop you giving the situation some serious thought in your free time. But if you come up with anything on Arliss Dyer's death, you have to let them handle it. They're a good crew and they think the world of you, but they won't stand for you stepping all over their murder investigation just because you think you could do better.'

It was an unfair assessment of his motives and they both knew it. But he let it stand for now. The message would have been the same regardless of his true objectives. In reality, it was hardly surprising she was unwilling for him to get involved any further. Alex Kasabian, Arliss Dyer, Julien Bellaire: there was only one connecting factor. And it was him.

Jejeune stopped by the detective's offices on his way out. They had retained the perspex dividers installed during the pandemic, giving the open-plan office the appearance of a series of cubicles. Danny's was at the far end. He looked up from his desk at the DCI's entrance and gave a wry grin. 'Come to hand yourself in?'

'I may have exceeded the speed limit the other night. I was in a hurry getting to Julien Bellaire's house.'

Maik head-tilted in the direction of Colleen Shepherd's office. 'We heard. Still, first offence. At least it wasn't a rare bird you were after.' He became serious. 'Your friend, sir.'

Jejeune acknowledged the comment with a look.

Salter realised it was the first time they'd met since the body in the Canon's Cross hide had been officially confirmed as Arliss Dyer. Danny hadn't offered his condolences, but the moment between them had been as eloquent as the most heartfelt of exchanges. The connection between the two men had only strengthened over Danny's shared experiences with Lindy in the Ray Hayes case, Salter knew. Bonds between these two men now would hold fast whatever the strains put on them. A few weeks of suspension would be nothing.

She nodded towards Shepherd's office. 'Sorry about that, sir.' They had all been summoned to an unhappy DCS Shepherd's office at one time or another, and there was a tacit understanding when you re-emerged; everyone else went about their business as if they had not heard the raised voices behind her door. But some comments couldn't be left unchallenged. 'I don't think that was right. To assume Lindy is just doing your bidding like that, asking your questions for you. It's insulting. She's an independent woman, not your wind-up toy. Plus, she's a journalist, she has every right to try to find out what is going on up at the Bellaire Institute. These hide fires, they're a legitimate news story.'

Any response Jejeune might have had was cut off by the sight of a lab tech popping his head round the door. At the sight of Salter, he seemed to hesitate, offering her an awkward grin before turning to Maik. 'Erm... any time you like for that... thing, Sarge.'

Salter turned to him quizzically as the tech ducked out of view. 'I asked him if he could help out with Max's DNA sample.' Maik held up his hands defensively. 'He needs it by the morning. I know how busy you've been, that's all.'

Jejeune saw Salter's features tighten slightly, but she fought back her rising anger as her eyes flickered in the departed tech's direction. 'It's fine, Danny. I'll do it tonight. No need to trouble anybody else with it.' She fixed on a strained smile and turned to Jejeune, indicating the newly painted walls. 'What do you think?'

Jejeune nodded non-committally. As far as he was concerned, the first rule of decorating was the same as for conservation: do no harm. In this, he'd be prepared to concede the new paint job had just about achieved its goal. 'I'd better be on my way,' he said tactfully. If the matter of Max's DNA collection was now behind Maik and Salter, the underlying issue might still require more discussion. 'The DCS wants me to hand over my notes, but I don't have them with me.' He looked at Maik. 'I'll give you a call. Perhaps we can meet up and I'll run through what I have.'

Maik returned his look. He understood: the words, the offer, and everything that lay beyond them. 'As you wish, sir. Just let me know the where and when. Oh, there was just one more thing. We lifted a lad for a series of vehicle break-ins and he was giving us a bit of lip about having outrun one of us earlier. Only, as far as I know, we have no record of a prior officer pursuit.'

Jejeune's smile suggested Danny might have been looking in the wrong place. Not that there would have been a record of a suspended-officer pursuit, either.

'Fair enough, then,' said Danny. 'I'll let you get on with your day. Unless there are any other offences you'd like us to take into consideration.'

'Not at this time,' said Jejeune with a faint smile.

Maik nodded. It was probably best, if you still had more offending to do.

The watching Salter marvelled once again at the unspoken connection between the two men. She knew she could not be the one to break it. And that was why, even before this exchange between them today, she had already known that she was going to have to be the one to leave Saltmarsh station.

41

Two inlets awaited Jejeune's glance out of the window on this overcast morning. The waters of the pale one trembled in the faint breeze, reflecting patches of the weak morning light that had already crept over the treetops. The dark one still hunkered under the shelter of the vegetation, awaiting the moment when the rising light would bring it to life. The only other movement in the cove was the Firecrest that had dropped in to explore the tops of the trees on the far bank. Jejeune watched the tiny bird through his bins as it fidgeted around busily. He drew his eyes away and looked around the conservatory. For the first time, Lindy didn't see joy in his gaze. Instead, as he scanned the empty space with its bare corners and unadorned half-walls, his eyes seemed to dim.

'I've been thinking,' said Lindy. 'I'd be okay with it, having an aviary in here. In fact, I think it would be nice, to walk out here in the morning and be greeted by a bunch of pretty little birds, all singing their hearts out. Let's face it, my projects, if I ever get around to starting any, aren't going to need any particular spot. I could do them anywhere. So...' she spread her arms out to encompass the room, 'all yours.'

Dominic stared out over the cove again. Beyond the window, the shaded side of the inlet crept inexorably towards the light. The Firecrest had flown away. During its entire stay it had explored an area probably no bigger than his desktop. But that had been its choice. 'Keeping birds in enclosures is necessary in some cases: research projects, captive breeding, even for education. But to keep birds in cages just for their beauty.' He shook his head. 'That can't be right.'

Lindy saw a shadow of sadness flicker across his features, and she knew this was not about Gouldian Finches, or any other kind of bird. 'You couldn't have saved her, Dom. Gaya Monde had probably made her decision even before she boarded that ship, possibly even before she had ever heard of you. Besides, she was half a world away when she killed herself. How could you have prevented that?'

'I could have had the head of station at Dumont d'Urville take her into custody.'

'Not unless you already knew that she was the one who had killed Kasabian.'

His silence made her look at him. She knew what his expression was telling her, but she couldn't bring herself to accept it. 'Seriously? It was less than two days into your investigation. Even for you that would be pretty remarkable. You're really telling me you knew then?'

He nodded sadly. 'Before that. When I saw the photographs of the site she sent to Julien Bellaire.'

'When was that, half an hour after you found out Kasabian was dead? How could you possibly have known then who did it?'

Jejeune looked out of the window. The waters of the cove were fully lit now. The erratic wind was creating a chequerboard of patterns on their surface: furrows, dimpled fields, smooth glassy patches. 'Severed,' he said. 'Gaya Monde told Bellaire in the video that the fuel line had been severed. That's why the snowmobile wouldn't start.'

'But that's true.'

'Yes, but when she came upon the body of Alex Kasabian, his hand was already frozen around the fuel line, with the damaged section inside his clenched fist. How did Gaya know it had been severed? It could have been spilt, or punctured, or corroded. But she said severed: cut in two, sliced cleanly.'

Lindy nodded thoughtfully. 'And since that wasn't evident from the photos she took, the only way she could have known is if she was the one who cut it.' In the silence that followed, the final piece slotted into place. 'And that video, the one of Kasabian's hand being unfurled after it thawed back at the base, that was the confirmation you needed. That was when you could see, finally, that Gaya Monde had described the cut correctly. The cut she couldn't see when the hand was still frozen.'

Domenic's look confirmed it. 'I shouldn't have waited for that video. I already knew. Even if I had asked the ship's captain to take her into protective custody earlier...'

'If she really wanted to take her own life, she would have found a way. You can't save those who don't want to be saved, Domenic. No one can. Your job, mine too, everybody's in fact, is to save those we can. But if she was going to commit suicide anyway, why lead you to her? In fact, why be so cryptic about everything in the first place? Why didn't she just confess to you? Or to the authorities in Dumont?'

'She couldn't. Nobody is going to believe a confession from somebody who is unwilling to reveal their motive. And she wasn't prepared to do that.' He looked at Lindy. 'All the while she was leading me to her guilt, she was trying to lead me away from the reason she'd done it. That's why she had to give me that trail of clues, to demonstrate to me that she had done it, that only she could have done it. It was the only way she could be sure I would believe her.'

'And yet, she was prepared to die without revealing why she killed Kasabian?'

He nodded. 'Imagine how important a motive must be if you're willing to go to those lengths to protect it.'

'The reputation of the project, you mean?'

Jejeune shook his head slowly. 'I don't think Gaya Monde would kill to protect a reputation. But she might to protect a person. She cared a great deal about her former daughter-in-law. This project was Tori Boyd's life's work. I think Gaya might have been willing to sacrifice herself to save that.'

Lindy gave the idea some thought. Gaya's decision was hard to understand out here in the anchored, rational world they inhabited. But in the solitude of that empty continent, all that space, all that silence, perhaps she had heard the whispers of different voices. 'But how would killing Alex Kasabian save Tori Boyd's work?'

'I think if Gaya Monde didn't do what Julien Bellaire wanted, he would have withdrawn his funding from the project.'

Lindy shook her head dubiously. 'I have to tell you, Dom, from all I've learned about him, he seems to be genuinely committed to fighting climate change. You really think Bellaire threatened to terminate the project?'

'A man with his money can always find a worthy cause. It wouldn't necessarily have to be this one.'

When all was said and done, money still was the ultimate influencer; but Lindy still wasn't convinced. 'I don't know, Dom, I can't believe he would walk away just like that. Besides what reason would he have for wanting Alex Kasabian dead in the first place?'

'I don't know,' admitted Jejeune. 'But it must have had something to do with those readings. A tech expert tells me fixing a satellite hack would be an easy task for a software guru like Bellaire. There is no need to go through an elaborate system of air-gapping and manual re-entry of data, not unless somebody wanted to have control over the readings being entered into the database.' He looked at her. 'You said if the readings didn't show any anomalies, you'd look into the monitoring equipment up at the Institute. Did you ever find out anything?'

Lindy shifted uneasily. 'I'm meeting somebody later on who might be able to help me with that.' With a bit of luck, she had managed to pass off her evasiveness as simply protecting a source, but it wouldn't hurt to change the subject anyway. 'You know, I have to say, Quentin Senior seemed to like my foreboding of petrels.'

'It does seem appropriate,' said Domenic. He didn't really feel like light-hearted conversation, but he knew Lindy deserved more than his self-indulgent regrets.

'I'm not sure that's always a requirement, though, is it?' said Lindy. 'I mean, there are some pretty eccentric ones out there.'

Jejeune inclined his head. 'True enough. You'd have to go a long way to beat capercaillie, for example.'

'A capercaillie of what?'

'Capercaillie is the bird,' explained Domenic. 'It's a large grouse. They're known for being particularly threatening towards humans that approach their breeding sites.'

'Threat—?' Lindy stopped herself. Sometimes it was better just not to ask. 'Do we see them here, these man-eating grouse?'

'No; in fact, it is entirely possible in the next few decades no one in the UK will be able to see them at all. They are still hanging on in Scotland, but every tract of forest that disappears sends them closer to extinction.'

'How sad,' said Lindy sincerely. 'Let's hope they can be saved. So what is the collective term for them, anyway, a mob?'

'No, that's Emus. It's a tok.'

'A tok? Is that even a real word?'

'It is,' confirmed Jejeune. 'It means a group of Capercaillies.'

Lindy covered her eyes with her hand. 'I blame myself,' she said, shaking her head. 'I have to remember, I'm dealing with birders.'

He smiled at her, but his heart was not really in it today. Gaya Monde was dead, and with her passing had gone the last chance for a prosecution in the Alex Kasabian case. A message alert chimed on his phone and he opened it to see an image of Arliss Dyer. It was an invitation to a memorial service, being organised by the local birding group. He stared at it for a long moment. Lindy recognised in his expression the same regret she had seen earlier.

'Come on, Dom. Even if you can convince yourself that you could have prevented Gaya Monde's death, not even you can hold yourself accountable for Arliss Dyer's.'

'Perhaps not, but I was the cause of it.' He kept his eyes on the photo. 'Did you ever wonder why Arliss was sleeping in a hide again the night he died?'

'Oh, Dom, you can't go there. You never got the call.'

Jejeune continued as if he hadn't heard her. 'He believed he had reported the threat to me. He trusted me to act on it.' He looked up at her. 'I was supposed to make it safe for him to sleep in hides again, Lindy. And I didn't. And that cost Arliss his life.'

Lindy flapped her arms by her sides in exasperation. 'That's just bloody ridiculous, Domenic. Arliss Dyer was lured to that hide by a phone call and given a free bottle of single malt to render him unconscious when he got there. That's what happened, and that was nothing to do with you.'

But Lindy knew remorse like this rarely responded to reason. Dyer had been Domenic's friend. He had known the man was in danger, and he had tried to protect him. He had put locks on the hides. He had posted notes. But none of that had been enough. And now, rightly or wrongly, Domenic was carrying that failure with him. She sighed sadly. She knew the only way he was going to relieve himself of his burden was by solving Arliss Dyer's murder. The problem was, as Colleen Shepherd had made dangerously clear, the moment he began looking into it, Domenic's career would be over.

42

Lindy lifted herself onto a stool at the bar of the Board Room. Paige Turner approached as soon as she sat down, and leaned easily on the bar opposite her. She reached a hand across to touch Lindy's. 'I've asked Tony to join us. I hope you don't mind. He would have been in here anyway. It would have been a bit awkward if we'd just left him and gone off for a chat on our own.'

Lindy hid her response behind a smile. Holland wasn't one of her favourite people, and the presence of a detective actively investigating the Arliss Dyer case wouldn't help her cause tonight. But Turner's point was unarguable. And she needed the woman to be as cooperative as possible.

She ordered a drink and Paige headed off down the bar. Lindy looked around. It was a quiet evening by most pubs' standards, but she sensed this place wouldn't often see the thronging crowds of other watering holes in the area anyway. Paige returned with Lindy's wine and looked over her head towards the door, where Holland had just entered. The constable joined them at the bar. Paige poured a beer and set it in front of him without being asked.

'So, not a bad place, eh?' he said as Turner moved off to serve a customer.

Lindy nodded and took a sip of her wine. 'Does Danny like it?'

Holland spent a moment looking at her. 'I think you can relax on that score,' he said. 'He's giving it a wide berth until they get some different beer in.' He held up his glass. 'He says the current stuff tastes like it's been regifted.'

Lindy looked puzzled. 'What's wrong with regifted beer?'

'I think he means after the original owner has already drunk it once,' said Holland flatly. He leaned towards her and lowered his voice slightly. 'Before all this kicks off, you should probably know I'm not on the case any more.'

Lindy raised her eyebrows in surprise. 'Any particular reason?'

Holland gave an enigmatic grin. 'I can't really say, I'm afraid. Nothing major, though.'

But Lindy knew better. The most common reason a detective was recused from an active case was because of a connection with somebody who was a person of interest. If that person was Paige Turner, things just weren't going very well at all for Lindy tonight.

'What sweet nothings are you whispering to her now?' asked Turner, returning to join them. 'Tony telling you how highly regarded he is at the station?'

'Me? I'm usually, what's that phrase, the thing they do with cheese?'

Lindy looked puzzled. 'You mean melt it?'

'Grate it,' said Turner. 'He means *persona non grata*.' She shook her head. 'I don't know which is more disturbing, the way his mind works, or the fact that I'm beginning to understand it.'

Lindy returned Paige's hand-pat from earlier. 'When I say I know what you mean, trust me, I do.'

Turner smiled. 'I understand you met my boss recently,' she said. 'Tori Boyd. What do you make of her? Only I think Tony is quite smitten.'

'You're the only one who's smited me,' he said gallantly before his expression clouded with doubt. 'Smote?' he asked Lindy.

'I really couldn't say, but whatever it is, it's not catching. Dom assures me he has no interest whatsoever in brilliant, drop-dead gorgeous women like that.'

Turner laughed out loud. 'Sounds like her ex felt the same way, judging from his antics when they were married. Still, we can only know what we are taught, can't we? Tori was saying his father left his mother when he was just a boy.'

'For a younger woman?' asked Holland.

'Do men generally leave their wives for older women in your experience, Constable?' asked Paige formally. She turned to Lindy. 'Honestly, the people they allow to carry warrant cards these days. It's no wonder you're non-grated at the station. Why don't you two head over to Chess Corner,' she said. 'It's a good spot for a quiet chat. I'll just let the gaffer know I'm taking a break and I'll join you.'

Holland grabbed the drinks and followed Lindy as she made a beeline for the table nestled in an alcove basking in the orange glow of the nearby fireplace. The chessboard tabletop was littered with the casualties of war, and Lindy began clearing them away into a box to give him room to put their glasses down.

'Never did get the hang of that game,' said Holland as they sat. 'I imagine the inspector'd be a dab hand at it though. Seems like the kind of thing that would be right up his alley.'

But Lindy knew better. The only opponent Domenic wanted to match wits with was the truth. For him, solving a case was never about gaining a victory, merely disentangling facts from the knots of lies and deception.

Turner joined them almost immediately. 'Not to be rude or anything,' she said, 'but I've only got about ten minutes, so we can jump right in if you like.' She turned to Tony. 'Lindy had asked me to look into the monitoring equipment on the buoys.' She addressed Lindy. 'In a nutshell, they're all perfectly accurate. I took random samples and checked them myself, and I also had them independently verified. They are all calibrated to hair's-breadth precision, and every one of them is functioning flawlessly. To be honest, I don't know how it would be possible to find a more sound set of operating equipment.'

But the reason for Tony Holland's recusal hadn't slipped Lindy's mind. She wasn't sure how, but perhaps a report like this might just suit Paige Turner's purposes. 'I wonder, did you let Tori Boyd know about my request?'

Turner nodded. 'She told me to provide you with whatever information you wanted.' She looked at the other woman frankly. 'She wasn't trying to hide anything, Lindy. She even invited you up to have a look around yourself if you wanted to.' Turner shook her head. 'But you won't find anything I didn't, I can assure you. I did a pretty thorough job. I wanted to. For Arliss's sake.'

Lindy nodded. 'You knew him, didn't you? And you were there when he made that call to Dom.'

Turner looked at Holland. 'Wouldn't this be sailing a bit close to the wind for casual conversation?' There was no hint of unease in Turner's carefree tone, but perhaps there was something less playful in her smile.

'I think Lindy is entitled to know what was said in the call,' said Holland, 'since the inspector is claiming not to have heard it.' He inclined his head. 'There's an argument to be made, anyway.'

'Okay, just so we're legal.' Turner had not quite succeeded in turning it into the joke she had intended. 'I heard the entire thing, start to finish. And I am absolutely sure about what Arliss said, about the hides all being in alignment, about that being the reason his hide was spared that night, about being concerned that the next target was one of the Brackets. If there's any suggestion that I was mistaken, or perhaps I might like to say I was—'

Holland laid his hand on the woman's arm. 'That's not what this is, Paige,' he said quietly. The gesture and the sincerity of his statement took Lindy by surprise. She was used to attention from men and skilled at detecting differing levels of intent. The way Holland had walked his eyes over her at the bar straddled the line between polite interest and something more. And yet he was undoubtedly making an effort here. It was in the small things: solicitously sliding his girlfriend's glass within reach, picking up her bag from the floor for her, an occasional gentle touch of her shoulder.

'Dom thinks somebody didn't want him hearing what Arliss Dyer had to say.'

Paige began to shake her head, but stopped in mid-gesture. 'The only odd bit about the entire message was right at the end. *I can recall what I heard*. He said it twice, as if he didn't want the inspector to think he might be mistaken about it.'

Lindy nodded thoughtfully.

'Can I just ask,' said Holland, going for a casual tone that remained a good way out of reach, 'does the DCI think Julien Bellaire may have anything to do with all this?'

Lindy was silent. But her look told him everything.

'How sure is he?' he asked.

'I think it's one of those situations where Dom – the DCI – knows, but he just can't prove it.'

Holland nodded. Intuition, he might call it with others. But with Jejeune, it always seemed a bit more. When he brought up a possibility, he did it with a certainty that suggested he had already considered all the possible alternatives you could come up with, and probably a few more besides. Holland drew in a breath. 'Only, over their port and walnuts at the golf club, Bellaire has been floating the idea with the chief constable that an officer who disobeys the terms of a suspension might be exhibiting a pattern of prior bad acts. He has been wondering aloud if that could lead to reviews of past cases, to see if there were any unsafe convictions.'

'Sounds like Dom might have touched a nerve,' said Lindy.

Holland nodded in agreement. 'Of course, Bellaire will never get away with forcing a review of all of the DCI's past cases. But everybody is still a bit jittery since Ray Hayes got out on an unsafe, and the fact that the brass at that level are even listening to him suggests what kind of juice the man's got.' He fixed Lindy with a stare, to make sure she was getting the message. 'It's the kind that could end a police officer's career. This here tonight, this is just a casual chat between friends,' he smiled at Lindy, 'new friends. But I don't think it would do any of us any good to go beyond it. If the DCI gambled on this and lost, Colleen Shepherd wouldn't be able to support him. Not with the weight of the suspension hanging over his head. She'd have to stand back and let them have at him.'

An uncomfortable lull settled over the table until Lindy broke it by tapping her palms against her thighs. 'I should be going,' she said, standing up. 'Thanks for this. Both of you.'

'I'll walk you out,' said Turner. She turned to Holland. 'You can stay and finish your beer. I'll be back later.'

As they got to the door, Turner leaned in confidentially. 'I'm not normally one to argue ends justifying means. As a journalist, I'm sure you've seen it lead down all kinds of slippery slopes, too.'

Lindy wasn't saying, but her look told Turner she was interested in seeing where this was going.

'But there are times when the outcome needs to be put first. I told Tony I wouldn't think any less of him if he was to give the inspector whatever he had on the case, if it was going to help solve Arliss's murder.' She paused. 'I mean, a mind like that, the DCI is usually going to be the smartest person in the room, isn't he?'

Lindy pulled a face. 'Yeah, well, sometimes they're very small rooms.'

Turner smiled but there was no mirth in it. 'I'm not sure where all this is heading between Tony and me. I'm prepared to find out, but if things don't work out, then maybe he slips back into his old ways: an endless round of quickies and meaningless one-nighters.' She paused. 'The thing is, when he was at Glover Boyd's, I think he saw how a life like that ends. All he talked about afterwards was Boyd's toys: his golf clubs and jigsaw puzzles and bicycle and photography equipment. All those things he'd tried to fill up those empty spaces with. I think Tony saw a vision of a future in the sad, lonely life of Glover Boyd, and it terrified him.' She shook her head. 'If he never does settle down, then perhaps the only thing standing between him and a future like that would be his job. He loves being a detective. He wouldn't sacrifice that for anything. I'm sorry.'

Lindy nodded. She understood. No matter how much you wanted to get to the truth, a career was too high a price to pay. It was a lesson she hoped Domenic might learn before it was too late.

43

Danny Maik considered his relationship with his DCS to be cordial enough, but a request for him to accompany her on a casual drive into the countryside wasn't something that had come up before. Like all good police officers, he'd learned to say nothing when he wasn't sure what was going on. And since Colleen Shepherd seemed to be locked in thoughts of her own, it made the drive out to wherever they were going a quiet one. Shepherd hadn't even asked the Jaguar's system to find some Motown for Danny. The scenery soon became familiar enough, but if he wondered why she had settled on this stretch of coast near Happisburgh for their outing, he didn't get the chance to ask.

'I've had to take Tony Holland off the Dyer case,' Shepherd announced suddenly.

Maik withdrew his gaze from the passing fields to look at his DCS. 'How did he take it?'

'He wasn't happy, obviously. But he only has himself to blame. In his haste to open up the suspect list to include people Dyer did know, he overlooked the fact that it has put Paige Turner even more squarely in the frame. She has no alibi for that night. Hers could just as easily have been the voice Dyer heard. She could have been Dyer's blackmail victim, if there was one, every bit as much as anyone else.'

Maik shook his head dubiously. 'I don't know, ma'am. When I interviewed her… unless she's very good, her grief over Dyer was genuine enough. She seems to wear her heart on her sleeve. I got the same impression when I first met her.'

Shepherd gave him a sideways look.

'Tony brought her in to the station to meet me when he first started seeing her.'

'He looks up to you, Danny. He needs your approval on so many levels. That's how it is for boys who grow up without a father figure around.'

And suddenly, he realised, they weren't talking about Tony Holland any more. Danny enjoyed the time he spent around Lauren's son, Max, but whether he was ready to assume the kind of role in the young boy's life that his DCS seemed to have in mind was a decision he had not yet made. He'd heard talk about relationships moving to other levels, but this was the first time he could say he truly understood the concept.

'Anyway,' said Shepherd, snapping him out of his thoughts. 'Given that we can't give Paige Turner a clean bill of health just yet, Tony had to be removed. I simply couldn't afford a situation where a personal relationship might compromise one of my officers' ability to do their job.'

If that was Shepherd's best effort at subtly introducing a topic, it was no wonder she had spent so long staring hard through the windscreen for inspiration. But Maik said nothing. It was a measure of how difficult this conversation was going to be that she had gone to the trouble of bringing him all the way out here. She would have somewhere specific in mind to get around to telling him what she wanted to say. He would wait patiently until she did. Which was not to say either of them were content to fill the rest of the journey with small talk. The trip settled back into silence again until she pulled the Jaguar into the car park. It was a place Danny recognised.

He had been here himself only a few days before, for a conversation with his DCI that was, in its way, every bit as difficult as the one he suspected he was about to have now.

They got out of the car and walked in silence to the edge of the cliffs, going out as far as safety would allow. They squinted their eyes against the low glare coming at them off the sea, but they did nothing to protect themselves against the blustery wind. They let it play about their heads, tousling their hair and reddening their cheeks, ignoring it in a way that marked them out as locals who'd stood and met these conditions a thousand times in the past. They looked at the freshest scar, where the relentless pounding of the seas had claimed the latest chunk of crumbling cliff face. 'Probably went in those high seas the other night,' said Maik.

Shepherd nodded. 'What is it they call them these days? High-energy storm events? I think we used to call them waves, didn't we?'

Maik smiled sadly. It was hard to believe so much of this coastline could have vanished in one man's lifetime. Like the Boatman's Arms and the Brackets, his past seemed to be disappearing at an alarming rate.

Shepherd drew her eyes from the sea to look at him. And she could see he knew. 'You understand why, don't you, Danny? It's not about your abilities, either of you. It's just that after that incident at the station... We could never again be sure about the two of you together.'

'It was a one-off, ma'am. I think everybody knows that.' Maik wasn't trying to change the course of proceedings. He knew Shepherd had already reached her decision. But the old soldier in him just wanted the record to be straight. If actions were going to be taken, they needed to be based on the right information.

'She has a little boy, Danny. She was prepared to leave him without a mother just to save you.'

He shook his head. 'No, she would never have done that. It was a spur-of-the-moment reaction, that's all. She wasn't thinking.'

'But that's just the point. Who's to say she wouldn't do the same thing again if a similar situation came up? In our business, those split-second decisions we make under pressure, they need to be free of any other complications.'

Maik said nothing. He had been in enough situations where a decision like that was called for. Shepherd's point was unarguable. You might not always think of yourself first, but you didn't let your actions put other people's lives at risk. Ever.

'Lauren says it needs to be you that stays. She says they wouldn't know what to do without you.' Shepherd gave a slight smile. 'She says this lot need a safe pair of hands to guide them, not some sarky cow who stands around banging on about the antics of her son all day long.'

Maik managed to find a smile of his own from somewhere. He knew the DCS had delivered Lauren's words verbatim. He could imagine her delivery: the expression, the steadfast gaze. Yes, it was what she would have said, and the way she would have said it. It would have all been heartfelt and sincere. But that didn't make it right. He shook his head slowly. 'I'll not have Max changing schools just because this lot need their hand held by a responsible adult once in a while.' He turned to look at her directly. 'I'll put my papers in tomorrow.'

It was the DCS's turn to fall silent. She watched the slow, incessant roll of the waves out at sea. She had known it would be this way. There was never going to be any chance Danny would permit Salter to be the one to leave. Men like Danny Maik didn't let others take on sacrifices like that. They held these things, these dignified gestures, these selfless acts, as their duty.

'There's no rush,' she said finally. 'I'm sure there'll be no shortage of interest when it's learned that you're on the market.' She smiled and looked at him. 'There's a surprising number of people out there who still think you're a half-decent copper. You know you'll have my highest recommendation.' She paused. 'Without the DCI and Tony Holland, we're wafer-thin at the moment. I'm not suggesting you stay on for the full duration of the DCI's suspension, but I don't think a few days here or there is going to make much difference, do you?'

He looked out at the sea for a long time. 'I'll stay as long as I'm needed, ma'am.' But his tone said the rest. He wouldn't linger when that time had passed.

It should have been over. There should have been a slow walk back to the car, perhaps a little light conversation between them, to show that life goes on, even after such a major upheaval. Perhaps simply silence as they both came to terms with it. But there shouldn't have been this awkwardness, this shadow that was causing Shepherd such unease now.

'The video from the hospital has come back from the lab,' she said. 'It's been authenticated. It shows Glover Boyd helping his wife into his van at the hospital emergency entrance at 8:43. Match that with the footage from the CCTV at their house, similarly verified, which shows him helping her out of the van again at 9:47, and you have precisely the travel time required to get from the hospital to the house. Add in the phone mast records of her calls, and you even have the exact route Glover Boyd took that night when he drove her home.' She looked at him. 'I'm sorry, Danny, the simple truth is, as much as you like him for this, the evidence clearly shows that Glover Boyd couldn't have been anywhere near that hide at Canon's Cross when it was set on fire.'

Maik shook his head slowly. 'It's him, ma'am. I don't know how, but it's him.'

Shepherd sighed, as if a final effort at something had been spent, and now there was nothing left. Except for this. 'They say anyone is capable of murder, don't they? And you and I have been around long enough to know that is true. But we also know that there are some kinds of murder that are beyond the capacity of certain individuals.'

They both knew what she meant. It didn't take very much to stop the human body from functioning; to stop a heart from beating, to stop lungs from taking in air. But for one human to deliberately decide to do that, to kill someone, not in anger or passion, but coldly, to look at another human being and know in advance that you are going to take their life, that took an act of will that not everyone possessed.

She turned away from the sea, her eyes watering with the wind, and fastened her gaze instead on the careworn façades of a row of buildings staring back at her from the street front across the open land. In the middle was an old hotel. It was hard to tell if it had survived the pandemic, but a single, weak light in its lobby suggested there was still a heartbeat in there somewhere.

'There's a point in a relationship at which you get to know a person well enough to be aware of what he or she is capable of. Possibly even better than they know themselves,' said Shepherd, still staring at the buildings. 'To set fire to a hide, knowing that someone inside is going to be burned alive...' She shook her head. 'Not many people possess that level of depravity.'

She regarded the row of buildings again, seeing in them something that had long disappeared. 'Faded glories,' she said sadly. 'This was quite a chic little destination once, you know.' There was a tremor of something in her voice that told Maik these were not just the casual observations of a disinterested out-of-towner. 'This was his lair, where he led his quarry, to wine them and dine them. And then, to add them to his list. A nice meal in the restaurant, a couple of drinks, and then up to the room. "Lover Boy". She drew her eyes from the buildings finally and looked at Maik. 'Glover Boyd is not your killer, Danny. There are things a woman can tell about a man she has known intimately. He doesn't have it in him to take a life like that.'

Behind them lay the exposed strata of rocks along the cliff face. They had held the Earth's secrets, tucked away in their past, until the pounding seas had jarred them loose and exposed the hidden truth for all the world to see. Maik realised what it had cost his DCS to tell him what she had held inside herself for all these years. And he knew she would only have done so if she was certain beyond all doubt that Glover Boyd had not killed Arliss Dyer.

He shook his head slowly. 'You know, I would have bet my Motown collection that he was responsible.' He gave a tight smile. 'Glover Boyd out, Paige Turner in. Probably just as well I'm on my way out of here, if my instincts are that far off.'

Shepherd found an ironic smile from somewhere. 'Technology, Danny. It's done for many a good copper's intuition. CCTV cameras, phone signal triangulation; the triumph of hard evidence over instinct. Policing has evolved, thank God, and our techniques have evolved with it, as they always do. Let's rely on the technology here, the data, the hard evidence. That's what will get us over the line with this one, if anything will.'

But Danny's mind was elsewhere now. He was thinking about how policing had evolved, and with it the techniques. It only made sense, when you thought about it. And that would mean it would be true of other disciplines, too. 'Mind if we get back to the station now, ma'am? There's one or two things I'd like to check out.'

Shepherd regarded him closely. She knew enough not to ask at this point what those things might be. Like his DCI, Danny liked to get a little way down the road before he invited you to join him on his journey. But when he had this look in his eye, he was usually on to something.

'Certainly, Sergeant,' she said. And with one more look at the faded, careworn façade of the hotel, she led the way back to her car.

44

A clammy warmth hung in the air, sapping the energy and making exercise like descending a steep coastal path to a rocky beach an effort. If you were a non-birder like Lindy, the promise of a fresh breeze once you arrived was probably just enough to draw you on. For a birder like Dom, though, there was a far more appealing prospect: a lifer.

'Black-browed Albatross, we think,' Senior told them as they arrived. 'A ways out now, but it was close enough earlier to get a quick glimpse at it. Tracked northwards, but it'll likely be back soon. It's been patrolling this stretch all morning.'

Senior's eyes shone with excitement, and Lindy was reminded of their earlier conversation about grabbing every opportunity to bird, especially as age began to take its toll. In that context, it was easy to understand the man's willingness to stand out here in this crushing humidity, on this uncomfortable rocky shoreline, for however long it took for his bird to show up.

'I have to say, an albatross just off the coast of Saltmarsh is not something I thought I'd ever see,' she told him.

'It's what we live for, isn't it, Inspector? Moments like this.'

'A lifer for you?'

Senior shook his great white head. 'No, new for my British list, but even if it wasn't, an amazing opportunity nevertheless. An albatross, no less, as you say, Lindy, right on our doorstep. If we are able to get a confirmed identification at some point, this'll definitely be one for the books.'

Lindy smiled again at the man's infectious enthusiasm. Even she was beginning to get caught up in the moment. Further along the beach, a clean-up crew was working dil- igently on an untidy trail of plastic strewn along the beach at the tideline. Occasionally one of them would look around at the beach and give a rueful shake of the head. They had been working tirelessly since Lindy and Dom had arrived, but the impact they had made was barely perceptible. Senior followed Lindy's gaze to the young volunteers. 'It's such a Sisyphean task,' he said. 'Did you know there's a study called the MacArthur Report that estimates that by 2050, the ton- nage of plastic in the world's oceans will exceed that of the fish?'

It seemed impossible that this could be true, yet neither of them could find the will inside themselves to doubt it. The statement filled them all with such a sense of overwhelming hopelessness it was a moment before anyone could speak.

'And yet, still they try, bless them,' said Senior. 'If they can save even one seabird, one Black-browed Albatross, I suppose their efforts are worth it.'

The mention of the bird seemed to stir a restlessness in him. 'I might head over to the point,' he said, 'see if I can get a squint down there. Back in a jiffy.' He paused as he shouldered his 'scope. 'Wonderful, eh? The chase, the anticipation. I tell you, there's simply nothing like it.'

He moved off, and Lindy let her eyes track Senior's dis- appearing form. 'I'm sorry I wasn't able to find you anything on the monitoring equipment, Dom,' said 'There just wasn't anything there to find. Every piece of equipment at the Institute was in perfect working order.'

Jejeune had raised his bins to scan the horizon. He lowered them now and gave her a smile. 'Thanks for trying anyway.'

'But I know inaccurate records or dodgy equipment were your last hope for a motive. With the data verified, and now the monitoring equipment, too, surely that's it.'

'It's okay, really.'

She shrugged. 'Well it's not okay for me, I have to tell you. Eric is not best pleased at the moment. I sold the investigation to him as a follow-up story to the earlier look into the rumours of equipment breaking down. I had no idea what I might find out, so I needed him to sign off in case anyone asked down the road whether I was pursuing a legit story. Now he's banging on about fruitless investigations and wise use of resources and budgets. I asked him if, next time, it would help if I already had the answers to my questions before I went out to ask them.' She gave a mischievous grin. 'It's fair to say that didn't go over too well, either. Honestly, there's no pleasing that man sometimes.'

An alert pinged on Jejeune's phone just as Senior began returning to them, hurrying unsteadily over the uneven rocks along the shoreline and already unshouldering his 'scope. The detective waited to receive the message from the man rather than the phone. 'Heading our way,' Senior told them breathlessly.

Both men raised their bins and scanned the seas to the north. Although the water was calm along the coastline, out at sea Jejeune could see the swells of white-tipped waves. Perhaps there was a flicker of movement behind one of them, a shadow drifting above the dark water. Senior flashed out a crooked finger in the same general direction. 'Here it comes now. I'll get the 'scope on it.' With lightning speed, he set up the 'scope and swivelled it onto the bird, tracking it as it skimmed low over the wave tops. 'Ah yes, you beauty. There you are.'

He stepped aside and Jejeune leaned in, catching several good looks as the bird bounced in and out of view behind the turbulent offshore waves. Could he have identified it himself from such a distant sighting? As an albatross, certainly. But beyond that? He didn't know. He took Lindy's arm and gently shepherded her towards the 'scope. Though she didn't share the men's enthusiasm, she could appreciate the significance of the bird's appearance, and the importance of what was probably a once-in-a-lifetime event. She watched the bird for a moment, but when it seemed to be fading out towards the horizon she stepped back to allow Senior further views. The older man followed the bird through the 'scope and Jejeune tracked the distant, dark speck through his binoculars until it finally disappeared from view altogether. In a way that none of them could have explained, they knew the bird would not be reappearing. It was gone for good, a prize for those who had seen it, and a disappointment for those still making their way over from the church car park.

'It's been lost, hasn't it, in this era of captured images and endless replays from every angle, the sheer joy of a single, fleeting sighting?' said Senior. He watched as the group hurried across the uneven ground, laden with 'scopes and tripods and telescopic photo lenses, ready to begin their descent to the beach. Their imminent disappointment seemed to sadden him, even in his elation over his sighting. 'A building, or a statue, or a mountain; miss them today and they'll still be there tomorrow, and the next day, waiting for you. But not a bird. There's a transience to a sighting that is irreplaceable. You get your opportunity, if you're lucky enough, but even as you're seeing it, you're aware that it's a thing to be cherished, like all of life's most precious gifts, like life itself, to be seized before it's gone.'

Further along the beach, the clean-up crew were taking a break, sitting on seats of bleached driftwood, sharing sandwiches and drinks. The trail of plastic lay like a carpet around them.

'I wonder why seabirds are so drawn to plastic,' said Lindy. 'It's not a food item for them. You'd think they might have enough sense to leave it alone.'

'Studies have shown that decaying plastic in ocean water emits a similar smell to that given off by algae when it's being eaten. Since the creatures that eat this algae are prey for the seabirds, the scent alerts them that food must be in the area.'

Lindy's head sank in understanding. 'Only when the birds dive in, instead of getting a mouthful of their real prey, they swallow decomposing plastic instead. How awful.'

'Indeed.' Senior looked at Lindy sadly. 'And of course, our friends the tubenoses, the shearwaters and the petrels and the like have some of the best developed senses of smell of any birds. They can detect the scent from great distances away.' He stared out over the water, seemingly mesmerised for a moment by the gentle, incessant roll of the foam-flecked waves. 'It's estimated a bird like the Atlantic Petrel has a species range of around thirty-five million square miles. If there's plastic in the ocean, these birds will find it. What was your noun for petrels, Lindy? A foreboding?' He nodded. 'Fitting. Though perhaps it's not just the future of humans they're warning us about. Perhaps the birds are tocsins for their own existence, too.'

He stroked his beard thoughtfully, holding on to the last handful for a long moment before releasing it from his clutches. With a sigh, he drew himself up to his full height, a precursor, Jejeune knew, to a rallying of his spirits. 'Still, a Black-browed Albatross today. Close enough on that earlier pass for some of the lens wallahs to get a few definitive shots, no doubt. Have to be verified by Rare Birds, but I'm confident enough to consider it a cause for celebration. Care to join me at the Board Room? I've had a word with the management and they've given me their assurance they'll have some drinkable beer in by now. Woodforde's Wherry might be a bridge too far, but I'd expect we might find Greene King in there.' He turned to Lindy. 'And I'm told the wine in there is quite acceptable, too.'

She looked to Dom but he smiled his apologies. On another day, he would have welcomed the chance to toast the sighting of the Black-browed Albatross. But he was on the verge of something important, and it couldn't wait. He withdrew a piece of paper from his pocket and handed it to the older man. 'I wonder if I can ask you to have a look at this.'

Senior took the paper and stared at it, nodding and mumbling to himself as he read through the contents. 'Antarctica. You'd have your Wilson's. West coast of South Africa. Tristan da Cunha.' He shook his head slightly. 'Hmm, Madeira Archipelago? Of course, Deserta Grande, the Bulwer's.' He handed the paper back to Jejeune. 'And afterwards, a swing west, perhaps. To your patch?'

Jejeune nodded. 'Followed by a final sweep north over Scotland, before coming down the east coast to dock in Norfolk.' He looked at Senior. 'Am I right?'

'You are,' confirmed Senior. 'All large colonies, some the largest known, in fact; the Cape Petrels off South Africa, the Atlantics around Tristan. Over to the Leach's colony on Baccalieu and finishing with a flourish, the European Storm Petrel colony at Mousa.' He shook his head in admiration. 'You couldn't plan a route to see more petrels if you tried. Don't know if I'd choose to do it that way, though. You'd see some fine spectacles, no doubt, but it would be hard travel. That's an awfully long time to be at sea. Catch some dreadful weather, too, I shouldn't wonder, tracking up through the middle of the Atlantic like that. Must be an extremely dedicated bunch of birders, by the sound of it.'

'I don't think they're going for the birds,' said Jejeune. He looked out at the clean-up crew. 'At least, not in the way we'd understand it.'

Lindy could see it now. Senior had provided Dom with the confirmation he needed, the final answer to his final query. The only question now was how much Domenic was prepared to sacrifice to act on it. But unfortunately, she could tell from his troubled expression that he had already settled on an answer to that one, too.

45

The choreography of the earlier visits was not to be repeated. Jejeune was met at the door of Julien Bellaire's house by the same taciturn personal assistant, but he was ushered into an unfamiliar room. It offered views of a different landscape, too. Through a sweeping bank of large windows, Jejeune could see the clifftop path he had walked with Lindy and Bellaire in the rainstorm. From here, the glint off the glass of the Institute's administration block was just visible.

Bellaire was already at the window when Jejeune entered the room, and he remained there, gazing out over his domain. 'It is a place of great natural beauty and wonder, our planet. But it has reached the point where it needs protecting, not just appreciating. There are so few of us in a position to make meaningful, permanent change. I do not understand why these efforts should be met with such opposition in some quarters.'

He deigned to turn, finally, but if he was waiting for Jejeune to respond, he was disappointed. This was Bellaire's stage. The detective would let the performance continue. For now.

'The captain has completed a thorough search of the *Oceanite*. Gaya Monde did not leave a note.' Bellaire tilted his head slightly. 'But it seems you were correct. The absence of any tools in Alex Kasabian's clothing or survival kit bag makes it clear that he was murdered. It can only be assumed that Gaya took her own life that night because she knew she was going to be arrested as soon as the ship arrived in the UK. I am curious, though, as to how she could have done this, Inspector. As a participant in the 300-Club event, she has an alibi for the time in question, does she not?'

'Gaya Monde is, quite literally, the only person at the base that night who could have committed the murder and survived. Everyone else involved in the event must have been in the sauna at some point. To take part in the walk without raising their body temperatures sufficiently would have been fatal. Only Gaya, fully clothed, sitting on a snowmobile a hundred yards from the base, had the opportunity to get out to the site of the murder and return.'

'But she would not have had time, surely. There was only ten minutes between each group. All reported seeing her there when they went out, and she remained there for the entirety of their walks.'

'They saw a shape astride a running snowmobile, as they were walking towards its headlight beam. I think Gaya hosed down a full snowsuit and left it outside to freeze into a body shape. After the first group went back in, she set it on the snowmobile with a helmet, scarf and mitts, drew up the hood of the jacket and left it there. When the second group came out, no one would have spoken to the figure as they approached. At those temperatures, a person's lungs are under too much duress to talk. With the snowsuit in place astride one snowmobile, she left for the monitoring site on another one, cut the fuel line and returned in time for the third group, coming inside with them when they were finished. Later, she retrieved the frozen snowsuit and put it in the sauna to thaw, where Scott found it the next morning. But I suspect you knew this was the plan. What you didn't expect was Gaya's report.'

Bellaire stared at Jejeune from across the room. His expression was trying for detached interest, but there was a nerve working away somewhere near his jawline.

'On that video, you reacted with genuine shock when Gaya Monde told you about Kasabian's death. I know. I have seen enough reactions to the news of a death to recognise the real thing. But that shock was because you were expecting a different account, one that said Alex Kasabian had died by accident. I think Gaya was supposed to report that Alex Kasabian's death was the result of unforeseen circumstances; regrettable, but blameless nonetheless.'

Bellaire seemed mesmerised by Jejeune. His eyes were locked on the detective, but his own features displayed no emotion at all. He simply stared at the other man. Jejeune waited, but Bellaire had no wish to speak. With an almost imperceptible hand gesture, he invited the detective to continue.

'Gaya was going to be first to the body,' said Jejeune. 'But she knew Kasabian's snowmobile would be checked by the others as soon as they arrived, and she needed a plausible reason why Kasabian's machine had left him stranded. I think she intended to substitute her snowmobile for his. Given the importance of gasoline down there, I'm guessing she intended to siphon the tank and make it look as if it had run out of gas. In the meantime, she could do a quick running repair on the severed fuel line of Kasabian's snowmobile and drive that one back to base; a stent and a couple of clamps would be enough to get it running again until she could repair it properly. Then all she had to do was place a radio with a defective battery in Kasabian's survival kit bag and wait for the others to show up. No fuel and a dead battery. Carelessness and bad luck; the same combination that has claimed so many other lives on that continent. Nobody would even question it. But by clutching the fuel line and tucking that bag under his arm,

Alex Kasabian ensured his death couldn't be staged as an accident. That's why Gaya kept asking if you were sure you wanted to record the session. She knew the report you'd be receiving wasn't the one you were expecting. She wasn't sure how you'd react.'

Bellaire nodded appreciatively and slipped his hands into his pockets. It was not the reaction Jejeune had expected. He had conducted enough interviews to recognise that this was the point at which a suspect would usually point out that there was no evidence to back up his theory. Instead, Bellaire stood impassively before Jejeune, with only the faintest upward curl at the edges of his lips. 'A man died,' he said flatly. 'Tragic, yes, but you and I know that sometimes bigger issues are at stake than the life of a single person. Can one individual life really be measured against the millions who are threatened by the rising temperatures caused by climate change?' He gave a mirthless smile, and stepped forward, closing the gap to his one-man audience. 'We seem to have reached a tipping point with regards to climate change, don't you think, Inspector? There is now broad consensus on the effect of human activities, ambitious commitments by governments, undertakings in alternative energy projects.' He raised a cautionary finger. 'But it is a fragile acceptance, one feels. There is a brittleness to it that could so easily be exploited by a concerted effort from sceptics. If they had evidence, for example, that some of the climate data was subject to question, data from a massive worldwide project, the truth of the matter would not be important, the insignificance of the anomalies. It would be enough to give oxygen to the doubters once again, cast doubt on the validity of all data and erode the public's hard-won trust.'

'I think most people are well informed enough to make a decision on the validity of the data being provided to them.'

'I am not sure I share your confidence that they can recognise the truth when they see it. I believe that to give the sceptics such a foothold would be a mistake the world would come to regret.'

Outside the window, the wide blue skies stretched out over an unblemished sea to an endless horizon. It was such a big world and the lives of individual human beings so small in it. But this was the canvas on which men like Julien Bellaire chose to paint their dreams. Jejeune looked around the office. He realised what was missing, the same thing that was absent in the other room. Art. Not a single artefact in either of the rooms had been created solely for its beauty. Where was there the place in a world like this for a foraging Nightingale, a soaring albatross? Perhaps it was better that the fate of the planet rested with this new breed of tech-lomats, people able to dispassionately assess the value of climate stability as they moved between their interconnected worlds of international economies and global geopolitics? But even uber-mortals like this could not be allowed to decide who lived and who died in the pursuit of their goals. 'Did Alex Kasabian pose a threat to the movement, I wonder?' asked Jejeune. 'Or only to the ambitions of one person involved in it?'

'If there is hubris here, Inspector Jejeune, it belongs to an individual with the desire to show the world how clever he was, to sacrifice good work, vital work, critical, all for his own glory.'

'I believe the blog Gaya sent was to tell you Alex Kasabian was going to be killed. She knew you would read the words *storm petrel* and translate them as *Oceanite*. I wonder, did it resonate with you, Mr Bellaire, the name of the bird?'

Bellaire remained silent.

'I think Alex Kasabian discovered the readings were inconsistent with the ones being manually entered by Tori

Boyd. And because of that, he had to die. That message told you that Alex Kasabian would not be able to reveal his findings to anybody, that he would be dead before the ship arrived. So all you had to do was make sure that computers receiving the readings were destroyed in a fire, and your problem would disappear with them.'

Bellaire spread his hands wide in an appeal for reason. 'And yet, the readings we report are entirely consistent with global norms. Our records are open for all to see. So for what reason would we want to alter them? It is upon this point, Inspector, that your entire premise begins to collapse.'

'Does it?' Jejeune looked at him frankly. 'You know, for an organisation so intent on openness, the outbound cargo manifest for the *Oceanite* proved a remarkably hard document to access.'

Bellaire had resumed his intense scrutiny of Jejeune now, his eyes narrow and his lips pursed tightly.

'But then, the work was contracted to another of your companies, wasn't it? One that doesn't operate under anywhere near the same levels of transparency as the Bellaire Institute. It seems the ship was transporting new buoys to be deployed on its way out.'

'Replacements for the ones to be collected and returned for descaling, in accordance with our environmentally responsible operating practices.' Bellaire tried an indulgent smile. 'This has all been explained to your colleagues during their investigation. The new buoys ensure continuity. Climate data cannot have large gaps of interrupted transmissions if it is to be meaningful.'

'I'm told that it would be considerably less expensive, and far more efficient, to conduct the descaling at sea, with the buoys still in place, and still transmitting.'

Bellaire looked at Jejeune with what might have been admiration. 'You have solved Alex Kasabian's murder, identified his killer, closed the case. And all from over ten thousand miles away.' He inclined his head. 'It is a truly remarkable achievement, Mr Jejeune. But the matter is now over. That Alex's death cannot receive the justice it deserves after all your efforts is, as today's much-overused word has it, unfortunate. But the fault does not lie with you.'

'I don't believe fortune had anything to do with Alex Kasabian's death. Nor with Arliss Dyer's. He was a friend of mine, Mr Bellaire. And if Alex Kasabian's murder is no longer prosecutable, Arliss Dyer's is.'

'But not by you, Inspector. Am I correct in thinking you are currently prevented from investigating active cases? Or did I misunderstand the chief constable? You were charged with investigating the death of Alex Kasabian and you have done so. To go further breaches the terms of your suspension, does it not?'

He raised his eyebrows and indicated the open door to the room, at which his spectral assistant stood ready to escort Jejeune from the house. Bellaire called out to the detective as he reached the doorway and he turned to see the man, dwarfed by the giant picture window behind him, and beyond it the vast vista of the world he wished to save. He was looking at Jejeune with an expression the inspector had not seen before; somewhere between an appeal to logic and a plea for understanding.

'A person with suspicions but no evidence would find themselves with a decision to make, wouldn't they, Inspector? They could recklessly put forward their unsubstantiated theories, destroying the public's confidence in vital work and thus doing the sceptics' job for them. Or they perhaps might

46

The tall grasses fringing the hide had already turned tawny and brittle. The heat had contributed to their condition, but so had time. They were approaching the end of their season, a point at which they would begin to die off. Next spring, there would be regeneration and they would climb again against the walls of the hide in a dense, almost impenetrable mass of green shoots. The energy that these plants would invest, the resources it would take, was almost impossible to comprehend. And all to return to their former state, changed and yet still the same. Change and renewal, cycles and continuity; it was true of the natural world, and of the human relationships that existed within it. Such as the one between Domenic Jejeune and Danny Maik.

The DCI was checking through the slats when Maik entered the hide. 'We've found ourselves here before, Sergeant, as I recall,' said Jejeune by way of a greeting.

'Not always from choice, though. As I recall,' said Maik wryly. He looked around the shadowy interior of the structure, cool against the day's building heat. 'Just a chat is it, then, today, sir?' Because, if so, he was asking, why weren't we meeting in that cosy little conservatory of yours? Or even the Board Room, over a cloudy beer by the fireplace?

'Yes, Sergeant, just a chat. But it would probably be best to record it anyway.'

Best for Danny, he meant. Jejeune was required by law to share what he knew. For Maik, it may be necessary to prove he hadn't done the same. The sergeant shifted uneasily, but he drew out his phone anyway, turning on the recording feature and setting it on the rough-hewn window ledge between them.

Jejeune checked through the slats again. He had brought his bins along to the meeting but he doubted he would need them. Most of the migrants had moved through and the few resident waterfowl, the Moorhens and the Teal, were as familiar as old friends. 'I went to see Julien Bellaire yesterday.'

Maik stared at his DCI. He had been in the office next door when Shepherd, at volume, had expressly forbidden this. Based on their recent conversation, he found it hard to believe she would have revisited her decision. He'd seen Jejeune come to grips with some fairly complex issues in his time. The fact that he could lose his job over this admission wouldn't have been one of his more perceptive insights.

'At his invitation?' asked Maik, offering his DCI the only lifeline he could come up with.

But Jejeune left it dangling. 'He wanted to discuss my findings about Alex Kasabian's death.'

Maik waited.

'And they were that Alex Kasabian was murdered by a woman named Gaya Monde.'

The red recording light on Maik's phone pulsed in the semi-darkness of the hide's interior. But it couldn't pick up the flicker of warning in Maik's eyes when Jejeune had mentioned the woman's name.

'She has since taken her own life. On a ship. The *Oceanite*. It translates as "storm petrel", by the way.'

The information left no impression on Maik. 'Did she make a confession, sir?'

'No, but there is compelling evidence of her guilt. I've included it in my written report.'

'And this is what you told Mr Bellaire?'

'I'm as sure as I can be that he was already aware of it, Sergeant.'

Maik inclined his head appreciatively. As ambiguous statements that could survive a charge of slander went, it wasn't bad. Still, a clarification wouldn't hurt, especially one on the record. 'Just to be clear, sir, Julien Bellaire did not admit to any involvement in Alex Kasabian's death.'

'No, Sergeant. He did not.' Jejeune gave a rueful smile. 'He did however, make numerous references to the fact that I wasn't there in an official capacity. He was aware that anything he said to me wouldn't constitute a statement to the police.'

Maik looked at the blinking red light of his phone again. 'Anything else of note you covered with him, then, sir?'

'Our discussion tended more towards the philosophical: the value of a single human life, the nature of hubris, the place of birds in this world. Of course, we did discuss his efforts to change the world's climate trajectory. His legacy genuinely does seem to matter to him. It's understandable, I suppose. All the money in the world can't buy you a place in history. Only your actions can do that.'

It had been well wrapped, but Maik had been with his DCI too long to miss it. 'The role of birds, sir?'

'Storm petrels. Know much about them, Sergeant?'

Maik considered the question for a moment, not to call up his knowledge, but to search for a connection. 'Pelagic seabirds,' he said. 'Portents of doom, according to Sergeant Salter. Courtesy of Wikipedia, I imagine.' He nodded towards the window slats. 'Any out there?'

Jejeune rejected the idea with a small smile. 'They feed in the oceans. They are attracted to the scent of a chemical called dimethyl sulfide, also known as DMS. Algae and other micro-organisms give off this smell when they're being eaten by small predators, the kind of things larger predators, such as petrels, like to eat. The thing is, this scent is also emitted by plastic as it decomposes in seawater.'

Maik's silence wasn't boredom, or impatience. He had no cause to wonder whether the inspector would get to the point. He realised he had missed the quiet, deliberate way Jejeune sometimes unfurled the wonders of the natural world to him.

'Petrels range the open seas, but when they gather, as they do when they're attracted by the scent of food, they can do so in their thousands.'

'Be a sight to see,' said Maik, to show he was still following along.

Jejeune nodded in agreement. 'The thing is, that much living biomass becomes an entity of its own, a force with the power to influence natural phenomena, to affect the surrounding atmosphere, even. Can you imagine, for example, what the presence of a densely packed grouping of several thousand birds must have on the ambient air temperature? Or in the case of pelagic seabirds, the water temperature?'

Maik recognised the pause as Jejeune's final circling before he landed.

'I think the buoys deployed by the Bellaire Institute are decomposing. Lindy said there was an industry rumour a while ago. Her investigation into equipment malfunctions yielded nothing. Only, the rumour wasn't that equipment was malfunctioning. It was that it was breaking down.'

Maik couldn't suppress a small smile. Perhaps the person transcribing the recording of this conversation might imagine that it was only because the DCI had so much time on his hands these days that he'd have the luxury of analysing a phrase like this so carefully. But Danny knew better.

'You think the smell of decomposing plastic attracted these birds to the buoys in large numbers, causing false temperature readings?'

'In the world of climate change data, the smallest margins are vital. A consistent elevation in sea temperature of even a quarter of a degree would be profoundly significant.'

'And you believe this is what Alex Kasabian discovered?'

'I don't imagine he knew the buoys were decomposing, and I'm all but certain he didn't know that the smell of decomposing plastic attract petrels. But he knew something was wrong with the data. He would have had baseline readings from the Antarctic site to compare to various monitoring stations around the world. I think he realised that only the Bellaire buoys were showing these increases.'

Outside, they heard the whistle of rapid wingbeats and Jejeune lifted the window slat to see a small rush of Pochards dropping into the marsh. The ducks drifted in lazy circles, preening themselves and diving to feed. Jejeune watched them for a moment before closing the slat again, plunging the hide back into a shadowy darkness. It surprised both men to realise how much light had flooded in through that single, narrow flap. For a moment, until their eyes adjusted to the darkness, the blinking of the red light was all they could see.

'I suspect they tried to reason with him,' said Jejeune, 'tell him the problem was already being addressed. The *Oceanite* was deploying new buoys at sites on the way down to Antarctica, and they would be gathering up the decaying ones on the way back. Tristan de Cunha, the Madeira Archipelago, Baccalieu Island; all locations with massive populations of petrels nearby. The *Oceanite*'s route home goes directly past them.'

Maik looked unconvinced. 'I've seen that operation to descale those recovered buoys, sir. It's a pretty elaborate bluff if they have no intention of returning them to active service.'

In the dim light of the hide's interior, Maik saw Jejeune's shoulders rise in an uncharacteristic shrug. He may not have everything right, the gesture was telling him, but he had enough to be sure why Alex Kasabian had to die. 'For all his social dysfunction, Kasabian was a dedicated scientist. He would have insisted the climate community, the wider world even, be informed that the data sets were inaccurate and the readings invalid.'

Maik regarded his DCI carefully. As he said, all this could have been included in his written report. He didn't need to request a meeting in a hide to tell Danny this. And he certainly didn't need to insist that their conversation was recorded. He waited. Jejeune flipped open the slat again, the blade of sunlight flooding in through the opening. In contrast to the fanfare of their arrival, the Pochards had slipped away in silence, leaving the marsh quiet and still. Tiny patches of light floated on the water like fallen leaves.

'That bird call I mentioned earlier,' said Jejeune. 'The Curlew Sandpiper. It's fairly distinctive, a soft, dry rippling. But it's very quiet, easy to miss in the wind noise if the bird was in flight. You'd have to be very good to identify it. Very good, indeed.' Jejeune cast his eyes downward in thought. And perhaps in sorrow, too. *"I can recall what I heard."*

Maik's eyes flashed a warning. Not now. Not after they had done so well, tiptoed around so carefully to get to this point. One mention of the open case, and this brittle, make-believe world of a casual conversation between two colleagues in a bird hide would all come crashing down around them. But Jejeune hadn't forgotten about the red light on Maik's phone, beating like a metronomic pulse into the shadowy interior. He was going to deliver justice for Arliss Dyer. And if it took a reference to a phone message he had never heard, that he should never have had any knowledge of, he was prepared to live with the consequences of that.

'Arliss wasn't telling me that because he thought I'd doubt him. *Find me the voice*, he was saying, bring the voice to me. *I can recall what I heard*. Let me hear it, just once more, and I'll identify it for you. That's what he was telling me. They said the hides were aligned, didn't they, the arsonist? It had to be some-body local, somebody with the knowledge of the landscape to recognise that. I'd have paraded the voices of everyone even remotely connected with the Bellaire Institute past Arliss's ears. And when he told me, I'd have believed him. It wouldn't have mattered how airtight their alibi was, how implausible it was that they could have been involved, how utterly impossi-ble. I would have believed him over all of it.' He locked his eyes on Maik's in a way that made it impossible for the sergeant to ignore his next statement. 'Anybody who knew my opinion of Arliss's hearing would have realised that.'

Yes, thought Maik, they would, wouldn't they? He looked at Jejeune's face, cloaked in the shadows of the half-light inside the hide. And he knew, from the look that would never be picked up by any recording equipment, never transcribed on any page. The person Jejeune had served up, between all those glances at the flashing red light, all the pauses, all the looks, wasn't the same person Maik had been pursuing. But he was just beginning to see how it could be. 'If you'll excuse me sir, I have to go,' he said as evenly as his voice would allow. 'Pressing business.' He reached for the phone from the wooden ledge and switched off the recording function.

'Of course, Sergeant,' said Jejeune. 'Give my regards to Sergeant Salter.' This last because that was surely who Maik was dialling with such urgency as he dashed through the door of the hide and into the blinding sunlight outside.

47

There were different kinds of loneliness, thought Maik. There was the comfortable loneliness he had existed in before Salter came along, a world of order and predictability that suited an old soldier with too many ghosts in his past. Until it didn't any more. There was, too, the sad loneliness of someone who had just lost a partner, and now drifted through the universe desperately seeking something, anything, to latch on to in order to prevent them spinning off into nothingness. And then there was this; the hollow, pointless existence of Glover Boyd, rattling around in a house that was barely a dwelling, let alone a home, flitting from one unfulfilling hobby to another as a way to fill the gaping hours of emptiness.

'I heard about your mother, sir. My condolences.'

Boyd nodded his thanks. 'We were not that close in our later years, but it's not those times you remember, is it, Sergeant?'

Maik let the man have his moment of sadness. He knew enough about saying goodbye to those you cared about.

'As welcome as your kindness is, I can hardly believe that is the only reason for your visit today. What is it that you'd like to ask me, Sergeant?'

Maik looked around, his eyes catching the jumble of abandoned pursuits on the far side of the room. 'As a matter of fact, Mr Glover, I was wondering about your wife's injury, the night of the fire at Canon's Cross. Ligaments, wasn't it?'

A wariness seemed to rear up in Boyd. 'I believe so, yes.'

Maik nodded to himself. 'I was talking to a doctor at the hospital recently, and she told me soft tissue injuries are notoriously difficult to diagnose. Mostly you have to rely on the patient's account; where it hurts, when, the amount of pressure it can bear. It got me to wondering – you don't think she could have been deceiving you about the discomfort she was in? You know, get a bit of extra sympathy, have you do an extra bit of running around on her behalf. You do still seem to hold a candle for her, sir, if you don't mind me saying so.'

'Do I?' Boyd asked carelessly. 'Yes, I suppose I do. The truth is, I have always loved Tori. I would have done anything for her. Except remain faithful. I'm afraid there was just never enough good in me to do that. And so I lost her.' He looked at Maik through sad eyes. 'Not all mistakes are created equal, Sergeant. Some you pay for forever.' He gave one of his trademark wan smiles. 'But no.' He shook his head firmly. 'I'd have to reject that idea. In my opinion, Tori was genuinely in a great deal of pain.'

'And your opinion would carry a bit more weight than most, wouldn't it, sir, given your stint as a paramedic? When was that, by the way?'

'My failed stint, you mean? Oh, I suppose it would have to be about ten years ago now. You know,' he said wistfully, 'I often wonder, if I'd have stayed with it, could I have actually made something of my life, done something useful with it?' He shrugged easily. 'Story of my life, really: missed opportunities and poor decisions.'

The breeziness was only a touch forced, but it was enough to tell Maik that finally, after flailing around for so long in this case, the end was in sight. 'So you never thought about going back to it, then?'

Boyd shook his head. 'Wasn't for me, sadly. People's suffering upsets me. A better man might have been able to put his personal feelings aside in order to serve the greater good. A bit like you chaps do, I suppose. But of all the things I may be, Sergeant, a better man is not one of them.'

Maik nodded. 'Probably need new training by now, anyway, what with the new techniques evolving all the time. That constable, Holland, the one who was here, he's just returned from a stint at the Met. Now he's banging on about all the new approaches they have down there. You know how it is.'

Boyd nodded uneasily. 'Yes. Can I get you a cup of tea? Something to eat?'

Maik declined with a polite smile. Unusual behaviour was just the sort of confirmation he needed now. 'Wears a bit thin at times, the cutting edge of the Smoke versus our unsophisticated backwater ways up here. But they got me thinking, the constable's comments. We can't be that far behind, surely? Not with the way the information exchange works today. I mean, everybody would want to be up on best practice, wouldn't they? That's how it is in the police force. Be the same in medicine, I should imagine.'

Maik looked at Glover without expression. A parade of emotions flickered over the man's features like shadows on a landscape.

'I'd actually gone to that hospital to ask how it could be that East Anglia General, one of the best healthcare facilities in the country, could be so far behind London hospitals in the treatment of soft tissue injuries.'

Boyd was still. Not even his eyes moved as he sat across from Maik. It was as if he had ceased to exist.

'But of course, they aren't, are they, Mr Boyd?' Danny took out his phone and leaned forward to show Boyd an image. It was a frozen frame from grainy CCTV footage. It showed Tori Boyd hobbling into the front door of her house with her ex-husband trailing in her wake. Boyd stared at it without reaction.

'The doctor said no one on staff at East Anglia General would have dressed a ligament injury like that. I asked who might have wrapped a leg that way, and you know what she said? Perhaps someone who trained in healthcare a long time ago, but hasn't worked in the field since.'

As he looked at Glover Boyd's crestfallen expression now, Maik knew it was over. This man wasn't going to be one of those who stared at you arrogantly and told you what he'd done, and how, and when. He was too weak to take ownership of his crimes in that way. But in time, he would tell Danny what he needed to hear.

'My DCI said recently that if he knew somebody was guilty, I mean really knew it, he would look hard enough at that person's alibi until it all began to fall apart.' Maik's stare wasn't unkind. It was an invitation, to share the narrative, to become part of it and, finally, to take it up. 'To my way of thinking, here's how it could have happened,' said Maik. 'You pick up Tori at the hospital and help her into the back of your van, all under the watchful gaze of the hospital CCTV. Then at some quiet spot, that lay-by near Gilbert's Hollow would be a possibility for me, you stop the van for a moment and take your bike out of the back.'

Maik liked the present tense. It added immediacy, to bring it all back, to put Boyd in the moment once again, reliving the emotions, the sensations, the guilt. But if Boyd was listening now with an intensity Maik had not seen in him before, he was still not saying anything.

'By this time,' continued the sergeant, 'Tori has removed the dressing from her leg, and since she doesn't really have any ligament damage at all, she takes over the driving, still chatting to all and sundry on her phone so the masts can track her progress. In the meantime, you bike south down the path to the Canon's Cross hide, uncover the petrol cans stashed there earlier, and set fire to it. Then you ride east across the marsh trail to the point where it emerges back onto the old coast road. Having looped around the northern edge of the marsh, Tori is now just in time to meet you. You throw the bike in the back of the van, re-bandage her leg, and drive into the forecourt of her house for the CCTV cameras to capture your arrival.'

Maik stopped speaking and raised his eyebrows in Boyd's direction. The slow, methodical, matter-of-fact delivery had pressed the rest of the world into the background, and now he had ceased talking, the silence seemed to surround Boyd, like an abyss that he was in danger of disappearing into. Maik nodded towards the bicycle in the corner of the room. 'I fancied I saw a set of tyre tracks up by the Canon's Cross hide that night.'

'But I imagine you'd have wanted to wait until daylight to take some photos. And all that overnight rain would have put paid to that idea, wouldn't it?'

So there was still some fight left in Boyd after all. It took Maik by surprise slightly. He would need to press just a little bit harder. 'The fire at Abbot's Marsh would have been straightforward enough,' he said slowly, as if giving it some consideration. 'But Canon's Cross, where a man died, burned to death, that one must be hard to live with.'

Boyd lowered his head and Maik saw the man's shoulders slump as the final dregs of resistance drained from his body. 'She asked me to help her. Said she needed me to, that I owed her that much. Guilt can be a formidable weapon in the right hands, Sergeant, and my ex-wife has become a past master at exploiting it. Of course, in truth, I suppose I was flattered to be called upon at all. I am not really the sort of chap a person would normally want on their side in a tight spot.'

Maik saw the regret in Boyd's eyes, the sorrow. But he knew he couldn't press. He couldn't put the words in the man's mouth. He needed Glover Boyd to say it himself. He waited, letting the pause bring the sort of pressure only silence can. But still Boyd wouldn't take that final step.

'You have an alibi for the night of the fire at the Institute,' Maik told him. 'We've confirmed you were with a woman at that restaurant. So what was it – after the one at Canon's Cross, you couldn't go through with another one?'

Boyd tried another valiant smile. 'Ah yes, true, Sergeant. I was nowhere near the Institute when *that* hide went up. Couldn't be relied upon, you see. All right for the grunt work. But for the truly important stuff,' he shook his head, 'I'm afraid Tori would never trust me with that.'

'So it's your statement that Tori Boyd set fire to that hide?'

'It's my statement that I didn't. One thing I am sure of is that she would never have trusted anything of that importance to anyone else. Always had to take care of the big things herself, Tori. Never did quite get the hang of that delegating business.'

Maik could see Boyd slipping away, into some dream world where his wife took care of things, of him. He had no choice now but to try to force the confession. 'You said you would have done anything for her, but that's not true, is it?' Maik paused. 'You wouldn't have killed for her, would you?'

'No, Sergeant,' said Boyd regretfully. 'I wouldn't have done that.'

He was so close now. One more step. 'You didn't know that there was anyone in that hide, did you? Your ex-wife set you up to kill Dyer. Murder involves a conscious choice, it involves knowledge. But she had that knowledge, not you. She guided

Dyer to that hide, she provided the bottle of whisky. Tori is the one guilty of murder, Mr Boyd. You were merely the weapon.' Maik drew in a breath. 'You spoke of missed opportunities. You have a chance to do something right now. You can tell me the truth about what happened at Canon's Cross.'

Boyd raised his head and shook it slowly. 'I've spent my life in a kind of no-man's-land, Sergeant, no good at lying, but equally terrible at telling the truth. I'm not sure I even have the ability to tell the difference any more. Do something right, you say?' He nodded sadly and looked at Maik. 'I'm sorry, Sergeant, I will not implicate my wife in this terrible crime. Which means, of course, I will not be admitting to it, either.'

Maik was stunned. He sat on the couch for a moment, staring at Boyd. But he knew the moment had gone. He couldn't find the words for a gracious goodbye so he simply walked out of the room and out of the house in silence. On the step, he took out his phone and began to text Lauren Salter. It was up to her now.

48

Lauren Salter had lived in these parts long enough to recognise a trap when she saw one. The recent dry weather had crusted over the runnels in the track down the incline, but she knew just below the surface lay a quagmire of gluey mud. The remnants of the rain that had so recently had this slope flowing freely with water were still waiting to suck her tiny Kia in up to its axles. She reversed the car into the shadows beneath the stand of hornbeams at the top of the hill and began to walk down, staying to the grassy verge on the edge of the track all the way.

Tori Boyd was dragging through the burned-out ruins of the hide with a long-handled grappling hook. She looked up as Salter approached. 'I see you've managed to get rid of the bandage,' said Salter by way of greeting. 'All better, now, then?'

There was something in Salter's tone that made Boyd stiffen slightly. 'You're on private property, Sergeant. You were asked not to return.'

Salter smiled easily. 'Well, I suppose I'd better crack on with the reason for my visit then, hadn't I? I'm here to arrest you for the murder of Arliss Dyer on September twenty-first of this year. You do not have to say anything…' She completed the recital but, like every other person Salter could remember arresting, by this point Boyd seemed to have other things on her mind.

'I have an alibi for that night, Sergeant, as you well know.'

'Not any more. We spoke to the nurse who dressed your leg in A and E.' Salter produced her phone and showed Boyd an image of herself hobbling to the doorway of her house. 'The nurse is prepared to testify in court that this dressing is not the one she put on.'

Boyd took the phone from Salter's hand roughly and stared at the image before handing it back dismissively. 'It's very dark. I'd hardly call that conclusive evidence.'

'My partner— my colleague,' she corrected herself, 'is talking to your ex-husband now, showing him that same image and telling him exactly the same thing I'm telling you. I'm expecting a text at any moment to tell me Glover has confessed. At that point, I'm going to have to insist you accompany me to the station, where formal charges will be laid.' She indicated the glass dome of the Institute's headquarters behind Boyd. 'If you'd like to leave instructions for Paige Turner, I'd suggest you do that now.'

The other woman seemed to hesitate for a moment.

'Unless you really think your ex-husband will refuse to cooperate with the police.'

Boyd's upright posture gave way slightly. Her look told Salter that they both knew that in the end, Glover Boyd's own interests would always come first. 'You know, he told me once that we would always be together because his love was stronger than my hate. As if all his times with people like you didn't matter. Perhaps to him they didn't, possibly to you, either. But they mattered to me, every single one of them. I'm afraid declarations of undying loyalty really didn't mean very much coming from a man who is constitutionally incapable of staying faithful.'

'Comes in handy, though, sometimes, that kind of devotion.'

'Arliss Dyer, you mean?' Boyd lowered her head in genuine sadness. 'Poor Arliss. A casualty of a wider cause. Like

Alex Kasabian. We couldn't allow the findings to be called into doubt, you see. If they are to continue their support for climate initiatives, people need to have faith in the data. They can't be hearing whispers that the science can't be trusted.'

Salter was content to bide her time until Danny's notification came through that he had secured Glover Boyd's confession. But it wouldn't hurt to get as much information as Tori Boyd was willing to provide. Particularly if she could edge her towards implicating somebody else. 'So the air-gapping arrangement wasn't about security at all. It was deliberately set up by Julien Bellaire to allow you to manipulate the readings being uploaded to the database?'

Boyd looked out over the bay, at the buoys in their cradle, gently undulating on the tide. 'As soon as we realised we were getting false readings, we began changing the results, correcting them, really, readjusting them back to where global norms suggested they should be. But once we had started down that road, there was no turning back. Gaya really did try to convince Julien otherwise at first. She said the academic community might forgive inaccurate readings, but they could never accept deliberately falsifying data. But Julien said the false readings couldn't be allowed to compromise the project, destroy all the work we are doing here, all the future good we can do. He said the Institute's reputation would never recover from it.'

'*Its* reputation,' said Salter. She shook her head. 'This was about Bellaire, surely? The Billionaire Bicyclist, the environmental hero of his age. The man who took on climate change and won. The awards, the achievements, the praise; all of it based on faulty equipment and flawed data? *His* reputation would never have recovered. Alex Kasabian's revelations would have cost Julien Bellaire his place in history. That's what this is about, isn't it, Tori? That's why he sanctioned Kasabian's murder?'

But Boyd's conviction, her utter belief in the importance of the project, would not allow her to let go of the idea that her actions were justified. 'We tried to convince Alex that Julien would put things right. But he threw our policy of openness back in our faces. He said the world had a right to know what we were doing and if we wouldn't tell them, he would, as soon as he got the chance.'

'So Gaya took care of Alex Kasabian?' said Salter. 'Leaving you to destroy the hard drives on those computers, since they were the only place the original data was held, the only evidence left of what you had done.'

'Yes, yes of course, that's right.' Salter didn't need Boyd's look to tell her she had missed something. It was there in her voice. 'Once again, we were compromised by this idiotic policy of openness. How could we possibly erase those drives, or go back and manually alter the data on them, with the whole world watching? Setting fire to the hide and destroying everything was the only option we had left. To destroy the only existing records.'

Salter knew she had to probe, to find out what she'd missed, but before she could speak, her phone pinged. She looked down at the text. *Didn't get it. I'm coming over. 10 mins.* Did Glover Boyd know she was here, ready to arrest his ex-wife? It could surely be only a matter of seconds until Boyd's phone rang and her ex-husband informed her that he had found some courage from somewhere and refused to buckle under Danny's pressure. She needed to get this over the line now. 'Gaya Monde sacrificed her life to protect this project,' she reminded Boyd. 'A man died in the Antarctic. Another man in a hide here in Saltmarsh. Aren't they all owed something now, some sort of justice? Something that will bring some meaning to their deaths?'

Boyd lowered her head and stared at the ground.

'That text was from my partner, Ms Boyd,' she said. 'He has concluded his interview with Glover. You and your husband killed Arliss Dyer, didn't you? Together. He could have identified your husband's voice, so you knew he had to die. You went and unlocked the hide at Canon's Cross and left the petrol nearby. And then you called him at the pub and told him the hide was open, that he could sleep in there. And then Glover set fire to the hide.'

Boyd raised her eyes and turned her unblinking gaze on Salter. Both women knew this was the tipping point. 'I used a burner phone. I called his mobile first but of course the damned thing wasn't charged. So I called the pub. I had forgotten Paige was working that night. I almost hung up, in case she recognised my voice. But the manager answered instead. I told Arliss the hide was unlocked and I'd left a tumbler in there for him. Cut-glass. He always did like a bit of decorum when he was drinking fine-quality Scotch. I wanted to make sure he went to the hide to drink the whisky, instead of stopping off somewhere along the way.'

The surfeit of details, thought Salter. It was so common, once a suspect had begun confessing. It was as if they felt they had to convince you of their guilt. But Salter had all she needed. She looked down at her phone and began texting. *Got it. Take your time.* She heard the ping of Boyd's own phone just as she pressed send. She looked up. The rusty, hooked end of the grappling pole was inches from her face. Boyd moved it closer and Salter backed up.

'Show me the message, now.'

Salter turned the phone to her and Boyd flickered a glance at the text, jabbing the end of the pole into Salter's cheek and pressing it there. She indicated her own phone. 'So typical of Glover,' she said, shaking her head slightly. 'The one time he chooses to show a bit of backbone and it has to be now, over this, when you'd expect any decent, reasonable man to cave in.' She tucked her own phone away and sighed. 'So now we're left with you being the only one who knows what happened.'

'I told my partner you'd confessed.'

'"*Got it*?"' Boyd shook her head. 'Could mean anything. Give me the phone.'

Salter handed it to her and she threw it a long way into the tangled undergrowth beside the building. She took the pole in both hands and levelled it at the sergeant's face. Salter held up her hands and took a slow step backwards, easing away from the hook just below her eye socket. Boyd extended the pole enough to compensate, adding increased pressure as a recommendation to Salter not to move any further.

'Take it easy,' she told Boyd, trying for a calmness that she couldn't find. 'You can recant your confession. Like you say, no one else knows. It'd just be your word against mine.'

'But not the detail about the tumbler left in the hide. That's something only the person who had lured Arliss there that night might know. And they would find it now, wouldn't they, if they started sifting through the debris, once you'd told them what to look for? Fragments anyway. Perhaps even one big enough to hold a partial fingerprint of mine. Move over towards the water.'

'Don't do this, Tori. My partner will be here soon. You saw the message.'

'Not a minute to lose then.'

The swishing noise came first, but by the time Salter realised what it was, the hook had sliced through the air and struck her on the temple. She fell to the ground at Boyd's feet. Unconscious.

49

Maik also saw the dried-up crust of the track on the incline, but he was in too much of a hurry to be delayed by it. He gunned the Mini and slithered down the slope, fighting to keep at least one set of wheels on the grassy edge for traction. On the dry ground at the bottom of the hill, the over-torqued car grabbed suddenly and lurched forward. Maik braked hard, stopping close enough to Tori Boyd to make her step backwards in alarm. He was out of the vehicle before she could even recover her composure.

'Where's Lauren. Sergeant Salter?'

Boyd was wearing heavy gloves and trailing a pair of long black electrical cables behind her. She was moving a lot more easily than the last time he'd seen her, as Maik might have expected from someone who no longer had a dressing on her leg. She lowered the cables to the ground and straightened up. 'Left, a couple of minutes ago.' But she didn't look at him as she said it. Instead, she seemed distracted by her task, letting it take all of her attention. Perhaps Maik didn't look convinced. 'She received your text. The one that said Glover denies any involvement in Arliss Dyer's death.' She looked at him. 'She decided there was nothing further she could do here.'

'Did she say where she was going?'

'To meet you, presumably.' Boyd shrugged. 'I really have no idea. But perhaps you could still catch her if you left now.'

For a woman who'd been on the verge of facing a murder charge a few moments earlier, Tori Boyd was surprisingly calm and disinterested. On the other hand, an attitude like this was exactly what somebody might adopt if they were trying to cover up a nervousness inside. But before Maik could pursue the point, a call from the top of the hill had him turning away.

Colleen Shepherd was standing beside her burgundy Jaguar, looking forlornly at the muddy channels Maik's descent had torn through the downhill track. She walked to the edge of the slope, calling his name again. 'Danny. Wait.'

Maik knew why. He had only moments now. He had to press. 'You had your ex-husband kill Arliss Dyer, Ms Boyd.'

'I believe Glover has just denied any involvement in the crime, Sergeant.'

'You got him to set fire to the hide at Canon's Cross, where you knew Arliss Dyer would be sleeping off a bottle of single malt. Then you set fire to this hide to destroy the evidence that you were falsifying data.'

Again, Shepherd's call reached them. 'Sergeant Maik, stop. I need to speak to you.'

Boyd looked at Maik: cold, detached, unshakeable. 'You have no evidence of any of this. Now, I need to get on with my work.' She lifted the cables again and began to pay them out towards the cradle of buoys.

'Glover won't be able to live with what he's done,' Maik called out to her. 'You know that.'

Boyd stopped and turned. 'He did nothing, Sergeant. He told you that.'

There was another call and Maik looked up to see Shepherd descending the hill. She was on foot, slaloming down sideways on, touching her hand down for balance like a skateboarder as she slithered over the slick, muddy grass. 'Sergeant Maik,' she shouted without pausing, 'stop the interview now.'

He spun his gaze back onto Boyd. 'It's them, ma'am,' he called over his shoulder. 'Tori Boyd and her ex.'

Shepherd was at the bottom of the hill now, mud-spattered, dishevelled, but as resolute as ever. 'Sergeant Maik, unless it is your intention to charge Ms Boyd with a crime, your interview is suspended.'

He reluctantly peeled his stare from Boyd. 'She and Glover Boyd are in it together. They killed Dyer because he overheard him planning to set fire to this place.'

'This comes from the highest level.' Shepherd looked at Boyd and then back at Maik. 'Unless you have anything firm, the investigation into the Bellaire Institute is to cease immediately.'

'Ma'am, it's them,' said Maik insistently. 'It's about falsified data entries. The readings from the buoys.'

'Enough, Sergeant. Evidence. Do you have any, or not?'

'No,' conceded Maik finally. 'No, ma'am, I don't.'

'Then if you'll excuse me, I have important work to be getting on with,' said Boyd impatiently. Released from Maik's stare, she finished trailing the cables to the edge of the wharf. Laying them beside the cradle, she began heading back to the administration building.

Maik crossed to Shepherd and leaned in confidentially. "I think Lauren may be on her way over to see the ex. He might talk to her. I think he will. A few more minutes, ma'am. That's all we need.'

Shepherd shook her head firmly. 'I'm sorry, Sergeant. It's over.'

Boyd approached the grey electrical box on the side of the admin building and withdrew the key from the chain round her neck. She opened the panel and flipped on the switch. She flickered a glance over her shoulder at the two officers before locking the panel again.

'Why didn't she wait?' Maik asked the question aloud, but it was addressed to himself. 'Lauren? To hear what I had to say?' Boyd was walking towards the cradle of buoys at the far end of the bay again, following the trail of the thick electrical cables that lay on the ground. He thought about her look, that sly glance over her shoulder. Why lock the electrical panel? And shouldn't it be DC, anyway, for electrolysis?

The uneasy silence that had fallen between them all was shattered by a loud car horn. All three looked up to the top of the rise where a vehicle was beginning to crest the incline. The descent of Domenic Jejeune's Range Rover wouldn't be pretty, but judging by the speed he was travelling, it would be fast.

The Beast's mud-filled tyres skidded as Jejeune jolted down onto the hard ground at the base of the incline. He slewed the Range Rover in beside Maik's Mini and scrambled from the seat. 'You have to stop her,' he said.

Shepherd ran to him. 'Back in the car, Domenic. This is an active crime scene.'

Boyd was moving faster now, not running but easing into a quicker stride.

'She's going to destroy the evidence.'

'Inspector Jejeune. Get back in the vehicle. That is an order.'

'The cable, the grid. Stop her.'

The urgency in his voice got through.

'Ms Boyd, please, stay where you are.'

Whether it was the authority in Shepherd's voice, or the uncertainty of the situation, Boyd hesitated, then stopped. Maik ran up beside her and escorted her back towards them.

'This is ridiculous. I'm not under arrest. I've been charged with no crime. I demand to be allowed to get on with my work.'

'You knew I would have trusted Arliss, didn't you?' said Jejeune. 'Perhaps another detective could have been convinced that he was mistaken. But you knew once Arliss had ID'd your ex-husband's voice from the hide that night, I would believe him.'

'Arliss said he couldn't identify the voice.' Boyd looked to Maik for confirmation. 'Paige Turner is a witness to that. She heard him say it as well.'

'But she heard something else, too, as you did. Arliss telling me he could recall what he heard. And you knew what that meant, even if Paige Turner didn't.' Jejeune stared into her eyes. 'You stopped him from contacting me once,' he said flatly. 'But you knew you wouldn't be able to prevent it for ever.'

Boyd spun on Shepherd. 'Am I missing something, Superintendent? Because I could swear I just heard you telling the sergeant here that the case against my ex-husband and myself was over.' She looked at Jejeune frankly. 'There's no evidence, you see.'

Jejeune nodded. 'Yes, there is.' He turned to Shepherd. 'You need to impound the buoys. They are your evidence.'

Boyd shifted uneasily.

'The electric current, it isn't to descale the buoys.' Jejeune turned to Maik. 'As you said, it makes no sense, if they are decomposing. They could never be deployed again. So why descale them?'

Boyd was staring at him now, defiant and hostile.

'Those buoys all have chips in them that store the data they record. Tiny electronic memories of the original temperature recordings that would be erased as soon as an electric current was passed through them.' He turned to Shepherd. 'Recover that data. There's your evidence.'

'I'm not listening to any more of this.' Boyd spun away but Maik grabbed her arm.

'Stop,' he said.

'I don't believe you have the authority to detain me, Sergeant.' She looked at Shepherd. 'This is private property. Julien Bellaire is the person who gives me instructions. Perhaps you'd care to discuss it with him.'

'Ms Boyd,' said Shepherd, 'I'm formally requesting that you stop your activities until we can examine those buoys.'

'Wouldn't you need a warrant for that?' She looked between Jejeune and Shepherd. 'I wonder, Superintendent. Would you be prepared to argue that your just cause is the result of a directive from a suspended detective?'

'Sergeant Maik, call Sergeant Salter,' said Shepherd, locking her eyes on Boyd. 'Ask her to get a warrant to impound those sea buoys and bring it over here, as soon as possible.'

Jejeune looked puzzled. 'Lauren Salter is here, surely? I just saw her car under the trees at the top of the hill.'

Maik snatched his phone out and dialled. For a moment, the world hung suspended in time. And then, from somewhere beside the hide, came the faint sound of Marvin Gaye telling them all how sweet it was to be loved by someone like Danny Maik.

50

Maik lunged towards Boyd and grabbed her by the lapels. 'What have you done with her?'

'Sergeant.'

The half-second it took for Maik to look towards Shepherd's call of alarm was all Boyd needed. She twisted free of his grasp and began sprinting towards the grid in the bay, pulling on her heavy rubber gloves as she ran.

Maik charged after her, Jejeune and Shepherd in their wake. Boyd raced towards the cradle, to the cable terminals that lay in front of it. The connectors waited, their jaws stretched wide like hungry sharks, ready to be clipped onto the metal grid.

They all heard the faint call at the same time. 'Danny.'

From somewhere deep within the field of buoys, Maik saw Salter struggling to her feet. She was standing on the grid, fighting her way across the slippery plastic skins.

'Get out, Lauren. Get off there. The cables are live. She's going to electrify the grid.'

'No, I can stop her.' Salter began scrambling over the buoys faster, straining and crawling to get across them to the approaching Boyd. The wet plastic slithered around under her feet, robbing her of purchase, and she stumbled to her knees.

Jejeune and Shepherd were still chasing, but neither was going to reach Boyd before she got to the cradle. Maik was closing the distance between himself and Boyd, gaining with every step, but he wasn't going to catch her either. Not running. He hurled himself full length at the woman's back. She crumpled under the impact and Maik collapsed into her. But Boyd rolled free, and regained her feet as Maik scrabbled for purchase: a leg, a foot, a piece of clothing. Anything.

Nothing.

Boyd was up and moving again, metres from the cradle now.

'Lauren, get out of the way.'

But she was there now, standing on the side of the cradle, fighting for balance as it bobbed and rolled in the water. Boyd stopped before her. And as she looked up at her, the rage rose; all the anger, the humiliation of every betrayal, every lie Glover Boyd had ever told her. It was all there in her outstretched arms as she shoved Salter in the chest as hard as she could, sending the sergeant flailing backwards. As far away as they were, the crack of Salter's skull on the metal grid was audible even to Jejeune and Shepherd. They saw her slump limply between the buoys. Still.

Boyd reached down and grabbed the connectors in her gloved hands and moved towards the grid.

This time, he got it right. Maik hit Boyd from the side, jarring her body so violently he knocked her off her feet, snatching the terminals from her hands as she fell, arms flailing, to the ground. But there was never going to be enough room for Maik to reach the ground, too. Not so close to the water's edge. His momentum carried him out into the bay, over the still surface of the dark water. And in. The flash of light and the crack of sound rose simultaneously as he broke the water's surface, terminals still in hand. And then, there was nothing.

Salter's vision was blurry, clearing so slowly it was a few moments before she could recognise what it was she was looking at. The medics weren't helping either. Having administered a dressing to her head and draped a blanket over her, they were now standing together so that they formed a screen. If the thought hadn't been so ridiculous, she might almost have believed it was a deliberate attempt to prevent her from seeing what was going on behind them. But she was managing glimpses, irritably batting away the blanket to clear her field of view. Craning this way and that to see round the standing wall of medics, she now hazily recognised the scene they had been trying to shield from her. There was a flurry of activity around the wharf. Not chaos, and definitely not disorganisation. But urgency, yes. And panic? Perhaps. But sadness, too. People she recognised with heads bowed and the stunned, empty look of those processing bad news.

The activity closer to her made no more sense. A team of medics had unloaded a stretcher from the back of the ambulance and were hastily raising it. But she was being helped to her feet, guided by the strong hand of an unseen helper under her arms. Why get a stretcher and then stand her up? And why were the medics with the stretcher moving away from her, to the far end of the wharf?

The confusion made her head hurt and she closed her eyes against the pain, stumbling as she made her way to the ambulance. And then, in the half-turn of righting herself, she saw images: a pair of electric cables lying in a pool of water on the ground, dripping and sparking, a woman being led to a police car. And shouts; something about a key, an electrical panel, about shutting off the power. And other people, standing around as if they realised there was no urgency, as if they knew cutting off the electricity now could not undo what had been done. However much they wished it, however much they hoped and prayed, they could not recover that split second of time before electrically charged terminals had hit the water, with a man holding on to them, one in each hand, falling in a slow-motion spiral through the electric-white flash into the water.

And then a montage of images appeared before Salter, all at once, unfurling in a succession of terrible slow-motion freeze-frames. A limp figure who had been hauled from the water and rolled unresistingly back from the edge of the wharf, where it lay, still and unresponsive. DCS Shepherd pacing back and forth, threading her fingers through her hair. Jejeune, his clothing soaked, squatting on his haunches, laying a hand on the figure's chest like a parting gift, and leaving it there. Salter wanted to be there, to kneel beside the figure, to gently raise the lolling head and gather him into her, to cradle him against her and just rock him, rock him, rock him. But she knew she could not do that. She was being led away from the scene, and could feel herself going along unresistingly. All she could leave for the man who had been willing to give everything for her were the uncontrollable sobs torn from her heart as she was ushered into the back of the waiting ambulance.

51

The significant moments of our lives are sometimes marked by the most innocent of actions. In and of itself, the packing up of items from a desk was a common enough occurrence in the detectives' offices. But to collect up the legacy of Danny Maik at Saltmarsh station, to take his contribution to this room, his monumental presence in it, and to store it away in a small cardboard box, was a matter of such profound consequence that no one watching Lauren Salter's silent labours could find the words to express their feelings. The appearance of DCS Shepherd seemed to break the spell, though she, too, clearly understood the reason for the silence that had fallen over the room. 'You don't need to do that now, Lauren. It can wait.'

'The longer I leave it, the harder it will be,' Salter told her DCS. 'I was thinking of shifting to a different desk myself, ma'am, if that's all right with you?'

Shepherd looked at the current configuration. In the open-plan, finding a desk that wasn't in the direct eyeline of this one, a workstation that didn't give Salter an unbroken view of an empty space – or worse, someone else occupying it – would be difficult. But the others would do what was necessary to accommodate her. If no amount of shifting furniture was going to change the new reality of the station, anything that could help would be welcome.

Shepherd crossed to the desk and picked up a day calendar: *Motown Greats*. A photo of the Supremes smiled back at her: youthful, vibrant, without a care in the world. The calendar date was two days ago. A lot had changed since then. So much. She thought about turning the calendar to today's date, but somehow she couldn't bear the idea of consigning this happy, carefree day to the past. She handed it silently to Salter and she tucked it in the box with the other debris of this broken time.

'The CPS is formally charging Tori and Glover Boyd with the murder of Arliss Dyer.' There was no note of celebration in Shepherd's voice. 'They've decided to cooperate with the authorities. They have both entered guilty pleas.'

'That doesn't sound like Tori Boyd,' said Tony Holland, grateful for the distraction from the gradual disappearance of Danny Maik taking place before his eyes. 'Was it her ex who caved?'

'It was a joint confession. The evidence against them is overwhelming. But they're saying it was because Tori Boyd believed Dyer was planning to destroy the admin centre. Something about him wanting to restore the site to how it was before, with the Brackets as hides again. As a clear threat to the project, he had to be stopped.'

Holland looked incredulous. 'And the CPS is buying that?'

'The Crown Prosecution Service doesn't make a habit of rejecting confessions in murder cases, Constable, however implausible the motives.'

They realised Salter had been silent during the exchange. Shepherd watched as she looked at a photograph in her hand. The sergeant seemed to lose the will to continue her task, setting it down on the desk again. 'How's Max taking the news?' Shepherd asked.

'Well, he knows I'm sad, obviously, but it doesn't seem to have stopped him marmalising Zelda or whatever his current quest is.' Salter paused. 'Life just goes on for kids, doesn't it? Perhaps that's a good thing, though. Perhaps that's the way to get through, just keeping pushing on.' She shook her head. 'All this is down to one man's ego. And there's no way Bellaire can face justice?'

'An indictment is unlikely. In order to show motive in the deaths of either Alex Kasabian or Arliss Dyer, we'd need evidence that the Bellaire Institute had been entering false data. Only Tori Boyd could give us that.' Shepherd paused. 'But she won't. As of now, it's still possible to argue for the integrity of the records that were entered into the Institute's system. Because of the air-gapping, and the fact that the computers holding the earlier readings have been destroyed, there's no evidence that false data was ever entered. There's an army of experts out there ready to argue that the readings from the Bellaire Institute are consistent with global norms.'

'But the monitoring software on those buoys currently in the bay all shows inflated temperatures.'

'Which is why, Tori Boyd is saying, their data was never entered into the system. They detected a problem and were about to fix it.' Shepherd held up her hands. 'We can't prove otherwise. As long as she sticks with this story, the reputation of the project remains intact.'

'I would think its reputation is a bit of a moot point, isn't it?' said Holland sarcastically. 'The project is over now, surely?'

Shepherd shook her head. 'Julien Bellaire is expected to announce the name of the new project director today. He's withdrawing his name from the Institute and stepping back from all public association with it. It's to be called the Gayatri Monde Institute of Global Climatology from now on.' Shepherd looked less than impressed. 'It's Tori Boyd's quid pro quo. As long as Bellaire continues funding the project, she'll stay silent about the false data and he remains a free man. As for Glover, I don't think he cares about Bellaire or the project. But he'll stay quiet to protect his ex-wife's legacy.'

Holland shook his head. 'A few people had him wrong,' he said. 'Me among them. I had him down as just some selfish twat with no thought for anybody else. But when it came right down to it, he wouldn't give her up, would he?'

'It probably took every ounce of resolve he's ever had, or ever will have.' There was no admiration in Shepherd's tone, only contempt. '"*Lover Boy*",' she said. 'I wonder if it really was love, in the end. Or just more guilt?'

The sudden commotion outside in the corridor had everyone in the room looking in that direction. Domenic Jejeune had said he might try to stop by, but his entrances were usually a lot more unobtrusive. Shepherd couldn't count the times he had simply appeared by her side, seemingly having materialised out of the ether. This didn't sound like somebody trying for a quiet entrance. More the opposite, in fact.

Paige Turner appeared in the doorway with a broad smile on her face. 'I was just coming in to see if you wanted to go for lunch, Tony, but look who I found loitering in these newly painted hallways.'

The face had a greyish pallor, but the unfamiliar sheepish grin was what struck them all the most.

'Danny,' shouted Salter. 'What are you doing here? I was coming over the hospital to see you this afternoon. I was just packing up a few of your things.'

'I'm out on a four-hour furlough. They've reset my heart rhythms after the jolt knocked them out of sync, and they've sent me out for a walkabout to see how I do. They want me back in for one more night's observation, but for now, they said I should be okay as long as I avoid anything too strenuous.' He looked at Holland's grinning face. 'I'm supposed to avoid any big shocks, too, so don't start telling me you're working hard.'

'You know, of all the things I'm going to miss about you, your sense of humour is the one I might be able to get by without,' said Holland, barely able to keep the emotion from his voice. 'I suppose you've come to see I don't steal any of your paper clips.'

'I think I can trust Lauren to make sure all my belongings make it safely to King's Lynn.'

Maik's dry delivery sent the clear message: *no fuss.* But if everybody still felt as if they needed to walk on eggshells around him, their pleasure at having him here was obvious.

Shepherd was first to broach the subject. As their leader, the task would probably have fallen to her anyway, but she took it on gladly. 'Defying science, Danny? Still, I suppose it's better than denying it.'

He raised his eyebrows and smiled gratefully. 'Dodging it, more likely. The doctor said the terminals were close enough together when I went in that the current preferred to complete the circuit through the salt water rather than through me.'

They were all aware that if Danny had fallen into the freshwater marsh on the other side of the flat expanse, there would have been no heartbeat to knock out of sync. Although they had lived all their lives by the sea, none of them had been aware that salt water conducted electricity. Perhaps predictably, only Domenic Jejeune, born and raised a couple of thousand miles from the nearest ocean, had known that the salt water would carry the current instead of it forcing itself through Maik's body. It had been Jejeune who had realised Maik was unconscious, not dead, and jumped in to prevent him from drowning.

The reflective silence was allowed to settle over the room for a moment before Holland brightened. 'Oh, hey, we were going to come over to the hospital to do this for you, but since you're here, we may as well do it now. It's our little going-away present; me and Paige.'

He called up a tune on his laptop and Maik recognised the familiar intro. Any second now, the unmistakable harmonies of the Supremes would begin to overlay the Funk Brothers' backing. He watched as Holland grabbed a desk stapler as a mic and Paige leaned in to join him in lip-syncing the lyrics: 'My World is Empty Without You, Babe'.

Shepherd couldn't tell whether the expression spreading over Maik's pallid features was meant to be a smile, but it grew still stronger when Holland grabbed Salter by the arm and had her shuffle-step to join the other two in an impromptu dance routine. Shepherd joined Maik at his shoulder. 'They were fairly short, weren't they, those old Motown songs?'

'Usually about three minutes, I think.'

'Small mercies,' she said drily. 'Still, I suppose we should be grateful they chose this one. Yesterday I heard them working on "My Guy".'

'The Mary Wells tune?' Maik's eyebrows reached for his forehead. Small mercies indeed.

As the soundtrack faded, the performers collapsed into self-congratulation and Maik managed something that sounded like applause. Salter came over and grabbed Danny's arm. 'Oh by the way, Max said to tell you he did well on his DNA project. It finally came to me, all that fuss. You thought... Glover Boyd and me.'

Maik rolled his shoulders, trying to shrug away the charge. But Holland knew better. That song in the car that night, the one about the illegitimate kid. 'Love Child'. No wonder Danny had wanted him to turn it off.

'It's okay, Danny,' said Salter. 'The timing was about right. But there was never any question who was Max's father. Why didn't you just ask me?'

'None of my business, really.'

She leaned into him slightly. 'That's not the way I see it, Danny Maik. Like it or not, my life *is* your business now, or at least as much of it as you'd like to be. And frankly, I'm hoping that's quite a lot.'

The others averted their eyes for a moment until the worst of Maik's embarrassment had passed. 'Right, well, I'd best be getting back.' He nodded at the stapler Holland still held in his hand. 'Leave you to your work.'

'I'll walk you out,' said Shepherd.

Maik was silent as they made their way along the corridor, but he paused at the doorway. 'Do you think Inspector Jejeune is right, ma'am? Do you think Tori Boyd would have still killed Arliss Dyer if she'd known he was suspended?'

There was a long pause before Shepherd answered. 'I'm not even sure Tori Boyd knows the answer to that. Eric tells me when they were all out birding together, she seemed genuinely fond of the man. Perhaps that would have been enough to save him, if she'd known it was some other detective she'd need to convince of her innocence, rather than one who was going to have unshakeable faith in Arliss Dyer's hearing. But in the end, the research work had to come first. And Dyer posed a threat to all that. So perhaps she had already determined he needed to die, regardless of who investigated his claims.'

Maik acknowledged the point with a tilt of his head. 'Well, I'd better be getting back to the hospital. Let them check how I'm getting on.'

Shepherd nodded sadly. 'Not too much, Danny and not too fast. Why don't you think about taking a break before you start your new duties? They'll want you to be at your best, and so will I. We can't have them saying I sent over damaged goods. I'd never hear the end of it at the superintendents' conference.'

She smiled. 'They're getting a good officer, Danny, but more than that, they're getting a good man. And so is Lauren Salter. All of us here at the station, we're better people for having known you.'

'I've served with a few good ones, ma'am, but none better. It's been an honour.'

Just enough, she thought as she watched his broad back disappear from view. *Just enough, and just right*. Typical Danny Maik.

52

A veil of haze hovered over the sea. Through it, a fine line of sunlight lay like a promise on the horizon. It would bring a warm day, but there had been a coolness to the early morning that reminded them a change of season was coming.

Jejeune wasn't sure why Colleen Shepherd had chosen this venue for their meeting. Her tone had been a touch guarded, which probably meant she was going to deliver the news he had been expecting. Perhaps the station was still too sad a place, too redolent of past successes and celebrations, for an announcement like the one she was going to make.

From his elevated position in the driver's seat of the Beast, he looked around. In the low morning light, the ruins of the nearby priory lurked like dark forces. Later they would emerge as the sentinels they were, forlorn witnesses to the disappearing stories of the past.

Lindy followed his gaze from the passenger seat. 'So, Bellaire's name is no longer going to be associated with one of the largest climate change projects in history? That's going to be hard for a man who likes the spotlight as much as he does. Still, I suppose at least this way, he'll be able to save what's left of his precious reputation, even if he doesn't get to write his name among the stars.' She looked out at the crumbling ruins once more and was silent for a long moment. 'They're not right, are they,' she asked eventually, 'people like Tori Boyd and Julien Bellaire? To say that people can't be trusted to come to the right decision on their own, that they need to be manipulated into it?'

'I think all you can do is provide the most accurate, most complete information you can. It's not up to anyone to tell someone else how to interpret the data, or where it should lead their actions. Science was never meant to do that. It is a tool for providing information. Ultimately, humans need to make their own decisions about what to do with it.'

'But changing the trajectory of the planet's temperature is not a matter of opinion, Dom. It's the only way human beings are going to be able to continue to exist. This is too big to get wrong, to delay while people argue over the details and politicians faff about with the niceties of the language. You can't just hope people decide to take it seriously in the end. If sceptics were going to point to the Bellaire Institute's flawed data as a reason not to act, and they definitely would have, isn't it somehow justified to take that option away from them?'

Outside the Range Rover's windows, the landscape was beginning to draw life from the rising light. Another day was on its way, with all its questions and challenges and moral ambiguities for humans to face. 'Once you start manipulating the message, even for good, or what you believe to be good, there are no controls any more. You're on the way to being the one who decides what matters and what doesn't.' Jejeune turned to look at her. 'Two men died because someone else decided it served a bigger purpose, because their view of the world told them it was necessary.'

Lindy nodded silently. He knew she believed taking another life was never the right thing to do, no matter how you tried to justify it. But he could tell that the bigger question, about manipulating humans to act in the right way, when the alternative was unthinkable; that was still troubling her. But perhaps that was a good thing. Perhaps it needed good, decent, intelligent people like Lindy to consider these ideas, to wrestle with them. Because when the right answers came, as they surely would, there would no longer be any doubting them.

A car drew up beside them. It was one they both recognised: a burgundy Jaguar. 'You go. I'll stay here. You know what she wants to tell you. It'll be easier if it's just the two of you.'

Lindy didn't say for whom she thought it would be easier. Perhaps she intended it that way.

Shepherd got out of the car and bundled a scarf around herself. As if by tacit agreement she and Jejeune began walking towards the cliff edge, into the stiff, buffeting breeze. They walked in silence until they reached the edge. For a moment they stood, shoulder to shoulder, looking out to sea.

'Danny mentioned he ran into you in a hide the other day.' Shepherd's expression suggested she was going to gloss over the improbability of such a chance meeting. 'He is adamant that you didn't ask him for any information about the Arliss Dyer case, and he confirms that he did not reveal one single fact about it to you. Furthermore, he said he's prepared to swear to it before a board of inquiry, if one was to be called.' She paused for a moment and let the sound of the crashing surf below fill the silence. 'It won't.'

Jejeune offered no reply. He continued staring out over the endless grey expanse of the sea, moving restlessly under the freshening onshore breezes. Danny also had a recording. If he hadn't mentioned it, it meant he wasn't intending to use it. Whatever was on there, like a quote, '*I can recall what I heard*', that Jejeune should have had no first-hand knowledge of, would remain between the two men alone. 'How's he doing?'

'Okay. It's a good thing for him you were at the wharf. Speaking of which, you having been explicitly warned off having any contact with Tori Boyd or the Bellaire Institute, I can only assume you had gone there for the excellent birding opportunities. Eric tells me it's a good place to see some rarity or other. Water Rail, is it?'

Jejeune nodded, still looking out over the water. 'If you're lucky.'

Shepherd turned to look at him sideways on. 'Oh, I'd say you are, Domenic. Extremely lucky.' She peered at him over the rim of her steel-framed glasses. 'You've taken on one of the most powerful men in the world and somehow lived to fight another day. But that's not to say your involvement in an active case has gone unnoticed.' The look was one he had seen many times before. 'There will be no second chances, Domenic. You know that. Why don't you take that poor long-suffering girl of yours on a holiday? Preferably one that doesn't involve bird-ing.'

'It'd be a long holiday if I was to see out the remainder of the suspension.'

'Perhaps that's no bad thing. It'll give you time to adjust to the idea of running a unit without Danny Maik.' She allowed a heartbeat's pause, but to Jejeune it seemed longer. 'He's applied for a transfer to King's Lynn. I have approved it.'

Jejeune was silent. He had been expecting the news. He had known it was this she had come here to tell him. But hearing it out loud like this was still numbing. Not even a month-long holiday would be enough time to prepare for what would await him on his return. He knew the department would survive without Danny Maik. Ecosystems continued to exist when a species disappeared, even vital, keystone species.

But they were changed, fundamentally, from that point on. Perhaps those changes were imperceptible at first, but their impacts gradually emerged over time. They were unpredictable, but he could never remember hearing about a time when the loss of a species resulted in things turning out better for an ecosystem.

Shepherd looked at the scarred cliffs, still bearing the evidence of recent further erosion. There were millennia of constancy in this landscape. Now she found herself wondering just how much of it would still be here next year. 'Change is inevitable, Domenic. The world around us is not static, it would be a mistake to expect our lives to be.'

Not so long ago, she had told him change was a chance to put our past behind us. But it also meant facing an uncertain future. They had both seen many officers come and go, but none would affect them as profoundly as the exit of Danny Maik. He had been everything to Jejeune and his DCS, a buffer between them when needed, a bridge at other times. Whatever else his departure meant, it would require a resetting of the relationship between Jejeune and Shepherd. Perhaps the silence from each of them now was their acknowledgement of this.

'We wouldn't have got there without him, this time. His instinct that Glover Boyd was involved, when everybody, and the evidence, was telling him otherwise.' Shepherd shook her head. 'Shoes to fill,' she said.

Jejeune nodded. *King's Lynn.* There would be talk of Danny being close enough to drop by, the distance and time minimised to ideal driving conditions. There would be reminders that his partner was still at the station, so there would be regular updates and meeting at social gatherings, perhaps even talk of a regular pub night, Fridays, say, after a long work week, for a laugh and a catch-up. At the Board Room, as soon as they

WILSON'S STORM PETREL

The Wilson's Storm Petrel (*Oceanites oceanicus*), also known as Wilson's Petrel, is one of the most abundant bird species on the planet, with a global population estimated to be in excess of fifty million pairs.

Named for the celebrated Scottish-American ornithologist, Alexander Wilson, the species has a circumpolar distribution throughout the seas of the southern hemisphere. Nesting on the Antarctic coastlines and nearby islands, the Wilson's Storm Petrel is the smallest warm-blooded species to breed in the Antarctic region. To avoid predation by larger birds such as skuas, it will approach its breeding site only at night, and will even avoid coming in to land on clear, moonlit nights.

Outside the breeding season, the Wilson's Storm Petrel is strictly pelagic, spending the rest of the year at sea as it moves into the northern oceans during the southern hemisphere's winter. Even in calm weather, the birds can make use of the slight breeze produced by wave action to become airborne. Flying low over the sea and pattering on the water surface as they pick up food items, they feed predominantly on planktonic invertebrates close to the surface. Sadly, the diet and feeding behaviour of the Wilson's Storm Petrel make the species particularly vulnerable to the threat of pollution in oceans, and many birds die each year from plastic ingestion.

Reversing the trend of bird deaths from ocean-borne plastics will take a great deal of effort, but if any further incentive was needed, humans might do well to remember that in marine mythology, killing a storm petrel was believed to bring an unbroken sequence of bad luck. Fortunately, a number of organisations, including the Sea Save Foundation, the Ocean Blue Project and Seabird Information Network, are committed to combatting the increasing problem of plastics in oceans, and have developed a range of strategies for individuals and corporations to reduce the impacts on wildlife. Further details may be found on the websites of these organisations.

ACKNOWLEDGEMENTS

I am grateful to Juliet Mabey at Oneworld for her ongoing support for the Birder Murder Mysteries. My thanks also go to my editors, Jenny Parrott and Molly Scull, for their enthusiasm, encouragement and guidance. Jacqui Lewis, Laura McFarlane, Paul Nash and the rest of the Oneworld team made light work of some tight deadlines and ensured the process of bringing the project to completion remained a pleasure throughout.

At WCA, Bruce Westwood and Michael Levine provided timely and much-appreciated advice, while the multitasking Meg Wheeler continues to do so much, so quickly, so well. My thanks to you all.

I am indebted to the captain and crew of the *MV Hondius* who safely transported me to Antarctica and back under the most challenging of conditions, and delivered some amazing experiences along the way. My thanks, also, to the Oceanwide Expeditions staff, particularly Sara Jenner, Christian Savigny, who quite literally wrote the book on Antarctic birds, and Hazel Pittwood, who helped me to identify so many of them.

Finally, as always, my love and gratitude go to my wife, Resa. Even by your own extraordinary standards, your ability to predict the exciting new developments for the series has been impressive. You continue to reach new heights in the art of being unwrong.